THE SPOILS OF WAR

By Gordon Kent

Gordon Kent

THE SPOILS OF WAR

HarperCollins*Publishers*

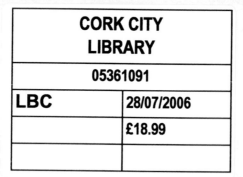

HarperCollins*Publishers*
77-85 Fulham Palace Road,
Hammersmith, London W6 8JB

www.harpercollins.co.uk

Published by HarperCollins*Publishers* 2006
1 3 5 7 9 8 6 4 2

A catalogue record for this book
is available from the British Library

ISBN-13 978 0 00 717874 2 (hb)
ISBN-10 0 00 717874 3 (hb)
ISBN-13 978 0 00 722926 0 (trade pbk)
ISBN-10 0 00 722926 7 (trade pbk)

Typeset in Meridien by Palimpsest Book Production Limited,
Polmont, Stirlingshire

Printed and bound in Great Britain by
Clays Ltd, St Ives plc

'Υπέρ τὰ ἐσκαμμένα ἄλλεσθαι

T. Cuyler young
Donald G. Cameron

They went further than seemed possible

Prologue

The Kosovo–Albania Border, 1997

The late afternoon rain sent the Albanian soldiers into the cover of the trees. Dukas thought the move was probably for the best. What he had seen of the Albanians scared him, and he was glad when they walked off up the road to the stand of oak trees, shouting at each other and carrying their rifles across their necks like ox yokes.

The rain beat on the windshield of Dukas's borrowed Land Rover and the wipers droned back and forth, harmonizing with the heater and the raindrops on the roof, washing away some of the mud accumulated in a nine-hour drive across "the former Yugoslavia." There was mud from Bosnia and mud from Croatia and a little mud from Kosovo, all washing off into the ruined tarmac of a road in Albania.

"Have a little faith, okay," muttered the Mossad guy in the back seat. Actually, there were two Mossad guys in the back seat, but one of them was so obviously a bureaucratic functionary that Dukas ignored him. Dukas tried to adjust his body language so that he was not telegraphing his views on the afternoon quite so blatantly. He looked back.

"When do you want to call this off?" he asked.

"Give the man another hour."

His name was Shlomo, he had said. Dukas thought the name was funny, but the man himself was serious. Now, he moved his hand slightly to indicate that, no, he didn't expect their quarry to appear either, and that, yes, they were going to wait an hour because he, Shlomo, was under the scrutiny of someone who had sent a bureaucrat to watch him.

Dukas liked Shlomo. And he didn't mind helping the Israelis, as long as his own investigations into Bosnian Muslim war crimes benefited from helping them. He pulled a headset up over his ears and keyed his radio.

"Roger, Squid, I copy you," the voice on the other end said. The Canadians he had picked up as an ops team thought it was hilarious that Dukas was attached to the US Navy, and they called him Squid at every opportunity.

"Give it another six zero minutes."

"Roger, copy." The Canadians were in cover along the Albanian side of the border. Dukas had looked for them a few times and failed, but they answered radio calls and they had stayed in their positions all day; now they would all be drenched in addition to tired. By contrast, the Albanians had a roaring fire going in the tree line; at dusk, both the smoke and the fire must have shown for miles. But Dukas would not have been allowed here without the "support" of the Albanians.

A column of headlights showed across the ridge to the south in Kosovo. Dukas and Shlomo had their binoculars up in an instant and then back in their laps. They both sighed on much the same note.

"He'll come in this lot," the bureaucrat said.

Dukas shook his head. Shlomo said, "No, David. It's just local militia crossing the border to buy weapons."

"Why can't he be in among them? He could be with them." The Mossad bureaucrat, who had introduced himself as David, sounded as if he believed that he could make his assertions true by repeating them. He had the makings of a politician, Dukas thought.

"He doesn't have that kind of contact."

2

"You don't know that." David sounded petulant.

Dukas listened to them and wondered what made their target, a Lebanese, so important that David would get his penny loafers dirty coming to collect him, especially as it was Dukas who would have to do the work and who would do the interrogation. As was almost always the case when he was working with foreign intelligence people, Dukas suspected that he was being used. He was a cynic. But he was usually right.

He cleared his throat. The two men in the back fell silent. "How is it that a Muslim Lebanese doesn't have contacts in Kosovo?" he asked.

"He's a city boy," Shlomo said.

"You guys said he was an arms dealer." Dukas turned to look into the back seat. It was dusk, and Shlomo's face was almost invisible. David was leaning forward into the last sunlight. He seemed excited.

"I said his efforts helped to put guns in the hands of the Muslims in Bosnia," Shlomo said.

The convoy of headlights over in Kosovo had descended the ridge and made it to the checkpoint at the Albanian border.

Dukas kept going. "Why does he sell arms to Bosnians and not Kosovans?"

David said, "Why don't you do your job and let us do ours?" His words hung there for a few seconds. Shlomo's hand twitched, as if he was going to try and withdraw the words his partner had said.

Dukas looked at his watch and turned to face the back seat again, bunching the skirts of his raincoat in his fist. "My job is to aid the UN and the War Crimes Tribunal in The Hague in the apprehension of war criminals."

He turned and met David's eyes, but the younger man returned his look with indifference. Dukas continued, "If the guy we're after isn't of interest to me, my job will include dropping you guys at an airport and driving *back* the nine hours it took me to get here. With nothing. And unless it suits me, my job has *nothing* to do with helping you do yours."

David held his gaze, and then his eyes flicked away as he seemed to lose interest. He shrugged.

Shlomo shook his head.

Dukas was considering a further lecture on the subject when he heard a radio tone in his headset.

"Yeah?"

"Palm Two has movement on the hillside."

Dukas looked over his shoulder through the rain-streaked glass reflexively; in fact, he couldn't see anything except a yellow smudge where the Albanians had their fire. "Just Albanians," he said.

"Palm Two says it's a sniper with high-res optics and a ghillie suit," reported the voice in his ear.

Dukas's head snapped up.

"What's happened?" Shlomo asked from the back seat.

The windshield wipers cycled. Fifty meters below them, at the checkpoint, an ancient white Zil was being searched thoroughly while its former occupants stood and smoked. One man had a briefcase. This drew Dukas's eye.

Surprise, surprise.

"That's our guy." Dukas waved. He was out of the car and moving. He stopped to clutch his headset to his ear. "The guy at three o'clock in the car being searched now. No, not in the car. Next to the car. Yeah! Briefcase. Take him!" He started down the rocky hillside, paused to draw a heavy revolver from his shoulder holster.

Shlomo caught up with him and they ran down the hill together, raincoats flapping like ungainly wings.

Boom.

The shot sounded like a cannon. Two Canadian soldiers, halfway out of their concealment, froze and looked around for the source.

4

In his headset, the Canadian voice said, "Sniper!" and then, "Palm Two, do you have a shot?"

Pop, pop.

Dukas was now a bystander, lying full length in the wet bracken between two stones with Shlomo wedged in next to him.

Pop, pop.

"Hawk One, this is Palm Two. He's gone. No hits."

"Is it safe to move?" Dukas asked. He was soaked; runoff from the hillside was going right down his pants.

"Wait one."

It took the Canadians ten minutes to clear the hillside. They found a small patch of dark khaki polyester and a one-inch square of flannel.

"That's off his ghillie suit," a black Nova Scotian sergeant said. He presented them to Dukas and Shlomo. "That flannel he used to wipe the optics on his rifle." He sounded as if he was from Boston.

Dukas knelt by the body. It was impossible to establish whether this was, in fact, the man they'd come for; a fifty-caliber sniper round had removed most of his head. Dukas began to search the corpse. The man had a wallet with American dollars and several forms of ID. His clothes were all international—a Gap sweatshirt with a hood, blue jeans. The briefcase was locked to his wrist; the keys were in his jeans.

Shlomo leaned in to see what was in the case and Dukas rotated it so that he could see everything.

"This guy was an *arms* dealer?" Dukas said.

Shlomo shrugged. "We make mistakes, too." Shlomo didn't seem surprised by the contents.

Dukas pointed with a booted toe at the remnants of the jawline and lack of a head. "Was that a mistake?" he asked.

Shlomo raised his hands. "I don't like what you're suggesting."

"You going to tell me that the *Albanians* shot him?" Dukas exhaled sharply. "With a fifty-cal?"

Shlomo glanced up the hill at the Land Rover. "It wasn't right, what David said, but he is political and thinks he rules the world, okay?"

Dukas knelt again by the briefcase and began to inventory the contents. He pulled plastic freezer bags from the zippered liner of his raincoat, assigned a chain-of-custody code to each item, placed it in the freezer bag, and stuck the number on the outside. Most of the items in the briefcase were Roman coins. He did the inventory carefully, because he was angry and he didn't want to do something stupid. Shlomo watched him for a while and then walked over to the car the dead man had arrived in and began to question the three other occupants in English and then in Turkish. Then Arabic.

In the inner pocket, Dukas found a red leather calendar book. Once, its edges had been gold-leafed, but it had been used for too many years. The calendar date was 1987. He flipped it open to the back—penciled addresses and phone numbers in Arabic and in roman script, in cities throughout the Mediterranean.

David thrust out a hand. "I'll take that."

Dukas hadn't seen him come down the hill, but it looked as if he had taken the longer and drier route on the tarmac.

Dukas didn't reply. He placed the calendar in a plastic bag, put a sticker on it, and wrote a number. He tossed the bag on the pile.

David stepped around him and bent over the pile. Dukas stood up suddenly, his hip grazing the younger man and sending him sprawling.

"Sorry," Dukas said, offering his hand. "I'm clumsy."

David crab-walked away and rose to his feet. His jaw worked as if he was chewing, and his face was red, but he kept his distance.

Shlomo came back from the car.

6

"He attacked me," David said.

Dukas shook his head. "A misunderstanding."

"He attacked me," David said, his anger causing his voice to rise. "He is interfering."

Dukas talked over David. "Get this guy out of here."

David began to use his hands. He wasn't speaking English now, but Hebrew, and he was speaking only to Shlomo.

Shlomo didn't move. David went on talking. Shlomo ignored him and looked at the briefcase and then at Dukas, his head bent slightly to one side as if he were asking a question. Dukas locked the locks on the briefcase and put the keys in the pocket of his raincoat. The Canadian sergeant was standing by the Zil, watching the three terrified Kosovans and smoking. From time to time he glanced at the two Israelis.

David wiped his hands on his coat, turned away from Shlomo in obvious disgust and faced Dukas. "Give me that briefcase."

"Don't tempt me to start this as a homicide investigation."

David raised his hand and pointed at Dukas. "You don't even understand what you are interfering with. Give me the briefcase."

Dukas walked past the younger man and started up the hill, then turned. Instead of anger, he found only fatigue and boredom, as if he had played this scene too many times. "This is evidence in a war-crimes-tribunal investigation. You never mentioned a briefcase in our memorandum of understanding. You told me that this guy was some kind of terrorist heavy hitter. I don't know why you wanted him dead, but he's dead. Now—"

"We wanted him dead? The Albanians shot him!" David shouted, turning to Shlomo for support. Shlomo said nothing. His attention had switched from Dukas to David. He eyed him with distaste, the way tourists look at panhandlers.

Dukas shook his head, looked away, glanced back at a flicker of movement. The younger man had taken a long sliding step forward and his hand hit Dukas's elbow hard, numbing it. Dukas dropped the briefcase but managed to pivot, block the follow-on blow, and stand over the case. Dukas had plenty of time to see that the Canadians were too far away to do anything. He risked a glance at Shlomo, who hadn't moved.

David crouched, a relaxed martial arts position. He looked confident. "Give us the fucking briefcase."

Dukas shook his head. He didn't think the briefcase was worth a crap to him or any of the cases he was making, but this was too stupid a point to concede. He picked it up and held it to him like a schoolgirl holding her books and hoped that the heavy case would deflect a blow.

Shlomo stepped up behind his partner and elbowed him in the head so that he sat abruptly on the wet road. Again.

The Canadian ordered all three Kosovans to the ground and started bellowing into his radio for backup.

"It would be better if you gave us the briefcase," Shlomo said. He sounded as tired as Dukas felt.

"Put in a request through channels."

David moaned.

"That guy's dangerous," Dukas said.

"More dangerous than you know, my friend." Shlomo wiped the rain from his eyes. "I think you'd better get out of here."

Part One

1

Tel Aviv, Israel, January, 2002

Abe Peretz told the old joke about the Polish immigrant woman and the boy on the bus. It was practically archaic, he said, from the early days of Israel, but still funny: A mother and her little boy are riding on a bus in Jerusalem. The boy speaks Hebrew but the mother keeps speaking Yiddish. A man sitting across the aisle leans over and says, "Lady, the little boy speaks wonderful Hebrew; why do you keep talking to him in this wretched Yiddish?" "Because," she says, "I don't want him to forget he's a Jew."

Outside, the night was coming down like a lavender curtain, darker to the east behind them but brightening into orange on the undersides of the clouds out over the Mediterranean. The apartment was high above Ben Yehuda but the sounds of the street came up; and the smell of evening, a swirl of salt sea and car exhaust and cooking food, rose with them.

"They say that if you breathe really deep, you can smell the desert," Abe Peretz said.

"Only if you're a Jew," his wife said with a smile. "You, you'd have trouble."

The Peretzes lived in Tel Aviv but had been there only a few months; the Craiks were old friends passing through. The two men had served on a ship together fifteen years before, when one had been new to the Navy and the other had been in too long; now Peretz was the FBI's deputy legal attaché at the US embassy, and Alan Craik, long ago that young newbie, was the Fifth Fleet intel officer in Bahrain.

Peretz grinned at the two guests. "Bea thinks I'm not Jewish enough. Funny, because I don't look Jewish." He winked at his wife; she overdid rolling her eyes and laughed and said to Rose Craik, who was visibly pregnant, "This one had better be a girl. Two boys are enough."

"Well, I'm concentrating really hard."

"Two *girls* are enough, too," Peretz said. His own two had just come in, still out of sight but noisy at the apartment's front door. "The quietest voice they know is the scream. If you think Italians are noisy, wait until you've lived in a—"

The two girls erupted through the glass doors to the terrace, both in T-shirts with slogans across their breasts that were meaningless to the adults, one in Hebrew, one in English. There was a lot of kissing and flouncing and shouting; the greetings to Rose were enthusiastic but forced, because Rose Craik had been a great favorite when they had been children but now they were grown up—in their own eyes, at least; and after a lot of shouting, in which Bea took a major part, they whirled out again and the terrace seemed astonishingly quiet.

"As I was saying before I was interrupted," Abe Peretz said. He grinned again. He grinned a lot, his way of saying that nothing he said was quite serious, or at least not quite as it sounded.

"As you were saying," Bea Peretz erupted, "it's time I started cooking if we're ever going to eat." She got up and gestured toward Rose. "Come help me." She was a big woman, getting a little heavy, but she had beautiful eyes and still-black hair that lay tight against her skull and then cascaded down her back. "You guys tell each other war stories so we don't have to listen over dinner."

Alan Craik smiled at his wife, who had as many war stories as either of the men—chopper pilot, ex-squadron CO, currently deputy naval attaché, Bahrain—and who now gave a little shrug and let herself be led away.

That was the day that the latest fragile truce between the Israelis and the Palestinians had self-destructed when a Palestinian militant was killed by a car bomb in the West Bank. The al-Aksa Martyrs Brigade declared that the cease-fire was finished. Before the day was over, two soldiers had been killed at a settlement, and the Martyrs Brigade took credit.

That was also the last day of a man named Salem Qatib, who, like the cease-fire, was a victim of both sides: first the Palestinians tortured him, and then the Israelis tortured him, and then he died.

"Bea's kind of bossy," Abe said. He looked at the fingertips of one hand, sniffed them—an old habit. "We talk too much about being Jewish, don't we."

Embarrassed, Craik mumbled something vague.

"No, we do. Since we moved here, Bea and the girls have got like the Republican Party—a steady move to the right." He gave a snort, certainly meant to show disgust. "Bea has a new bosom buddy named Esther Himmelfarb. I mean, it's good that she's found a friend; Bea doesn't usually get close to people. And the woman helps her a lot—she knows where everything is, knows who to see, what to say, but—" He waved a hand. "We keep kosher—that's new. The girls want to go live on a kibbutz, even though the kibbutzes are all turning into corporations and the days of boys-and-girls-together-taming-the-desert are long gone. It's a romance. All three of them have fallen in love." He sniffed his fingers.

"You don't like it here?"

"I'm not enchanted by living on land that the former owners gave up because they had a gun at their head. And now they're sitting out there in refugee camps, watching me eat their dinner."

13

"The Palestinians don't exactly have the cleanest hands in the world."

"They're absolute shits. Just like a lot of Israelis. But overall, Israel gives me a royal pain in the butt because they're the occupying power and that puts a special responsibility on you to behave better than the other guy—and they won't face up to reality." He shot Craik a look to see if he knew which reality he meant. "You can't say 'No right of return, no reparations' and be a moral entity." He rested his arms on the terrace railing and put his chin on them. "That's why Bea says I'm a bad Jew. Because I won't join in the national romance."

Craik slumped lower until his spine was almost ready to fall off the seat, his long legs thrust out toward the edge of the terrace. He had his own doubts about Israel, but he had to shut up and do his job: in two days, he was supposed to meet with Shin Bet, Israel's military intelligence, to get their input on an operation in Afghanistan.

Fifty miles south in Gaza, three men were beating the Palestinian named Salem Qatib. Two would hold the victim while the third hit him, and then they would slam him against a stone wall and shout, "What else? What else?" They were Palestinian, too.

"Your husband looks like hell, if I'm allowed to say that, Rose," Bea Peretz was saying.

"He's stressed out, is all."

"What's he doing in Israel?"

"Oh—Navy stuff. You know." She hesitated, added, "He got a couple of extra days on his orders to try to sort of run down."

"Israel's a great place! Really. Even Abe thinks so." She was pounding dough down on a board, making it thin. "I wish you could meet my friend Esther. She makes you

14

understand how you can love this country. We all want to stay for good."

"The Bureau'll go along with that?"

"There's other jobs, Rose. Some things are more important than what you do for a living." The way she said it, Rose felt as if Bea had said it before, maybe many times—the detritus of an old argument, washed up on this woman-to-woman beach. Rose sampled a bit of something made with chopped olives and murmured, "We are what we do for a living, to some extent."

"And we can change!" Bea hit the dough a tremendous *whack!* "You were going to be an astronaut once. You didn't make it. You didn't die."

Only where nobody but me can see, Rose thought. She said, "Anyway, maybe Abe's not so invested in it as I was."

"Oh—Abe!" Bea cut the dough into squares with great slashes of a knife. "Abe could sell bread from a pushcart and be happy! He lives in such a fog—"

"How's Rose coping with not being an astronaut?" Peretz said to Alan Craik. They were still on the terrace, new drinks in their hands, the sky almost blue-black.

"I think it almost killed her, but—you know Rose. Get on with life." He sipped at his weak gin and tonic. "She's going to be deep-select for captain."

Peretz looked out at the sky for a long time, and when he spoke it was clear that he'd hardly listened to the answer to his own question. "If I get a transfer, I don't think Bea'll go with me. Or the girls."

"Well, if they're in school—"

Peretz bounced a knuckle against his upper lip. "It's a hell of a thing, to watch a family go in the tank because of—" He sighed. "It's never just one thing, is it. Bea and I have always had a— You know, the relationship has always been noisy. But suddenly— It's this damned place. Jesus." He stared at his fingers. "Religion's soaked into the goddam soil here. Like Love Canal."

Salem Qatib, who had been beaten, lay in one rut of a Gaza road. By and by somebody would have driven along the road and run over him, but a Palestinian who knew about the torture and who was a Mossad informer got on a cell phone and alerted his control.

Over dinner—candles, no kids, Israeli wine, lamb and grains in a recipe that was millennia old—the Craiks tried to talk about old friends and old days and things that didn't have to do with Israel or being Jewish. But as more wine was poured, Bea didn't want to talk about anything else, as if they had a scab that she wanted to scratch and watch bleed. She cited her friend Esther often—"Esther says." Even Nine-Eleven, the topic of conversation everywhere in those days, brought her back to Israel. "Now you know what it's like!" she cried. "Now you know what the Arabs are!" She gestured at Abe with a fork. "You'll say next that we should be more understanding, because al-Qaida blew up the World Trade Center because they're misunderstood!"

Abe started to say that he never said, and so on, and she interrupted, and so on.

"Bea enjoys being a caricature," Peretz said, smiling to show it was a joke and failing. "Bea, beautiful Bea, light of my life, could we talk about baseball?"

"Esther says the Palestinians are terrorists and invaders and we ought to throw them out and keep them the fuck out!"

"'We,'" Abe said, smiling at them.

"Arafat is a monster. He's paying the terrorists, killing women and children, and pretending to want peace. Esther says they live out there like animals; they live in kennels; they're barely able to read and write and they say they have 'universities,' my God!"

16

"When our great-grandparents lived in the shtetls, the Russians called them animals; they couldn't read or write; they—"

"And they came here and they made the desert bloom! They built real universities! They made a nation!"

"On land that they took with the gun," Abe said wearily.

"Because it was ours!"

Abe looked at Alan and gave an apologetic shrug. The silence grew longer, and Abe said, falsely cheerful, "What d'you hear from Mike Dukas?"

Maybe because she had had too much wine, Bea broke in with, "I'll never forgive Mike Dukas for saying that Jonathan Pollard was a traitor! Never. Never, never, never!"

"But Pollard *was* a traitor," Abe made the mistake of saying.

He was probably going to explain that somebody who sells American secrets to another state, even if it's Israel, is in fact a traitor, but Bea said in a suddenly quiet voice, "I know what *you* think," and she turned away and began to talk to Rose about having daughters.

Then things were easier for a while, and they got through dessert, and Alan looked at his watch and at Rose, and when Bea brought in coffee everything would have been all right if Rose hadn't asked for cream, and there was embarrassment and confusion, and Abe explained the kosher rule of thumb and ended, smiling as at a great joke, "It's a dietary law, which I'd be happy to explain the logic of if I understood it myself."

Bea said, "If you were half the Jew you ought to be, you'd understand it."

"But I must be a Jew—my mother was Jewish. Okay, Bea?"

She dropped her voice to a purr. "Abe means he's *a modern* Jew. Just like everybody else—no funny foods, no embarrassing hat, no accent—*oy veh!* that he should have an accent!—he should be taken for a Presbyterian, maybe.

17

Assimilate, right, Abe? That's the magic word, right? Assimilate European high culture and never look back— Dostoevsky, Mozart, and Wittgenstein, right?"

In the embarrassed silence, Alan said, "Who's Wittgenstein?"

She stared at him, broke into loud laughter, then patted him on the cheek. "I love you, Al—you're perfect."

Alan looked at his wife and got the slightly wide-eyed look: *Say nothing; we'll leave soon.*

Salem Qatib lay on a table now. A big Israeli was leaning over him shouting *Shit!* again and again, and then he screamed at another man, "You stupid asshole, you've fucking *killed* him!"

Acco, Israel

Rashid Halaby sat in the dark with his back against a wall that had been built when Augustus was Caesar. The fancy American flashlight that his mother had given him for his birthday had a new battery, but it was running down now. He had his cell phone, but the signal couldn't penetrate the layers of rock and mud brick above him. He was hungry. He was filthy. He was thirsty and had no water. His ribs hurt every time he took a deep breath or moved in a certain way, from a fall.

Salem, his best friend—taken. Beaten.

Rashid had run from the dig in Gaza, fought the men who had tried to stop him. He had run and left Salem to their attackers. Then he had hidden, then hitched a ride with workers from a kiln going back to their homes in Israel. He thought he might have killed a man—a Hamas man. With a rock hammer.

He couldn't go home.

His hand dug almost of its own volition, scrabbling in the ancient dirt. He built a little pile of worthless artifacts; the bones of a small animal, some shells, a coil of brass or bronze wire, something that might have been a bead or a carbonized grain of wheat. And a bronze arrowhead with a distinctive cast barb, the type that the Scythians had used. Salem Qatib had taught him all that.

Sitting in the dark, he cried. Once he started, he couldn't stop, and it went on and on, because too many bad things had happened. He wanted out. He needed to find Salem.

2

Acco

It was after midnight when Rashid emerged from the tunnels under Acco. He left by way of new digs into the crusader city; they were unguarded and had opened new routes to the surface for him. One came up just outside the north walls, close enough to the sea that he had to wade the last few yards through water filthy with refuse in his wavering flashlight. He washed as soon as the water looked clean. Then he picked his way along the stone shoring intended to keep ancient Acco from washing into the Mediterranean until he passed the walls and entered the industrial zone to the north. There he climbed up into the over-lit modern night and squelched his way to a bus stop. By the time a bus came, he was nearly dry. Neither of the two passengers gave him a glance.

He was going to the apartment of Salem's girlfriend. He didn't like her, but he had nowhere else to go. She would tell him what had happened. She would know where to find Salem.

Even his feet were almost dry by the time the bus dropped him a few meters from her apartment, a heavy building with too much concrete and too little glass. From the street, he could see a paid security guard in the lobby. He had been here before, many times. Salem had virtually lived in her apartment after he met her.

He walked around the building, hungry, thirsty, and every time he slipped his side gave a pulse of pain like a knife-jab. Yesterday, or perhaps two days ago, he had had everything a man his age could want—a job, a place to live, a wonderful friend—

Before he could start crying again, Rashid pushed himself up the steps and into the lobby. The guard did not raise his head from his Koran, and Rashid went by. The building had elevators that actually worked. Rashid hit the up button and waited. When the doors opened, he entered, panicked briefly when he saw a man coming up from the garage with him, and then made himself press the button for sixteen. The man smiled at him and then frowned at his shoes, good American basketball shoes now caked with filth and still damp.

"I got lost," Rashid said.

The words hung in the air between them. Rashid knew immediately that talking had been a mistake. The other man looked away. The elevator came to a stop on twelve and the man got out, looking at Rashid as he left and then at the digital floor display as if to check where Rashid was going.

Rashid felt his hands begin to shake. He clenched them.

The doors shut.

Rashid was sure that the man intended to call the desk when he reached his apartment. If Saida refused to see him, he would be taken, perhaps handed over to the police.

The doors opened on an empty corridor. Rashid stumbled forward, rattled and apprehensive. Saida was a hard woman, but she wasn't bad.

A slut, his mother said.

He got to her door, still confused about what to say when she answered, and knocked. He should have called before he came, but he had little money, and in movies, people could be traced by their cell phones. He knocked again, put his ear to the door and knocked as loud as he dared.

The elevator departed behind him with a loud hum and

whir of hydraulics and pulleys. He listened to it as it ran all the way down to the lobby without stopping.

He knocked again.

She wasn't home.

The stairwell was locked on the ground floor, he knew. He didn't want to face the security in the lobby by going down the stairs.

The elevator was coming back up.

He tried to turn the handle of her door. Locked, of course. He tried again, as if strength could break a lock. Suddenly, his apprehension turned to panic at the approach of the elevator and he put both hands on the knob and wrenched at it, throwing his weight against the door.

The knob suddenly turned freely, and he stumbled through and the door slammed shut behind him. He tripped and fell sprawling with a crash as loud as the slam of the door. His flailing hands found paper, clothes, pans—

The balcony light shone through the sliding doors at the end of a short hall. The floor of the entire apartment, bigger than the place he shared with his mother, was covered in papers and trash. Every item in every drawer, every sheet of paper, had been rifled and tossed on the linoleum.

The lock had been forced. That's why he had got in so easily.

Two thoughts seemed to occur to him simultaneously: that whoever had done this might still be there, and that the lobby security might be coming up in the elevator, might enter and assume he had robbed her. The association of the two thoughts froze him on the floor.

The elevator ran and ran, a pulse-like vibration allowing him to count the floors.

It stopped. The doors opened. It was this floor; someone got out and walked swiftly up the hall, and then back down it. Rashid held his breath, sure, *sure* that it was the guard. Unable to move. With nothing between him and arrest but an unlocked door. The man moved and stopped.

And moved.

And stopped.

Rashid saw the guard's feet under the door against the light of the outside hall. In his mind, he prayed. *Inshallah, Inshallah, Inshallah.*

Allah's will was that the guard should walk on. He moved down the corridor a few more doors, stopped, and came back.

The elevator doors opened and closed again and the car began to move.

Rashid breathed.

What if she was here, dead? That was a foolish thought, born of fatigue and the alien landscape in which he suddenly found himself. It was like finding himself on the set of an American horror movie.

He couldn't push it out of his mind. In movies, the dead person was always in the bathroom. The bathroom was the next room on the hall.

He wished he had a weapon. He forced himself to crawl to the light-switch and threw it. All the lights came on, revealing the destruction of Saida's effects more cruelly than the hallway lighting had done. He peered into the bathroom and saw no body. Emboldened, he moved into the kitchen, found a clean glass on a paper on the floor, and drank her expensive bottled water from the refrigerator. He drank three bottles before he was done; then he ate a sandwich that was days old but tasted wonderful.

Saida's absence left him with no options. No money, no place to go, no one to beg for help. But his brain began to run again, and the panic drew back to the edge of his consciousness.

He had to get out of this building.

He had to get money.

He had to find Salem, although it was increasingly clear to him that Salem was in deep trouble. Rashid knew he

23

had found something—something wonderful. Salem could not hide his feelings from Rashid. And he had taken things from the dig—Rashid had seen them in a gym bag in Salem's car.

The men beating Salem at the dig, pounding him with their fists and the flat of a shovel. Yelling abuse. Telling Salem he was a thief. And Rashid, Salem's loyal friend, had run away and hidden in the old tunnels under the city.

He went into the bedroom. The epicenter of the apartment's wreckage. He started to go through the piles of clothing the searchers had thrown on the floor.

Salem's clothes were in a separate pile. Rashid dug into it for Salem's Navy coat; he didn't wear it in Gaza, where American sailors would hardly be popular, but he often wore it in Israel where the opposite was true. Up in the padding of the shoulders was Salem's emergency stash. Salem had shown it to him, once, with a joke.

"It's my fly-away money," he had said.

A thousand dollars in American bills, crisp and neat. And a tiny hard rectangle that felt unfamiliar. Rashid pulled it out and tried to remember what it did. He took another swig of water and remembered. He was holding a flash card, the memory of a digital camera. And Salem had hidden it.

He pocketed it with the money. He took the peacoat, because it was warm and dry and it was Salem's. It made him feel taller.

He still had to leave the building. He poked through the rubble of Salem's life with Saida and found a pair of his boots, rubberized duck shoes that Salem had seldom worn because, he said, they hurt his feet and were too hot. They fit poorly, but with the peacoat they made him look like a young man of means. They gave him the confidence to take the elevator and face the man at the desk.

As the elevator descended, he found he was calm. Perhaps too tired to feel more fear.

24

"She's not home," the guard said when Rashid emerged. The tone was on the edge of accusation.

"I know," Rashid replied, walking steadily to the doors. Whatever the guard might have wanted to ask, Rashid kept going, volunteering nothing, a tactic that seldom failed him, until he was out on the street in the cold winter rain. When the guard finally opened her apartment, he, Rashid, would be the obvious suspect. Then the police would join Hamas in searching for him.

His life here was done. He was going to find Salem, and the place to look was back in the occupied territory. So be it. Rashid felt the crisp bills in his pocket and headed for a bus stop.

Naval Criminal Investigative Service HQ, Naples, Italy

"Aw, *shit*!"

Mike Dukas was looking at a message directing him to do something—*urgently*—and his people were already stretched thin and he didn't have time for Mickey Mouse. His hand hit the phone.

"Dick," he growled, "get in here."

"Your wish is my, mm, suggestion."

Dick Triffler was the ASAC—the Assistant Special Agent in Charge, NCIS Naples. He was a tall, slender African American with an oddly high voice and a manner so precise that he seemed to be doing an imitation of somebody—Clifton Webb, maybe, or William F. Buckley. He had worked with and for Dukas off and on for years and had always been eager to transfer someplace else; Dukas had been astonished, therefore, when Triffler had *requested* to be ASAC when Dukas had taken over Naples as Special Agent in Charge. Asked why, Triffler, who had been running his own long-term investigation on the West Coast, had said, "I thought I needed a challenge."

Now Triffler came in, buttoning a black blazer over a blue-on-blue striped shirt and a thick silk tie that, in an office where Dukas was wearing an ancient polo, made it look as if the Prince of Wales was visiting a homeless person. "You rang?" Triffler said as he sat down, pulling one knife-creased pant leg over a knee.

"I got a Rummygram telling us we *urgently* got to get the closeout details on some poor ex-Navy bastard who died in Tel Aviv. What the hell, is this any way to run a war on terrorism?"

"What war on terrorism?"

"The one we're waging twenty-four-seven throughout the universe. Isn't that what all this paperwork is about? Jesus Christ, I've got five drunken sailors in foreign jails, three sex abusers, a phantom shitter on the *Fort Klock*, and we're supposed to be looking under the beds for al-fucking-Qaida! Now I've got to scrape up somebody to do scut work in fucking Tel Aviv! Let the naval attaché do it!"

"You're venting again. That's what I'm here for, isn't it—to listen to you vent. As you know, naval attachés have better things to do, like looking for a good place to have lunch, and dealing with dead sailors in foreign places is our charge."

Dukas sighed. "Well—yeah, it's our business—so who's near Tel Aviv? The *Jefferson*'s already in the Canal. Athens office is too busy. We got anybody who can take a day and go?"

Triffler's laugh was deliberately false. "How about Al Craik? He's in Tel Aviv even as we speak."

"How the hell do you know that?"

"Your wife told my wife."

Dukas stared at him, stuck his lips out, raised an eyebrow. "That's some network you got—two wives. You ever think of going into intelligence?"

Triffler stood—an impressive unfolding of long-boned limbs. "Am I done being vented at? You get in touch with Al."

"You giving the orders now?"

"Somebody has to do it."

Dukas scowled at his retreating back and then put out his hand for the phone and called Fifth Fleet, Bahrain, to ask where Commander Craik was staying in Tel Aviv.

Washington

In the Department of Defense's (DoD's) mint-new Office of Information Analysis, the workday went on longer even than in the White House. The atmosphere of the place was that of a great business enterprise at the top of its game—buoyant, aggressive, determined, and overworked.

For a thirty-five-year-old named Ray Spinner, the place was salvation. He'd got bounced from the Navy for passing privileged information to his power-lawyer father; Dad had placed him in OIA to make it up. Now, Spinner reeled through his workdays in a frenzy half joy and half terror (Could he measure up? Could he be hardline enough? Did he dare to ape the bosses and wear power suspenders?). It was better than the Navy had ever been, but scary.

Sitting in a cubicle among twenty other cubicles, he was watching a message come up on his computer. New data came first to people like him; he knocked out the obvious bullshit and passed the rest up the line. The criteria had little to do with either authenticity or reliability and everything to do with usefulness to the office's main goal—just then, getting something going in Iraq. He had already made the mistake of knocking out a report from a defector who said he had overheard a third party say that sarin gas was being manufactured nights and weekends in a Baghdad elementary school; it had been made very clear to him that this was precisely the kind of intelligence that was wanted, and if he made the same kind of dumb-nuts mistake again, he'd find himself handing out towels in the men's room.

Spinner therefore really bore down now. The bit he was

27

looking at struck him as a no-brainer—forwarding of a Tel Aviv police department memo about some dead A-rab.

> Yarkov District police tonight reported death of Salem Qatib, Palestinian, resident West Bank. Held US student visa 1994-95, ex-US Navy reserve.

Meaning that the informant thought the dead guy might be of interest because he had US connections. *Wrong.* The real question was, Was he a terrorist? *Well, let's see.* Spinner brought up OIA's own list, which was different from the CIA's and the FBI's and much longer, and he didn't find Salem Qatib as a terrorist but did find him on the Purgatory list ("not in Hell, but nearby") of people "tracked for conflate background"—that is, for combining at least two suspicious factors. Like being Palestinian and having served three years in the US Naval Reserve.

As a cryptologist.

Hey, whoa!

Cryptologists had high security clearances and were tracked for years after they left the service because they had had access to sensitive stuff—codes, for example, that might not be changed for a long time. So Qatib must have been tracked, and he appeared to be clean, but OIA still had him on the conflate list because Palestinian plus cryptology equaled possible spy, right?

So. It wouldn't do to make another mistake. Which he could do either by bumping this one up the line (but the word was that the White House was tired of the Palestinian problem), or by killing it (but maybe there was a secret interest in Palestinians that he didn't know about).

Naval Reserve. That meant that the Navy would have to do a red-tape write-off—certify that the guy was dead, close his files, tie up all the loose ends of debts and pensions and all the other petty crap that the bean-counter mind could think of. So who did that?

The Naval Criminal Investigative Service, that's who.

Nearest office to Tel Aviv? Athens. He looked at the Athens roster, didn't recognize any names—Spinner liked to deal with friends—and noted that Athens was actually under NCIS Naples, so looked there. And my God, Mary, look at that— the Special Agent in Charge, Naples, was an asshole named Mike Dukas!

Spinner grinned.

Mike Dukas had been the prick who'd got him read out of the Navy.

So Spinner forwarded the Qatib report to Michael Dukas, SAC NCIS Naples, blind-copied to his own boss at OIA, with the terse order, "Check implications anti-terrorism and terrorist connections and report back ASAP." He put the name of OIA's head at the bottom—a stretch, but permissible. He sent it Urgent.

Up yours, Dukas. He could just see the overweight, glowering, blue-collar Dukas hunched over the message, trying to figure out why he'd been told to jump, and to jump urgently.

Spinner grinned. He stood, stretched, looked over his cubicle wall at a guy going by wearing red suspenders. Yeah, he'd look drop-dead good in those.

Tel Aviv

Alan Craik was sitting on a hotel-room bed, a telephone in his hand. His wife, mostly naked, came out of the bathroom and turned, her back to him, to rummage in a suitcase. He grinned at her back. "Sexy buns."

On the telephone, a voice barked, "Dukas."

"My God, you mean I was holding for *you*? If I'd known it was you, I wouldn't have waited."

Rose ran back toward the bathroom, an irrelevant nightgown fluttering from her shoulders.

"I got a favor I want you to do me."

"The answer is no."

"No, the answer is yes. There's nothing to it; it'll give you something to do in Tel Aviv while Rose shops."

"How the hell'd you know where I am?"

"Rose talked to Les a couple days ago. Les talked to Triffler's wife. You can't have secrets, man." Les—Leslie—was Dukas's new and pregnant wife; she and Rose were pals. "Anyways—"

"Yeah?"

"This is strictly routine—I gotta have somebody from the Navy get a death certificate. A guy died, ex-Nav. Find out what the story is, blah-blah-blah. Anybody could do it."

"Get anybody."

"There isn't anybody! Look, the guy died; we gotta make it possible to close out his file, notify next of kin, all that. Just do it, will you?"

"Meaning what?"

"Piece o' cake." Dukas told him where to go in Tel Aviv—the main police building on Dizengoff Street—and the victim's name—Salem Qatib.

"That's an *Arab* name."

"Palestinian."

"Mike, a Palestinian who's ex-US Navy?—in Tel Aviv—?"

"Just do it, will you? Fax me the death certificate and anything else you get. And don't overdo it—forget you're an intel officer and just be my errand boy. I'll fax the dead guy's paperwork to the embassy."

He would have objected, but Dukas had hung up and his wife came out of the bathroom, and when she saw his face, she said, "Now what?"

Bayt Da Border Crossing, Gaza

Rashid spent the bus drive across Israel handling his papers and his Israeli passport, and imagining how he might handle the border crossing. He was dirty—even his eyes felt dirty—but the other passengers going to Gaza weren't much cleaner.

When he had worked on the site, it had been easy, because he had been in Salem's car and Salem had a work permit—bogus, in that it mis-stated Salem's reasons for being in Gaza, but real enough and issued under the seal of the Palestinian Authority. Salem knew how to get such things.

In two hours of tired worry, Rashid concocted a simple story to cover his visit; a girl he had met in Acco, the need to see her again. True enough, if he substituted Salem for the girl. He rehearsed his story to himself, staring at his passport and his travel documents, until the bus slowed to a stop in the morning line at the border crossing. The bus was half empty. Rashid felt alone, and his anxieties were pushed into his stomach and his limbs. He had to put the passport down because it showed the trembling of his hands.

The bus inched forward in the line, surrounded by barbed wire and graffiti-covered concrete, steel reinforcement rods rusting away in long brown streaks. The stink of leaded gasoline fumes filled the air around him, came in through his open window and bit at his throat.

Before they reached the checkpoint, armed Palestinian Authority security men came on to the bus. One of them took the passenger list from the driver and read through it. Another, younger, officer checked through the documents that passengers had; passports, work permits, sometimes only letters from a possible employer and an identity card.

The man with the passenger list made a call on his cell phone. The bored young man with an AK on his back flipped through Rashid's Israeli passport.

"Where do you live?" he asked.

"Acco."

"Purpose of your visit?" he asked, looking carefully at Rashid's travel documents.

Rashid hadn't seen him ask anyone else these questions, and he started to tremble again. "I'm—I'm going to see a—girl."

The man laughed. He was only a little older than Rashid.

Rashid relaxed a little, and then the man with the passenger list pointed at him. "Rashid Halaby?" he said.

The younger guard nodded, held up Rashid's passport. "Take him."

Tel Aviv

Dressed and waiting for his wife, Alan Craik was thinking not of her but of how thoroughly their world had changed since September eleventh. He was not thinking in sequence, not being rational or logical, rather letting his mind leapfrog from idea to idea; in fact, there was no logic, only the sequence of time itself, certainly no meaning. September eleventh obsessed his world, but he was oddly not quite of it: he had been on an island in the Gulf of Oman on September eleventh, miles from a television set, and he had not seen those images as they had burned their way into the world's consciousness. He saw them later, to be sure; he had been shocked, saddened, angered, but he had missed the raw outrage—and the fear— that had gripped so many people. The difference was that he had not seen the horror live on television:

The island was rocky scrub and sand. There were goats, lots of them, many apparently wild. People walked into and out of this landscape as if passing from another reality into his and then out again. The sky came down like gray, hot metal and the sea, a smell wherever he went, was rarely visible. He was doing the red tape on the setting-up of a Navy sonar station, a job that could have been done and done better by a lieutenant with some sonar experience, but he was out of favor at Fifth Fleet, out of favor with the new flag and the new flag captain. The flag captain had said that there was no place for him there anymore and they'd expedite a new duty station for him but they didn't want him as their intel, didn't want his kind, whatever that meant. But he knew what it meant: a risk-taker, a man who thought that out on a limb was where intel was done best.

He was out at the site, watching the goats, the odd Bedouin. Nothing was happening. He was thinking that they didn't need him there at all. Right at that moment, they didn't need him anywhere. Then his cell phone rang and the world changed. It was Sully, a CIA security thug who was a bully but the right man to have if people started shooting at you. Sully pushed people around verbally by saying the things that you didn't say when the dynamics among people were fragile or explosive—sex, politics, religion—and now he said, the very first thing he said, "Al-Qaida just re-elected George Bush to a second term." Then he had explained that a jetliner had crashed into the World Trade Center and other passenger aircraft were missing and bad shit was going down.

The event had jerked him from the job at Fifth Fleet to one as a Temporary Additional Duty case officer at Central Command, Qatar. He had been twice to Afghanistan since then, three times to Kuwait, once to Pakistan, once to Iran, all in the four months since that remarkably, perhaps fantastically, lucky, successful, outrageous al-Qaida hit. He had gone from vengefulness to resignation, then to a kind of skeptical sadness.

"Penny?" Rose said.

He took her hand. "I was thinking that al-Qaida did things right, and we're going to do things wrong."

"Still chewing on it."

"Aren't you?"

"I don't want to go rushing back to a squadron to throw myself at bin Laden, if that's what you mean."

She'd been really hurt, he knew, by bailing out of the astronaut program. The Navy had lost some of its zest for her; he thought that it was that loss that had let her get pregnant again, driven her, maybe, back on her kids and on him. "There'll be plenty of time to go to a squadron," he said. "Years."

"Another war, you think?"

"Oh, yeah. Lots of them." He stood up, kissed her. "Bin Laden has arranged our futures for us."

33

"We make our own futures." She believed in self-determination.

"I thought so until this happened, but now—" He shook his head. "I keep wanting to look up to see who's jerking my strings." He straightened his clothes, pulling on himself as if he were rearranging his body, and they went to the elevator. He told her, in a different, heavier voice, that he was going to run Dukas's errand while she shopped for presents for their kids. "I'm going there now and I should be done by two, and we'll have a late lunch and then I'll mosey over to the embassy and arrange to have them send the stuff to Mike."

"I want to see a movie. Let's go to a movie."

"In Hebrew? Anyway, I've seen *Harry Potter* as much as I can stand."

"It might be more interesting in Hebrew."

On the street, he warned her for the third or maybe the fifth time of what to look for to avoid car bombs; he told her to duck if anybody started shooting, because half the crowd in any given spot would be armed; he told her to be careful of the baby. She told him he was a fuss-budget and she loved him and she'd see him at two o'clock.

He was back to thinking about September eleventh. "Everybody's scared here," he said. "Scared people scare me."

Naples

Mike Dukas flicked a paper across his desk to Dick Triffler. "What the hell is an Office of Information Analysis?"

Triffler studied the paper. "It's a secret office in DoD to do an end run around the intel agencies."

"What the hell?"

"Folks who don't like it call it the Office of Intellectual Paralysis. Folks who do like it think it's the latest thing in what they call 'intelligence reform,' which means doing the Alley Oop around worn-out old shitkickers like the CIA, the

FBI, and the Naval Criminal Investigation Service. We are, and I think I quote, 'tired, old, liberal, and nitpicking.' It's do-it-yourself intel."

"How come you know all that and I don't?"

"I read *The New Yorker*."

"Some secret."

Triffler looked up over the rims of his reading glasses. "*The New Yorker* has an excellent track record. You should read it."

"I don't have time to read. So why the hell is this secret bunch of bureaucrats sending me a message to do what I already did anyway, namely get things moving on this guy who died in Tel Aviv?"

Triffler took off the glasses. "You're a bureaucrat, too, after all."

"That's the worst thing you've ever called me."

"No, it isn't. You just didn't hear the others. Done with me?"

"I smell fish. Rummy's errand boys don't send me messages by name. Somebody's after me. Well?"

"Sounds right."

"Check it out, will you?"

Triffler sighed. "If I say 'Why me?' will you do it yourself?"

"No time."

Triffler sighed again. "The black man's burden," he said. He went back to his own office and got on the phone to a friend who taught public policy at Howard University. The woman was deep into Washington's Democratic political scene, a good bet for elective office if she ever wanted it. "I need some information," he said.

"Are you the Dick Triffler who's tall, thin, and a dynamite dresser?"

"My word for it would be 'elegant.'"

"Your wife is so lucky."

"Tell her that."

"Information is my middle name, honey; what d'you need?"

"There's a new office in DoD called Information Analysis. I want to know who works there."

"This administration's pretty tight in the ass, hon."

"You'd win my undying gratitude."

"That your best offer?"

"At this distance, I'm afraid so."

"I'll see what I can do."

What she did was call a grossly overweight but unpredictably vain man in the office of a member of the Congressional Black Caucus. He had been an aide for a decade, knew where bodies were buried and who had held the shovel. He loved information, which he hoarded and then dealt like cards in a game of cutthroat stud.

"What're you offering, chickie?"

"Well, I was just offered undying gratitude, how's that?"

He laughed. "For gratitude, I don't even give out the correct time."

She cajoled, joked, reminded him of her usefulness in promoting legislation for his member.

"You promoting my member, sweetie? You haven't set eyes on my member yet!"

"Spare me the Clarence Thomas jokes. You going to get me what I want or not?" She let an edge show in her voice; he got it. Business was business, after all. He'd need her, she was saying—each in his turn. He sighed. "You one tough lady. I'll get back."

The fat man slicked his wavy hair back—shiny, very like Cab Calloway's, he thought—and checked his reflection in a window and called a guy he knew at the Pentagon. "Whose dick I gotta lick to pry loose a list of folks in some shithouse called the Office of Information Analysis?" he said.

*　　*　　*

36

Tel Aviv

Tel Aviv is a city of beautiful women and ugly architecture; the first make up for the second. Craik found it a pleasure to walk.

The police station on Dizengoff Street was on a par with the city's other buildings, but at least it looked as if being a cop was a good thing—clean, solid, windowless. The entrance didn't invite you in but announced that going in, with the right credentials, would be easier than getting out with the wrong ones.

He showed his passport and his part-timer's NCIS badge. "Commander Craik, US Navy. About the death of Qatib, Salem."

The policewoman at the inquiries desk spoke better Hebrew than she did English, but she wrote some things down and got on a telephone. Meanwhile, a plain-clothes detective was looking Alan over and probably realizing that he wasn't armed—Alan, like most of the men in Tel Aviv, was wearing a short-sleeved shirt and slacks—while Alan was looking him over and deciding that the extra tuck on the right side of his shirt covered an in-the-waistband holster, and his slightly cocked left foot might suggest an ankle gun.

People went by as if they were heading for a somber event, heads down, moving fast. The space was big, harshly echoing, lighted with banks of fluorescents overhead; the noise of footsteps was like some sort of clattering engine. *Move, move,* the noise, the atmosphere seemed to say; *get in and get out, don't linger, we're serious here.*

"Commander Alan Craik?"

The man was blond, chunky, purposely likable. He had a Browning nine-millimeter in a very visible shoulder holster and he smiled as if he really was glad to see Alan. Maybe he was simply glad to see anybody who would allow him to strike an item off his to-do list. "Detective Sergeant Berudh."

37

They shook hands. Berudh led him toward a bank of elevators, one hand behind Alan's left arm; he was chattering about the building—how big it was, how many different offices it housed, how many crimes they covered a day. "You're US Navy," he said abruptly. "Not from a ship, I think."

"No, not from a ship." Habit kept him from saying where he was stationed just then. Which was absurd, of course, because the Israelis would already know. And they were allies. More or less.

Berudh was silent in the elevator, surrounded as they were by worried-looking people who were certainly not police. The elevator smelled of nervousness, Alan thought. Then two young women got on, smiling, bouncy, and chattered as the elevator rose. They worked there and seemed to say, "What is there to be nervous about?"

"Only the police are at home in a police station," he said when they got off.

"And why not? Everybody's guilty about something." Berudh led the way down a corridor. "Most of them are here for permits, licenses, getting papers stamped, but they feel guilty. Actually, it makes the job easier." He held a door open. "You're NCIS?"

Alan explained that he had a badge but it was left over from earlier duty. "The special agent in charge of NCIS, Naples, asked me to do this for him."

"Scut work," Berudh said and gave him the smile. Berudh spoke American English with a slight accent, clearly knew American slang. "We work with NCIS when there are ships in Haifa, stuff like that. Sailors come down here, get in the usual trouble sailors do, we have to arrest them, blah-blah-blah. But we're all friends."

He was leading Alan through a room that had half a dozen desks in it, fluorescent lights overhead, a computer on each desk and a man or woman working at each one. More guns were in evidence here, some hung in their holsters on chair-backs.

"Okay." Berudh sat behind the only empty desk, pulled a metal chair over for Alan. He offered coffee or tea or soda, told a quick joke, surprised Alan by asking to see his ID. "I know you ID'd yourself at the door and at reception, but it's a rule. Death is serious business, isn't it?" He looked over the passport and the badge, made some notes, and sat back. "Okay."

He had a thin pile of photocopies and computer printouts. He began to hand them across the desk, naming each one as he did so—"Initial contact sheet—log sheet—physician's report—death certificate—telephone log, that's only to show when we notified your embassy—" The pages were clean, all typed, neat, efficient, but in a language Alan couldn't read. Berudh explained that Qatib, Salem, had begun his police connection as an unidentified corpse in Jaffa, another of Tel Aviv's sub-districts, then been logged in as a homicide, then identified from missing-person calls placed by his family.

Alan could have taken the papers then and left, but a perverse sense of duty made him ask questions he wasn't at all interested in. "How come if he was found in Jaffa, you're handling it here?"

"Question of internal politics." Berudh made a face. "Yarkov District claims control over all cases of wrongful death. Not that we handle them all. Our homicide people are very territorial."

"How long had he been missing?"

"Unh—" Berudh half-stood and leaned over to look at Alan's pages. "You've got a page from our missing-persons log—it's small type, very dense—" Alan held up a page; Berudh squinted at it and said, "I think the first call came in about eleven p.m." Berudh rattled through a translation of the missing-persons page: a woman's voice had made the first call, identified herself as a girlfriend; the victim hadn't turned up for dinner at his cousin's. They looked at the physician's report. The man had been dead an estimated seven to twelve hours when the doctor had examined him.

"But no autopsy," Alan said.

"No, no, no. Arabs are against that."

"Can I see the body?" He hoped the answer was no.

"We released him to the family pretty much as soon as the doc was through with him. Off to the West Bank." Berudh raised his hands. "Coffin was closed."

Something pinged in Alan's brain but didn't quite connect, and he said lamely, stalling until the connection was made, "You don't have a suspect."

"At this point, no. Mugging? Girlfriend? Palestinian in-fighting?" He shrugged. "This guy was in your Navy, but a Palestinian can be into anything. Hamas, Fatah—he could have had a suicide belt stashed someplace, chickened out, got punished. They're all fanatics."

Alan signed a paper that said that he had in fact received all the stuff in his hand, and Berudh, smiling again, gave him a dark blue plastic folder with something in Hebrew on it and *TLVPD* in English in white letters. "It'll keep them neat; they blow in the wind, you know; we always have a breeze, it's the sea—that's Tel Aviv, my friend, the Fort Lauderdale of the eastern Med—" He was seeing Alan to the elevator, explaining twice how to get out of the building, assuring him that if there was anything, *anything* he could do—and was gone.

In the vast lobby, assaulted again by the clatter of echoes, Alan crossed among the worried people heading for the eleva-tors and looked with relish at the thin slice of the outdoors that showed through the guarded entrance. *Guilt.* Even when you weren't guilty of anything, you felt it. He thought of September eleventh: *Yes, it's guilt, as if I could have stopped it.* Which was nonsense.

It was at that point that his brain made the connection

40

he'd missed earlier. According to the two-page file Dukas had faxed him—Qatib's short personnel record and an ID sheet—he had had family in the States. But the body, Berudh had said, had been sent to the West Bank. Maybe the family had moved back? Or the parents had divorced and one had come back? Or—?

Instead of leaving the police building, ignoring Dukas's plea not to be an intel officer, he went to the information desk and said to the same young woman, "I'd like to talk to somebody in Homicide." Why hadn't he asked to see Berudh again? he wondered. *Because you check one source against another.* He pointed at the signature on the first page in the blue folder Berudh had given him. "This person," he said, figuring that one way in was as good as another.

3

Gaza City, Palestinian Authority

He wasn't sure where he was—somewhere in the territories. The interrogation room smelled of mold. It was underground, the white paint on the walls peeled away from the concrete in long strips, exposing the rough surface beneath. It was too bright, lit by a pair of hot halogen lights, so that cockroaches threw sharp shadows on the floor where they scuttled.

Rashid had been waiting there for three hours. He had surprised himself by falling asleep. He had woken up to find that the persistent itching on his leg was an insect that had crawled up his jeans. He panicked, flailed around the room getting the unclean thing out of his clothes.

Then he sat, his arms crossed on his chest, and waited.

He heard steps in the hall, conversations, snatches of laughter, once, a startled scream.

More steps in the hall, sharper, and the click of a woman's heels. His door opened.

There was a man and a woman. The man was middle-aged, thin, smoking. The woman was younger, but not by much, wore heels and a short skirt.

Men with guns brought two chairs.

"I am Colonel Mahmoud Hamal and this is Zahirah," the man said. "You are Rashid George Halaby?"

Rashid nodded.

"You know who I am?"

Rashid shook his head.

"Perhaps you have heard me called the Tax Collector. Hmm? I am responsible for the security of our Palestinian Authority in regard to antiquities. You work for Hamas?"

The question pierced through Rashid's other fears; something to be dreaded, something for which he had not prepared an answer. So he said nothing, tried to keep his eyes down. He had heard of the Tax Collector. Salem had mentioned him—feared him, even.

"How long have you been with Hamas?" Colonel Hamal was looking at a manila folder.

Rashid looked at him with lowered eyes. The colonel was wearing a suit, had a silk tie, and a heavy gold ring on his finger. Rashid blinked to keep tears off his face.

The colonel waved the folder at him. "You are Rashid George Halaby. You live in Haifa. You run errands for Hamas. You had two brothers killed in the Intifada by Jewish soldiers. Your father died in Jordan in a riot. Your mother teaches at a Muslim school. Why not just say these things?"

Unbidden, Rashid's eyes rose and met the colonel's. The man smiled.

"You have an Israeli passport. As far as I can tell, you have never been arrested in Israel. Are you a Muslim?"

Rashid nodded.

"How do you come to have an Israeli passport?" the woman asked. Her voice was warm, her Arabic slightly accented.

"We live in Acco. Not Haifa." Rashid spoke softly, as if he was afraid he might be overheard. They must know these things. Haifa was an Israeli town. Acco had a big Palestinian population, one of the biggest in Israel. "I'm a Palestinian."

The man waved his hand, his attention still on the documents. "Acco, then. Either way, you are not from Gaza or the West Bank. You have an Israeli passport." Hamal threw it on the table in front of the boy. "Why didn't you proclaim it? I have no jurisdiction over you."

Rashid couldn't think of a reply. He couldn't think at all. All answers were going to lead to the same place—*Hamas, Salem, Hamas, Salem. Had he killed the man with the hammer? Did they know?* He shrugged, the motion stiff. Rashid rubbed the back of his hand over his face, rubbed his lips. The arresting officers had not been gentle.

"What were you doing here?" Hamal paused for effect. "In Gaza?"

"Working. With a friend." Rashid thought that sounded harmless, but both the man and the woman smiled.

"What were you working on?"

Rashid's lips trembled.

"How long have you been with Hamas?" Hamal asked again.

"Since my brothers died." Rashid answered savagely.

Hamal nodded. He smoked for over a minute. "You were working with a friend. Digging, perhaps?"

Rashid didn't know what to say, because these people seemed to know so much. And he had no idea what they wanted. But after too long a hesitation, he said, "Yes," softly.

The woman leaned forward across the table. "Is your friend Salem Qatib, Rashid?"

Rashid gave himself away with his reaction, and read it on them. But the mention of the name caused much of the fear to drop away. They were in it now. He raised his eyes, met hers. She was attractive; her eyes were big and friendly. She wore scent.

"Yes," he said.

"How well do you know Salem Qatib?" Colonel Hamal asked.

Rashid squirmed. "We are friends."

Hamal rustled his papers and glanced at his watch.

"He—he played with my oldest brother—when they were boys," Rashid said.

Hamal didn't look up from the dossier in front of him.

"Then—then he went away to—America," Rashid said. "When he—Salem—came back, he came to visit my mother."

The woman nodded her understanding.

Rashid went on, "He wanted to offer my brother a job, but Ali—was dead. So he took me instead."

"Tell me about that job." The woman leaned forward, and her scent covered the smell of mold and made the room a better place. It was not a smell of sex, but of flowers.

"We dug. For old things, antiquities." Rashid knew he was committed now, had said too much, but their expressions didn't change and he had nothing to lose. They were interested in Salem. So was he. "Salem would identify a site, and we would dig by hand. If there were things, then other men would come, but we would do the fine work." Rashid tried to express the fine work by brushing the table with his fingers. "With a toothbrush? You know? And sifting. The other men would never sift, they wanted to use a backhoe for everything."

"And Hamas told you to take the job." Hamal was leaning forward too, his cigarette smoke cutting through the woman's perfume. She waved at the smoke, but her eyes stayed with Rashid.

Rashid wrapped himself in his arms again and sat quietly. Because it was true, and because it was a betrayal of Salem before he even knew Salem.

"You had to, yes? Your mother would have asked you to do this work for them." Zahirah sounded concerned. Perhaps she, too, despite her modern clothes, was a mother.

"They took care of us when my father died."

"Of course. And you—what? You reported to them on what Salem found?"

Rashid put his face in his hands. He sobbed, "Not after we were friends! I—" he gulped air, swallowed the word *loved*. "We were friends."

45

She nodded. Hamal leaned across her. "You were at the dig at Tel-Sharm-Heir'at?"

Rashid nodded. He could see the dig, the pit facing the sea, and everything covered with blue tarps against the winter rain. The row of burial urns that started them on the site. The stone structure nearest the sea that had electrified Salem.

"You were there when Qatib was beaten?" Hamal asked.

"I—ran." *The beach full of men. Salem kneeling, hit with a shovel. The bearded man he hit with a hammer.*

Zahirah nodded. Hamal made a mark in the manila folder.

"Salem Qatib is an archaeologist, yes?" Hamal asked.

Rashid was still on the beach in his mind. His hands were shaking again, but his voice was steady. "He went to school in America."

"He entered the Masters program in Archaeology and Ancient Studies at the University of Michigan," Hamal said. "Which means that he is, in fact, an archaeologist. I would like to hear you confirm that, Rashid."

"Yes, he is an archaeologist."

"He is conducting an illegal dig."

"Are there legal digs here?" Rashid surprised himself. But he wasn't as afraid as he had been.

The woman, Zahirah, raised her carefully plucked brows. The man smiled, grunted a laugh. "Digs are legal if we license them. Hmm? And if not—then we seize them."

Rashid looked at the table in front of him, because he now knew who had taken and beaten Salem. His sweat turned to ice, his relaxation vanished.

"You—" he began. He started again. "Where is Salem? Have you arrested him?" And he thought *Do they know I hit the man with a hammer?*

Hamal took a drag on his cigarette, exhaled to the side, away from Zahirah. "We seized the dig at Tel-Sharm-Heir'at. We do not have your friend Salem. Do you know that Salem Qatib was abducted that night? After my men took the site?"

Rashid put his hands out, grabbed the table as if he might slide off his chair. "No."

"He was taken by Israelis, Rashid. Do you know anything about that?"

"No! No!" Rashid's head went back and forth between them.

"And they killed him." Hamal's voice was brutal.

Rashid sat in shock.

Tel Aviv

Alan Craik and a woman detective named Miriam Gurion were sitting in a cubicle in the homicide detectives' "room," really a space big enough to play basketball in. She was in her late forties, he thought, her face lined by sun and wind, her hair gray. She spoke English well but with an almost-swallowed "r" that sometimes disappeared into her throat.

"How do you know I was lied to?" he said. He watched her eyes, which met his honestly enough but flicked away to each side; she had the head movements, too, of the watcher who is always checking the periphery. The watchfulness of a cop in a place where bombs go off. Or of a detective of homicide who thought the walls had ears.

"The 27-14," she said. "The 27-14 is a routine piece of paper, but it has to be signed when we say it's a homicide—and that's my name on it, and in fact I signed it." She leaned toward him over her messy desk and lowered her voice. "Two years ago."

Behind her, three cat photos and five people photos were stuck to the cubicle wall; the people, he had already figured out, were the same two, young and older, one also in a wedding dress—her daughters?

"Let's go for coffee," she said.

"Yeah, but I don't—"

"I don't say another word in here." She was almost whispering. She led him out a side door of the building to a sidewalk café a block away, not mentioning Salem Qatib or the paper or what she had meant by "two years ago."

He ordered coffee, she a soda. While they waited, she lit a cigarette and puffed and simply shook her head when he tried to talk. She blew out smoke and he unconsciously waved it away. "Oh, you're one of those," she said and turned sideways to him, holding the cigarette low on her street side. The waiter put the coffee and the soda down between them and hovered, and she made a shooing gesture. When he was gone, she said, "Tell me about this detective who gave you the papers."

"What's your interest?" he said.

She grunted. "My interest is my job." She puffed, exhaled out of the street side of her lips. "My interest is in living in a good country, where the cops don't tell lies. This detective you talked to told you lies."

He told her about Berudh, described him, his office. She said, "Mossad." When he looked skeptical, she said, "He has to be a Mossad liaison. We have to work with them, but they're bastards. So *they* lied to you." She got out another cigarette, played with a cheap lighter, said, "I didn't want to say these things at Dizengoff Street. You understand. But faking a homicide file, that's serious business."

"You don't know it's faked."

She sighed. She held out her hand. He didn't get it. She moved the hand impatiently, then lit her new cigarette, put the hand out again. He gave her the blue folder with the papers Berudh had given him.

Miriam Gurion opened the papers on the café table and put her head low over them as if she were near-sighted. She smoked and turned pages, separating them into two stacks. "This is bullshit," she said. "You believe in feelings? I get bad feelings." She stubbed out the end of the cigarette and burrowed for another in her huge handbag. With her head, she indicated one of the piles she had made. "These papers, you see them?

They're authentic—I know, because they're from a case I had two years ago. That's what I meant, I signed the 27-14 two years ago—these are all from another case." She touched the other pile. "These are new, mostly *dreck*. See, your Berudh or somebody dug out my old case, probably scanned the file into a computer, printed it out, blocked out the name and the date, typed in new ones, rescanned—and here we are! A nice case file on somebody named Qatib, Salem, to give to the nice American officer who only wants to get it over with so he can go home. Eh?"

She lit a new cigarette and leaned back, smoking, her eyes on the street, and then she said without looking at him, "I don't believe this crap about your guy, what's his name—Qatib—being taken to the West Bank for burial. The family is in the US, you said? So the burial story is bullshit. I think maybe so is the story about people calling him in missing; we'll check this. Right now." She got a cell phone from the over-stuffed handbag. Alan figured there was a gun in there somewhere, too; could she ever find it if she needed it? She punched in numbers, said to him, "I think we need to work together." Then she was barking Hebrew into the cell, touching new numbers, making another call.

When she was done, she threw the phone into the handbag's open maw and stubbed out the cigarette and lit another. "The file on my two-year-old case is checked out from storage. Okay? Also, there's nothing in the missing persons log for any calls last night about Qatib, Salem." She put a hand on one pile of paper. "All bullshit."

"Okay. Why?"

"You tell me, darling." She blew out smoke. "What a bloody mess! I'm going to have to open a file, new case, plus file a complaint against your Berudh, plus I got no body—" She sat back and puffed, then looked at the papers she had said were from her old case and said, "Maybe we go find a body." Smiled.

"Qatib?"

Her open hand, turned upward, floated over the table. "Why do they pick my case to do their faking? Chance? No. Something against me? No. Then why? Very fast work, darling, doing all this between about midnight and this morning. So they pick my case because a lot of the work is done for them already, *nu*?" The hand closed into a fist. She laughed. "Two things: somebody knew my old case, remembered it, and maybe there was a connection. Like the same people found the body? Or turned it into a body? Mmm?" She ground the cigarette into her saucer. "Let's take a ride to Jaffa."

The coffee was terrible, and Alan didn't mind leaving the café, but he didn't get it. "What's in Jaffa?"

She waved the waiter toward her and scrambled in her bag for money; Alan was late in reaching for his own. "Two years ago, a body was found in an old military barracks there. He was young, Palestinian. I got the case. Mossad waved me off when I seemed to be getting somewhere. Now that case file is being used for the body of another young Palestinian. And here is Mossad again." She stood. "Maybe Qatib, Salem, ended up in Jaffa."

He looked at his watch. He had only an hour until he was supposed to meet Rose. Dukas had told him not to behave like an intelligence officer. He'd done enough. "I think I'd have to have more to go on than that."

She gave him a look that might have been disgust and then sat again and got the cell phone out. She did the numbers, held up a finger, eyebrows arched, as if saying *Watch what I'll pull out of my ass now!* She waited, sighed, jerked upright and began to bellow Hebrew into the phone. Then she listened, said something that sounded awfully like the Hebrew for bullshit and closed the phone with a distinct, though small, bang. "He's pissing his drawers, he's so scared!"

"Who?"

"The guy, darling, the guy who runs the place in Jaffa where they found the body two years ago! He knows something, and I scared the piss out of him! Are you coming or not?"

He felt as if hands were dragging at him to pull him down into his chair, but he stood and said, "Let's go," which was not what he wanted to do at all.

Gaza

Both the colonel and the woman had left the room. Alone, Rashid cried a little, silently, straight-backed. He had feared this very thing, that Salem was dead, when he saw Saida's apartment. And now it was proven true.

The woman brought him tea, and he drank it. The colonel came back with Rashid's backpack and placed it on the table with a plastic zip-lock bag that held the contents of Rashid's pockets when he was taken.

When they started again, their tone was different, as if he had passed a test and now they were all on the same side. They asked him questions, hundreds of them, and he answered as best he could; about Salem, about Hamas and their interest in the dig, about the dig itself at Tel-Sharm-Heir'at.

They gave him food. They didn't ask anything about the man he had hit with the hammer.

After several hours, Hamal appeared satisfied. It was Zahirah who was still interested in the dig and everything about it, so it was Zahirah who asked the question that changed everything.

She asked, "Where were you for the last twenty hours? Why were you coming back to Gaza?"

And Rashid told her. He was past concealment, except where he tried to cover his act of violence at the dig. He told them about hiding in the old ruins under his home town of Acco. And he told them about going to Saida's apartment. And eventually, he told them about the flash card he had found in Salem's coat.

51

They brought in his belongings. He showed them the card.

Hamal lit another cigarette. "Who else had been in her apartment, Rashid?"

Rashid shrugged. "It was all pulled apart," he said slowly. "Everything ruined."

And Hamal raised his eyebrows at Zahirah and said, "Hamas."

Zahirah nodded, and then turned back to Rashid. Her voice was especially gentle, almost tender. "Who is this Saida?" she asked.

After a moment Rashid said her surname. "Frayj. Saida Frayj. She—Salem." He stopped in a conflict of desire to incriminate and desire to protect. While he struggled to find words, his interrogators exchanged glances.

Hamal left. Zahirah stayed, asking questions about the dig, about the stone structure, about how long Salem had been interested in it. Rashid tried to be careful. They could be lying; Salem could be in a cell just under Rashid's feet. He tried to cover Salem; he told Zahirah that Salem had only just found the stone structure.

"Do you know what it is, Rashid? That stone structure?" she asked.

"A tomb?" He knew what Salem had said about it. He didn't want to betray too much.

"A very particular type of tomb, Rashid. A tholos tomb. A stone chamber made by Greeks and no one else."

"Oh," he said, trying to sound surprised.

Then Hamal returned with a laptop computer. He turned it on, inserted the card, and in a minute he had the card opened. He and Zahirah crouched over the screen, which was hidden from Rashid by the angle.

"There we go," Hamal said.

Then he laughed. Zahirah turned her face away.

Hamal began to stare intently. He swore. "Zahirah, look at what she's holding. Look at it!"

The woman did as she was told. She breathed in sharply,

leaned forward, reached forward to touch the screen. The vivid colors on the screen lit her face, so that she looked younger and more mysterious to Rashid. She played with the keyboard, spun the screen so that Rashid could see the image.

On the screen was a naked woman, her breasts prominent and glossy in the harsh light of the camera's flash. She was handsome, her features strong, her nose long and fine, her eyebrows heavy and black, and her eyes were filled with reflected light. They glowed red at the centers. She was smiling.

Saida, the slut.

In her hands was a two-handled cup. It was gold.

"Do you know this woman?" Hamal asked him.

Rashid spat, "Saida."

"This came from her apartment?" Zahirah asked.

"Taken inside the tomb," Hamal said. "Look, here and here. Those big stones—you can see where the flash just shows them."

They both looked at the image, and then the next, and then more, often turning the screen for Rashid to answer questions; Saida in jewelry, Saida holding a dagger, Saida with the cup again, Saida with a bottle of champagne.

Rashid became angrier and angrier. He did not tell Hamal that he had seen a canvas bag full of these things in the car—that would have been betrayal. But he didn't hide that Saida was a greedy girl who his own mother called a slut and a whore, who was not Muslim but a Christian from Bethlehem, and who always wanted money and good times.

They both listened intently to his anger and his enmity. In the end, he ran down like an old battery, his sentences more disconnected, his gestures subdued, until Colonel Hamal rose to his feet and Zahirah patted his hand.

They took the computer and left.

*   *   *

Tel Aviv

After the glitter and bustle of Dizengoff Street, Jaffa might have been in another country, another time. It had to some extent cultivated its look—old streets, winding passages, the Camel Market—but it was genuinely old, partly Arab, its back turned on the aggressive newness of central Tel Aviv.

"Over there, the Pal'yam blew up the two British patrol boats," Miriam Gurion said. She gestured vaguely toward the water. "In 1946," she said, in case his knowledge of Israeli history wasn't as good as hers. In fact, he didn't get it and said so.

She stopped, her head back, eyebrows arched, a pair of unflinching eyes looking into his. "We had to fight the British to get what is ours. We've had to fight everybody. Come on."

They had come in her car, which she had left almost carelessly at an angle near a curb as if she was saying *I dare you to ticket me*. Now, she led him toward a battered chain-link fence with old razor wire looped along the top. A gate big enough for a small car stood partway along, a concrete guardhouse behind it. The guardhouse wouldn't have withstood a car bomb, he thought, but what terrorist was going to get media attention by bombing an almost derelict site? It was in fact a moribund Israeli navy barracks, a former British facility that had faded into obsolescence as Israel had matured.

The fence was lined along the bottom with wind-blown plastic bags and papers; weeds grew inside; broken concrete paths connected buildings that looked mostly abandoned, with signs that identified in fading paint military offices that no longer existed. He saw one that said *Fourth Royal Marines Enquiries*. Others, in less faded paint, were in Hebrew.

The teenaged guard came to attention and looked at their ID and made a call. The site was modern enough for that, at any rate. The result was surprising: a middle-aged officer with a rather menacing, gnome-like face dominated by a hawk's-beak nose came hurrying around a corner, still adjusting his hat on his head. Alan's reaction was that the guy was only a lieutenant and much too old for a lieutenant, and his menace was all bluff.

"Mosher," Miriam Gurion said quietly to Alan. "A *shlemiel.*" She went toward Mosher as if she was going to beat the life out of him, and he actually stopped, and the look on his face went from menace to guilt to fear in one pass. He said something, and she rapped out a burst of Hebrew that caused him to flinch. He tried to recover, said something that sounded like pleading, and she erupted into more scolding Hebrew.

She grabbed Alan's arm. "Come on." She began to march him away from the gate. Lieutenant Mosher watched them and fell in behind, uttering more pleading noises.

Alan glanced at his watch, saw that he was going to be late meeting Rose. "Where are we going?" he said.

"To look at a body." She snorted. "I said to him, 'Mosher, where's the body?' I thought he was going to piss himself. I said, 'It's right where the other one was, isn't it, Mosher.' I thought he was going to cry." She shook her head. "A nice man, actually, but a *shlemiel.*"

They were striding along the building that had once belonged to the Fourth Marines. The windows were mostly dark, but he saw fluorescent lights burning in one second-floor room—Mosher's office, or some negligible naval function that had been banished here? A door was open at ground level; as he looked, a man stepped into it, heavy-set, ridiculous in long, baggy shorts. He might have been some idler in a small town, curious about outsiders. Alan nodded but the man didn't respond. Maybe the sun was in his eyes.

What had once been a parade or exercise ground opened to their right, its gravel partly consumed by grass, and beyond it three identical buildings that would have been barracks. Their windows were boarded over now.

Alan wondered what Lieutenant Mosher had done to get such duty. He was well over age for a lieutenant, he thought. They walked up a slope and then down the other side. "Here," she said. She was pointing at a low mound perhaps ten feet high and forty feet long, at the end nearer them a trench that seemed to cut it into two unequal parts.

Ammunition storage, Alan thought. And that was what Mosher, suddenly speaking in English, was explaining. The British and then the Israelis had used it as an ammunition bunker; then it was judged to be obsolete and it had been used for other things—at one point, the base canteen—and it had served until the Gulf War as a repository for hazardous waste.

"Then Saddam started throwing Scuds and they were ordered to have a bunker, so that's when they put in the air conditioner." He was talking to Alan. "But it's empty now. Unused. Empty!"

Alan wondered why he could hear an air conditioner running.

The beginning of the trench was a flight of concrete steps down to the ex-ammo dump's steel door. Above it, a window-sized air conditioner wheezed away. She said something in Hebrew, and Mosher worked at the door with a big ring of keys.

Alan smelled death as soon as the door rasped open. Apparently Mosher did, too; he said, "Air-conditioning is not adequate." He was sweating and swallowing a lot.

The interior was cracked, unpainted concrete. It curved over-head to a height of ten feet, darkening where it sloped down to meet the floor at the sides. A line of five electric bulbs in wire cages ran along the center of the ceiling, connected by old-fashioned BX cable. Desks stood in the shadows, their chairs stacked on them along with big typewriters and wire baskets and solid shapes that might have been books. The air conditioner whined. The air smelled of damp and mold and death.

Miriam Gurion led them to the far end. An old tarpaulin, stiff as a tarred sail, was mounded up there. "I never saw this in my life," Mosher said. He pulled the tarpaulin, which was heavy and unwilling; Alan grabbed it and helped him lift and fold it back and then pull it completely clear to reveal the dead man.

Naples

"I got your list."

Dukas looked up from his paperwork. Triffler was standing in front of the desk, his coming into the office unnoticed, his words meaningless. Dukas frowned. "List?" he said.

"The bunch in DoD. Information Analysis?"

"Oh, yeah, yeah—" Dukas came back from the Land of Paperwork. "That was quick."

"The black DC network. We use drums."

"You know, it doesn't help for you to keep saying how black you are. In fact, you're about as black as my Aunt Olympia."

"We keep saying it so you guys won't." Triffler was hitting keys on Dukas's computer. "I networked this, but I figure you don't know how to access it, which is why I came here in my very own person."

"I like stuff on paper."

"We know you do, Mike. We all laugh about it all the time." He punched a last key, his long, thin body curved into a bow because he was standing, and a list of names came up on the screen. "*Ecco*, as they say over here—the roster of OIA."

Muttering that Triffler did good work and he thought he'd keep him around, Dukas swung his chair to face the screen and started scrolling down. There were only forty names, and he didn't have to read all of them.

"Well, well, well."

"A hit?"

57

"You done good." Dukas tapped the screen. "Spinner, Raymond L. Ha!" He was smiling. "How stuff you do does come back to bite you in the ass!"

"Shakespeare said something like that."

"What d'you know about Shakespeare?"

"Andrew's a freshman at Brown. A parent's got to keep up."

Dukas looked fleetingly troubled; perhaps he was thinking that when his yet-to-be-born child was a freshman some- where, he'd be ready for Social Security. He jerked himself away from the thought. "This guy—" Dukas tapped the screen again. "Raymond Spinner. I busted this guy for passing internal fleet information to his daddy, who swings in Washington. I persuaded him to cash out. And now he's washed up on a beach in DoD—I think Daddy's been at work again—and he thinks he's going to fuck me over." Dukas grunted. "Well, well, well."

"You're going to do something ugly."

"Surely not." He smiled at Triffler. "I'm going to be a good little bureaucrat." He began to draft an email as a reply that piggy-backed on the one he had received:

From: Michael Dukas, Special Agent in Charge, Naval
Criminal Investigative Service, Naples, Italy
To: Deputy Assistant Secretary of Defense, Department of
Defense, Office of Information Analysis
Subject: Your request.
Message: Per 1347.5 Sec. 11, please locate your place in
chain of command and justify referenced request.
Recommend GS-10 Raymond Spinner expedite.

"What's 1347.5?"

"How the hell should I know?"

* * *

58

Tel Aviv

"Light," Alan said. He could see that a nude body was lying there and that there was shiny metal along one side of him, but he couldn't see enough. Miriam was burrowing in her handbag and she came up with one that Alan recognized as of a type advertised in the pricier gun magazines—high-intensity, small size, big price.

The body was lying on a rolling litter, like a low gurney; it supplied the metallic reflection he'd seen. The damage to the man was sickening.

"Beaten," Miriam said.

"Cause of death?"

"I'm not a doctor." She was shining her very bright light on the eyes and prying one of them open; then she focused on the mashed lips, which she parted with a ballpoint pen so she could study the teeth. "Really bad," she said. She pressed on the chest, but nothing happened. "I thought maybe water."

"Torture."

"Mmmm."

They worked their way down to the feet, which, like the legs, were less damaged than the head and upper body. He pointed out two round marks on the left leg. "Cigarette."

"Your guy?" she said.

He took the ID sheet that Dukas had faxed to the embassy. Two head shots, front and profile, were in the upper right corner, the size of passport photos. Faxed, smudged, they didn't look like the battered mess on the table. Alan read down the sheet to Distinguishing Marks and said, "Two-inch tattoo of fouled anchor, left forearm." He thought he had to explain it to her. "A fouled anchor is an anchor with a rope twisted around it, sort of. Two inches is about—five centimeters."

She was holding the dead left arm. "Yes."

"Surgical scar, right abdomen, appendectomy. About—four centimeters."

"Yes, okay."

"Three moles, prominent, smooth, dark brown, left side of chest, triangle pattern about—seven centimeters."

She hung her head over the dead man's chest, her light bright on his waxy skin, turned her head toward Alan and said, "Now aren't you glad you came?" She dug into the big handbag, which she dropped on the gurney, shining the light into it, and pulled out a plastic phial and then a sterile packet and then a box big enough to have held half a dozen cigars. She took a swab from the packet and swabbed the inside of the dead man's mouth and put it into the phial, then clipped hair from his head, put it into another phial, and unpacked a small ink pad. Alan figured she had an entire evidence kit in there.

"Won't your forensics people do that?" he said.

"Mossad, darling, Mossad."

Alan switched his light off and straightened, his back sore from bending. "How did somebody get a body in here?" Alan asked Mosher.

"Many people work here over the many years. Keys—" He made walking motions with his fingers.

"But you didn't know the body was here?"

"Me?"

Oddly, Alan believed him. Mosher was a schlemiel, and probably a nebbish, too, and he knew he was being used, and he was scared.

"Do you—does anybody live on the facility?"

Mosher shook his head as if the idea disgusted him. "Where would they live? Some buildings don't even have water. I live in Tel Aviv. Most of my people are IDF reservists. It's nice duty—you go home to mama's cooking."

"You have a duty officer at night."

"A petty officer."

"Who checks everything."

"Yes, yes—"

"And guards on the perimeter?"

He shrugged. "Kids. Good kids. But—"

"Who else has space on the facility? I saw a man back there—"

Mosher backed away, his hands up to ward off threat. He shook his head and bolted out the door.

Alan found Miriam outside, standing on the top step, a cell phone at her ear and a roll of crime scene tape in her left hand. She gestured at him to help; he took the tape and together they taped off the entrances to the stairs and the steel door. Miriam went right on talking to somebody in Hebrew.

"I called it in to Homicide," she said. "They're sending a team. Let them fight with Mossad." She was lighting a cigarette. "How come you don't smoke?"

"My wife persuaded me my kids deserve better."

"Nice wife?"

"Wonderful."

She held the cigarette at her side, away from him. "I had a nice husband for a while. Then I scared him off. Two kids. One's a wifey in London; one's a doctor in bet-Elan." She blew out smoke. "Actually I threw my husband out. He started playing around." She looked aside at him. "I'm embarrassing you."

"I don't embarrass that easy."

She patted his arm. "We'll get along." She got on the phone again.

Alan stood on a little hill, looking down at the entrance to the bunker, thinking of the dead man inside. Tortured, beaten to death. It turned his stomach. It always did.

He and a master chief named Fidelio, whom everybody called Fidel, had been in northern Afghanistan before the bombing began. He had had half a million dollars in US cash, but he was there because Fidel spoke Farsi and Pashto and they needed an officer to go with him. They were in the western part of the Alliance territory

61

buying help for the US attack that was yet to come. As it happened, the warlord they had been sent to spoke Turkmen, so they needed somebody local to translate the Turkmen into Farsi so that Fidel could translate it into English for Alan. They were sitting in a stone house in a room hung with carpets and carpeted under them, sitting cross-legged, tea and food in front of them. Outside, it sounded as if somebody was beating a rug, except that there were screams. Alan had put a quarter of a million US in a pile next to the food, and the general said, "How many men will the US send?" The screaming went on, and the thumping, and Alan frowned at Fidel and then at the sound, and the general muttered something and an aide left the room and the thumping and the screaming stopped. Then they made the deal. The general and his army would fight for the US, and he expected weapons and trucks and petrol and some heavy weapons. Alan said through the chain of interpreters that the quarter-million dollars was for those things, and the general sighed and said back through the chain that his expenses were very high. Most of his money, Alan thought, came from Iran; his men had Iranian weapons and Iranian uniforms, and there were men wandering around speaking Farsi, according to Fidel, who were probably Iranian intel. Still, none of that mattered; his job right then was to get the general to say yes, and they'd worry about Iran later. The general had said yes; Alan said yes. The general and Alan and Fidel all shook hands and smiled a lot and the pile of money disappeared, and when they went outside, there was a bloody body on the ground, and a frightened man was being made to look at it and some soldiers started to shout at him and push him around. He was next.

Thinking of it, Alan wanted a cigarette, and he might have asked her for one, but Miriam said, "You and I are going, darling," and he didn't want to push the intimacy of her "darling" by sharing one of her cigarettes.

"So soon?"

She laughed and told him to be nice. "I'll drive you back, start the paperwork, come back here. It's my case now."

"And you'll inform me."

"I will, of course I will—" She was leading the way toward the gate. Alan asked if Mosher would get into trouble and she said she supposed he would. "But nothing serious. I think he really didn't know."

"It isn't much of a job."

"He made a mess once; he's only waiting here to get out."

An SUV was slanted into one of the parking spaces by the gate, but he barely noted it. She pointed at her car and they started for it. They crossed the street, and he heard the SUV start up behind them but paid no attention, and then the big vehicle was beside them and the doors opened and three men poured out. He was grabbed by the arms before he could react; he shouted, but they were pulling him into the car. He saw her trying to get a hand into her bag, and a man punched her hard and sent her sprawling, and then Alan was on his back on the floor of the SUV and it was starting to move, the doors still open and his feet sticking out. Somebody kicked his legs and there was a lot of shouting and the doors slammed.

4

Tel Aviv

Rose Craik didn't worry when her husband wasn't at the hotel at two because she assumed the job had taken longer than he had expected. The possibility annoyed her, nonetheless; she wanted him to climb down from his work for a day, to try to forget the war that now seemed to consume him. She didn't really want to see a movie; she wanted him to see a movie.

Or not forget the war, not merely the war in Afghanistan; rather, the altered military world into which he had been launched by September eleventh. He felt guilt, she knew, because US intelligence hadn't anticipated the attack; he felt a deep, not very well defined anxiety about America itself. When he had said, "Scared people scare me," she knew that he was trying to express that anxiety for her, perhaps for himself. Sometimes he seemed stunned by the attack's intricacy and its success; other times he was puzzled by the reaction to it. "We've had terrorism against the US for twenty years. Everybody knew al-Qaida was out there. Why is everybody over-reacting?" And the job was grinding him down—literally; she had watched him get thinner over the months.

Bored now, frustrated, she telephoned home—Bahrain— where a Navy friend was keeping their kids; she said they were fine. She called her office; she was missed but they were getting along. She watched some Israeli television. At three o'clock, she allowed herself to worry.

At three-twenty, the telephone rang. Intense disappointment when it wasn't Alan, then a catch of breath when she heard a woman with an accent who said she was with the police. Rose's gut dropped. The woman said that they had to talk. She was in the lobby—could she come up? Rose was an attaché with all that meant about classified knowledge, being an American in a foreign place. Hotels, even in Israel, weren't necessarily safe; a public place was better than a room. "I'll come down."

The woman was heavy-set, hard-eyed, maybe a little flamboyant in her loose hair and her bright scarf. She had a bruise on the left side of her face from eye to chin, the eye puffing and darkening. "Miriam Gurion, sergeant, Tel Aviv police." She held up ID.

"Is it about—?"

The woman put a finger to her lips.

If anybody in the hotel lobby thought it was odd that a woman was holding up a badge and a card, nobody gave any sign. Rose took the card and studied it, handed it back with her own diplomatic passport. She glanced around the lobby, looking for the signs of a watcher, threat, anomaly. What was the woman afraid of?

Mrs Gurion—she said she was Mrs, not Ms—led her to a deep sofa in an alcove that allowed them to see the doors. When they sat, the sofa gave a kind of sigh, and mounds of pinky gray fabric swelled around them.

"I think your husband is okay, but the situation is not good." Tears came to the woman's eyes. "I am so ashamed. It is my fault—all my fault—" She gulped. "They took me prisoner!"

Rose's heart raced but she leaned forward. "Is he all right?"

"I was with your husband. We were doing a job, maybe you know about it, a man who was dead—"

65

"Where is my husband?"

The woman shook her head. "They took him from the street. They give me this." She waved fingers at her bruised face. "Four men in a big car." She started to cry. "I don't know where they took him. They put me in another car and we drove around and around. Then they put me out in Ayalon. The bastards!"

Rose shook her head. "I don't understand—who would— Was it the Palestinians?"

"They wouldn't dare. An American?" Her laughter was edged with contempt. "Who dares to snatch an American off the street in Israel? Gangsters? Not possible." She took out a cigarette. "They might dare to take a policewoman, but not an American." She eyed Rose. "He says you made him quit."

"I don't—oh, smoking. Go ahead." She tried to be patient as the woman fiddled with a lighter, but she burst out, "How bad is it?" Her brain was turning over possibilities, actions: should she telephone the embassy? The Navy in Bahrain? Mike Dukas? It was confusing because the woman was the police, the first ones she would have called.

"It is Mossad; it has to be Mossad; nobody else dares. You know what I mean, Mossad?" She told Rose how she and Alan had spent the hours he had been away—how he had found her at the police station on Dizengoff Street; she had told him what she knew; she had taken him to a place where the body had been hidden. "Then, when we come out, they grab him. And knock me down and drive me around. I am not pleased."

"How bad is it?"

The woman blew smoke. "These are some very stupid people, but how stupid they can be, I don't know. My idea is that they can't be stupid enough to do something large. But, when they find he is an American officer, they may be frightened."

66

"Scared people do stupid things."

"Just so." The woman met her eyes. The look was open, curious, challenging. "You are brave?"

"I'm a naval officer, too."

The eyes appraised her, made some judgment. "So." She screwed the cigarette into an ashtray. "The formalities you can forget—reporting to the police, I mean. I did that. They told me to shut up. Now you must do whatever things will bring weight on them. Understand?"

"Pressure."

"Yes, okay—pressure. I say it is Mossad." She took out another cigarette. "It is Mossad. Press."

"I can call my embassy—"

"If you call as a citizen, they will be days doing anything. I know. You have friends? You can—" she made a motion—"do you say 'pull strings'?"

"Yes, that's what we say. And yes, I can. Why won't the police help?"

"When your husband and I had seen this body, this dead man, I called Homicide. They didn't come. Why? Because some voice came from up high and said don't."

"But they attacked *you*. You're *police*."

"Exactly, and so my superiors are, mmm, confused. Not very daring people. They are angry because of this—" She flicked her fingers at her bruised face again. "But beyond a certain place, they have to ask themselves, 'How far dare we go?' The right thing is not always the right thing, understand?" She touched Rose's hand. "I was afraid you would be one of those screamers, you know?"

"No, I'm not a screamer." She stood. "Except when I get mad. What are you going to do?"

"Try to find your husband. I keep you informed, I assure you."

Rose nodded, hugged herself. "I'll go pull strings."

* * *

The naval attaché in Bahrain was a senior captain who was as politically astute as a presidential campaign manager. He would make admiral but not as a battle-group commander; he'd probably wind up at NATO or the National Security Council, and he'd probably serve as attaché again at some even more vital post than Bahrain. Rose had worked for him for almost two years, respected him, liked him in a cautious way, trusted him within certain bounds. Now, she got herself on a secure phone at Abe Peretz's office in the American embassy. The Bahrain attaché wasn't available until she told his aide that the matter was important enough to affect US-Israeli relations—something she'd worked out for herself on the cab ride.

"Rose, what is this?"

"Sir, my apologies for taking you away from—" Her voice was trembling, and she tried to control it.

"No apology necessary, but you know how things go here. What's up?"

"A policewoman has told me that my husband has been grabbed off the street by agents of Mossad." She waited a beat; when he didn't speak she said, "If it really happened that way, at the very least the US should make a stink at a high level. An American officer—"

"Alan was grabbed on the *street*?"

"He was carrying out an assignment for NCIS. I don't know the details; he said it was routine, just a bother."

"You're sure he's missing."

"He's two hours late." She saw how flimsy the story might sound, but she called up an image of Miriam Gurion's face and eyes. "The policewoman who told me is a sergeant. She gave me ID. I don't have any reason not to believe her."

Again, there was silence. Then he said, "You get confirmation. Get confirmation of the policewoman. This is an ugly business, Rose. We can't—you can't—be accused of going off half-cocked. You've got to nail it down." She waited, not wanting to push him, and he said, "What can I do?"

"Tell me how to get in a pipeline to somebody important so that when I can prove all this, somebody'll be ready to holler."

"I can do better than that. I'll flag a buddy at State. You nail this down, Rose—nothing can go until you do. And don't let it get to you, okay? If the policewoman is right, Mossad will be treating him like a visiting head of state."

She said *Oh, yeah* to herself but babbled something aloud about gratitude, and then he was gone.

At NCIS, Naples, Mike Dukas was on another line, but Dick Triffler was available.

"Hey, Rose, what a pleasure."

"Somebody's grabbed Alan." She told it fast, again fighting a tremor in her voice. "What do I do?"

"Okay, the police know and aren't doing anything. You've called your boss. You better touch base with the embassy in Tel Aviv, no matter how cautious they'll be. You have to—" Peculiar sounds came through the phone, then his voice saying something to somebody else, and then he was back. "Mike's getting on the line from his office. Mike? You there?"

"Rose, what the hell?" Dukas sounded anguished—not for Alan, she knew, but for her. Dukas was in love with her, an old, old story; the whole world knew it. "You okay?"

"Mike, Alan was grabbed by Mossad. He was doing your damned errand in Tel Aviv!"

"No way, it was a routine—"

Triffler broke in. "Routine jobs go wrong, Mike; shut up. She needs advice."

"But you're okay?" Dukas growled.

"I'm fine. Guys, I want to bring pressure to bear. What do I do?"

69

"Mossad won't hurt him," Dukas said. "They won't dare. But—Jesus. What a stupid thing to do! Well, if they're that stupid, they may get scared. What you gotta do, babe, is get State to launch a demarche. You understand 'demarche'?"

"It's diplomatic shit."

"Yeah, very heavy diplomatic shit. It's when your government tells another government that it's shot itself in the foot. If Mossad really snatched a US officer who was on US business, demarche will be the least that will happen. The Israelis will be seeing eight billion bucks a year threatening to grow wings. So that's what we do, babe—push the right buttons." Dukas's voice was hoarse. "Dick, who do we know at DNI now?"

Triffler mentioned a couple of names at the office of the Director of Naval Intelligence, and Dukas told him to get on to them. "Get all the details first. Rose, give us everything— where, who, name of policewoman, time of day—"

She poured out what she knew, and then Triffler was gone and Dukas was making rather helpless, soft noises to her, and she said, "What can *I* do?"

"You still got an in with Chief of Naval Ops?"

"The CNO I worked for is long gone. He's at some think tank now—"

"Tell him to call current CNO and lay it out."

"But—they're busy people—"

"Babe, it's *their Navy*! You don't get it. A US officer was snatched by another government—they'll go ballistic! Now, get on it." His voice softened. "And stop chewing on it. He's gonna be okay. Trust me."

"Oh, Mike—" Her voice broke.

At the same time, the deputy to an assistant secretary of state got a call from the US naval attaché, Bahrain. As he listened, his normally worried frown contracted to a grimace. After he hung up, he stared at the telephone for

70

five seconds and then dialed the private number of the assistant secretary.

"Dick, I think you better alert the Secretary that Israel may have just stuck a firecracker up our ass."

Half an hour later, Rear Admiral Paris Giglio, retired, telephoned the current Chief of Naval Operations in Washington. They had served together in the first Gulf War; although never close friends, they got along. And they had the common bond of men who have done the same tough job.

"Jig, it's been a while! You want the job back?"

Giglio made negative noises and got right to business. "I want to bring something to your attention, Ron."

A pause, and then a cautious "Shoot."

"One of your officers was snatched off a street this morning in Tel Aviv. It hasn't made the news but I have this direct from the guy's wife, a super officer herself who served with me. She has good reason to believe that he was snatched by Mossad."

"What?"

The Navy had its own reasons for reacting passionately to an Israeli insult. The long institutional memory still resented the 1967 Israeli attack on the USS *Liberty* that had left thirty-seven sailors dead.

Five hours after Alan Craik had been pulled into the SUV in Tel Aviv, the Director of Naval Intelligence was on a secure line to the head of Mossad. He went through no polite protocols, listened to no formalities. Instead, he read a statement. "We have good reason to believe that your agents kidnapped an American Naval officer, Commander Alan Craik, from a Tel Aviv street shortly after noon today. Commander Craik was on US Navy business and was in your country with clearance and full knowledge of your government. His orders included exchanging classified materials with your office. What you've done is inexcusable and unacceptable, and we

71

demand that he be released immediately or the severest consequences will follow. Do you understand me?"

Coldly, unemotionally—but clearly—the Mossad officer said that he did.

An hour and forty-three minutes later, Alan Craik was delivered by an unmarked government limousine to the door of his hotel. Also in the limousine, besides the plain-clothes driver, were two special agents of the Institute for Intelligence and Special Tasks, or Mossad—Shlomo and Ziv, no last names. Both made a great effort to smile as Craik got out of the car, and both apologized yet again for "this unfortunate incident." They extended their hands.

Standing on the sidewalk with his left hand on the limo door, Craik waited until they had run down and the smiles had run out and the hands had drooped, and then he leaned in and said, "Fuck you!"

Demarche

From: The Secretary of State of the United States of America

To: The Minister for Foreign Affairs, the State of Israel

The government of the United States wishes to state in the strongest terms that the detention in Tel Aviv of Commander Alan Craik of the United States Navy by agents of the State of Israel is unacceptable. Not only was Commander Craik in Israel with your government's knowledge and permission, but also he was seeking legal details concerning the death in Israel of a former member of the United States Naval Reserve, Salem Qatib. This treatment of a decorated member of our armed forces is an insult to his honor, to that of his country, and to the memory of the dead man.

The government of the United States wishes the State of Israel to understand clearly that it requires that investigation of the detention of Commander Craik be pursued to a quick and satisfactory conclusion. It also wishes to make clear that it will itself continue to pursue the investigation of the death of Salem Qatib to its conclusion, in which it expects all cooperation.

5

Washington

Ray Spinner was thinking about a pretty woman named Jennifer when his phone rang and a man named McKinnon asked him if he could step around to his office for a sec, please? That McKinnon had an office was enough to suggest his status; he also had a title; but, most to the point, he could end Spinner's career with a word.

"Sir."

McKinnon looked up from a crowded desk. He was fifteen years older than Spinner, infinitely more impressive in Washington terms: eight years in State and then Defense in the Reagan administration, four more in the National Security Council and Defense under Bush One; then exile to an Ivy League professorship during Clinton. He had published two books. His name was never in the media—a contradictory achievement in a media-mad town, but one that had put him where he was, because some specialties require reticence.

"Yeah. Shut the door. Sit down." He made a point of closing a folder, the point being that he was allowed to see it and Spinner wasn't. But Spinner had had time to make out "Classified Special" and "PERPETUAL JUSTICE." Perhaps oddly, "perpetual justice" didn't sound unusual to him; it sounded like a lot of other code names in those days.

Spinner sat. It was like being back in college, he thought, called into the professor's office because of a bad paper.

McKinnon was balding and thus big-domed, unquestionably an "intellectual." Spinner found himself sweating. Until then, only his father had been able to make him so nervous.

McKinnon handed a single sheet of paper across the desk. "That yours?"

Spinner had only to look at the From and To. It was the blind copy of the message he'd sent Mike Dukas in Naples about the dead Navy guy in Tel Aviv. Suddenly, the message didn't seem like a very good idea.

"Well, you see—"

"Is that yours?"

"Unnh—yes. You see—"

McKinnon shut him up merely by hunching his shoulders. His jacket was off, revealing a pair of the red suspenders that Spinner so admired. He also wore one of those baggy shirts that you learn to recognize as expensive. He said, "So what's the story?"

"I got the initial, uh—" Spinner cleared his throat "—initial data that the person in question—the name is there on my message—"

"Qatib."

"Right."

"Arab name."

"I suppose."

"No 'suppose' about it. You don't understand Arabic? You don't know Arab culture?"

"Well, my background—"

"Your background is the Navy; I know all about it. I don't expect much as a result. You were saying?"

"Unnh—the person—Qatib—died in Israel and because, because he had US connections—studied here, Navy reserve— I checked the Purgatory list. He was on it. So I thought, unnh—" He glanced at McKinnon, whose eyes were fixed on him. "I thought I should pursue it."

"Good for you! Exactly what you should have done. And?"

Encouraged, Spinner told him about NCIS and the dominion of the Naples office.

"Who is this Michael Dukas?"

Spinner thought of lying and saying he'd picked the name out of a directory, but he suspected that McKinnon already knew who Dukas was. This was a test, he decided. The prof already knew the answers. So Spinner said, "He was a nosy bastard who framed me and forced me to resign my commission."

McKinnon leaned way back in his chair and inhaled deeply, as if he wanted to smell Spinner's answer. He tapped a pencil twice on his desk and, without looking at Spinner, said, "So, you saw that we needed more data on Qatib. Good. So you dumped it on somebody you don't like, and sent it over the title of the deputy assistant. Not good." He looked at Spinner, a comical expression on his face—mouth rubbery and pulled down at the corners: clown grimace. "C minus."

They stared at each other until Spinner had to look away. He knew he was about to be fired.

"You're here because your father has clout," McKinnon said. "Okay, I can live with that. Believe me, you wouldn't be here otherwise, because a military background is the last thing we need. Correction: second last; what we need last is somebody with a background in intelligence." He leaned forward again. "You know what's wrong with military people?"

Spinner tried to think of all the things he'd found wrong. "They're dorks?" he said.

McKinnon laughed. Actually laughed. "That's one way of putting it. They're *mediocre*. And they're *tentative*. And they're *self-seeking*. Ranks, medals, privileges. They're fucking bureaucrats in fancy clothes, and they're *not smart*. They're *timocrats*." He looked to see if Spinner knew what a timocrat is, saw he didn't, smiled with delight. He stood; Spinner suspected that he was reverting to his academic self, that all he lacked was a blackboard. "There are only so many smart people in the world, and they don't gravitate to the military; if they get into the military by mistake, they soon get out. Therefore, policy can't be left to the military. They're like mechanics—they can fix the car, but they can't design it." He leaned back against the wall. "Smart people come *here*. They come here because we recruit them. We've been looking at some of the people here for as long as ten years. Why?"

Spinner knew he wasn't supposed to answer.

"Because people—ordinary people—can't run a democracy. You know Plato?"

Spinner clawed back through his undergraduate classes and came up with *The Republic.*

"Right. The current president of the United States is the modern version of the philosopher-king. He is surrounded with a group of special people. Smart people. They must inform him so he can make wise decisions, and they must keep him from getting wrong information that would harm those decisions. They must also advise him on how to manage information about his decisions so that the people will accept them."

Despite himself, Spinner frowned. Wasn't there a contradiction there somewhere?

"To advise wisely, to screen out the false, to manage the true. Do you know who Leo Strauss was?"

Spinner, committed now to the truth, shook his head. McKinnon shook his head in response, as if disgusted, but he grabbed a piece of paper and scribbled on it and shoved it across. "Read Leo Strauss," it said. Spinner said he'd go right out and get some.

"You won't understand it, but keep reading. Strauss is—" McKinnon stared off at the bewildering problem of what Strauss is. "Have you read Alan Bloom? No matter. The point I'm trying to make is that there is a deep philosophical basis for what we do here and for the way we do it. You have to keep reminding yourself that we are special people and that

77

we have a special responsibility. This is not just another dick-off government job!" He sat again, wearily, as if his lecture had exhausted him. "I want you to take this Qatib thing and run with it. I've got you screening inputs now; I'd have kept you there, frankly, but you went ahead and sent this message and I'm going to see if you're equal to that act of folly. It's a test, okay? Let's be frank. It's a test. I have a suspicion you can't cut it at this level, but because of your father, who's given us good data, and because you lost your Navy job getting data to him, I want to be fair. Open a file on Qatib. Run with it."

"I didn't know how much Israel would be—"

McKinnon waved a hand. "Israel's neither here nor there." He raised the hand, index finger pointing up. "The *big* picture. Israel will take care of itself if we fix the big picture. The key to the Middle East is Iraq. You don't understand that; it took me six years to figure it out. Don't sentimentalize about Israel." He looked down at something on his desk, looked up again, said with a quick smile, "Don't sentimentalize about anything." McKinnon sighed. He chewed a thumbnail. "Imagine you have to brief the philosopher-king on this Tel Aviv thing. That's the standard. But don't bean-count and don't nitpick. Think *policy*." He said nothing for so long that Spinner stood, assuming he was dismissed. McKinnon, however, didn't look at him but said in a gloomy voice, "The policy is that we will democratize the Middle East by democratizing Iraq, and anybody who gets in our way is an enemy. That includes the military and the State Department and the fucking intelligence establishment."

Spinner wanted to say that McKinnon had just told him that Israel wasn't either here or there. Now he seemed to be saying that Israel *was* either here or there. But was it here? Or there? On that note, with McKinnon staring into a corner, he crept out of the office.

*   *   *

Tel Aviv

An hour after his release, Alan Craik was spent. He had been screaming at Mike Dukas. His voice was hoarse by the time he slammed down the phone, his rage a blast against the friend who had given him the supposedly trivial job that had led to humiliation. He had been snatched off the street like a beginner, held prisoner, shamed. Made helpless.

Then an aide to the Chief of Naval Operations had called, then an assistant secretary of state, then Abe Peretz, and a general from CentCom, and the ambassador to Israel. Their message was that they were behind him and that the wrong that had been done him would be paid for.

His fury at Dukas ran down and became contemptible.

"I lost it," he said. His face was in his hands. He was sitting, disheveled and sweaty from the day, on the hotel-room bed. "One of my best friends, and I trashed him."

She sat next to him and hugged his shoulders. "Mike understands. It's okay."

"Christ." He looked at his hands. They were trembling. "What's the matter with me?"

"You need a rest."

He was thirty-eight. The face he lifted to her looked older. "What do I do?" he said.

"Call Mike back."

"I can't."

"Apologize. Then work with him to get back at these bastards." She got up and passed in front of him, and he followed her with agonized eyes as she picked up the telephone and dialed and waited. He heard her speak to somebody in the Naples office and then she held out the phone to him. "Mike," she said.

He put the instrument to his ear but said nothing. He was listening to his own breathing and perhaps to Dukas's, as well. Finally, he croaked, "I'm sorry, man." He was suddenly choked with tears.

79

"Well, it was an experience."

"It wasn't meant for you. It was—"

"Jeez, it sure seemed to have my name on it! You kept calling me Mike and using the word *bastard*. Sounded like it was for me."

"I'm sorry, I'm sorry—it's them, but I can't get at them—"

"I know, kid, yeah, shit. All is forgiven. Forget it."

"If I could take it back—"

"You can't, so forget it. I'm still the guy you've slogged through the shit with. The truth is, now you've calmed down, I put the phone down for a while and let you rant while I did something else. Anyway, look, you're right: I sent you into something without checking it out, and you got slammed. It *is* my fault. So forget it. The real question is, what do we do now?"

"Declare war on Israel?"

"Ho-ho, naughty boy. I suspect the gubmint has about shot its wad, expressing its displeasure in a demarche. What happens from now is what we make happen. So what d'you want to make happen?"

"I want to nail several Israeli skins to the barn door."

"Okay, but you gotta ID them. You got names?"

"The two ass-kissers who delivered me to the hotel were named Shlomo something and Ziv something. No last names. I don't know the shmucks who had me in the hotel room, but my guess is they were grunts—dumb, clumsy, a couple of them didn't even speak English."

"I need first *and* last names."

"They didn't *give* last names. Don't hassle me!"

"Okay, okay! You done good."

"I want to *hit* somebody."

"Don't. I'll take over from here."

"You're going to follow up?"

"After the chewing-out you gave me? Christ, I'll have the tooth marks on my ass for life! Actually, I've already had

80

the order to pursue 'with utmost diligence,' plus State sent a demarche to the Israelis that was the diplomatic equivalent of your blast at me, and it ended with a promise to follow up. That's my warrant. I'm off to see the wizard as soon as I can clear my desk."

"You're coming to Tel Aviv?"

"No way are the Israelis going to fuck me out of a country clearance on this one; they're too scared. So you leave, I arrive, life goes on."

Alan gave the telephone a feeble grin. "You're a good guy, Mike."

"I've ordered up a forensics team. We'll do a number on the dead guy, Qatib. Who, by the way, was a cryptologist—you know that?"

"You didn't bother to tell me. Serious business?"

"Maybe. I mean, the Israelis, a former cryptologist, a body—like, they'd be dee-lighted to have our codes."

"Oh, shit."

"My favorite expression."

They talked some more, but mostly they repeated what they'd said. Dukas's parting words were, "Hang in there, kid."

And Alan said, "Dov—one of them was named Dov." That was all he could remember.

When Alan hung up, his hands were still shaking. Rose put her arms around him. He was enraged because he had to go to the embassy next morning to be de-briefed and to get a medical check. She told him it was all routine; everything would be okay. "It's over. We're okay. We're okay." She held him tighter. "You still going to do your meeting tomorrow?"

"You're goddam right I am!" He stood. "It's the reason I came! Not all this fucking Mickey Mouse—" He didn't say that the clandestine meeting to exchange information with Shin Bet might erase some of the humiliation of the day.

*　　*　　*

81

Dukas put the phone down as if he were placing it on a box of eggs. He pushed his lips out, shook his head, then looked up at Dick Triffler.

"That bad?" Triffler said.

"Bad. Wouldn't you be? I sure would." He sat back in the desk chair, his weight making the springs groan. "The Tel Aviv cop woman says it was murder. She doesn't say how, so we need the forensics before we jump to a conclusion; she and Al both say there was torture, too." He shrugged. "Peretz says the FBI is already on it. I told him to spread the word there that this is our case and everything will come to us, and if it doesn't, I'm going to scream all the way up to the White House. I talked to Kasser." Kasser was the head of NCIS, Dukas's immediate boss. "We're to make the Qatib case a top priority. It's what this office is here for until we close it. Okay?" He looked up through thick eyebrows at Triffler. "Craik's out of it—he's got some secret thing of his own tomorrow and then he's outa there. Somebody has to go to Tel Aviv and ram an investigation down the Israelis' throats."

"Mike, I just got here. We're still unpacking boxes!"

"It's either you or me. That's direct from Kasser. The one who doesn't go runs the office. Which do you want?"

Triffler, rarely flustered, looked at his hands and pursed his lips. Dukas thought about it, then said, "Okay, I'll go. Soonest, Kasser says. Can't possibly go tomorrow. Saturday?"

"You've got the meeting with Italian security at Sixth Fleet Saturday—remember, Saturday's the only day everybody can make it?" Before Dukas's well-known contempt for meetings could erupt, he said, "Mike—you called the meeting! You said it was 'essential to cooperation on matters of joint concern!'"

"Okay, I'll go Sunday."

"When are you going to brief me on running the office?"

"Okay, I'll go Sunday night! Jesus." Dukas swung forward.

He grabbed a yellow pad and a pencil—the computer at his elbow might as well not have existed—and began to write. "I want everything we can get on Salem Qatib. Maybe he was murdered because he was porking somebody's wife, but Kasser says we gotta know how important it is that he was a cryptologist. You know what it'll cost if somebody got Navy codes out of him? About a hundred and fifty mil. So we want everything on that—what codes he knew, where he worked, where he studied, who remembers him. I want a *detailed* bio on him, not the summary. Check with FBI and CIA to see what they got on him. Don't dick around—remind them of the demarche and who's driving the bus. Okay?"

"We need to know what was going on in his life in Palestine."

"Yeah, I'm working on that. Peretz and the policewoman. But listen—" He pointed the pencil at Triffler. "If the police-woman's right, Mossad killed the guy. That's a heavy, heavy idea. Rumor to the contrary, they don't just kill people. Killing's pretty rare; you need authorization, preparation. Unless it's a mistake."

"What does Craik say?"

"He's too mad to make much sense. FBI'll de-brief him tomorrow morning, maybe they'll get more. He's supposed to get a medical check; that's got him pissed, too. He got a couple first names of the guys he thinks are Mossad, plus he thought the guys who snatched him were pretty much thugs. Maybe rent-a-goons. They kept talking to him in Hebrew and pushing him around until they looked at his wallet and realized what they had. When somebody showed up who spoke English, he was apparently all over himself explaining that they had mistaken Al for a Tel Aviv cop. Which makes you ask, why were they so ready to snatch a Tel Aviv cop?"

"I'm the one who opens the case file?"

"You bet. Go to it."

Triffler looked at his watch. It was after seven in the

evening. "This is just like working for Mike Dukas," he said. "I suppose you don't care that I have choir practice this evening."

"Choir practice! You just got here!"

"My voice is very much in demand."

Dukas hunched down over his work. "You can hum 'Amazing Grace' while you work. *Quietly.*"

6

___

Gaza

A guard, far more courteous than the last pair, took Rashid to a shower, and then to a room with a bed. He heard the guard turn the bolt from the outside, but at least the room was not in the basement, and it had a window on a dusty yard.

The night was cold. He lay with a single thin blanket and shivered, listening to the sound of knocking and ringing in the building's steam pipes. He was exhausted, but the bile of betrayal—his own, others', perhaps Salem's—rolled around his guts. He shivered. His teeth chattered. Eventually, he slept, and in his dreams he ran and ran, while Salem called for help behind him.

Washington

Late in the day, McKinnon astonished Ray Spinner by poking his head into his cubicle and saying, "You'd better read this."

Spinner saw the word *demarche* and From and To. He read the whole thing—naval officer, Israeli government with one foot in dogshit, naughty-naughty. It occurred to him that the Qatib business, which he had tried to kick sideways, was suddenly much bigger and much more important than he had thought.

McKinnon was leaning on the carpeted wall. "State's got its balls in an uproar because Mossad was doing its job, apparently. About this Qatib, so your instincts were right in asking for follow-up. Full Marks. Some Navy guy got his pants caught in the gears, or something. Find out what happened and keep me current. One way or the other, the Qatib thing will expand and make at least a nice little case study." He handed over another piece of paper. This time, he was grinning.

A reply, Spinner saw, from Dukas direct to the Assistant Secretary—*Oh, my God!*—with some sort of bureaucratic blah-blah-blah. Spinner looked at McKinnon. Was he going to get fired *now*?

"Questions?" McKinnon said.

"What do I do about Dukas's message?"

"That's a dumb question, but you're allowed *one*. Tell him to fuck off with the jokes and get you the data. That clear?"

"My pleasure." So he wasn't fired. He could feel sweat below his eyes. He tried to smile. McKinnon laughed and slipped out, and Spinner could hear him still laughing as he went up the row of cubicles.

In Israel, that was the day that an elderly man was kidnapped and murdered. The al-Aksa Martyrs Brigade claimed credit. It was also the day that two Palestinians shot into a car, killing an Israeli woman.

7

Gaza

In the morning, a guard took him to wash, and then to the courtyard to pray with other men, all of whom seemed to be guards, not prisoners. He tried very hard to concentrate his mind on the glory of God. After prayer, he ate with them.

Then they took him to an office. Zahirah was there, freshly dressed and made up. She had glossy enlargements of the photos from the flashcard in neat rows on her desk and taped to the wall behind her.

She also had Rashid's passport and backpack. The presence of those two items on a corner of her desk gave Rashid hope. He sat quietly while she worked away at her computer, typing rapidly, a pencil clenched in her lipsticked mouth; she grabbed the pencil to scribble notes that she pasted to her computer screen.

"Do you want to help us, Rashid?" she asked after ten minutes. "We intend to find out exactly what happened to your friend—to Salem. And then, if it is within our power, to avenge him."

You were the ones who beat him first! Rashid's brain was already split in two; half wanted to help the Palestinian Authority, and half viewed that Authority as the enemy of every Palestinian.

"We can help you," she continued. "If you will help us.

Hamas will not help you; they have lost the dig, and all they will care about is the lost money. They cannot go outside of Palestine to ask questions. So they will likely concentrate on you." She paused for effect. "And on your mother—who we can protect. We can. You can, if you help us."

Rashid had no loyalty to Hamas; they had paid the bills after the death of his father and brothers, and his mother loved them, but they had shown their true colors when he worked for Salem. He had very little loyalty to Israel; years of Hamas propaganda and experience of Israeli police methods in Acco combined to make Israel more of an enemy than a home. The thought of travel, anything *outside* the constant war that was all around him, was more tempting than anything he had heard. And the possibility of avenging Salem, even indirectly, might help him deal with the fact that when Salem had needed him, he had run.

Still, he hesitated. Even with nothing to go home to, no job, no future, he still hesitated to commit to the Authority.

Zahirah held up the clearest photo of the slut Saida disporting herself with the gold cup. "Rashid, listen to me, please. This Saida—she has left the country. Yes, we know that. She has gone to Cyprus—perhaps Crete; I'll know in an hour. I think she has many of these items. I think she intends to sell them on the black market.

He raised his hands. "What would you have me do?" he asked.

Zahirah smiled broadly, showing most of her white, even teeth. "You have a clean Israeli passport. You speak English. You know Saida. We want you to help us find her and bring her back."

That sounded so appealing that Rashid answered her smile with his own. Excitement began to rise within him. "I think I could do that."

Zahirah began to make piles of documents atop the photos. She pressed a buzzer under her desk and in answer a young man appeared at her door. She waved to him.

"This is Ali, your keeper. You have much to learn. You will have to leave tonight. The colonel will want to see you before you go."

Ali wasn't much older than Rashid—Salem's age, in fact. He smiled at Rashid, who looked down at the ground to hide his confusion. Then he smiled a little in return.

Ten minutes later, he was learning to use a cell phone for clandestine communications. And he had chosen a side.

Washington

Spinner's new status was symbolized by a message that was waiting on his computer in the morning. It had been routed to him by name—major development, to be a name and not the generic "Screener"—and included the information's source, also a first for Spinner. The information had come from "Habakkuk," who was passing information from "Deborah."

Deborah/Habakkuk/Routing
Subj: American officer detained by Mossad
US Naval intelligence officer Alan Craik was detained yesterday by, supposedly, Mossad officers. Cause may be his involvement in illicit investigation of death of Palestinian terrorist named Salem Qatib. Craik released last evening unharmed but feathers very ruffled. Release the result of efforts by his wife, Rose Siciliano Craik, also naval officer and also possible intelligence agent (Ass't Attaché, Bahrain). Real reason for their presence in Israel not known. Evidence here of US condemnation of Israel for Craik detention. Question: why so much attention to death of one terrorist?

Spinner frowned at this. He read it again, and then again. He knew who Alan and Rose Craik were because Craik had served on the Fifth Fleet staff in Bahrain. What made him frown was the apparently private knowledge that the source had of the Craiks—"feathers very ruffled. . . . Release the result of efforts by his wife. . . ." How did somebody know that? And yet know at the same time about the demarche? ("Evidence here of condemnation of Israel. . . .")

Spinner wrote a note on a memo pad and clipped it to the message. The note said, *Who is Deborah?*

And it occurred to him—the stirring of, perhaps, an instinct for intelligence, and the reason that the CIA insists on vetting all agent reports before they are disseminated—that Deborah wrote reports that revealed too much of himself. Or was it herself?

Tel Aviv

The Craiks were taking Miriam Gurion to lunch. They had wanted to take the Peretzes, too, but Bea had said that she couldn't make it, and Abe had called back to apologize and say that Bea "was busy advising Likud on how to be Jewish," and he had explained a bit lamely that in fact she was busy all the time with things he didn't understand. "Maybe she's found a younger guy, who knows?" The upshot of his call was that Rose was embarrassed and asked him to come to lunch, anyway.

Now they were sitting at a table in a crowded room in what Miriam said was the best Yemeni-Ethiopian restaurant in Tel Aviv. "Noisy, but the food's worth it," she had said. And she was right. It was definitely noisy, and the food was definitely great.

Alan felt awkward, bellowing the details of his detention over the bellows that surrounded them, trying to keep his rage from bursting out, but the other three kept shooting questions at him as they all forked down spicy lentils, ground lamb with fennel, cold mashed tomatoes with cumin and hot peppers. He told them of the capture, the hours in a room, the sudden release.

"So what about the dead guy?" Abe shouted.

"Not here," Miriam said.

Alan shrugged. "Later," he said to Abe.

When they were stuffed and groaning and happy, Miriam led them down the street to a shabby café and took them to a table at the back. "Cop place," she said. "You know, when cops take a break?"

"I think we call it 'cooping,'" Abe said. He had to explain to her what a coop was.

She said, "Well, this is a coop. A cop coop." She laughed, a big laugh that surprised Alan, who had seen only her serious side. "Okay," she said to him when black coffee and a plate of tiny cakes had appeared, "talk about the dead man Qatib. But talk quietly."

After Alan, with interpolations by Miriam, had explained who Qatib had been and why Mike Dukas had asked him to do the supposedly routine closeout, Abe said, "I don't get it."

"Neither do we, darling. None of it hangs together."

"Mossad doesn't do such things." Abe seemed embarrassed. "As a rule. I mean—no offense, Mrs Gurion, but you know how these things work." Miriam was making noises like a revving engine. "Well, you know what I mean—they'd need a big reason to do something like this."

"Not to mention snatching my husband off the street," Rose said.

"That is because he is so handsome, darling," Miriam said, patting Rose's hand.

"They never said I was handsome," Alan muttered.

"What did they say?"

"Everything they said was so stupid, I couldn't believe it was happening. I really had a hard time believing they were

Mossad." He rubbed his chin, felt the beginning of stubble. "But they were."

"Of course they were!" Miriam's eyes widened and narrowed quickly. "Because now they are on me. Yesterday morning, I was on the case, good; yesterday four p.m., I am off the case; this morning, I am on the case again. Why? First, Mossad calls TLV police, get that woman off the case. Then Mossad calls TLV, oh we're so sorry, we were wrong, do put that nice lady on the case. Why? Because you scared them." She gestured toward Alan with a coffee spoon, then looked at Abe. "You say you need a big reason for all this. No. I say there is no big reason. I say they were stupid people doing a stupid thing." She gave a sudden, rather girlish grin. "That is what I tell the very pleasant man who calls me from your friends in Naples."

"Dukas?"

"No. Mister Triffler. You know Mister Triffler?"

They smiled. Abe examined his fingers, gave her a sly look. "Okay, they were stupid. But why did they kill Qatib?"

"Because that is most stupid of all! We have to live with the Palestinians, whatever happens—interrogations must not kill." She put her chin up, said almost defiantly, "The Supreme Court of Israel ruled in 1999 that torture is illegal."

"Al said the dead man had been beaten."

"Yes, badly, badly. But beating, I don't know—if he died of beating, do you think Mossad beat him to death? Are they that stupid?"

"Either way, the question remains, why do any of it? Who was he?"

She gave an elaborate shrug. "He was a Palestinian." She put down the spoon. "I have work to do at Dizengoff Street." She began shaking hands all around.

When she had gone and Peretz and Alan and Rose were walking back toward their hotel, Peretz said, "Interesting woman. Think she'd be open to a contact?"

"What, recruit her? No, I don't."

"No, nò. But—I liaise with cops; she's a cop. What I'm thinking—this thing isn't going to go away. State told the Israelis we'll pursue the investigation and expect them to do the same. I just got word Dukas is sending somebody to follow through. I'm going to wind up in the middle of that, no matter what happens." Peretz stepped around a woman who was staring into a store window. "And you're leaving."

"You bet your ass I'm leaving." He said that he thought that the investigation was really Dukas's and NCIS's, not Peretz's, but it would be impossible to do from Naples.

When they were parting, Peretz said, "Mossad has a long arm, Alan. And a long memory." He looked like a wise professor repeating an important point to a slow pupil.

Alan looked at his watch and nodded. "I'll remember." He was on his way to the meeting that was his real reason for being in Tel Aviv; he couldn't wait for it to be over so he could get out. He left Peretz nodding to himself, conscious that the man had more to say, and too focused to listen to it.

Naples

Dick Triffler was leaning against the wall in Dukas's office, arms crossed, one ankle over the other and the shoe resting tip-down. He'd taken his jacket off, but his shirt was crisp and white and his tie was a thick Italian silk in a shade of blue that could have been used for a late-night sky. "Tel Aviv's already giving us static about the forensics team," he said.

"Jeez, I thought they'd pretend to stay scared for twenty-four hours, anyway." Dukas made a face. He was wearing the same dark polo shirt and tired chinos, and his feet, in running shoes that looked like purple bathtubs, were crossed on his desk. "How much static?"

"They 'question the necessity.'"

Dukas made a growling noise. "Okay, message ONI, try to get them to lean on it."

Triffler nodded.

"How about the policewoman Craik was working with?"

"Sounds nice but very cautious. Clearly thinks I'm trying to recruit her with my magic wand. She says that she's got the Qatib case now but she's just doing the preliminary work. She's been promised the body by the end of next week."

"What the hell, what end of next week? What're they gonna do, clone it before they turn it over? The cops should have had the body already!"

"'Administrative complications.' Mrs Gurion says she doesn't dare turn them off completely."

Dukas made the face again and toyed with a pencil. "You tell her I'll be there Monday?"

"She was beside herself with delight."

"When NCIS was investigating Pollard, the CIA finally broke down and gave us a Mossad organizational chart and a personnel roster. What I want to do is get on to head-quarters and pry that stuff out of them. Specifically, I want to know all the operational people named Shlomo and if so what they do. I'm trying to find out what the hell Mossad's interest could be in Qatib if it wasn't cryptology. Can do?"

"If they'll give it to me."

"HQ will give us anything we want right now because a Navy guy was kidnapped and Mossad is in the shit."

"For twenty-four hours, anyway."

"Yeah, so move quick."

"You know how many guys in Israel are named Shlomo? It's like Bill."

"Yeah, well one was with me in Bosnia in ninety-seven.

A Shlomo, not a Bill. We gotta start somewhere."

Dukas made a call to The Hague. He wanted a former French cop named Pigoreau, who now worked for the World Court and who had been Dukas's assistant in a war-crimes investigation unit in Bosnia. Pigoreau wasn't in the office yet—banker's hours, Dukas thought—but would be in soon, he'd call back, etcetera. And did an hour later.

"Mike! Marvelous to hear from you!" Pigoreau had a great French accent—you expected an accordion accompaniment.

"Hey, Pig."

Laughter. "Mike, you're the only guy I let call me Pig. You know, in French this is a big insult—*cochon*?"

"In English, it's affectionate. The Three Little Pigs. Porky Pig. We got a chain of supermarkets called Piggly-Wiggly."

"Okay, I take it as an endearment. What is going on?"

Dukas reminded him of the operation with the two Israelis in Bosnia. Pigoreau didn't remember it at once—he hadn't been involved, but he had had contact with everything that went on in that office—and it came back with some prompting. Finally he was able to say, "The guy died!"

"Yeah, that's the one. We wanted him, and he got shot."

"I remember. A long time, Mike."

"Yeah. What I need is, Pig, I want to know what the Israeli involvement was."

"Oh, *mon dieu*—Mike, that stuff is buried a thousand meters deep someplace."

"Yeah, but it's get-attable. You guys are bureaucrats; you don't throw stuff away."

Pigoreau laughed again. "I try, Mike. This is serious business? Okay."

"Leave a message on this phone. You're a good guy, Pig."

"*Cochon*."

Dukas hung up and thought about how much he didn't want to go to Tel Aviv. On the other hand, it would get him out of the office. And it was his job.

Tel Aviv

Tel Aviv's sunlit concrete was a nightmare environment for spotting surveillance. Alan Craik was looking for surveillance because he was gun-shy from the events of yesterday, and because that's what he had been taught to do in a hostile environment. And this was now a hostile environment.

He was on his adversary's home ground, a colossal disadvantage. And the city's modernity eliminated narrow streets with blind corners and back alleys in favor of broad boulevards. Heavy buildings set a bomb-blast's reach away from the street gave potential watchers plenty of room on the wide sidewalks, among the hundreds of vendors and the thousands of pedestrians, to stalk him at will.

If his opponents had all these advantages and deployed a large, diverse team to watch him, he would never see them. If they were lazy, undermanned, or too uniform—that was another story. Especially if he could lead them into an environment where they were out of place, ill-dressed, just wrong. That was his technique, perfected in the souks and western hotels of the Gulf States. He planned his routes to cross the invisible social boundaries that define class and trade, profession, education. His route today went from his hotel to the diamond district, through the towers and business suits of the insurance brokerage houses, in and out of the library and the museum of the University, and on to his meeting.

He made his first watcher ten minutes into the walk. He spotted her early, a slight young woman in a drab scarf with a face like Julie Andrews. He gave her that name in his head, an automatic catalogue of everyone who gave him a glance or appeared interested in his progress. Her rugby shirt, jean shorts, and tanned legs were unremarkable on the busy sidewalk three blocks from his hotel.

What could be more natural than the American officer

cruising the diamond district for his wife? But Julie Andrews drew stares from the conservative, Orthodox men on the sidewalk. She stood out like Jane Fonda in Hanoi. Alan felt his heart swelling in his chest, the first sweet rush of adrenaline hitting him. His snatch, the terror of it, the humiliation retreated with this little victory.

He'd never spotted a real surveillant before. And these were Israelis, probably Mossad. On their home ground.

Take that, you bastards.

Alan showed them how boring he was, how unconcerned he was that he'd been their prisoner sixteen hours earlier. He had to fight the temptation to show them that he had spotted them. He wished he had a camera—maybe Mike would care? The embassy? He'd have to file a report, anyway. Embassies took this kind of thing seriously.

Leaving the huge concrete octagon of the university library, he scored another victory. He'd spotted the possibilities of the library on his first trip to Israel. Doors everywhere, and one small, but legitimate, exit to a garden whose real purpose was to illuminate the chancellor's plate glass window. The garden had a narrow walkway that led out past the graduate residence and directly downhill to a protected bus stop.

When he arrived at the bus stop, he had the intense satisfaction of watching Miss Andrews run down a ramp behind him, talking into the collar of her shirt, stopping to talk to a youngish man he hadn't spotted, and then, to be treasured and retold forever like a find in a yard sale, he got to watch a third person, a stocky middle-aged male in a T-shirt, climb into a waiting van with a heavy aerial and speed away through the bus lane, the paunchy occupant staring at Alan openmouthed through the passenger window from four feet away.

Alan got the license number. It didn't matter a damn, it shouldn't have done anything to balance the indignity of yesterday, but his mood was lighter. His shoulders were squarer, and he found that he was whistling when he approached the meeting. His watch said he'd enter the lobby on time to the minute.

The man in the hotel lobby wasn't anyone's idea of a military intelligence officer. He was short, heavy to the point of fat, dressed in a khaki bush jacket, faded jeans and sandals that had been worn to paint something orange. His head was bald and almost perfectly round. His hands were huge, which, combined with his round head and his dark glasses, gave him the look of a garden mole.

Alan had expected an officer in uniform. Or perhaps a slender, sunburned man in shorts. He expected the Shin Bet to be different from the Mossad—but not this different.

The man's smile was warm and penetrating, too warm to be feigned. "Commander Craik?" he said. "Benjamin Aaronson. Call me Ben." Alan's hand vanished in one of his, and then they were in an elevator headed up, their recognitions exchanged.

"Your wife like Tel Aviv? Ugly city, but great shopping." Ben held the door to a room—no, a suite of rooms. There was a laptop on a table big enough to seat a board of directors. He closed the door behind them, set the bolt. "You got fucked over by Mossad yesterday." It wasn't a question.

"Yeah." Alan tossed his backpack on the table. He was surprised by the wave of anger that accompanied the admission, as if having to confess that he'd been snatched put him at a disadvantage. A rare insight—Alan could suddenly see that it was a macho thing, like getting mugged. His masculinity—to hell with that.

"Well, we're sorry. We're really sorry, and you beat the odds by showing today—half the guys in my unit said you'd walk. Wouldn't blame you."

Alan swallowed a couple of comments, all unprofessional. "Not something I'd really like to talk about," he said.

"Sure." Ben opened the laptop. "You have some files for me."

Alan opened his backpack, removed a data storage device and put it on the table, tore off a yellow sticky from a pad on the table and wrote a string of numbers from memory. "Files are on the stick. There's the crypto key." He shrugged. "I don't really know what's on it."

Ben plugged it into his laptop, replaced his black sunglasses with bifocals, and peered at the screen, hunting keys with exaggerated care as he typed the digits. "You want some food? There's enough in there to feed my whole unit."

"You the commander?" Alan asked. He was looking out the window, wondering if he should have ditched the meeting.

"Um-hmm." Ben was scrolling now, looking very fast at the documents Alan had provided. "I'm the colonel—you think they're going to send some stooge to meet you?" He smiled over the screen. "Relax, Commander. This is going to take some time."

"You have stuff for me, too, I hope."

"That's what 'exchange' means." His attention went back to the screen.

Maybe it was the residue of yesterday, but Alan had expected something more adversarial, something like bargaining in the souk. He already thought he'd been put at a disadvantage by coughing up his stuff first, but it didn't feel like that. Ben felt more like an aviator than a spy.

"You always been an intel guy?" Alan asked.

"No. No, I started in a tank. I was a crew commander in Lebanon in '83." He continued to scroll while he talked.

Alan nodded to show that he knew what had happened in Lebanon in 1983.

"Everyone goes into the military here—that means everyone is supposed to, you know? Except that there's religious exemptions and too many rich fucks who send their kids to Europe or the US or Canada to evade military time— you know that?" He looked up, his eyes bright above his bifocals.

This isn't just small talk. Alan took a chair and sat opposite Ben. "I guess I thought everyone served."

"That's the myth. Here's the reality—the kids getting hit by rocks in the West Bank aren't the kids whose parents are in Parliament."

"That sounds familiar." Alan was surprised he let that slip. He didn't criticize his own country to foreigners. It was a rule, a navy rule.

Ben's eyes were back on the screen. "A lot of this is pure shit, you know?"

Alan got to his feet. "Look—"

"Don't get on your tall horse, Commander." He looked over the screen again. "Your President is a good friend of Israel, but he's a terrible intelligence manager. Yes?"

"He's the commander-in-chief," Alan said without too much emphasis.

"Politics and intelligence, they go so naturally together and they are terrible bed mates, yes? You know what I am saying, Commander?"

Not a clue, unless this is another recruitment attempt. What the hell is he talking about? "Not sure I do, Ben. Call me Alan. Okay?"

"Sure. I'm saying that good intelligence is the truth, yes? The truth we see on the ground? And good intelligence officers tell the truth."

Alan gave a cautious nod, already worried about where this was going. Was it yesterday making him shy? He was growing anxious because a friendly foreign officer was trying to make professional talk in a hotel room.

He caught himself watching out the window. Ben read on. He began to read snatches aloud.

It didn't take Alan long to understand what the man meant

when he said "shit." He read a report summary on an interrogation conducted in an unknown location. The target of
the location was referred to as "the terrorist." The summary
sounded as if it had been written for a Hollywood movie.
Ben read several of these without comment, although his
English was good enough to convey his amusement—and
his disgust.

Alan fought with anxiety. Followed a train of thought out
of the room. Back to Afghanistan. Brought himself back to
the room.

After twenty minutes of this, Ben went on as if he had
never stopped. "Politicians want the truth to serve their
own ends—their own ends. Not the truth. Not the truth
you saw. And they never see the people—the dead ones,
the results of prolonged interrogations." He pressed a key.
"Okay, you brought what your people said you'd bring. Not
your fault that it's shit, but it is. My contact says you'll be
the officer in charge on this operation—one of the pieces
in Perpetual Justice. Who makes up these names, eh?" He
took the bifocals off his nose and wiped them carefully on
his bush jacket's tail. Then he pressed a few keys and spun
the laptop to Alan, so that he had the keyboard under his
hands and the screen lit up before him. It was an older
model IBM, he noted.

"What we're giving you is shit, too." Ben's voice had an
edge. "Political shit, just like yours. I wanted to talk to you—
really talk. You think this is a set-up, don't you? It's not.
We're providing a lot of the material to support these
Perpetual Justice ops—and some of it is a pile of crap."

Alan tried to feign unconcern, but his shoulders were tight
and he felt as if he'd been strapped in an ejection seat for
seven hours. "I'm uncomfortable with your choice of topics,
maybe."

Ben polished his glasses again. "Will I surprise you if I
say we know you quite well, Commander? Africa, Silver

Star, some not-so-secret decorations. You are an operator, yes? And my guess is, you are a believer." He smiled, changing his round head into the face of everyone's friend. The perfect friend. "As I am. A true believer in a complex canon of—of what we are." His turn to look out the window.

Alan started through the files to cover his mixture of pleasure and fear. How could he not be flattered that they knew his career? And *why did this seem so much like a recruitment attempt?*

The reality outlined in the files drew him away from Ben's words. His part of Perpetual Justice was a snatch operation against a suspected al-Qaida moneyman, and for the first time he saw a parallel between what had happened to him yesterday and what he was about to do. That hadn't really pushed through Alan's conscience until that very moment, a twinge:

The big SUV had powered through the streets as two men in the front shouted at each other. A big man in the back had had a gun. Alan had registered these things at a distance because he couldn't form a coherent thought. When his brain had finally turned over, it had started on an endless loop of threat and fear. Captured. Torture. He had been conscious of just how many secrets he knew and could betray—operations, Afghanistan, fear—panic. Who has me? Why? I've been captured! Torture. Prepare myself. Who has me?

He snapped back to the computer. His hands were trembling. He did not raise his eyes to meet Ben's.

The documents in front of him were recent surveillance findings of the target, clearly much altered. They'd had a certain amount of information deleted, but they were thorough, carefully annotated. Exactly what he'd need to plan his operation.

The next file was a clean summary of the target's ties to al-Qaida and his location in the financial hierarchy. To Alan, it was like reading an academic paper with no footnotes. Everything was neat and tidy—the target's role, his family relations, his bank accounts. To Alan, it stank. Intelligence was never that simple. Terrorists were never that simple. He looked up, straight into Ben's smile.

"Okay, you pass. You really are an intel officer. You had me worried."

"This is like a document you send to a briefer."

"Give that man a cigar." Ben paused, clearly pleased with his phrase. "There's more of the same. It was pushed on us. We decided to tell your people through you. I'm going to talk out of school—that's your phrase, yes? Okay, out of school, under the rose—we're a secretive lot, we have a great many phrases for this. Okay? The surveillance reports, his location—I'll back those. My people, or people I know, did those. The background, the bank accounts, the summary—not ours, okay? I can guess, but I won't—you don't want to criticize your president. Same-same. Right?"

Alan was scrolling down the summary, looking at an Excel spreadsheet on banking that looked impressive as hell. Except that it was unsourced.

"Jesus." Alan looked up self-consciously. "Ah, sorry."

Ben smiled. "I think I've heard the name before."

Alan's eyes went back to the document and he grimaced. "I don't get it. All this unsourced stuff."

"But when you deliver it to your Central Command, it will *become* sourced. From Israeli military intelligence. Very trustworthy, yes? Maybe in some circles, more trustworthy than your own CIA?"

Alan murmured "Jesus" again without thinking.

"We decided we wouldn't do it without telling somebody—and somebody is you, Commander. They try and fuck us. Okay, we're proud in the military. We don't trade shit unless we *mean* to fuck somebody. We ask for you. 'Send the guy running the operation.' So we—so I can have this conversation. There it is. It's political. Somebody wants this man. Is he al-Qaida? I have no idea. But I think if he is, there would not be all this amateur shit in the package."

Alan shook his head slowly. "I haven't seen what I brought you."

Ben held up his hand, balanced it, teetered the palm slowly up and down. "Same-same. Some shit."

"I didn't see it. Not my stuff."

"Of course not. Me, I'm a meddler. I won't do one of these things, these 'exchanges,' without reading everything."

Alan shrugged. "We're not like that."

Ben smiled. "No? What's to stop a double agent from filling that data stick with stolen secrets on stealth technology and giving it to you to pass? Nothing simpler."

That idea had never occurred to Alan, whose hands froze on the keyboard.

Ben continued, "May I give you a piece of advice, professional to professional? If they won't let you read the material, refuse the meeting. Let them find another Patty."

"Patsy," Alan said automatically. "Does our stuff pick up authenticity, too? I mean, what I delivered—"

"Will be devoured by our politicians. Because it comes from *US intelligence*."

Alan started pressing the keys that would dump the data files into his stick. "I don't like being used."

Ben nodded. A slow smile spread over his face. "Good. I was afraid you wouldn't listen." He paused and said, "There's more than one Israel."

"I'm getting that idea, yeah."

"I wish we had more time to talk—" Ben said. He rose to his feet. "You are in a hurry."

Alan collected his bag, rested his hands on the seat back. "Maybe I'd be more receptive if I hadn't been grabbed by other Israelis yesterday." He shrugged, nothing to lose. "Or followed here by a surveillance team."

104

Ben winced. "Not mine."

Alan shrugged again, because it made no difference. "Thanks for the heads-up on politics. I believe you. Okay?" He was tempted to unburden; life since Nine-Eleven had left him with more reservations about his own profession than the rest of his career combined, but Ben was not the man. "You going to be in trouble over this? You know I'll put in a contact report."

Ben smiled. "As will I. May I tell you something that will surprise you, Commander? This is the start of something. I dislike the politicization of intelligence. I love my country. I will not sit still. Now, I fight back. And not just here."

When they shook hands at the door, Ben gave him a slip of paper that proved to have his real name—Colonel Benjamin Galid—and a phone number. "In case," he said.

Alan left before it could get any worse. Because he no longer knew what to believe, except that too much of it had resonated.

That day, a Palestinian gunman killed six people in Israel and wounded a score of others. The crowd beat him and the police killed him. The Martyrs Brigade took credit for the attack.

That evening, the Craiks left Tel Aviv for Bahrain.

8

Cyprus

For the first two days on Cyprus, Rashid didn't even look for Saida. He spent the Sabbaths of three religions living from phone to phone. His new friends, Zahirah and Ali, had moved him briskly around the island, passing him from one Palestinian business to another. He learned a routine and some basic habits of caution. And each day, at times he had memorized back in the concrete building in Gaza, he used a cell phone or a pay phone to call certain numbers where his new friends waited to help him. If he used a cell phone, he discarded it after the call. If he used a pay phone, he could never use that one again.

Sometimes, it was very exciting. Other times, it was like living with his mother.

In Famagusta, he found a tourist shop with novels in English. He bought a book called *A Perfect Spy* from the money he had taken from Salem's coat, which he kept carefully separated from the money given to him by Ali for "operational expenses."

The English in the novel was difficult, but the story was excellent. It passed the time between movements.

On Sunday, Zahirah directed him to the ferry docks at Kyrenia.

"Your friend has purchased a ticket on a ferry to Athens," Zahirah said. She sounded very pleased. "You will go to the

106

ferry, purchase a similar ticket, and follow her. Call us once you have located her."

He arrived early in the evening and watched the passengers go on board, and he never saw her. When the ferry was less than an hour from sailing, he called another number for instructions. This time Ali directed him to board the ferry. He seemed sure that Saida would be on it. And he taxed Rashid with an unnecessary communication.

"Locate her," his new friend said. "Don't approach her and don't let her identify you. Don't call every time you are nervous. Call when you have something to report."

Rashid did as he was told.

Washington

Standing in front of his mirror, Ray Spinner had thought he looked terrific in his new red-white-and-blue suspenders. Saturday seemed just the day to wear them—only the real gunners there on Saturday—but when he got to work he had a spasm of insecurity and didn't dare take his jacket off. Five minutes later, he went to the men's room and removed the suspenders and put them in a pocket, where they made an unsightly bulge. Plus his pants wouldn't stay up.

Back in his cubicle, there was a message from McKinnon: *See me.* Spinner slipped the suspenders into a desk drawer and headed out at speed. It occurred to him—momentary flash of anger—that but for McKinnon, he'd be wearing the suspenders and wouldn't have to hold his pants up with one hand.

McKinnon was standing behind his desk reading a book. He was wearing brown suspenders and looking both professorial and powerful, as if he might have been one of those Oxbridge types who were also MI5 in the days of Burgess and MacLean. "Hmmm?" he said without looking up.

"You wanted to see me."

McKinnon read a few more words and looked up over his

glasses and apparently recognized Spinner. "What's new in Israel?" he said.

"It's cryptology. The dead man was a Navy cryptologist; it looks like he gave up what he knew to his Palestinian buddies and Mossad got hold of it."

"What's your evidence?"

"Message traffic is heavy. It all says cryptology."

"Are *you* sure?"

Spinner hesitated. "Of course I'm not sure!" he said. He was shocked that he let his own annoyance show.

"That's a start. I'm not sure, either. When the hounds start chasing their tails, I tend to be a little skeptical. I think maybe something else is in play." He smiled one of those meaningless smiles that lift only the corners of the mouth. "Off you go."

Spinner blurted out, "Do you know something I don't?"

McKinnon was back in his book. "I certainly hope so." He waved Spinner away.

Back in his cubicle, Spinner frowned at the carpet-covered wall for some minutes and thought that he really shouldn't take it anymore. McKinnon was a supercilious shit. On the other hand, he liked and needed the job.

He had gone to a Barnes and Noble and bought Leo Strauss's *The City and Man* because it was the thinnest Strauss book on the shelf. He had been dipping into it. It was *heavy* going for a man whose idea of a book was a thriller. He had almost self-destructed on a paragraph that went on for two pages. He was put off by sentences like "For Aristotle political inequality is ultimately justified by the natural inequality among men," because he had been raised on "All men are created equal," but he assumed that no matter what sentences like these meant, Strauss would pull a democratic rabbit out of his philosophical hat. He didn't want to face the possibility that neither Strauss, Aristotle, nor Plato was in fact democratic.

Naples

By Saturday, Dukas had Salem Qatib's bio and knew that he had studied classics and archaeology at the University of Michigan but hadn't taken a degree. Dukas tried to get the university on the phone, but on weekends academics are resting their brains. He made notes on what else he knew about Qatib: emigrated to the US with his parents at fourteen; his father returned to Palestine when Salem was seventeen and the parents later divorced; Salem did his Navy stint then and followed it with his college work, remaining a reservist. Then he'd gone off to Palestine himself and had kept a fairly clean record, except for whatever Mossad knew about him and was now not giving up—their current stance was "Who, me? Never heard of him!" The CIA had Qatib's name but was saying that other than his being a Palestinian and having attended an anti-settlement rally in Gaza, they weren't interested in him.

"Well, somebody was interested in him," Dukas said to Triffler.

"Or Al Craik's police lady is wrong about the Mossad involvement."

"You think Al was kidnapped by four guys who just happened to be in the neighborhood?"

"Stranger things have happened." Triffler checked his watch. "We have a meeting downtown in half an hour."

Washington

After lunch, Spinner had a message from McKinnon: *See me.* As in, *Here, Fido.* It really pissed him off, because he wasn't as big a dork as McKinnon was making him feel. (Was he?) He got the suspenders out of the drawer and put them on and, coatless, suspenders flashing signals like a police-car bubble light, strode up to the great man's office.

McKinnon was standing by the window studying a report with a gold seal on the cover. He looked up and acknowledged the suspenders with the sort of smile you give somebody else's baby.

"You wanted to see me."

McKinnon pointed at a piece of paper on his desk and went back to reading. It was a message to McKinnon's boss—this put things pretty high up the ladder, only one step down from the Assistant Secretary—to the effect that a rumor was spreading in the Palestinian territories that a Palestinian had been murdered for hiding something he'd found on a covert archaeological dig, and the Israelis were involved. Spinner read it twice and looked up. He was confused, but he was also irritated. It was like a guessing game. He decided to go the straight way forward. "I don't get it."

"Socrates would be proud of you." McKinnon closed the report but kept a finger in his place. "Check it out—see if it has any connection with your dead man."

"Archaeology?"

"That's what it says."

"I don't get a connection between the Palestinian Authority and archaeology."

McKinnon extracted another sheet of paper from a folder. It was only part of a larger message:

2. An inside source tells me that there is some brouhaha going on just below the cabinet level about the detention of the American officer. His story was that he was doing routine work on the death of a Palestinian who had been in the American navy. The upshot was a mess that is not quite a scandal but may have repercussions because he says Mossad was involved. Mossad's story is that the dead man was killed by the Palestinian Authority for illegal digging in a site in Gaza and they had nothing to do with him. Some people here are pleased because Mossad have got way above themselves and are a pain.

110

Without looking up, McKinnon said, "Check it out. If you find a connection, get back to me and we'll see where we go next."

"Who's the source?"

"If I wanted you to know, I'd have told you."

Spinner felt his anger rise. "What do you want me to do?"

McKinnon looked at him as if Spinner were a newly discovered species. "Do you think we might have a departmental library? Do you think they might have a file on the Palestinian Authority? Is it possible that there would be something in there about archaeology?" He looked at Spinner with an expression—head slightly tilted and turned aside, eyes wide, mouth pursed—that made Spinner wonder if he was gay. For a moment, anyway. "Or," McKinnon said, "you could just go out on the street and start surveying typical Americans."

Spinner, feeling himself blushing purple, turned and started out. McKinnon's voice followed him. "You have to earn those suspenders, you know." Then he laughed. "Extra brownie points for working on Sunday."

9

Washington

Ray Spinner was still at the Pentagon on Sunday. He surprised himself, being there more or less voluntarily, but he was finding a peculiar satisfaction in pursuing a thread through the tortured labyrinth of conflicting books, old news reports, classified summaries and estimates, and open sources like *Facts on File*, which he had never even heard of until a librarian pointed him at the many volumes on the shelves.

He had skipped dinner. Not that dinner meant much to him unless there was some woman he wanted to impress; otherwise, he was a fast-food consumer. Food was fuel; the rest—flavor, appearance, ethnicity, spice—was window-dressing. Still, he looked at his watch and grunted in surprise and only then realized that his gut was empty and unhappy.

The thread was illegal antiquities. He had followed it, back and forth, sometimes losing it, sometimes going along a false trail after the wrong thread, from the general of "illegal art" to the particulars of Palestine, theft, archaeology, contraband, and a dozen other subsets. What he had learned was that big money was involved. *Big* money.

There was an illicit worldwide trade in art objects, and not the least of it was antiquities from the Middle East. The flow was large and constant; the sums at the buyer's end could be huge. Before an object reached the buyer, however, it passed through many hands, each of which had to be greased;

112

each hand got less than the one next up the chain, but every-body took a cut. At the far end was a digger—Spinner had stopped researching stolen art because the operative word was archaeology, where the crime was not theft but illegal digging—who dug the object up and got a pittance for it.

What lay between digger and ultimate buyer was not a network, not a pipeline, but an erratic zigzag. The final buyer might be in Japan or the US; the swank dealer who sold him the object might be in London or New York or Zurich; but the line from there back to the digger might touch Lebanon, South Africa, Brazil, and Singapore.

Money. It was all about money. Big money. Only at the buyer's end was there any suggestion of love of art or history. For everybody else on the zigzag, it was all about money.

And that was why both the Palestinian Authority and Hamas were involved. It was extraordinarily difficult for both to get money, especially in the form of hard currency, and extraordinarily hard to move it. Neither had a major industry; neither had an educated work force; and what trade they could generate was often crushed by Israeli red tape or military action. Archaeological finds, on the other hand, represented relatively easy money, and they were easy to move—illegally. The Middle East was built on eons of humanity, millennia of civilizations that were piled one on another like rags in a bag. Dig down in Palestine and you might find a First World War cap badge or a Roman coin; keep digging and you might find a crusader's sword-hilt or a piece of first-century Chinese jade; keep digging, and you might find foundations, bones, buckles, clasps, pins, pots, tools, even whole statuary, from Egypt or Syria or Babylon or Crete or India.

So the Palestinian Authority had an archaeological section, which "licensed" research in the territory and its part of the West Bank and Gaza. It took its share and used it "for the general benefit," which meant that some wonderful stuff had entered the zigzag and wound up in Tokyo and Beverly Hills.

One classified report that Spinner had found dealt with a hoard of Roman coins that a Palestinian smuggler had been trying to move across the Bosnian border in the mid-nineties to sell, it was believed, in Greece; he had got caught and had been killed in the melee. Two Mossad agents had been present— a sign of how seriously Israel took this sort of financing of its principal problem and enemy. One analyst, however, had opined that the biggest obstacle for the Palestinian Authority was not Mossad but illegal diggers within the Palestinian territories themselves who didn't get a license and who didn't share their finds with the Authority. With a bulldozer and a few dozen men, they could pillage a site in twenty-four hours. But it was a dangerous business; both the Authority and the Israeli government were after the looters. People died.

Spinner boiled this down to a couple of pages. By ten o'clock Sunday night, after a couple of candy bars from a machine, he was ready to put it on McKinnon's desk. He ended his report with the suggestion that it looked as if something was happening in Israel that tied together the illegal digs, Mossad, and the death of Salem Qatib, and that the best way to find out was not to wait to get some sanitized and over-interpreted summary from the CIA, but to send their own man to winkle out the truth first-hand.

Spinner even had somebody in mind.

Eastern Aegean
Rashid found Saida as evening fell over Chios. He saw her on the top deck while the ferry was negotiating the harbor entrance. Once he had seen her, his apprehensions of missing her turned into a different set of apprehensions as he struggled to watch her without detection in the relatively limited passenger spaces of the ship. But she didn't disembark at Chios. Growing bolder, he managed to follow her to her

cabin. On the door was a computer printout with her name and her destination: Lesvos. Rashid went down to the main deck and looked at the ferry's route map; Lesvos was the next stop, an arrowhead-shaped island close to the coast of Turkey.

He spent a long time looking at the map. Lesvos was a big island with a bay, the Bay of Kalloni, filling what might otherwise have been the interior, making the island look as if it was hollow. The dotted line representing the ferry route ran into a city facing the Turkish coast, Mytilene. Mytilene also had an international airport.

Standing next to the map on the wall was a stand loaded with tourist brochures in Greek, Italian, French, and English. Rashid found a brochure for the island as a whole and separate brochures for individual tourist attractions: Mytilene, of course; an ancient fortress town called Molyvos on the north coast; a petrified forest; the resort town of Kalloni on the bay of the same name; and a brochure on Skala Eressos, a town on the west coast; that made him blush. "Visit the birthplace of Sappho!" it began. Rashid had never heard of Sappho and hadn't made the connection between Lesvos and Lesbians, but by the time he read a paragraph and looked at a picture the connections were clear and he hurriedly replaced the brochure, worried that someone else might have seen him. The rest of the brochures he kept.

Rashid went back to his cabin and waited. Six hours later, he was fifty yards behind her when she disembarked at Mytilene, and he followed her to the bus station across from the museum. She bought a ticket and walked down the waterfront to a tourist bar. Rashid left her there and went back to the bus station, nearly empty at this hour, and approached the ticket counter, where a fat man with a heavy beard sat watching football on a very small television.

Rashid's English was good, but he spent a minute planning what he wanted to say, and then he walked up to the fat man.

"Do you speak English?" he asked.

The man nodded, his eyes on the screen.

"I, ahh, I missed my, ahh, sister?" Rashid found that his carefully planned sentence was dissolving in the face of the fat man's indifference. "I miss her getting off the ferry."

The fat man nodded. He waved a hand over his shoulder.

The gesture meant nothing to Rashid, whose store of boldness was already dwindling. "Did she bought—buy—a ticket?" he asked, glancing back at the entrance.

The man gestured again.

Rashid looked up, following his arm, and saw the times for the buses. They all followed the same route; Mytilene to Molyvos to Skala Eressos and back to Mytilene. Rashid couldn't read the Greek, but he puzzled out the English.

"Can I buy a ticket?"

The fat man shrugged and turned to him, his eyes on the television screen until his whole body had turned to face the ticket counter.

"Okay," the fat man said. "You go to Skala Eressos like her?" He smirked.

Rashid didn't understand the smirk until he remembered the brochure. "Sure," he answered.

"Twenty-one euros."

Rashid paid from the money he had been given in Gaza.

"When can I, umm, get on? Board?" Rashid had already decided he had to board the bus. If he let her go, he might not find her again.

The man shrugged again. "There is your bus, yes?" He was pointing outside, to where an old Volvo bus sat across the street, blocking the view of the harbor. "The driver is asleep, but you go on. If you like. Yes?"

Rashid took his ticket and went out across the street to the bus and climbed aboard. The driver was asleep in his seat, and a chorus of snores emerged from the body of the bus. Rashid went as far back as he could, pushed his backpack into the overhead luggage nets, and lay down across two seats with his peacoat as a blanket.

It didn't occur to him that it was Salem's peacoat, and he was following Salem's girl.

By that time Sunday night, Mike Dukas was in the air between Rome and Tel Aviv, and Alan Craik was on his way from Bahrain to Tajikistan.

Part Two

10

Molyvos, Lesvos

Jerry Piat had arrived on Lesvos at the end of summer with one suitcase, disconcerted by the number of American tourists eighteen hours by ferry from Athens, but they were gone before October came in. He took a house in Molyvos high on the hillside below the ancient citadel, so high that it made his legs burn with effort to reach it. He rented the house from an agency in Athens, paid in cash, and was never asked for identification.

Mrs Paleologos, the woman who cleaned and brought him milk, assumed he was a writer, and he obliged her by purchasing a five-year-old laptop on a trip to Athens and carrying it around. It served him as well as an artist's palette would have served an earlier generation.

He didn't have a car. When he needed to go to Mytilene, the main town, to catch the ferry, he went by bus or cadged a ride. He avoided the use of his passports and his credit cards, avoided identifying himself whenever possible, paid cash. When he needed to transport an item for his new business, he rented a truck from a fisherman—for cash. He also taught himself a good deal of Greek.

Jerry Piat was not a writer. He was a man with a past, and the ebb and flow of that past had washed him up on Lesvos, and now he dealt in antiquities.

Piat's attempts at Greek provided the people of the town

with a good deal of amusement. Their greetings, cautious at first, had become more complex and involved saint's days and festivals as he mastered the rudiments of the language in November. The greetings kept him on his toes. And he endured a good many of them, because it was his delight to ramble through the town from the citadel at the top, down the precipitous streets too narrow to support the most economical European car, past the simple beauty of the small square with its one ancient tree, through the arch of vines that covered the eighteenth century market, down the tourists' streets lined with closed jewelry shops, closed trinket shops, and closed, but busy, potters turning out wares for the next season, past the Bronze Age walls and the two archaeological digs, and into the fishing port where the town's fleet sold their catch, three hundred feet below the citadel's walls.

Piat ate fish most evenings because they were fresh, cheap, and delicious. He drank ouzo for the same reason. And he had punctuated his walks with stops in the town's single real café, perched exactly between the real town and the tourist town, so that the windows of its small main room looked down on the port two hundred feet below and the gate of the Turkish outworks. Piat went there every day, opened his laptop, played with it for a while, and then drank coffee and watched the sea.

Piat had found a way of making money while doing very little work. He found that he enjoyed learning about his work more than he enjoyed doing it. He'd wasted his college time learning trivia to pass. Now he read about the past with interest born of avarice. There was a lot of money in antiquities, and none of it was traceable. That mattered to Piat.

Piat knew he would have to move on in the spring, but for the moment, life was better than he had expected. He surprised himself by the moderation of his drinking. After a month on Lesvos, his hands had stopped shaking for the first time in years. His face gained flesh. His brain enjoyed learning the language. He watched the late tourists and the locals and the visiting lesbians from Skala Eressos, and he thought, *All I need now is a girl.*

It was the warmest January in years. He knew this because all the locals had told him so every morning for three weeks. Several days, he wore shorts. Old habit and a temptation to virtue led him to put on beat-up shoes and run down the steep streets, out along the two archaeological digs and off among the sheep and the olive trees that inhabited the volcanic landscape beyond the town.

This morning he ran uphill, climbing slowly with the town appearing and vanishing on his left as he pushed himself through the switchbacks on the road that, if he ever went far enough, would take him to the hot springs at Thermi. It had become a goal, almost a fantasy, that before he moved on, he would run the seven miles to the springs and lie in the hot water where Sappho and Alcaeus had bathed. But probably not together.

He turned again, the town emerging behind a crag, legs burning with the effort. This was the highest he'd gone, and now he was running from turn to turn, telling himself that he'd go back at the next one, then the next. High above him, he heard the growl of a distant engine. He pushed on, looking for a place to get clear of the road. Sixty yards on, and he had to climb again, and then he saw the vehicle, the daily bus from Mytilene. He pushed himself into a sprint and ran off the road to the left on a broad shelf of green. He could hear the bells on sheep somewhere below him, and the roar of the bus.

When Rashid woke, the bus was moving, climbing hills into the dawn.

123

After a moment of disorientation and another of panic, he spotted Saida sitting near the front, her dyed-blond head cocked down as if she was reading. He took the heavy English paperback out of his pack and started to read. His eyes wouldn't stick on the page—he had to keep looking at Saida to make sure she was still there. She never turned her head.

He was aware that they climbed for a long time through olive groves and naked volcanic rock before they finally passed the summit of the road with the sea far below to his right and started down, switchback after switchback, the Turkish shore visible in the distance across the strait. The bus stopped twice for sheep straying on the road and slowed once for a thin man in shorts.

Piat pulled up, put his hands on his hips, and breathed. The bus came past slowly, gears clashing around the switchback, the windows reflecting the blue of the sea behind him. He waited for it to pass, disappointed now that he had quit before he was really ready. He let it go in a cloud of leaded gas fumes and waited for it to get well clear before he started the much faster run down.

Three miles. Still a long way to go before he was ready for Thermi.

Then the bus was passing a modern petrol station, a street of bars and restaurants, and they came to a stop on a cobbled square with an old walled town above them and the sea stretching away on the other side of the bus beyond a black sand beach.

The driver stood up and shouted, "Molyvos!" He said something in Greek and pointed up the street. In English he said, "One hour." Then he got down into the street and lit a cigarette.

Most of the passengers stayed where they were.

Saida took her bag and got off. Rashid had to scramble to follow her. By the time he had his book back in his bag and got off, she was already well up the cobbled street, her pink coat vanishing through the old Turkish gate into the old town. Rashid reached the gate and looked up the street. It curved away to the right and divided around a sharply angled stone building. She was nowhere to be seen.

He walked up to a wedge-shaped house at the intersection of two streets and followed the larger street to the left up an incline so steep that his thighs were burning before he had gone a hundred steps. The way narrowed and narrowed again, with cross streets as small as in his home town of Acco appearing at irregular angles. Molyvos was a maze, a steep maze, but it reminded him of home more powerfully than anywhere he had been in three days and he pushed on, confident in his ability to negotiate an old town. He liked Molyvos. People nodded to him as he passed and he nodded back.

Despite his confidence, he was aware that they were locals, and he was the only tourist.

He grew hot as he climbed, then cold as the wind hit his sweat, and he pulled Salem's coat on. He looked at his watch every few minutes. He stood at the intersection of two relatively large streets and tried to think like Saida. She had taken her bag; she intended to stay. And she had moved as if she knew where she was going.

He turned left and down, back towards the tourist section. Assuming that Molyvos was like Acco, the tourist section would congregate almost all of the businesses and all the hotels. He followed his new street across the hill, pausing at occasional terraces to look down. Twice he caught glimpses of a row of shops screened by grape vines. The vines were alien to him, but he took the next street downhill to find the shops.

He no sooner emerged onto the street of vines and shops than he saw her pink coat and her backpack farther down the street. She was wearing fashionable shoes; he could see that the blocky heels made the cobbled streets difficult for her to walk. He started to overtake her rapidly. He stopped to look in shop windows, an activity that he himself found inadequate to cover his presence because he and Saida were virtually the only tourists on the street, but she took no notice of him, never looked back, just glanced from time to time at a paper in her hand.

Rashid looked at his watch. They had less than fifteen minutes to catch the bus, if that was her intention. He felt exposed on the street because the town was so empty, but as long as she kept moving he could not afford to drop any farther back. He began to be frustrated by her inability to find whatever she was looking for.

It never occurred to him that she was wasting time on purpose.

Piat's house didn't have a shower, and the water pressure this high in the town was pitiful anyway, so he stood in his kitchen and sponged himself with a washcloth. Then he washed his shorts in a stained plastic bucket so that they'd be clean again tomorrow, or at least clean by his standards. He pulled on an old black polo shirt and an ancient pair of jeans, pushed his feet into shoes, tucked his laptop into his backpack with a bottle of water and headed off to find coffee.

A hundred feet lower in the town, he walked into the chocolate shop. Sergio, one of the brothers who ran the place, was moving chairs out to the balcony that hung out over the lower town with nothing but a pair of two-hundred-year-old wooden supports keeping gravity at bay. Piat captured the table with the best view and slid carefully into his usual seat. The balcony was very small.

Sergio flashed a smile.

Piat smiled back. *"Tha thela Elleniko, parakalo."* The first

Greek he'd learned. He loved Greek coffee; heavy, sweet, complicated.

Sergio nodded. *"Effkaristo."*

Piat opened his computer and started going through the dozen files he'd downloaded at the internet café in the fishing port the night before. He deleted all of the email he'd received, most of it spam and the rest not worth his time. He had pictures from a lot of merchandise for sale in Athens; a casual scan showed that none of the pieces on offer were worth the time it would take him to get to Athens. By the time his day's work was done the muck at the bottom of the cup bumped against his teeth and coated his tongue. Real Greeks seemed to know how to avoid this. Piat raised his head to order another cup.

With ten minutes left until the bus would depart, Saida turned downhill and entered a brightly painted café with red window frames and a bright blue door. The sign advertised chocolates in English and Greek. Rashid found a potter's workshop up the street and stood outside watching the potter, glancing over his shoulder at the chocolate shop. He could see her through the window, her pink coat obvious.

A girl in a pink coat was just coming up the steps from the street. Piat appreciated her in a single glance, from her skinny legs to elegant face, her hard eyes and heavy brows. She wasn't beautiful, but the careful display of young flesh at leg and hip had its effect. He smiled at her without thinking. She looked like an angry Audrey Hepburn. The thought made him laugh.

She smiled back, crossing the interior of the café without breaking eye contact.

Piat was on guard before she reached his table.

"Mr Furman?" she asked. She had an accent he couldn't immediately place. She also had a silver ring in her navel with a gold bead on it, and from her wrist dangled a shiny paper bag from a tourist shop. She had a heavy backpack.

"Yes," Piat answered.

She put the shiny bag on the table in front of him and gave him a smile that curled the corners of her lips down while her eyes just touched his under heavy brows. "I'll be back. Please wait."

She left the bag and went out, dazzled Sergio and asked for the washroom. Piat suspected she was unable to keep herself from flirting with men. And he suspected her. Furman was the name he used for a handful of transactions in Athens. It didn't belong here. He considered bolting.

He decided that bolting was pointless, got Sergio's attention, and raised his cup. Sergio nodded. Out of ex-professional paranoia, Piat looked through the café at the narrow street outside, found its emptiness unreassuring, and fidgeted, trying to recollect everyone who knew him as Furman. Pointless.

Coffee came, and he drank. He looked at his watch twice, wished for a cigarette as many times, looked out at the street and down at the fishing port. The bus was loading a handful of passengers.

Dusty alarm bells rang in his head. Piat got up, slid out from behind his table, off the balcony, and down the stone steps to the lower room that was closed in the winter and held the café's malodorous bathroom. It also had a second door that led to a lower street. Piat had seen it as a potential escape route the first time he'd come in, because old training made him catalogue such things.

Of course the bathroom was empty. The girl was gone.

The bag she had left was big enough to take seriously as a bomb. Piat went back up to the bag and the last decent sip of his coffee. He gave the bag a cautious squeeze. Then he finished his coffee. After some reflection, he took out his folding knife and cut the bottom off the bag very slowly.

Not a bomb. Only a single CD in an envelope with a yellow sticky note attached. The sticky note said:

Saida2310@Yahoo.com
Just yes if u want it and we'll meet.

Piat wanted to know what *it* was, but he didn't choose to put the CD into his own computer. He closed his laptop, put it in his backpack, took the bag and the note, and left some euros for Sergio. Sergio was Greek and male, so he jutted his chin in the direction the girl had gone and shrugged. Piat shrugged back. He looked past Sergio's cash register at the upper street, automatically noting the sparse pedestrian traffic—two women walking arm in arm, a young man in a blue coat watching a potter. Then he was out the door and moving.

Rashid stood and waited. The bus's departure time came and went. He began to be afraid. And then the man she had spoken with came to the door, looked right at him, and walked off the other way at a brisk pace.

Rashid's stomach felt like a washing machine with a heavy load. He suspected she was gone, feared she was gone, but he couldn't see how he had missed her. He was frozen outside the potter's. Instinct pushed him to follow the thin man. Hope made him hesitate outside the door of the café. He took a long look inside. She wasn't there. There were stairs going down to a basement. Rashid hurried down the street to the end of the building and found one of the irregular cross streets ran back along the lower side of the chocolate shop, with a steep cliff falling away beyond. There was a lower door. She had walked down the stairs. She was gone.

Abandoning any notion of stealth, Rashid ran back to the corner and then down the main street, through the Turkish gate. A glance to his left proved that the bus was gone; a glance to his right showed the slight form of the man she had met going down into the fishing port.

Rashid followed the thin man.

Piat walked down to the fishing port with his mind on the girl. She was too young to be a professional, he thought, unless somebody out there was using children to track old men. But he didn't like that she had his Athens business name or had tracked it to his café in the islands. Somebody in Athens, somebody with whom he did business, had blabbed. He went through the Turkish gate trying to deduce who that might be.

The whole thing could be a set-up, but it was pretty damned elaborate if that was true, and Piat didn't think that a real attempt to grab him would be elaborate. Lesvos was a quiet island with a law-abiding population, but it was a long way from serious police and security services. It was full of smugglers and drug-runners and various other illicit activities, and Piat assumed that if any of his old enemies wanted him, they'd either grab him off the street or shoot him. Elaborate traps with young girls and computer codes hardly seemed necessary.

For the first time in weeks, though, it made Piat want to smoke. He pushed that temptation down and went into his cybercafé. They knew him here, too, and in winter he had the whole place to himself. He paid for an hour, sat at one of their machines, and pushed the girl's CD into a drive.

The drive whirred. A window invited him to open the new disk in various formats. The window told him that he was going to see photographs. He chose a slideshow and clicked on it.

The drive whirred again. Piat waved at the young man at the counter for a cup of coffee.

The first image appeared on the screen, with three more

in smaller windows displayed below. The disk was virtually empty, but Piat didn't register that yet, because he was unable to take his eyes off the picture on the screen.

The picture showed a cup with two handles like wings.

The cup had a wide base and a narrow, cone-shaped stem that rose gracefully to a wide bowl with the handles. The base and stem were gold; the exterior of the bowl was niello, an ancient enamel treatment, with crisp black, silver and gold designs spiraling down from the top. The bowl had a heavy rim of gold, marked with symbols, and there were more symbols scattered among the scenes in the spiral.

It was fabulous.

Piat breathed out, slowly, and looked around the café to see who might be watching his screen. Old paranoia. He went back to the picture, then looked at the other three, each a close-up of one of the panels of the spiral.

Mycenaean. He knew a cup like it, in the Walters collection in Baltimore. Except that the Walters cup was clay, and this was gold. *Three thousand years old.*

He couldn't fault the art. On one panel, a man with a figure-eight shield strained to thrust his spear into another man in heavy armor. The armor was consistent; the shield was correct. The same armored man appeared again in the second panel in a chariot. The chariot wheels had four spokes. He catalogued these details automatically, because he had already fallen in love with the piece and then faced the reality that it had to be a forgery.

Niello. Like Schliemann's finds at Mycenae. There weren't a lot of craftsmen in the world who could produce something like that. It wasn't like faking pottery. He clicked through the four pictures, looking for signs of wear. The niello's black background work had flaked away in several portions, and there were dents and very small scratches in the surface of the cup.

At one level, he wanted it to be real.

At another, he knew it had to be fake.

And then there were the symbols on the rim. Piat knew Linear B when he looked at it. As far as he knew, there were only three or four uses of Linear B on objects in existence. That made it an enormous risk for a forger to try, especially as there were very few scholars who could read Linear B.

It took him thirty minutes on the internet to prove to himself that most of the visible symbols in the photos were real symbols from Linear B. The inscription, if it was an inscription, started (or ended) on the rim and ran around the spiral design down to the base. Much of it wasn't visible in the photos he had. But what was visible was real, or at least correctly executed.

Piat knew a man in Athens who could read Linear B, or said he could. He had joked to Piat that he was one of forty people in the world who could decipher it.

Piat drank his now-cold Nescafé and stared out the window. If the cup was real, its value would be immense. Even if fake, the possibility of a major profit was there. It would cost him two days, but he had other business in Athens anyway.

He took the CD out of the drive and put it in his computer case. He used the internet to check the ferry schedule to Athens. He'd catch the bus returning and take the night ferry from Mytilene.

He sent a short email to an Athens IP and signed it "Jack."

He spent half an hour making a careful sketch of the cup. He provided only rough approximations of the scenes in niello, and he left off the Linear B writing. He made the sketch directly on his laptop and wasted an hour fiddling with the shapes to get the dimensions close to correct. Because he was good at sketching with pencils, the process on the computer struck him as unnecessarily cumbersome, but he had six hours to kill.

132

When he was done, he wrote a short email to a man in South Carolina who bought high-end antiquities of doubtful origin. He kept the message ambiguous but included the sketch. His work completed, Piat finished his cold Nescafé, made a face, and glanced out the window.

He noticed that the young man in the blue coat, first seen at the café, was loitering outside the door of the cybercafé.

11

Tel Aviv

By the time Dukas had flown from Naples to Rome to make the Alitalia flight to Tel Aviv, the FBI had started an investigation in the US into Qatib's residence there, and Abe Peretz in Tel Aviv was exchanging messages with Dukas and Washington and Naples about what he was learning—or not learning—in Israel. The Tel Aviv police were being cooperative, he had said, and Mossad, after Alan's blast at them, were making all the right noises. But noise was all that they were producing so far, and when Dukas had left home that Sunday he still hadn't known any more about the Mossad involvement than Craik had told him.

It takes as long to fly from Naples to Tel Aviv via Rome as it does from New York to London, but the schedules are not as kind. Dukas got to Tel Aviv at four on Monday morning, checked into his hotel and slipped into the clean, cool sheets in his socks and underwear and slept hard until his wakeup came at eight. A recorded voice told him the time and said it was seventeen degrees and cloudy, and he growled aloud into the phone, "Where am I?" He lay back and thought about it. *If this is Monday, I must be in Tel Aviv.* He tasted as if he'd spent the night licking envelope flaps.

He took a shower and brushed his teeth as if he were getting ready to visit the dentist, but the taste of travel persisted. Half-dressed—black polo shirt, red boxer undershorts, socks—he sat on the bed again and called Triffler at home in Naples.

"Just checking to make sure you're awake."

"I'm out the door in three minutes. This isn't a secure phone."

"Of course it isn't secure! I'm on a goddam hotel phone. I wanted you to know that I got here safely and am okay because I knew you'd be worried sick."

"You were in our prayers all night."

"I'm surprised the subject line got past the divine spam filter. The reason I called, I think we better talk when I've touched some bases here. Can you stand by secure at ten your time?"

"My boss gave me a million things to do."

"Yeah, bosses are assholes. Can you?"

"It'll be a chance to catch you up on the most recent hysteria from the puzzle-masters. Ten o'clock."

"Be there."

Dukas pulled on a pair of chinos that, with the polo shirt, made him look like an overweight ex-boxer. He hadn't brought a gun, so there was no reason for a jacket. He'd *look* better in a jacket, he thought, but he was more comfortable the way he was, and his memories of Israel were that jackets were as rare as ascots.

He was headed for breakfast when the telephone rang.

"Seventeen-forty-six," he said, giving the room number instead of his name because of a caution that was habitual but irrational.

"Mister Michael Dukas?"

Dukas had a good ear for voices. This one he hadn't heard for almost eight years, but he remembered it—deep, not too heavily accented, a little slow. He couldn't have put a name to it, but he knew it, and it called up a place and a time and a death. And a name that had maybe been a cover name— Shlomo.

"Yes?"

"You won't remember me, but we met some years ago in—"

"Bosnia, the Kosovo border. Shlomo."

A hesitation, a sound between a chuckle and a gasp. "My name now is Shlomo Eshkol." Dukas waited. Was this also the Mossad smiler who had led Alan out of captivity? "I am downstairs. I wonder if we could meet."

Dukas was cagey, wanting the guy to talk, thinking that even good operational people sometimes used their own first names when they were clandestine, so maybe this really *was* a Shlomo. He said, "I'm heading out for breakfast. This is business, not social, right?"

"You may say so."

"Don't spoil my breakfast. I'll be right down."

Shlomo Eṣhkol—if that was his name—looked much as he had in Bosnia, probably a little more lined and battered, although Dukas remembered him as seeming a little used even then—what his wife called a face that looked as if it had been stepped on. Dukas let his hand be shaken and then let himself be persuaded that they wanted to go to the hotel coffee shop.

"You one of the guys that snatched Al Craik?" Dukas said as they sat down.

"Not so. I'm one of the guys who brought him back to his hotel."

"Samey-samey—same by association."

Eshkol made one of those guy-to-guy faces of denial—mock frown, slightly pouted lips—and raised a hand as if to push the words away. Dukas moved the hand aside so forcefully that Eshkol's arm banged on the table.

"Don't give me that shit! You guys—the *Institute*—snatched an American officer off the street and you're not going to brush it off with a little Middle Eastern body language! It isn't over—for me or for the US government." Dukas surprised himself with his anger; it was as if the anger was delighted to have a real face and a real name to put to Craik's humiliation at last.

"I was not one of those who grabbed him!"

"But you were one of the ones who cleaned up after them, right? To me, you're all the same guys." Eshkol's face seemed to lengthen; lines of tension showed as muscles clenched above his jaw. He was an angry man, too. Dukas, unfazed by anger, didn't look away but in fact leaned closer. "You and I got along in Bosnia. I thought you were an okay guy. I don't think you're an okay guy in Tel Aviv. You don't like it, be just as mad as you like. Go away, if you want. Tell your bosses you're not getting off this easy."

Eshkol's face looked as if it had hardened into flesh-colored cement. He was wearing a golf jacket—so much for Dukas's idea that men didn't wear jackets here, except that he had thought when he saw it that the reason Eshkol was wearing it was that he was packing—and Dukas was waiting for him to produce the gun from its cover. Instead, after a couple of seconds of frozen anger, Eshkol broke into a smile and said, "You know who my boss is?" He laughed and studied Dukas's face like a man waiting to see when somebody would get the joke. "Well?"

"I don't do guesses."

"Bosnia. The guy who was with me."

Dukas remembered—the offensive type who'd thought that the way to deal with all enemies was to kill them. "He worked for you, I thought."

Eshkol nodded. "Now I work for him."

Dukas glanced down at the menu. "Okay, you got my sympathy." He saw that the restaurant offered Belgian pancakes, which, for an American in a Jewish country, would probably do. "You understand my position?"

"You don't forgive."

"Don't forget it and don't let your boss forget it." He closed the menu and looked around for a waiter. "What d'you want?"

"To make contact."

"My ass."

"This is on my time; they don't know I'm here. Look, Dukas, listen to me—I'm trying to be straight with you. As straight as—you know, as straight as I can be." Eshkol stared into his eyes. "I want to help you." Dukas looked back and shrugged.

Eshkol ordered tea while Dukas ordered the pancakes, sour cream, syrup, coffee, brown toast with Negev strawberry jam, and, as an afterthought, two poached eggs. When the waiter had hurried away, Eshkol laced his blunt, thick fingers together and said, "There are things I cannot tell you. You know how it works. But there could be things I would choose to tell you because—okay, I'll be straight with you—we made a mistake and behaved badly."

"Was Salem Qatib's death about crypto?" The Israelis shared some US codes; would of course know Qatib's background.

"We didn't know he was ex-US Navy."

"A Palestinian with a US crypto background, you didn't *know*?"

Eshkol sighed. "We had it, but it was in a file. Nobody looked."

"Nobody cared."

"Not until he turned up dead."

Dukas shot him a look but got nothing back. "What else've you got on Qatib?"

"Michael—I can call you Michael, okay?—it isn't some one thing that we have on Qatib. He was a *Palestinian*. He had bad contacts in the Palestinian Authority and Hamas; people around him had contacts with Fatah and Hamas. It's a hundred things, a thousand things."

"He was a terrorist?"

"No, frankly, I think he wasn't a terrorist. My boss maybe wants to think he was a terrorist, but he wasn't a terrorist."

Dukas gave him a flat, blank look—the thousand-yard stare. "I'm here to find out how and why Salem Qatib died. His *death*. That's what I want. Facts. Documents. Interviews. I want the guys who killed him. I'll *get* the guys who killed him." He went on staring at Eshkol, thinking that the man wasn't quite what he seemed but probably was telling the truth when he said he wanted to help. The trouble was, the help was coming through about a hundred layers of gauze. "Why'd you torture him?"

"I didn't torture him! Michael—believe me. There was no torture."

"You were there?"

"No—"

"Were you there when he died?"

"It's the same as with Commander Craik; these things, they were done by other people."

"So why do you say there wasn't torture? You weren't there, how could you know?"

Eshkol muttered that torture was illegal in Israel. The waiter put plates in front of Dukas, a big one for the pancakes, a smaller one with the eggs, a very small one for the toast. He set down a kind of lazy Susan with jams, a bowl with the sour cream, a pitcher of syrup, a coffee cup and a pot. When he had satisfied himself that everything was there, he put Eshkol's tea down and disappeared, and Dukas said, "Qatib died of torture."

"How do you know of what he died?"

"If Craik says the guy died of torture, I believe it."

"Only an autopsy would tell you if he died of torture."

"Which is why I've asked for a forensics team and which is why the body is being turned over to the local cops—yes?"

Eshkol made another gesture. Dukas decided Eshkol used

139

gestures when he didn't want to commit himself. "When do you guys turn the body over?"

"Not my—"

"Not your department. You weren't at the torture; you weren't at the snatch of Craik; you don't know about the body. What do they pay you for?" He was mopping up egg yolk with a forkful of pancake, which he now waved in front of Eshkol. "I asked for a forensics team, your government negatived it as not needed. I've asked for it again. You don't know about that, either?"

Eshkol spread his hands. "I don't!"

Dukas finished the pancake and egg yolk and started spreading jam on a piece of toast. "What's your specialty?"

A vague wave. "Investigation."

"Of what?"

"Michael—this is classified—*you* understand—"

Dukas chewed, staring at him. He was thinking about Bosnia. Two Israelis, "helping" (ho-ho) the US and the UN capture a Palestinian. Who got shot dead and who just happened to be carrying a case full of antique coins. "Money?" he said. And he thought, *Antique coins*, and Salem Qatib had studied archaeology, and he wondered if there was a connection. He would have to pursue his attempts to get in touch with people at Qatib's university. "Money?" he said to Eshkol.

"Following the money, yes, maybe. We do that, sure."

Dukas made a mental note to goose Triffler about the Mossad personnel roster, and he said, "You were interested in Qatib because he had access to money? What, he was laundering money for the PA? Getting money? What?"

Eshkol waved a hand.

"What's your boss's name?"

A shrug. "Michael, I can't—"

Dukas finished eating and sipped coffee and looked at Eshkol, who started chattering about football. Dukas let him run down and then said, "We ought to talk sometime," and, seeing Abe Peretz in the coffee-shop doorway, waved and said he had to go. Peretz had agreed to pick him up to take him to the embassy and walk him through the formalities. Eshkol's eyes had followed Dukas's and he said, "Somebody you know?"

"My ride."

"I thought I could drive you places, Michael. Put you in the picture—"

Dukas was writing his room number on the check. "I don't think I want to be in that picture, thanks." He stood. A little late, Eshkol got to his feet and leaned close and said, "Better if your friend doesn't know who I am."

"No, it isn't."

Dukas introduced them but relented and didn't use the word Mossad. Nonetheless, it was the first thing he told Peretz once Eshkol had detached himself from them. By then, they were in Peretz's car and headed for the embassy.

"I worked with him on a thing in Bosnia," Dukas said. "He's trying to snow me."

"Mossad got their wrist slapped by Jerusalem because of the demarche, so they'll make nice for a while, but don't expect too much."

"I don't expect anything. Where's my request for the forensics team this morning?"

"Ambassador signed off on it *again*, TLV cops okayed it, and a great silence falls."

"They going to nix it again?"

"Why shouldn't they? We didn't ask for our aid money back the first time."

"It stinks."

Peretz laughed. "I forget what it's like to come here from the real world. What you have to remember, Mike, is *everything* here is about security. They eat and breathe security— or insecurity, depending on how you look at it. From a

141

security aspect, they don't see much reason why a foreign forensics team should look at a dead Palestinian."

"'Foreign,' as in we-pay-your-bills foreign?"

"That cuts no ice here. There's Israel, and then there's the outside. We give them money, but it doesn't buy anything. They *let* us give them money."

"I'd forgotten how foreign aid works."

When Dukas had been shown around the embassy and introduced to the chief of staff—a woman—and the deputy naval attaché and the coffee machine, he was taken to an office that was temporarily vacant and told it was his to use. There was no computer; the file cabinets were locked; and the telephone didn't work.

"I need a STU and a phone." A STU was a secure telephone device.

Peretz was embarrassed. "You'll have to use mine. Security."

"So it isn't just an Israeli hobby."

"Since Nine-Eleven—"

Dukas snorted.

Peretz handed him a computer-printed sheet—Dukas's schedule. "We're meeting Mossad at one o'clock. A make-nice confab; they're going to turn over 'significant documentation.' Ambassador wants to meet with you at four; CIA chief of station at four-thirty." Peretz looked at him over a pair of wire-rimmed glasses. "She's worried about turf, so just keep telling her it's a Navy issue." He dropped the paper in front of Dukas.

Dukas saw that he was invited to a reception at five-thirty and a free showing of a new Leonardo DiCaprio movie in the embassy's theatre at eight. Whoopee. "I want to meet right quick with this policewoman that clued Al to the Qatib shit. Can you arrange that?"

Peretz said he could.

Dukas sat down with a stack of messages about Qatib and

cryptology. He'd seen most of them in Naples, but he had to go through the whole mess, checking out what the Tel Aviv embassy had been getting and giving. The Navy, NSA (who owned cryptology), and the Bureau were all nuts on the crypto question; again, it was the near-hysteria of the post-Nine-Eleven world. When Dukas had made his way through the pile, he concluded that nobody knew much that they hadn't known three days before, but a lot of people were really stirred up.

"I smell fear," he said to Peretz.

"As in, 'Let's for God's sake not make another mistake.'"

"As in 'Is my ass covered?'" He didn't say that he smelled something else—the sour odor of desk jockeys jumping to conclusions.

At ten o'clock Naples time he got on the STU to Triffler, who was laughing because the hysteria had now spread to the Pacific: Salem Qatib had gone to a three-month school at Monterey and then done a two-week training cruise on a surveillance ship. "Pac Fleet are doing handsprings trying to prove that the guy couldn't have learned anything remotely useful to anybody. 'Negligible value' is used three times in one message. It's a real plug for Navy education."

Dukas told him about meeting Eshkol. "Which set me thinking. Where's that Mossad organizational chart?"

"I've been promised it for today."

"Oh, shit, promises. A little break—remember I said I knew a guy named Shlomo? Now he says his name is Shlomo Eshkol. I was on this quickie with him in Bosnia. Nice guy, at least he seemed to be back then. He waylaid me at breakfast, was trying to 'help' me—his word—but he's in it and he's got a bean up his nose about something. Maybe guilt; such things happen. I'm trying to backtrack the Bosnia thing with Pigoreau to find out just what his interest was there; all I know at this point is, the guy they were after was smuggling antique coins."

"I don't see a connection."

"Doesn't seem to fit with the death of a former Navy cryptologist, no, but coins are money. Maybe it's money."

"Maybe just coincidence."

"There's no such thing as coincidence."

"May I write that down?"

"When you get the personnel roster, put somebody on checking every Shlomo. *You* check Shlomo Eshkol—specifically, is there a real Eshkol or was he bullshitting me? Then check his boss, too. Here's how it works—he says his boss was promoted over his head, so you're looking for somebody who eight years ago was in a lower grade and is now higher. I want the name and I want the title."

"Do you know that I'm doing my job *and* yours here?" Triffler's fluty voice sounded long-suffering.

"And doing it brilliantly. You've been at it for—what? Two hours? Poor you."

As he'd been telling Triffler what he wanted, his brain had made one of those irrational leaps that brings either real illumination or foolishness: the reason that Eshkol had come to his hotel was precisely so that Dukas could ask for the information he wanted Triffler to get. That is, Eshkol had given two clues—a supposedly real name and the fact that his boss was somebody who had used to work for him. From there, any intel specialist could probably track them. What Eshkol wanted Dukas to know—or so it seemed at that moment— was that Eshkol's and his boss's specialty had something important to do with Qatib's death.

It may have been reverse jet lag, but Dukas's gut was telling him that it was lunch time in Tel Aviv, or at least brunch time, and in the course of his research into the possibility, he found that while Tel Aviv may be short on great architecture, it abounds in good restaurants. He settled right then for a recommendation from one of the embassy marine guards, a place called Susannah where he could pig out on mutton meatballs,

144

felafels, and tabouleh; dinner, he was told, could be had at a hundred places, from Spagettim (fifty varieties of spaghetti) to Kimmel (pork and bacon with Italian sausage—this was Jewish?) to Chimichanga (Mexican, what else?), with Russian, Thai, French, Italian (a place called Bellini that specialized in pasta putanesca particularly appealing to him), and dozens of others waiting in the wings.

A week in Tel Aviv was beginning to look not so bad.

12

Tajikistan

The leased 747 turned for the second leg of its approach, and Alan could look through the scarred window at the airport below. He nudged Fidel in the seat next to him and tapped the Plexiglas. Fidel leaned over, looked, muttered, "Jesus."

"Changed a little," Alan said over the sound of the engines.

"Changed a fucking lot, Commander."

Alan looked out again. When they had flown in the first time, the airport had had two crossed runways and a terminal with some one-storey buildings huddled around it. Now, both runways had been extended and a third was under construction, and two prefab hangars were almost completed, as well as two inflatable structures and a row of mobile homes. Fidel took another look and sat back, buckling his seatbelt, and said, apparently irrelevantly, "I tell you a guy offered me seven-fifty a day to come back here as a civilian?"

The connection was clear: Tajikistan, Afghanistan, war itself were big-money items now.

"You going to do it?"

"I got two years on my enlistment. Maybe then. What d'you think?"

Fidel spoke Pashto and Farsi; he was trained in demolition, weapons, and tactics; he was an intelligence professional. Why shouldn't he make a bundle, like everybody else on the civilian side—except that the Navy had paid for all that

146

training? Before Alan could say anything, Fidel added, "You could make a lot more than that, Commander."

He knew. He'd already had offers from an ex-Navy friend who ran his own security outfit. "I know somebody who'd be happy to get you if you want to go that way," he said.

They were humping luggage through an unfinished landscape of plywood walls, new concrete, and exposed metal grid work when Fidel came back to the subject. "You not too interested in doing this when you leave the Navy, are you, Commander?"

Alan frowned. He was looking for somebody who was supposed to meet them with transport. "I'm not what you'd call enthusiastic about anybody doing this as a civilian, I guess." He shifted his grip on his flight bag. "There's a reason we talk about 'citizen soldiers' and not about citizen mercenaries."

"Man's got a right to make the most he can of his skills."

"And the Navy lets you do that."

"Not for the same money, they don't."

"That's a different question." He spotted their ride, a Marine captain he had worked with before. As if by common consent, he and Fidel stopped talking about big money and leaving the Navy, but Alan kept on thinking about it as they drove through the roadblocks and checkpoints and construction delays of the now huge air facility, where, he guessed, a lot of the people he saw were civilians doing what the military used to do. Almost to himself, but loud enough for Fidel to hear, he said, "There's a reason we want people who do what we do under orders. There has to be control. Very tight control." He was thinking of the four men who had snatched him off the street in Tel Aviv. They had been out of control, he thought. And he was thinking of the man who had called himself Ben, and what he had said.

They'd been given one of the mobile homes as a temporary briefing room. They were scheduled to fly out in a few hours;

he had to nail everything down now, because they'd break into separate parts and take different aircraft. Besides Fidel, who would stay with him, he had two SEALs, one Marine, and one army special-forces sergeant. Altogether, they comprised Team Nineteen, which existed only for this mission and would fade away when it was done.

"The President signed a special finding four days after Nine-Eleven, authorizing what we're going to do. It's new, and it's right at the edge, and I want you all to understand what the rules are." He looked around at the blank, tough faces. "We're tasked to snatch a man who's supposed to be an al-Qaida officer, detain him and interrogate him and then turn him over for further detention." He didn't tell them about his own doubts and the more-than-doubts of the Shin Bet officer in Tel Aviv. Alan had taken the suspect data to CentCom and told them about Shin Bet's doubts, and they'd told him the information was the best they had, and he was to go ahead with the operation. One colonel at CentCom had even pointed out to him that the information had been provided by the Israelis so must be reliable. Exactly as Ben had said. Now, masking his own uncertainty, he said to the four men in front of him, "The operation means violating the sovereignty of another country. Anybody got a problem with that?" The faces remained blank. "It means kidnapping somebody who isn't involved in what we're doing in Afghanistan. Anybody got a problem with that?"

The sergeant raised his hand from the wrist. "This target involved in Nine-Eleven?"

"That's what we're supposed to find out. He's on the list because our people think he is. Problem?"

"No problem."

It was a question, that laconic answer meant, of cause: there might have been a problem about snatching somebody who minded his own business, but snatching somebody who was connected to Nine-Eleven was self-justifying. The rules—the old rules, the pre-Nine-Eleven rules—bent under the weight of the event. Alan was not himself convinced of the morality of it: if you argued that cataclysmic events justified cataclysmic actions, then you might justify all sorts of things. But maybe, he knew, he was too aware of what had happened in Tel Aviv, of having been the victim. The people who had grabbed him had felt justified, he was sure—by an idea of security or threat. Frightened people, he had said, did stupid things. He fought the notion that what he was doing now was stupid, or at least ill thought out—that its consequences were unforeseeable. He remembered saying to Fidel a month before, "If you fight like your enemy, you become your enemy." Now, he said, "You four guys get the hard work. You grab the guy and bring him to us in Kandahar, and we interrogate him."

"Where is he?"

"Iran."

He showed them, on the laptop, maps from a CD that had been prepared in Washington. They had it down to the street and the house. The target had been living in Herat, in Western Afghanistan, and funneling Iranian money to the Northern Alliance—the good guys now allied with the US—but the suspicion in DoD was that he had been bin Laden's man the whole time, and some of the Iranian money had been skimmed to go to the Nine-Eleven operation. Or that was the paranoid view. Or at least it was the suspicion or the notion or the invention of the people in Washington who had sent the information to Shin Bet to pass it to CentCom. Now the target was supposed to be in Mashhad, Iran. "You fly from here to Ashkhabad, just over the border in Turkmenistan. The Turkmen are on our side."

"It says here," one of the SEALs growled.

"You the Turkmen speaker?"

"That's me."

"You don't think they're on our side?"

"I think if we're paying enough, they're on our side. If

149

you think they won't let the Iranians know we're there, you're playing with a cracked bat."

"The geniuses tell me they're on our side."

The SEAL shrugged.

"You four go in a truck convoy. There's a major route to Mashhad, a lot of Russian stuff and a lot of contraband that comes through Turkmenistan into Iran. There's a local contact I'll brief Sergeant Fosca on separately. You make the snatch and signal, and you'll be picked up."

"By what?"

"Chopper. CIA is moving teams in that area putting down passive radiation detectors. One of their choppers will take you out."

The other SEAL said, "Better if they took us in, too."

"I think the idea is to minimize risk. The Iranians have good radar."

"Yeah," the sergeant muttered, "they got it from us. I thought the Iranians were our buddies these days."

Alan wanted to say, *That was last month when we needed them,* but he muttered something about reality and Iranian paranoia.

"Why's this guy living so close to the border if he's an al-Qaida biggie?"

"Maybe that's the only place the Iranians will let him live. Maybe they want us to take him off their hands." Except that until a couple of months ago, we weren't the kind of people who crossed borders to grab people. Now we are.

He started to go into details, went into them by layers, deeper and deeper. Fidel handed out false ID, Iranian, Turkmen, and US money, local clothes. "You fly into Ashkhabad as four Americans. You drive into Iran as four truckers from the Stans. When the chopper drops you back in Ashkhabad, you fly the guy to Kandahar and turn him over to me. Then you guys are done."

150

The sergeant grinned without humor. "And we go home, right? Sure we do."

They ran through weapons, fallbacks, bailout and communications. The other SEAL was the comm man; he got his own briefing packet, too, and a pack the size of a book-bag with his communications gear. Later, they all shook hands and said see you later, see you; it was dark by then, and Alan and Fidel stood around to watch the others' aircraft take off, lights dimmed and few, roaring down the runway and then heading high in an evasion route, and they were gone. Alan felt empty, bereft of adrenaline and filled only with anxiety. He didn't like the operation; he didn't like briefing it and staying behind. He didn't like the dodgy intelligence it was based on.

"Kandahar's a hot zone," Fidel said when the last hint of the plane had faded.

"Pretty hot."

"Taliban was really big there."

"That's what they say."

Fidel sighed. "Would I like this better if they were paying me seven-fifty a day?"

The Aegean
The ferry from Mytilene to Athens takes eighteen hours. Piat took two books, a cheap nylon raincoat, and his laptop. The youth in the blue coat followed him on the ferry, and Piat had time to study him.

He also had too much time to study the cup. On his third time through, he decided he was already obsessed and started rationing his viewings as if they were cigarettes. He translated a few lines of Xenophon, cheating with the computer translation too often to learn much. He devoted time to watching his pursuer.

At the institution that trains young Americans to be spies, or more properly, case officers, attendees are taught to give a nickname to every surveillant: Copper, for a guy with red hair, or Blacksock for a man wearing shorts and dark socks. Piat was a graduate. He had already christened his young man "the Swain." The Swain was young, too handsome to avoid notice, and tended to cling to Piat when distance would have served.

Off Naxos, the weather changed for the worse, and cold winter rain fell into the sea and on the old volcanoes and made the observation decks too miserable for passing the long hours between Piat's rationed glances at the cup. Jerry went below, wondering if he could handle a cigar without instant reversion to smoking a pack a day. He settled for alcohol in the ferry's bar. The Swain didn't follow him there.

He succumbed to the temptation to drink Scotch. It hit him harder than he expected. The rain had brought heavy swells, and he staggered back to his cabin and started to compose a spurious provenance for the cup. He felt the urge to get laid but lacked the sobriety or energy to pull it off. He fell asleep with the knowledge that he had drunk too much.

Tel Aviv

Dukas and Peretz were five minutes late for their make-nice meeting with Mossad, but nobody seemed to mind. The atmosphere was almost jolly, kept earthbound by a sincere apology from the Mossad honcho for the unfortunate mistake involving Commander Craik. Dukas was looking at people's name tags and realizing that nobody who had been connected with Craik's snatching was there—not Shlomo Eshkol or the man who had been with him in Bosnia and was now his boss or any of the four thugs Craik remembered. He gave Peretz a fake smile that meant *We're being stiffed*. Inwardly, he was thinking that this was another reason Eshkol had come to his hotel—he had known what this meeting would be like and he had known that anybody connected with the Craik debacle or Qatib's death was being kept away.

They were in a conference room with big windows that looked into big windows across a narrow street. At the end of the long table was a metal cart loaded with five banker's boxes. These were apparently being held back as the Big Gift, like the gold watch at a retirement do; meanwhile, pretty women danced in and out with coffee and tea and trays of sweets while classical music played from invisible speakers.

"Social occasion," Dukas growled to Peretz.

Mossad had laid on five people, two of them women. Peretz had warned him that they would be liaison personnel, not operational ones. He already knew three of them through his job, he said—nice people, but out of the loop. The man in charge was named Marcuse and was wearing, of all things, a suit.

The Israelis took turns saying, first, how sorry they were and then, second, how cooperative they wanted to be. Finally, Marcuse pointed a splayed-fingered hand down the table at the cart. "A down payment on our desire to make amends," he said. He had an accent like Hollywood's idea of a Russian. "We are still searching, but this is the first intake under the headings cryptology, navy, and Palestinian military penetrations."

Dukas was having a hard time not showing his disgust because he was still jet-lagged and his threshold was low. Peretz jumped in before he could say something undiplomatic and assured everybody that cooperation was what the US most wanted right then, and they appreciated deeply the thought and care that went into sharing the Institute's files. Dukas, aware then that Peretz would be here when he was long gone, and Peretz would have to go on working with these people, forced himself to smile and said he really appreciated their effort.

Everybody smiled.

"We shall have more tomorrow."

"And more the day after that, I bet," Dukas growled. Everybody smiled and nodded.

"Salem Qatib," Dukas said. The smiles were replaced by looks of polite incomprehension.

153

"I've come to investigate the death of Salem Qatib. So far, I haven't seen even a death certificate."

Marcuse said that that would be a police matter.

"As would the surrender of the body, huh?"

Yes, yes, of course.

"I've asked to be allowed to have an American forensics team. How're we doing on that?"

Smiles again. Not their responsibility. Ministry of Foreign Affairs.

"Well, as long as you guys are in liaison, let's liaise. I'm liaising you to find out where my forensics team is, okay? Folks, this is a serious matter. My government told your government how serious it is just last Thursday. Are we on the same sheet of music here?"

The message would of course be communicated that the US believed that the forensics team was of the first importance.

Dukas asked for a Mossad organizational chart. Polite bullshit. He asked for a personnel roster. Indulgent laughter. He asked to interview the people who had been present when Salem Qatib had died. Looks of incomprehension.

"I'm batting a thousand," Dukas said to Peretz.

On the way back to the embassy, a panel truck followed them with the banker's boxes of documents. Dukas looked back at it and thought that if some Palestinian wack-job chose to blow up the panel truck, his investigation wouldn't lose a thing of value.

"They're burying us in bullshit," he said aloud. "Standard operating procedure."

Washington

Ray Spinner waited all morning for McKinnon to summon him to talk about his idea of sending somebody to Israel, but the summons didn't come. He made reasons for walking by McKinnon's office, thinking maybe the man was out, but there he was, listening to somebody on the telephone.

McKinnon looked up, but if he recognized Spinner, he gave no sign. Spinner went back to his cubicle and tried to work on other projects. He felt betrayed, but he knew that what had betrayed him was his own faltering self-importance. Why, after all, should McKinnon pay any attention to an idea that came from—let's face it, Ray—a munchkin?

He took the Leo Strauss book out of his attaché and put it where anybody going by could see it, just in case. He did some work, then actually read a little Strauss—he couldn't hack it for more than fifteen minutes at a time—but had to stop to ponder what was being said. "The proper work of a writing is to talk to some readers and to be silent to others . . . the proper work of a writing is to arouse to thinking those who are fit for it. . . ." Did that mean that it also was supposed to bore the pants off everybody else, which was what Strauss was doing to him, although he didn't want to admit it? Was this the same as what was meant someplace else by "persuasion"?—"To bring about the needed change on the part of the city, of the non-philosophers or the multitude, the right kind of persuasion is necessary and sufficient. . . . The multitude of the non-philosophers is good-natured and therefore persuadable." Did this mean using PR on them? Wasn't that what Hitler had done? He wanted to ask McKinnon about it, but of course he didn't dare—McKinnon might say that he was incapable of understanding, therefore not qualified, therefore he was fired.

Spinner grabbed lunch in the cafeteria and was back at his desk before one. At one-twenty, McKinnon materialized at the entrance to his cubicle and said, "Come on," as if they'd made a date to go somewhere. If he saw the Strauss, carefully left face-down and open, he gave no sign. Spinner scrambled up and hurried into the corridor and almost knocked down a woman who was carrying a laptop and a lot of paper and who didn't seem at all pleased with him.

McKinnon shut the office door as soon as Spinner was

155

inside. "I've been talking to the Assistant Secretary," he said. "You want to go to Tel Aviv, right?"

"Well—I made a suggestion—an idea—"

"It's a good idea and it's a bad idea. The Qatib thing has got very big very fast because of the cryptology thing. We like it that maybe it doesn't have anything to do with cryptology, if *we* can show that it isn't cryptology, but if it's something else, then we want it to be *us* who finds it. Good job on the archaeology, by the way. But it's a bad idea because we don't send people places, except at the upper level where they're making official visits. All that spy crap is what the agency people do. Look what it got them—Nine-Eleven." He sat behind his desk. "You want to go?"

"Sure!"

McKinnon looked at him. "To do what?"

"Get the whole story."

"And what's that going to do for the price of fish?"

"To get the truth. Not what the intel people feed us."

McKinnon looked at a paper on his desk and shoved it aside and said, "What're the implications? On a bigger scale, I mean."

Spinner had actually thought about this. "Well, better understanding of Israel and its problems. Insight into how the Palestinians are paying for terrorism. Maybe a step toward stopping them."

"The focus here is on Iraq."

"Well—" Spinner didn't understand the Iraq thing, which was mostly happening at a much higher level. "Terrorism," he said.

"You think Saddam Hussein is financing Palestinian terrorism by buying antiquities?" McKinnon was being sarcastic.

"Saddam pays big bucks to martyrs' families. And as a matter of fact, some Iraqi officials are pretty involved in selling treasures from the Iraqi national museum." Spinner had learned a lot the day before. "They're skimming a lot,

156

I'm sure, but some of it must be finding its way back to the Iraqi weapons programs."

"But no connection to Israel."

"Saddam's Israel's biggest enemy."

McKinnon looked away and rubbed his lower lip with a finger and put one calf up on the desk. He was wearing beautiful shoes, Spinner thought. Four hundred bucks if they cost a nickel. McKinnon said, "If we send you, it isn't going to be with a lot of spy crap—you understand?"

Spinner grinned. "No exploding cigars?"

"No nothing. You go in clear, as yourself, no fancy communications plans or one-time-only code books or disappearing ink."

Spinner frowned. "Diplomatic passport?"

"Absolutely not!" McKinnon made a despairing sound.

"I thought, in that case, a cover identity—"

McKinnon whipped his leg down and leaned forward so fast it seemed that he was going to lunge right across the desk. "No! We don't supply that stuff, understand? Cover identities and passports have to be approved by the goddam CIA; country clearances have to come from State. If we so much as ask for either one, the whole huge machinery of bureaucratic intelligence will start to grind. In twenty-four hours, they'll own the operation and their agent will go and you and I will be sitting here with our thumb up our ass!"

Spinner didn't really know what a country clearance was, although he'd heard the term. He understood cover identities, however, and he thought they sounded pretty cool. He was disappointed that he wouldn't be using one.

"You have a passport?" McKinnon said.

"Sure. From my Navy days, but it's just a regular passport."

"Photo in uniform?"

"Unh-unh." Or was it? He wasn't sure.

McKinnon grunted and looked unhappy. "The Assistant Secretary has made it my call whether you go." He was hunched down, his head seeming to have sunk into his shoulders. "How do you see yourself operating once you get there?"

"I thought we'd have, unh, people on the ground? Agents?"

"If we had people on the ground, there'd be no need for anybody to go!"

"Yeah, but there are the people who supply us with the data. 'Deborah.' 'Habakkuk.' Others, maybe?"

McKinnon squeezed his mouth between the thumb and fingers of his right hand. He looked *really* unhappy. "Forget Deborah. Deborah's Habakkuk's private source; we're not allowed to ask anything about him or her."

"Well, Habakkuk, then."

McKinnon sucked air between his upper front teeth and pulled the piece of paper back in front of him. "Who do you think Habakkuk is?"

Spinner wanted to shout *How the fuck would I know?* but murmured that he had no idea.

"Exactly. That's the point. If you or somebody goes and gets in touch with him, then he loses that anonymity." He sighed. "Habakkuk came to us. Came, actually, to somebody outside the government who got in touch with us—" he waved a hand—"half a dozen years ago. He's very dedicated and he's very committed, but you might as well understand that he doesn't come for nothing. We pay for everything we get from him." He looked up to study Spinner's face. "We're not dealing with rabid idealism here."

"Oh. I'd have thought otherwise."

"Would that it were so. Anyway, if you go to Habakkuk, it'll cost us. That's not in itself a problem—there's money in a, mm, fund—but there's the question of making the money available, and so on. We can't have you running around Israel with a half a million dollars in your pocket." He laughed.

"Half a million!"

"A manner of speaking. More like several tens of thousands. You get what you pay for. Well—" He leaned back. "That remains to be seen. A detail. So." He put his hands behind his head. "You contact Habakkuk. Then what?"

"Ask to be put in touch with people who traffic in illegal antiquities and with the people who try to stop them."

"No to the first, maybe to the second, as well. Habakkuk won't know anybody in the antiquities trade. He's an academic. He's not in the government but he's in Likud. He gets around a lot, so maybe he can help and maybe he can't. Then what?"

"Then I talk to them and try to track Salem Qatib."

"*How?*"

"I don't know. The police? See, I thought I'd have some sort of special status—a diplomatic passport, maybe some sort of letter or ID—"

"Forget it."

Spinner began to have more respect for the machinery of the intel agencies. They were able to make such contacts, present themselves in useful ways, because they had status and sources and cover. Going as a private citizen—let's face it, as a tourist—rather limited the possibilities. "Maybe it's a bad idea," he said. He thought about trying to deal with people who spoke only Hebrew. But on television, Israeli officials always spoke English. Granted that they sounded like they were choking on a mouthful of matzo, it was still English.

McKinnon sucked more air between his teeth and thought about it. "I guess we could put you in touch with Habakkuk. He has a certain number of contacts. Habakkuk, for a price, *might* be able to come up with something." He wasn't really talking to Spinner but to himself. "It would be nice to score one on State Research." The State Department's Office of Research was its in-house intel agency.

McKinnon glanced at Spinner with a sudden smile, surprisingly boyish. "You know what the Assistant Secretary's first reaction was? 'Fire that guy!'" McKinnon's laughter bounced around the room. Spinner cringed. When McKinnon had stopped laughing, he said, "Then he sort of warmed to the idea and finally said, 'What harm could it do?'" He sobered and leaned forward again, hands joined. "A lot of harm. If you fuck it up and the US gets its foot in the dogshit, don't come home."

"I'm going?"

"Didn't I say that? Yes, you're going." McKinnon pulled the piece of paper toward him for the third time. "Here's your travel itinerary. You're not on official business, so you don't have to fly a US carrier, but Continental is the most convenient one." He pushed the paper toward Spinner. "Draw some money from Monica—you know Monica? Monica the Money Maiden? The ticket is paid for, but get enough to put ten thousand into your credit card account. You could maybe get something to pay Habakkuk from an ATM. I'll give you the dope on contacting him before day's end. Make sure your passport is up-to-date." He stood. He smiled. "You leave at seven from BWI. Don't pack a tux and don't take a gun."

Joke.

"Do take Leo Strauss."

So he had noticed.

Late in the day, a new message came in from Habakkuk with a report from Deborah. It said that an American named Michael Dukas, who worked for the Naval Criminal Investigative Service, was in Tel Aviv and was looking into illegal archaeological activity in connection with the death of a Palestinian, but American naval codes might be involved, too. Dukas was anti-Israeli and anti-Semitic and could only do his country harm.

Spinner had been trying to talk to Dukas for two days; he kept getting the message that Dukas was out of the office on a case. Now he knew where.

*   *   *

160

Tel Aviv

Dukas reached the University of Michigan by phone in the middle of Tel Aviv's afternoon. He got bounced around but landed in the registrar's office, where a woman told him that they didn't give information about students over the telephone. They'd like to have a letter on letterhead, preferably signed by his superior. Ten minutes later, Dukas took advantage of his courtesy meeting with the ambassador to tell him this amusing little story of the rigors of investigation, and the ambassador got the message and at once put somebody on it. Twenty minutes after that, Dukas got a call from the registrar himself, offering any help they could give and saying he hadn't realized it was a matter of national security. Dukas gathered that he'd had a chat with somebody at the State Department.

"A former student of yours, name Qatib, that's Q-A-T-I-B, first name Salem, as in Salem—like the town in Massachusetts. Yeah, Salem Qatib. He was a student in '95-'96. My question is, what did he study and who did he study with?"

The registrar would get back to him.

Dukas met with the CIA chief of station, who was a dynamic, interesting-looking woman in her forties whom Dukas would have liked to know better if he hadn't felt guilty about his wife. Peretz had said the woman was political; right enough, but she had energy and dedication and he'd have liked to spend the afternoon with her, talking Israeli policy. Maybe spend the night. However, it was clear she had other priorities and almost certainly another guy; after a few minutes of talk, she said, in the tone that meant she was looking toward getting rid of him, "There's a lot of traffic about your case. How big is it?"

Dukas didn't see any point in putting down smoke. "There's a lot of noise right now. Maybe it's only noise. Maybe it's only an ex-Navy guy who got crosswise of some bad people and got dead."

"Because of crypto?"

"I dunno. That looks right, but—"

"Doesn't feel right?"

"Doesn't connect the dots. Palestinians after US crypto? Hard to believe. Mossad after US crypto? Easy to believe, but the guy has lived here for five years and I can't find where they've even said hello to him."

"What can I do?"

This seemed like a real offer. Dukas was surprised. Post-Nine-Eleven cooperation? "Can I take that as a rain check on future needs?"

They left it at that. At that point, Dukas didn't see what he'd want from her in the future, but then—

The U of M guy didn't call back until after seven, Tel Aviv time—it was almost his lunch hour in Ann Arbor, so he must have been working hard—to tell Dukas that he had the information he'd asked for.

"Great."

"Mister Qatib worked toward a master's degree in archaeology but didn't take the degree. He studied Introductory Classical Greek, Introductory Geology and Soils, and a number of archaeology courses with Middle Eastern emphases. Does that help?"

Dukas said it did, but it didn't, because he already knew that Qatib had studied archaeology, and, right at that point, archaeology looked like a dead end. But no deader than cryptology. And cryptology looked moribund enough that he put in a secure call to Ted Kasser, his boss in Washington, to tell him to try to drag the Navy back from any changing of codes until he'd learned more. "I don't think it's worth a hundred and fifty million bucks' worth of recoding until I know more."

The NCIS head said in his dry voice, "We don't want to be wrong on this one, Mike."

"Exactly my point—we don't want to be wrong."

Kasser chuckled, a sound like two dry things rubbing together. "The tendency here is to avoid being wrong by throwing money at it."

"The tendency among us taxpayers is to tell the Navy to wait up until we have some facts."

Kasser chuckled again. "Facts! What are they?"

Miriam Gurion would normally have been Dukas's type—big, forties, intelligent. However, there was no answering ping when he looked at her, and he decided that if she was his type, he wasn't hers. One reason—and it surprised him—was that after he'd spent fifteen minutes with her and Abe Peretz he saw that Abe *was* her type. Or Maybe Dukas was reading the signs wrong, but what he saw was two people who were working too hard at not seeming to know each other very well.

So where would that leave Bea Peretz? He'd find out later: he was supposed to be having dinner with the Peretzes. But Abe's behavior seemed odd, as perhaps it always does in a friend who is supposed to be happily married. Or had Alan Craik said something about that? Yes, something about Israel coming between Abe and Bea; Dukas had barely paid attention, his focus on the Qatib case.

"Homicide are working hard," Miriam Gurion was saying. They were in a small meeting room in the embassy. "They have done the forensics on the place where we found Qatib's body. It is too clean, they say. Wiped down."

"Mrs Gurion is the lead investigator," Peretz said. He was sitting as far from her as he could without being in the corridor, Dukas between them.

Dukas said, "I'd like to see the place where you guys found the body."

"I told you, it's clean. When the Mossad thugs snatched Commander Craik and me, somebody higher up—" she pointed toward the ceiling—"went right to the top of TLV

and got them to squash Homicide. I'd already called downtown and asked for a team; they were actually on the way.
One reason they're being nice to me, they're so angry
with Mossad—one guy told me the team were halfway to
Jaffa, they got the call to come back. Not what cops like
to do."

"I want to see the site anyway." Dukas was hunched
forward, fingers laced, feeling deep fatigue but still able to
focus. "What about the Mossad guys who snatched you?"

"Mossad magic."

Dukas asked a question with a look.

"Disappeared," she said. "Poof."

Dukas studied his hands. He wanted to get through this
without sounding accusing, especially if she and Abe had
something going—you didn't want to imply that another cop
had done anything less than brilliantly. "You're sure they
were Mossad," he said.

She bristled but didn't bellow or spit. "Of course."

"How are you sure?"

Her eyes narrowed. "They tell me they are Mossad. They
warn me what Mossad will do if I continue. I know how the
bastards operate!"

"They got there pretty quick," Dukas said. "To grab you
and Craik, I mean."

"Well—Commander Craik and I were a half hour, something like that, in the facility. That's not so quick."

"To come from where? Middle of the day, traffic—Jaffa
easy to get to?"

"Well—" She glanced at Abe Peretz, as if this was something they'd already discussed. "Mossad's all over Tel Aviv;
you don't know half the time that they're Mossad—private
companies, offices with nice names. They could have been
next door."

"Why do you think they used this clapped-out naval facility
to hide the body?"

Again, she glanced at Peretz before she said, "I hoped the forensics would tell us that. No good."

"They'd used it before, you told Craik. The case two years ago, the one they used the paperwork from to fake this one. Same people?"

"Well—" She seemed uncomfortable. "We're checking other entities that had offices there in Jaffa. It could be that—" She shrugged. "It would explain everything very nicely if Mossad were already on the site."

"My idea," Peretz said. Then hurriedly, as if he'd said the wrong thing, "Sergeant Gurion and I have had several phone conversations about the case." He waited, cleared his throat, muttered, "My idea that maybe they were already inside."

Miriam Gurion jumped in. "Two years ago was a gang-banger; we knew who he was, what he did. It was peculiar he wound up there, but not impossible, so we started to work it—and the order came down from above, stop."

"Craik said you knew the guy who commands the facility in Jaffa."

She turned red in splotches, one heading for her cleavage, if it had been visible. "I got to know him in the old case."

Believable—unless she was banging him, too? Or had been, maybe. Dukas said, "Did he think it was an inside job?"

She looked at him. She didn't try to turn her eyes away. But she said nothing.

"How well do you know him?"

Her eyes flicked to Peretz. *Okay, she hasn't told Abe if she was banging the guy.* Dukas decided not to pursue that right now; instead, he said, "Two bodies—in the same place? The first one was also in this ammo bunker or whatever it is?"

She nodded. "They said they found the body along the perimeter and put it in the bunker to keep it cool. Just inside the fence. At the back of the facility; it's quite deep. It had been there several days before it was found, they said." She burrowed in her purse for something, found it—a paper-wrapped mint. "I thought he'd been shot outside the fence, crawled under it and died." She sucked on the mint. "That's what I was supposed to think."

"Now you don't think that."

"I don't know what I think now." She gave him the frank look again, accepting her own flaws, daring him to make something of them. "There wasn't any reason to put a gang-banger together with Mossad. Until we got the order to stop."

"Is there now?"

She shook her head. "The case is still open; I put two people on it, maybe we'll get something. He wasn't an Arab, though. No connection with Qatib. But maybe some connection with Mossad. Like an informer who got jumpy, maybe?"

They were all silent. Dukas said, "The guys who grabbed you and Craik were stupid. Maybe that's the common denominator—they're stupid."

"Mossad aren't stupid."

"Maybe they aren't Mossad."

"They're Mossad. When we pushed, Mossad pushed back."

Dukas sat back. "In the States, we have people who do contract work for the intel agencies. Usually ex-something else—Navy SEALs, special forces, like that. They can do stupid things if they're working offsite. Unsupervised. You got people like that?" In fact, he knew they had. Al Craik had also suggested as much. He turned to Abe. "How about you use your best offices to find who Mossad's got under contract but at arm's length?" He turned back to Miriam Gurion. "You could check with your friend at the facility to find if he has anybody like that there, can't you?"

"I don't like to trade on a friendship."

"Have you already asked him?"

166

She gave him the look, and he saw that in fact she had. She said, "He's very afraid." She didn't like saying it.

As gently as possible, Dukas said, "It's a police matter."

She looked at Abe, looked away, burrowed in her purse again. "I think something has been said to him. That's only a guess."

Dukas waited. "I think you need to ask him to go downtown."

She winced.

Later, when she'd calmed down and he had turned the conversation away from the guy he was now sure was her old boyfriend, she told them that they'd found that Salem Qatib had had a girlfriend who lived in Israel. They were trying to track her down; she was sure they'd locate her in a day or so. Did Dukas want to talk to her?

"Do I! Yes and yes." He waited.

"We might learn something important."

"That would be a nice change."

Bahrain

Rose Craik had her shoes off and her feet up and she was enjoying a half-and-half Guinness and Italian beer, her reward to herself for being pregnant and overworked. She had had a hell of a day at the embassy; the naval attaché was off in Riyadh, and she was filling in while doing her own job. Now, the kids were eating, and she had ten minutes to fall apart.

So she telephoned Leslie Dukas.

"Hey, I had a minute and thought I'd check in. How's the kid?"

"Three months and counting. Do you always feel like you weigh two hundred pounds?"

"No, later it's three hundred. You hear from Mike?"

"Yeah, but you know."

"The real thing in bed is nicer."

167

"Yeah."

"Al's silent, of course, but he's supposed to be back Friday."

"We still on for Saturday?" The Craiks were going home for thirty days' leave; they were flying through Naples and had made a date for dinner with Leslie and Mike Dukas.

"If everybody gets there. Our treat, by the way."

"I thought I'd ask Carol Triffler, too. They're nice. But we better make it Dutch, so many people."

"He isn't away, too, is he?"

"No, he's running the office while Mike's in Tel Aviv."

"Well, that gives us one man, at least. No, hon, it's our treat. Alan wants everybody to experience this restaurant he knew when he was a kid there, Dante e Beatrice. *Very* Neapolitan."

"Oh, boy—one man and three kids. With two more on the way."

"So it'll be a nice party. The Neapolitans love families." They talked some more about who was paying, but Alan had left pretty strict instructions because he'd lived in Naples and knew the restaurants, and Mike and Leslie were new there and didn't. It all sounded normal and uneventful, like get-togethers being planned all over the United States, she supposed.

If her husband got home in time from Afghanistan. And if Mike Dukas got home from Tel Aviv. And if she lasted through the week, pregnant and overworked. She got herself into bed and fell deep asleep, dreaming of responsibility and examinations for which she hadn't taken the courses.

Then it was after three in the morning in Tel Aviv, where Mike Dukas had had dinner with the Peretzes and then crawled gratefully into bed; after two in the Aegean, where Jerry Piat was in alcohol-induced slumber; after five a.m. in Afghanistan, the eastern sky just showing hesitant paleness, where Alan Craik was snoring in a sleeping bag on a pile of straw; and it was the time of exhausted sleep on Ray Spinner's flight to Tel Aviv, the movies over, the lights low, the cabin staff's smiles wan.

That day, an Israeli missile killed a Hamas official in the territories. Israeli soldiers killed five Palestinians.

13

Athens

Piat awoke with a dry mouth and found that his laptop had run its battery down. He drank some bottled water, showered, went to the restaurant and forced himself to eat. Outside the windows of the restaurant, rain battered the breakwater at the entrance to the harbor of Piraeus.

Piraeus had once been a separate city from Athens, the two so far apart that battles could be fought between them. From Piat's vantage in the restaurant, the two had become one continuous city, from the thriving, dirty port, a forest of cargo cranes in the foreground and ugly concrete high-rises on the surrounding hills, to the Acropolis of Athens rising like a promised land in the distance, barely visible in the rain.

Jerry waited in the restaurant with a second cup of coffee, and deliberately disembarked late, forcing his amateur pursuer to reveal himself or risk losing him on the pier.

Piat only had one small bag, and he carried it on his shoulder over an old wool sweater and his hideous yellow nylon slicker. He walked down the gangplank without having to wait. As he descended the three decks to the exit, he saw only the Swain and two Americans with heavy bags.

On the pier there were only three taxis left. Piat took the first one, climbed in, and dickered over the fare to practice his Greek. While he listened to the driver, he watched the Swain get into another taxi and smiled to himself.

The traffic was worse than he had expected. He commented on it to the driver.

"The Olympics," the driver said, as if that explained the line of scooters passing them on both sides.

"The Olympics are three years away."

"We won't be ready. This city—heh." The driver waved his hand in contempt for Athenians.

"Where are you from?" Piat asked.

"Ahh! Athens! Always Athens." The man brightened. "Do you like Athens? You have been here before?"

Piat spent the rest of the ride listening to the wonders of Athens. From time to time he looked back to see that one of the other Piraeus taxis was following them in the traffic. Piat did not make a habit of losing surveillance. He had been trained in a hard school, and he knew that in most cases, ditching the tails only made them angry and anxious.

But in this case, his pursuer was alone and terribly inexperienced. Piat had been watching him on and off for twenty hours, and felt he knew the young man well. Piat was tempted to get out of the taxi at a subway stop and vanish, but he felt lazy and he didn't see the Swain as much of a threat. He got out of the taxi near the ancient Agora, found a café with internet connections, and hooked up his laptop. While he paid for his connection and the use of a power outlet, he watched the Swain climb out of his cab. Piat was tempted to wave because the boy was unable to spot him. Piat downloaded his email. The Swain spotted him at last, his look of relief visible through the rain. Piat watched him make his way to a phone kiosk. *Calling the girl, no doubt.* Piat deleted offers to sell him cut-rate Viagra and wondered how a consortium of teenagers had acquired such a remarkable object as the gold cup.

The last email in his queue was the one he wanted. *Barry.* His friend with the Athens IP had answered him less than an hour ago. Piat read the message and looked up over his

171

screen at the Swain, who was still on the phone, copying something onto a piece of paper in the rain.

He closed his laptop, put it in his bag, and pulled on his raincoat. Time to lose the Swain. There was a major subway exchange less than a block away. He left a euro on his table and went to the door. Habit caused him to pause in the doorway and sweep the square of the Agora with his eyes.

One of the tall Americans from the ferry was standing across the square. Piat hesitated for a fraction of a second, his left foot already moving towards the subway station. He pulled his eyes away from the tall man. He already had the impression that the man was watching the Swain. He also had the impression that the tall man was a professional. So he swung his bag onto his shoulder and turned up the hill into the warren of streets that made up Athens's oldest neighborhood, climbing toward the Acropolis like every other tourist.

He walked around the Agora itself, paused to look at the remnants of the Roman attempts to improve decadent Hellenistic Athens, and left the ruins behind him. He turned right between shops selling copies of antiquities, up a broad street lined with closed restaurants, their chairs piled high on wet tables. The street was virtually empty, and he told himself that he had only himself to blame. *Wrong part of the city for this, old boy*, he thought. He could have taken his cab to the center of the city and been in the middle of an international business center, but he had been lazy.

The Swain was a turn behind him. Piat was no longer interested in him. He didn't think the tall men were with the Swain. It was just a hunch, and not one he'd bet his life on, so he gave the Swain an occasional glance when turnings allowed and tried to plan his next move.

The rain was hard enough now that his legs were already wet. It was a miserable day, and he was not surprised to find that the main path to the Acropolis was empty, the only life on it a damp trio of kiosks selling tourist maps. He stopped and bought one, an expensive map coated in clear plastic. The Swain stopped and stared at a wall. A flicker of movement a hundred yards down the hill showed that the tall man was still there, and Piat labeled him "OD" for his military-style, olive drab raincoat. Then Piat pulled his own nylon raincoat closer, wished he had gloves, and started up the last, hard climb to the Acropolis, staring at the map.

The professionals wouldn't come up into the Acropolis. If they were really on him, they would form a ring around it, a "bubble," and wait for him to come down. The Acropolis was a trap; there was only one way up and down, as many an attacker had found in the last three thousand years. Piat made his plan while he climbed.

He passed through the ticket kiosks, paid an exorbitant fee, and started up the steps. Now there were people. Not as many as Piat would have liked, but enough. There were two school groups and a dozen adults. Piat climbed the steps while striking up a conversation with a schoolteacher. He made a joke about his bad Greek and got an instant friend.

The Swain climbed behind him, alone.

Piat didn't waste time looking for OD from the top. He went through the museum, paused in his usual wonder, glanced at his map again, and wished for a cigarette. The schoolteacher rattled on in rapid Greek about the missing parts of the frieze of the Parthenon. Piat sympathized, but he moved on. Outside, the rain had slowed to a cold drizzle. Piat would have preferred a real downpour to obscure visibility, but he was committed to his plan. His theory was that OD had friends, and that they were watching the Swain. If that theory proved false, Piat was ready with a second plan. If the theory proved true, he would scout OD's team thoroughly and vanish.

Pulling up the hood of his raincoat, he dashed up the steps from the museum, around the ugly scaffolding surrounding the Parthenon, and back down the steps of the portico.

As he expected, his sudden departure from the museum left the Swain well behind him. Piat got to the base of the portico steps and turned left, towards the ancient theaters. He walked through a maze of paths and trees, away from the Plaka, onto the broadest path. Just where Piat expected to find him, a heavily built man in a red Gore-Tex coat was talking on a cell phone, his head down and his eyes on the path behind Piat. He was speaking Hebrew.

Gotcha.

Piat passed him and turned down a set of steps between the amphitheaters on the lower slopes. As soon as he was screened from Redcoat by the ruins of the Theater of Dionysus, Piat stripped off his raincoat, rolled it, and put it in his backpack, all without slowing his pace.

He had slowed to a sedate pace when he became visible again from Redcoat's vantage point, but Redcoat was focused on the Swain, who had appeared at the foot of the Acropolis steps and was looking around. Piat trudged uphill. He no longer noticed the rain.

Piat turned north on a new path, passing just fifty feet below the Swain. He had now completed a reverse, and was about to go back down the hill of the Acropolis just the way he had climbed it. As he reached the entrance, he could see OD standing with his foot up on a concrete bench. He, too, was focused on the Swain. He had a cell phone in his hand.

Piat passed him and continued to the point where the main path descended into the Plaka. His heart was beating hard from adrenaline, but he was pleased to note that he wasn't breathing hard despite the speed of his progress up and down the Acropolis. He ambled down the hill, past the three tourist kiosks where he had bought himself the map and then straight on across the top of the Plaka, glancing down every set of steps that descended to his left to make sure of the way.

He had expected a third man, and even a fourth. He found

the third waiting at the top of a narrow set of steps that went down to the residential Plaka, smoking a cigarette. Piat had to pass within three feet of him, and the smell of his cigarette lingered in Piat's nostrils for a long time.

Piat could read a surveillance team the way an experienced quarterback can read a defense. The one he had just passed through were professionals, but they were undermanned and lax and edgy, an odd combination. He was sure that the language he had heard from Redcoat was Hebrew. A real Mossad team would have had six or even ten people, and they would have kept their cordon much further back from their prey. Piat could understand how the Swain could encourage laxity, but Piat's teachers had told him to always act as if the threat was real, and he had just been that threat. That team, whoever they were, had not been ready.

However, Piat was in the land of hubris and he had no intention of succumbing. He went down a set of old, slippery stone steps, their treads too well worn for rapid movement, into a tiny square shaded by a single tree. A sign under the tree stated that the Venetians had used the square for the cannon of their breeching battery in 1683. He suspected it had been a very small battery. He took an inside table at the tourist taverna and ate lunch, watching his back trail and admiring the eleventh-century Byzantine church beyond the tree.

He took his time with his food, which was surprisingly good, emptying the mandatory bowl of olives with relish and attacking his calamari when it came. In between bites, he used the tourist map to create another set of paths to make sure, doubly sure, that he was clean. He added an errand that he had planned to do by email. Better in person. Anything dark was better in person.

He left the taverna and walked straight down the hill, through another square, this one crowded with stray cats, out of the residential Plaka and into the modern reality of urban Athens. In the street of icon makers just off Syntagma Square, he stopped in front of a narrow shop with an iron grille on its window. Through that window, the discerning tourist, if he could see past the grime, could make out several well-rendered modern icons in various styles. Piat had been the discerning tourist years before. He was again.

The proprietor was hunched over a workbench. He rose at the sound of the door and threw a stained sheet over his work. Piat was pleased to be recognized and received a substantial embrace.

"Mikhail!" Piat said with enthusiasm.

"Sasha!" The proprietor was barely middle-aged, his relative youth always a shock to Piat because other icon makers all seemed to have been born old. "You did not say you would come. Is the telephone broken?"

Piat shook his head and shrugged. "Working on anything interesting?"

"This and that." Mikhail painted excellent modern icons. He restored icons for museums and select friends. Several times, he had created old icons himself.

Piat looked at the most recently completed work, a small icon in the Macedonian style of St. George killing the dragon. He pointed at it. "Very nice."

"The style of home is always the best style," Mikhail said. He shrugged. "Nothing *interesting*, Sasha. I try not to do anything so *interesting* anymore, yes?"

Piat nodded. "Sure. I like this, Mikhail. I'm in a hurry; too much of a hurry to dicker. How much?" He pointed at St. George.

"For resale, Sasha?"

"Never. For a friend, who is sick. It will go on his wall."

"A good man?"

"He is." *That is, he was before he became a drug addict,* Piat thought to himself.

"Two hundred euros. No bullshit."

Piat opened his bag and withdrew a copy of his computer sketch. While Mikhail wrapped the icon of St. George, Piat wrapped a hundred euros in the sketch. He took another two hundred out of his wallet and handed them to Mikhail all together.

Mikhail raised his eyebrows.

Piat nodded fractionally. "Sometime I'll ask your opinion of something I have," he said. "I want to know if it's a fake."

Mikhail shrugged. "Hard to tell. You'll have to bring it to me."

Piat nodded. "Perhaps you could just tell me if it *could* have been faked."

Mikhail's eyebrows shot up. "That is not so hard." He hugged Piat again, but he didn't open the folded paper while Piat was in the shop.

Piat paused on the steps of the icon maker and looked both ways. The street was not empty, but no one on the street was a threat. He walked up to the main drag and took a taxi to the subway station, traveled uptown a distance, and disembarked. He repeated the process, a very short cab ride followed by a subway journey.

Nothing. Very satisfying.

When he was sure he was clean, he stopped in a bar, went to the toilet, and placed fifty grams of hashish from Lesvos into the wrapping of the icon. He had a little trouble because his hands were shaking. He settled them with a shot of Scotch. Then he went to meet Barry.

Tel Aviv

A little heap of message slips lay on Dukas's borrowed desk on Tuesday morning. One was from the security officer to tell him that another six boxes of documents had arrived for him from Mossad; another was from the embassy secretary to say that two translators had been assigned to him, as all the documents sent over so far were in Hebrew.

"A waste of the taxpayers' money," Dukas growled.

Peretz had left a message to say that they had a date with Miriam Gurion at ten to visit "a site of interest," which Dukas hoped would have something to do with Qatib or the supposed girlfriend Gurion said existed. Other messages were fluff—two invitations to embassy birthday parties, one from somebody he never heard of to attend the opening of a US-Israeli exhibition of paintings about terrorism. Two of the messages, however, had meat on their bones: Pigoreau had called from The Hague at ten the night before to say that he had news; Triffler had called from Naples.

He called Triffler first.

"I was told yesterday afternoon you were in a meeting," Triffler said. "Does that mean the head or a date?"

"I was in a meeting." Dukas told him about the meetings with Mossad, the chief of station, the ambassador, and Miriam Gurion. "I was in lots of meetings."

"I find it ominous that Mossad is being cooperative."

"It's so ominous it stinks." He told him about the boxes of documents. "What've you got for me?"

"The Mossad personnel roster. I've found a name and a title. You gave me Shlomo Eshkol. I think your other man is somebody named David Tar-Saloman, and he's the head of—you ready?—the Antiquities and Arts Section of Mossad."

"Arts plural, like in fine arts?"

"Plural. Maybe they also cover poetry and modern dance."

"Antiquities, though, that's good. Or that's bad." He told Triffler about the conversation with the registrar at the University of Michigan.

"Do I see a pattern emerging?"

"Well, it could be better than cryptology."

"CNO is thinking of changing the comm codes in the entire fleet."

178

"I told Kasser yesterday, not yet."

"I'm sure they'll listen to you."

"Dick, send a message to DNO over my name. Tell them we have no hard evidence of code compromise; we're working on it; premature action could be worse than no action."

"Did you just think that up?"

"It's boilerplate for any crisis. Fill in the blanks. 'We have as yet not confirmed evidence of blank. We continue to devote our maximum energies to blank. Premature action can be more harmful to the national purpose than no action at all.'"

"Blank."

"Blankety-blank."

"It sounds almost presidential. But I'm telling you, Mike, Washington's in a cryptology tizzy. If they go ahead and change the codes, it'll be over and done with and we can, as they say, achieve closure and put it behind us."

"For umpteen million bucks and a lot of bruised reputations if we find that in fact Qatib was killed because of something else. Like arts and antiquities."

"Which is only a theory and is unsupported by facts, like evolution."

"And which we're not going to share with anybody else until I know more."

"Meanwhile, I have a message from NSA suggesting that you aren't doing your job very well."

Dukas sighed. "They're probably right." They talked for a while about the implications of a master's degree in archaeology and a Mossad Arts and Antiquities Section, and finally Triffler said, "I think I ought to be tasked to look into Palestinian involvement in illegal antiquities. It might tell us something, and it would get me out of the office."

"I left you in the office so I can be out of the office."

"Well, as acting SAC, I feel I deserve all the perks of the position. Actually, I did some Web surfing from home, and there's several people here in Naples who are very big in an international effort to stop the illegal trade in those fine old things that get dug up here and there. There's a UN office, for example, plus a couple of professors and the director of the Naples Museum. If I flashed my badge and sang them something from Monteverdi, I bet they'd level with me about antiquities coming out of Israel."

"Go for it. But don't sing, okay?"

"It's my secret weapon."

"Well, save it for when somebody tries to mug you."

Then he called Pigoreau, who was on the other line but would call back, and who did so in three minutes. Pigoreau laughed. "I was getting coffee, Mike. Would it be better if she had told you that?"

"More human, anyway. Whatcha got for me?"

"Oh, something—let me see—" Pigoreau was silent, then muttered something that Dukas didn't catch, then said, "I keep an unkempt desk, as you remember. I am really an *homme engagé*, not a desk jockey." Pigoreau had been an Olympic speed skater and then a detective, and only in the last couple of years had he been promoted to inaction. "Okay, I got your operation in Bosnia. They emailed me a file. But why do you want the file? You were *there*, Mike."

"But I saw it from inside. What I had was a UN warrant to grab a war criminal who was crossing into Kosovo. I get these two unknown Israeli guys laid on me by the people up the line. 'Observers.' I may have run into something involving one of them here."

"Hold on—" Pigoreau made small *mmm, mmm, mmm* sounds that might have been humming, except that Dukas couldn't detect a melody. Maybe it was French hip-hop. "Ah. Okay. Mike, this is what I would call *bien vague*, so I think there's been some redaction, okay? but what's here is that two quote representatives of the State of Israel unquote were added to the operational unit for quote purposes of observation

180

unquote. Except that up in the background section it says the guy who got killed was heading for Palestine."

"Which they didn't tell us at the time."

"Well, he was on the list for an atrocity in Bosnia. A Palestinian who'd been in Afghanistan against the Soviets and came into Bosnia when the Serbs got ugly. So he was a legitimate target for you and me. Only it was the Israelis who spotted him."

"So they let us do their work for them, which was—" Dukas hesitated. "The guy got killed. What happened to the stuff he was carrying?"

"What stuff?"

"He had an attaché full of gold coins."

"Roman? There's something here about Roman artifacts."

"What happened to them?"

"'Claimed by the State of Israel and returned to the State of Israel when acceptable proof of ownership was provided in 1999.' Long after you and I left, Mike."

"Yeah. But significant."

"This was helpful?"

"Very helpful."

Helpful enough that Dukas could see that Shlomo Eshkol and David Tar-Saloman of the Mossad Section for Arts and Antiquities had been in the field for a long time and that they took it seriously enough to get somebody killed. Their names had faces that he remembered from Bosnia; Eshkol's, older, had appeared at breakfast yesterday. So here were two real people who seemed to be connected with the snatching of Al Craik and maybe, therefore, with the corpse of Salem Qatib. And then?

Athens

Barry lived on the slope of the Acropolis opposite the Plaka, in a house that had probably held a large family in the eighteenth century. It was very small. It had a heavy wooden door with a central bell that annoyed Piat, so he knocked.

The woman who opened the door was tall and strong, with heavy eyebrows and no makeup, as if middle age held no terror for her. She narrowed her eyebrows the moment she saw Piat. "Look, Barry, it's what's-his-name." Mara was angry, as always. "Do you *have* a real name? Come to fuck him up again?"

"Hello, Mara." Piat sounded sad. His history with Mara went almost as far back as his history with Barry. Some of it had been happy. A lot of it had been like this.

"Jack!" Barry came around a low couch, all six foot four of him, using a cane. "Jack! Man, it's good to see you." He inclined his head towards Mara, who was already disappearing into the apartment's microscopic kitchen. "Pay no attention, okay? You know how she is."

The apartment stank of old food and unwashed dishes. Barry hobbled to the couch and waved his hands impatiently at the pile of manuscript pages on a chair. "Just throw them on the floor, will you, Jack?"

"Like hell, Barry. Jack, just wait a minute, okay? Barry, I've been on that fucking paper all day and I'll be damned if it's going on the floor." Mara came back into the main room. She sorted the papers with angry inefficiency. "Still smoke, Jack?"

Piat looked rueful. "Not at the moment." Mara always left him confused. He never knew what to say. "I—I think I've quit."

"Bullshit, Jack. You'll *know* when you quit." She chuckled. "You bring him drugs? Look, Jack, I'll fucking kill you if he's high tonight, okay? Barry's straight and he's got a job editing. So—"

Barry stood up to his full height. "Mara, get out. Jack, I'm sorry. Mara, you are humiliating me. This is—"

Mara just laughed. "He sure hopes you've got a kick for

182

him. Whatever. I'll be in the bedroom." She looked at Piat, not so much angry as pleading.

It seemed like a reenactment of all the other times. The fifty grams of hash in the icon sat in Piat's backpack, with the weight of all his other sins.

"Beer?" Barry asked.

"Sure." Piat sat carefully in the chair that Mara had cleared. One arm was smeared with old food, and there was a Styrofoam container of what had once been spanikopita on the floor next to the chair.

Barry opened two bottles with his hands and passed one to Piat.

"You have a job?"

"God, Jack, it's not much. Editing graduate crap at the university. Crap! Bad translations, bad use of evidence, trite, repetitious—crap. But it's just temporary. I'm writing a book—" He looked at Piat for approval.

Piat tried to give it. Barry had been writing various books since Piat had first met him. "Yeah? That's great, Barry. What's it about?"

"Scythians, Jack. Scythians! No one's ever put all the archival material together. There's material in Persian, Greek, Chinese; I read them all! And the archaeology is all in Russian. Easy. I just need the money to get some research material, that's all." While he spoke, Barry was carefully getting onto the couch. He was a big, tall man whose knees could barely support his weight, and the process took some time.

Piat didn't like to watch it, because he'd been there when Barry's knees had taken the damage. He knew he deserved a share of the blame.

So did Mara.

"But you don't care about my academic crap, do you, Jack? You see any of the old gang? How's Mark? God, remember how he could drink?"

Dead, thought Piat. Barry and Mark had been closer than they ought to have been, back in the first days in Afghanistan, when Barry was a young archaeologist and linguist recruited as a lowly border-crosser and Mark was a senior case officer. But they'd both gone to Yale and they were both New England gentry. And Mark had died in Angola, for nothing. Not the tale he told Barry.

"Mark's good. You read the papers, Barry. It's not a happy time at the company. Mark'll retire soon."

"Sure, Jack. Did he ever marry that girl you told me about?"

Piat hesitated a second, promising himself that he would *not* fabricate new twists in anyone's life for Barry, because Barry's encyclopedic brain never let a detail go. *What girl did I make up?* "I guess not, Bear. I don't even remember telling you that."

"Hey, Jack. No one calls me *Bear* anymore." He laughed. The laugh was a little outside the normal, a little too wild. "Or *Tschaarsi*. Nobody calls me Tschaarsi anymore, either. Think the Taliban left any of our boys alive?"

Piat shrugged. "They're all driving taxis in Manhattan, Bear." *Except the boys who* are *the Taliban.*

"Get me something a little stronger, Jack, will you? There's a bottle of Irish whiskey in the spice cupboard."

"Hey! Barry, that's my bottle!" Mara's voice floated out of the bedroom like the god's from the machine.

"Why don't I just go out and get us a bottle," Piat suggested. He already wanted the stink of the apartment out of his nose.

Barry just waved one of his big hands. "Ignore her, Jack. Pour us a couple. What about Dave? Dave Hammond?"

Piat waved the bottle. "You didn't even like Dave."

Barry laughed. "So maybe he's dead?"

Piat snorted. "Dave" was a man named Clive Partlow, a slippery son-of-a-bitch who had, of course, risen to a position of real power. "No, Dave is thriving in the current environment."

"You can pour me a stiffer shot than that, Jack. What about you? Are you thriving? You look better than you did last summer."

"Yeah." Piat stooped to hand Barry a full juice glass of Black Bush.

Barry drank a gulp of it immediately. Barry looked considerably worse than he had last summer, when Piat had needed a bolt hole and had used Barry—as Piat had so often used Barry.

"Still living the antiquities cover?"

"You know—" Piat began.

"—you can't talk about it. Jack, this is me? Anyway, it tickles me, the idea of you doing anything with antiquities. You can't even read classical Greek, can you?"

Barry never meant any harm. He was a genius, and his condescension just flowed off like normal conversation. Once, Piat would have risen to it, but today, Piat just smiled, with his Loeb edition of Plato in his pocket. "Nah. I never did classics like you."

"And Mark, and Dave. Dave was a shit, Jack, and I doubt he's changed, but he could think. You have to give him that."

He could avoid operations where people got shot at, too. You have to give him that. Piat had a suspicion that Barry's knees and Partlow's cowardice were linked, but he'd never really wanted to know the answer. Old news. "He was a thinker."

"Of course he was, Jack. We all were. I have to say, the idea of militant intellectuals has some appeal. Why should they all sit in the ivory tower? Hmm? Aeschylus? You have heard of Aeschylus, Jack?"

Piat smiled. "I think I've heard of him."

"The greatest playwright of ancient Greece, if you ask me. His brother died at Marathon. He fought at Salamis, maybe at Plataea. You know what it says on his grave stele? Nothing about winning for the best play at Athens or Delphi. Just

185

that he fought in the front rank at Marathon. That's all. That's what I'm saying."

With a certain self-loathing, Piat leaned forward. "You're like that, Barry."

Barry shook his head. "I'm no Aeschylus, Jack."

"You went and saw the animal, though, Barry. In Iran and Afghanistan, when we needed you." Piat could remember being able to do this without feeling like a leper. Every case officer's job; provide the love. He took a mouthful of Irish whiskey.

Barry raised his head from the Afghan pillow on the sofa. "Thanks, Jack."

Piat could remember when that head had been like the head of a Greek statue; big, handsome features and a mane of blond hair. Now the flesh sagged and all the color was gone, and so was most of the hair.

Barry waved his glass. It was empty. "A little more, if you don't mind, Jack? And get it off your chest! What did you come here for?"

Piat crossed to the kitchen and brought the bottle back. While he was pouring for Barry, Mara flung herself out of the bedroom. She had a raincoat on.

"Feel free to drink my booze. I'll just go out." She closed the door with a crash.

"God, I'm sorry, Jack. She likes you, you know. She's just—" Barry waved his glass again. "Just unhappy. I need to write this book, Jack. I need to give her some of the things she wants. A house. God, a life. I've wasted mine, Jack. And she's stuck to me—stuck *by* me. God, I owe her." His head slumped down.

Piat took another hit of the Irish whiskey. It was getting to him fast. He sat more heavily than he had intended. "I've got a little work for you."

Barry chuckled. "I knew you would, when you said you might do an antiquities cover. I thought 'He doesn't even read Greek!' Mara laughed, too."

186

"This is a little harder than reading Greek, Bear."

Barry raised himself on an elbow and grinned at Piat. "I don't do a lot of border-crossing these days, Jack. And I'm out of practice with explosives."

Piat smiled without warmth. "Just an inscription."

"Sure, Jack. Sure. Persian? Elamite?"

"Linear B."

Barry had his glass at his lips. He choked a little, and some whiskey ran down his chin. "Linear B? Really? Something new? Or just a rehash? Are you forging something?"

Piat really laughed. "I'm glad you think so much of me, Bear. No, it may be real and it may be fake. You've got to tell me. Can you—read Linear B?" He choked off the word *still.*

"Jack. John Chadwick died in 1998. You know who he was?"

"Never heard of him, bud."

"He and Michael Ventris deciphered Linear B. Ventris died in the fifties. Now they're both dead. I suspect that means I'm the best Linear B scholar in the world."

Piat took another drink of whiskey. He never knew what to make of Barry when he was like this. He knew that it was his job to ask questions and let Barry enjoy his fleeting superiority. Looking at the ruin on the sofa, it was hard to be confident that there was anything left in there at all.

Barry swung his legs off the sofa. "Give, Jack. Let me see it." His eyes were avid, hungry.

"This doesn't get out to *anyone*, Bear. This is serious no-shit secret, okay?"

"Cross my heart, Jack. Now give."

"Okay, but one more time, Bear. This is important. Keep it to yourself."

Barry glowed a little; a genuine smile and movement with purpose made him look younger and more confident. "I know it's important, Jack. That's why I do it, huh? And the money, of course. How much for this?"

Piat went to his backpack and took out the CD. Barry's computer occupied a place of honor on a nearly clean white Formica table under the windows. The big windows let in a little gray light, but their only view was the elevation of the next high-rise, just a few feet away.

He put the CD into a drive. Barry made his way heavily across the room, his breathing audible over the machine noises of the computer.

Jerry had the picture up before Barry landed heavily on the swivel chair. Barry looked at the first picture for a long time.

"Do you think it's real, Jack?" he breathed.

"You tell me, Bear."

Barry flipped through all four slides. Piat had thought hard about only giving Barry one, or two, or trying to copy the symbols by hand, but that had all seemed counterproductive. Barry would keep his mouth shut, or he wouldn't.

"God," Barry whispered. "God, I hope it's real."

"Yeah," Piat said. "Yeah, me too."

"The Linear B is all real. I can't see any symbols that are faked."

"What's it say?"

"Ask me in a week, Jack. Linear B is the writing system for a very early form of Greek. It's a syllabary; every symbol represents a syllable. No one quite knows what the rules were; no one is quite sure what it all means, not even me." He smiled. This passed for self-deprecation, with Barry. "Give me two days. I'll have a rough draft. There's an easy word; *Da-na*. See? Already making progress."

"What's Da-na, Bear?"

"The Danae, Jack. The Greeks. The long-haired Achaeans. Go read your Homer." Barry turned from the computer, his eyes filled with fire from the reflected gold of the cup on the screen. "I can do it, Jack. But how much? Mara's going to ask."

Mara's going to ask had a ritualistic aspect. Barry was greedy, but he didn't like to show it. Another of Mara's burdens. Piat was ready with a figure, as usual.

"A thousand bucks for the Linear B. Another thousand for some advice on it. That's for later. And then maybe a contingency fee."

"Jack, you realize this is perhaps the sixth *object* with Linear B ever discovered." He pored over it again. "The others are all terra cotta."

"I know."

"Really? Done your homework for a change, Jack? It's brilliant. This was an important object. Now it's a miraculous one. This translation is worth a lousy two thousand bucks?"

"If it's real, maybe more."

"God, let it be real. You have this cup?"

"No."

"You can get it?"

"Maybe."

"Jack, get it for me. God, Jack, if this is real, I can get a job at any university I want. Cambridge! Oxford! Yale! Anywhere I want. Just one paper."

Piat realized that he hadn't thought the whole thing through. "It's very likely fake, Bear."

"I won't hear of it, Jack. Look at the niello! Brilliant! Who could fake that?" Then, almost accusingly, "Where's it from?"

Piat didn't think to dissemble. "Palestine." He shrugged. "That's a guess. It's complicated."

"Bullshit. Palestine? Roman crap. Hellenistic crap. This is Late Helladic Palace Culture, Jack. Not from Palestine. I'd say it was from Crete. Maybe Turkey."

Piat smothered a yawn. He could smell the whiskey from his breath on his hand. "Tell me if the inscription is real, Bear. Then we'll talk."

"But you'll let me see it? Write about it?"

189

Piat was trying to figure if he could. He owed Barry; fair enough. Would a paper hurt the cup's value, or help it? He was trying to think through a haze of Irish whiskey.

"If it's real. If I get it. Then we'll talk." Piat hesitated. "It's not simple, Bear."

"It never is," said Barry. He swung the chair around. "Jack, look at me. If this is real—Jack, do I have to say it? This could change—my—life."

After that, the evening went as usual. Barry played with the inscription, commented on the scenes on the cup, drank more, accepted the icon and hung it, and then consumed some of the hashish.

As usual, Mara came home, smelled the hash, and walked into the bedroom without a word. She didn't give Piat her usual withering look. Piat wondered if she really intended to kill him. She had it in her.

As usual, Barry smoked too much on top of too much booze. Mostly he talked, and what he talked about was how brilliant he was. But there was more to Barry than just the crap—he came out with good jokes, he remembered to be a host, he went back to drunken run-ons.

Piat went off to find the loo (the cleanest room in the apartment) and came back to find Barry rifling his backpack. He didn't apologize—to Barry, all was fair if it led to more hash—but he did pull the tattered copy of Plato's *Republic* from a side pocket and flourish it.

"Plato and Xenophon. You really are catching up on your reading."

Piat said nothing. He was too drunk to make a coherent argument, and he didn't want to expose himself to Barry's taunts about education.

"Contemporaries, of course—probably knew each other. I always wanted to prove that Xenophon was a character— maybe the tyrant—hard to prove. Make a fellow famous, though. A chair at a really big university."

"Xenophon's too much of a gentleman to be the tyrant." Piat couldn't resist rising to Barry's bait. He took another pull on the beer he had. Beer? Where had he got beer?

Barry kept flipping though the Plato. "The tyrant—here it is—the tyrant always looking for a new war to keep the people from noticing that he's taken away the democracy; the people trading their liberty for a little security. All around us, really. Democracy, tyranny, I wonder if that'd get me a chair. A book—democracy and tyranny. Make the arguments—I need another hit—uhh."

In mid-sentence, still rhapsodizing about the chair he would eventually receive, he fell asleep.

As usual, Piat threw a tattered quilt over him. He got up and swallowed the last of his whiskey. Then he copied the disk on Barry's machine, left Barry the copy, and threw the original into his pack.

Mara stepped out from the bedroom. She had her hair down, and a bulky wool sweater so big it came over her hips.

"You fucking bastard."

"Guilty as charged."

"He'll do your little job for you, you know. He'll do fuck anything for you, you monster. He'll quit his job and work until his back is on fire. And he'll expect me to rub it and take care of him. All so he can still be needed by the boys."

Piat was moving to the door.

"Jack?"

Piat turned around.

"To hell with all that. You want to fuck?"

Piat had his hand on the doorknob. *As usual.*

Tel Aviv

Dukas was only a little surprised that Abe Peretz was going along on the journey to have a look at the apartment that belonged to Salem Qatib's girlfriend. It was, after all, a nice day to get out of Tel Aviv; as LegAt, Peretz had an interest both in what the police were doing and in what Dukas was doing; he had every right to go. And after an evening with the Peretzes, Dukas thought he was right in his guess about Abe and Miriam Gurion: the Peretzes, he thought, were an unhappy couple. The evening hadn't been helped by the presence of a woman, presumably a widow—invited for Dukas's sake, perhaps—named Esther something-or-other, a new but apparently close friend of Bea's. Backed by the woman, Bea had seemed to sharpen the edge of everything she said; Abe had seemed to withdraw from them into some kind of passive-resistant imitation of good humor. So Abe was going along with them to Acco, not very much to Dukas's surprise.

It was only an hour and a half along the coast highway, might have been less if Dukas hadn't made plain his dislike of speed. Israelis, he'd already decided, were even worse drivers than Italians. Abe had laughed at him but slowed down; Miriam Gurion, in the front next to Peretz, had shaken her head. But she seemed as glad to be out of the city as Abe, and soon she was chattering about the case and about Salem Qatib's girlfriend, whom they hadn't been able to find yet even though they'd located her apartment.

"She's not in the apartment?" Dukas said.

"Nobody answers there. It has police tape across the door, the local man said. But his people didn't do it, so—" She shrugged.

"Have they been inside?"

"I think in fact they have but they're afraid to say. If it was Mossad that put the tape on, then the local cops were there and taking part, but it's 'national security.'" She turned and put her serious eyes on Dukas. "You know 'national security?'"

"We have a temple for its worship in Washington."

"We have hundreds."

After a while, he asked her if she'd got back yet to the guy who ran the naval facility in Jaffa. She shook her head and muttered something without turning around. Dukas thought she wouldn't lean on the guy until he leaned on her, but he wasn't ready to do that yet. But something smelled there, and he wanted to know what.

They went around Haifa in heavy traffic, Miriam saying "This is Haifa," and so on, as if she felt some responsibility to tourism, and then they were on a starker stretch of coast. "Crusaders," she said, and told him things he didn't care about—Acco when it was called Acre, the Crusades, the Knights' city under the modern city. He was glad when they got to the apartment building.

Dukas expected a local cop to be there, but Miriam said the visit wasn't formal, and, anyway, they would have to break into the apartment. "We're not really here." Dukas looked at Peretz, who gave him a sheepish smile and a shrug. *Great to have the LegAt and the visiting NCIS guy grabbed for breaking and entering.*

"You bring your wrecking bar?" Dukas said.

"I brought a set of picks." She gave him a surprising grin. "In Homicide, you learn a lot of skills." She jingled the picks. "Get some tools, too."

She said something to a security man in the lobby and showed him her badge; the security man looked worried but didn't say anything. Miriam told him something in a voice too low for Dukas to hear, but in the elevator she said she'd told him that if he called anybody, she'd arrest him. "Mossad probably scared him out of his wits. Of course, I can't arrest him because this isn't TLV. He probably knows that, but it will make him careful."

"What if Mossad show up?" Peretz said.

"We'll be gone by then."

She wiggled a pick into the lock and started to fiddle with it and the door opened.

"You're good," Dukas said.

"The lock was broken. Somebody here before us."

They stopped just inside the door. "Yes, somebody's been here before us," Peretz said. The place was trashed. The crudest kind of search had been carried out—stuff ripped out of drawers, the drawers themselves turned over and thrown on the floor; tables upended; sofa cushions ripped and tossed aside. A team of pros would have done it with a lot less mess, Dukas knew, could in fact have done a search without leaving any trace at all.

"Amateurs," he said.

"Mossad are not amateurs."

"Then it wasn't Mossad." He pointed at a muddy footprint. "*Real* amateurs."

Miriam was frowning. "It isn't what I'd expected."

They moved through the ruined flat without touching anything, then separated and took different rooms. It was a small place but fairly nice; the woman had tried to decorate it, make it pleasant. She had owned a lot of clothes, Dukas found, also a lot of men's clothes, which told him she was probably not a cross-dresser but had a guy pretty much living in. Dukas looked at the labels, felt the fabrics. He asked Miriam what some of the labels meant.

"Cheap," she said. "Trendy but inexpensive."

"Like the malls. Okay."

Peretz had been in the kitchen. "She wasn't much of a cook." He made a face. "What's in the fridge is spoiled."

They all moved that way. "Somebody was thirsty," Miriam said. She pointed at a glass and three empty water bottles on the kitchen sink. Dukas got toilet paper from the bathroom and took the glass and the bottles and put them one at a time into a plastic Wal-Mart sack that had been part of the litter on the floor. He looked at Miriam Gurion. "You guys do a forensics check on these things, okay?" He put the sack by the front door.

He went back to the bedroom and separated the male and female clothing with a foot. The job was easy; he guessed that the clothes had been originally separated in the closet and the drawers, and the searchers had made separate piles of them. Or fairly separate piles. Or—

"I think maybe two searches," he said to Miriam, who was still in the kitchen. "I think maybe somebody went through the clothes again—no, only the guy's clothes—after the first search had been made, and he kind of mixed things up a little. Dropped some guy things in with hers, but only on top."

"If there were two, Mossad wasn't first. If they'd been here first, nobody else would have got in. But Mossad wouldn't have made this kind of mess."

"Three searches?" Dukas said. "Popular girl."

"Popular man, I think."

Dukas nodded, looked at Peretz, then Miriam. "Salem Qatib," he said. "*Very* popular man."

Dukas went back and went through the male clothing. It, too, seemed anonymous—youthful, cheap, more or less fashionable, with a lot of jeans and T-shirts. "Where's the dirty clothes?" he shouted.

"Bathroom." Peretz had been cruising the whole apartment, not focusing on anything in particular. "Somebody dumped it in the shower."

A white-painted woven hamper had been turned on its side under the bathroom sink; beyond it, the plastic shower stall was halfway open, clothes covering its sea-green floor. Dukas poked through them—more blue jeans, separable by size and cut into his and hers; a couple of pairs of men's bikini briefs, half a dozen pairs of panties and four brassieres; some blouses. He dragged out the blue jeans. The man's were caked on the cuffs and knees with soil; one of the man's T-shirts had a smear of dried mud across it, too. Only one pair of the woman's jeans suggested anything like the same contact with the earth—a muddy knee and two spots where her buttocks had met raw dirt.

"He digs, she watches." He went back into the bedroom and rooted around for shoes, found the man's desert boots. Mud-caked, like the jeans.

"Mister Holmes, do you have a handy file on eighty-seven kinds of Israeli soils?" he called to Peretz.

Miriam understood the joke, laughed, understood also what Dukas was getting at and came into the bedroom. She broke off some dirt from a boot and rubbed it between her fingers. "Sandy," she said. She shrugged, laughed. "Everywhere in Israel is sandy."

"Qatib was an archaeologist," Dukas said.

If this was news to her, she suppressed any reaction. "He didn't have a job, so far as we know. So far as we can tell, the woman supported him."

They moved out to the long corridor that ran to the sliding doors that gave on a tiny terrace. Miriam had been looking at the places where other people had already looked for evidence—the bottoms of drawers, the toilet tank, the under-side of the kitchen countertop. There was nothing. "The place is useless. Either there was nothing here or somebody else found it."

Peretz, who had been out on the terrace, ambled in and pointed at a tangle of wires and a surge-protector bar. "She had a computer."

"Or he did."

"She wasn't poor."

"What did she do?"

"We found her on a labor website as a 'contract polling specialist.' We think that means some kind of freelancer. I thought until I saw this place that maybe she was one of those girls who come up to you at the shopping center with stupid questions about what you buy, but now I think she made more money than that. Maybe she really was some kind of specialist."

"Or maybe *he* made more money than you think." Dukas went back to the clothes and then so did the others, and they went through them garment by garment, looking at the seams, feeling for anything hidden. Nothing.

On the drive back to Tel Aviv, he asked Miriam Gurion how a Palestinian with a degree in archaeology could make money. She laughed. She talked about the laws against illicit digging, the laws against moving artifacts out of the country. She talked about the breaking of those laws and the financing of terrorism with the profits. "Of course, with a lot of corruption along the way. With the Palestinians, they want their cut even if they're strapping on a suicide belt." She settled her shoulders. "Palestinian idealism." She snorted.

When they dropped her at Dizengoff Street, Dukas got out and followed her a few steps so that they were away from Abe, and he said, "I don't want to make your job any harder, but I want to talk to the guy in Jaffa." He held her eyes. "I'm going to talk to him, one way or the other."

"You have many other things you can do."

"And I'm doing them. But I mean to do this, too."

"You should focus on your case, Mister Dukas. If we learn anything more about Jaffa, we'll inform you."

He held her arm because she was turning to go into the police building. "Don't let your personal life get in the way of my case."

She flushed and her jaw tightened. She was going to say something nasty, he thought, but she swung her head back and flared her nostrils and didn't say it or anything for some seconds. Looking at him, she frowned, and he guessed that she understood what he believed about her and the man in Jaffa and Abe Peretz. "It's painful for me," she said.

"I can see that. It isn't my doing."

She glanced at the car, its motor running, Abe turned away to look at the street. "All right, I'll fix it up for you. Do I have to be there?"

"I need for you to get me into the facility and introduce me. Then you can take off."

She drew her arm away but didn't leave. "That guy and I—it became personal. It's embarrassing for me now." She glanced at the car again.

"I'm here to find who murdered Salem Qatib. Your personal life is your business."

She gave him a smile with one side of her face. "I hope so." There was a certain sad gallantry to the words. It made him sorry again that she hadn't found him her type.

On the way to his borrowed office he stopped at the room where the translators were working on the pile of crap Mossad had sent over. When he looked in, one of the translators, a dark-haired kid with the sad face of a basset hound, looked up, saw him, and scowled. Dukas raised his eyebrows in question. The kid pinched his nose between a thumb and index finger. Universal sign language.

Dukas answered emails, most of which implied that he wasn't moving the investigation along fast enough. He read two draft reports on the implications of recoding the entire US Navy. These were so discouraging that he went down to the snack bar and got two slices of microwaved pizza and a milk-shake-in-a-can and a super-large bag of Cajun-style potato chips and slopped back to the office and pushed the paperwork aside and tried to cheer himself up by eating and making notes, cop notes, for a report he knew he'd have to write one day. Regrettably, they added up to a lot of nothing.

What—you've been here a whole thirty-six hours and you haven't learned anything yet? What a shmuck!

He made a bad-smell face. *What am I doing here?* He doodled on a pad. *What I'm doing here is trying to set right a lot of crap, like my best friend gets kidnapped, my country gets insulted, and an ex-Navy guy I never knew gets murdered. So what have I set right?*

Nothing.

He looked at his notes about the visit to the girl's apartment. Mud-stains on her ass, mud on the guy's knees and his boots.

He called the University of Michigan and got put right through to the registrar, who gave him the name of a woman in archaeology and actually managed to switch him to her line. He was put through to a Professor Gianetti. She sounded pretty nice, a little nasal, kind of bouncy. He asked her how you got mud on your blue jeans. She laughed at his question.

"In my business, you spend most of your time on your knees!" She giggled.

"Digging?"

"Depends." She sobered. "If it's something local and small, you might do your own digging. Get out the old shovel. You do that mostly standing up until the hole gets deep and then, yuh, you might get on your knees and dig. To get down there, you know? But mostly if it's a big dig, you got people to do the heavy lifting—you hire local people. I just got back from Belize, we're digging a Mayan site on the coast? I had ninety locals. They dig trenches—you know how that works? You make a grid— Never mind. The point is, when they find something, that's when you get on your knees. You don't want somebody with a shovel going after an artifact. You're on your knees, mostly upside-down in the hole, working with a trowel, then a spoon and a toothbrush. My favorite weapon is a watercolor painter's red sable brush. Very soft, it won't scratch even decayed bone, right? But it's just stiff enough to brush dirt away."

"I heard that illegal diggers use bulldozers."

"Oh, God, do they ever! That's to get down to the layer where stuff is, but they destroy a ton of stuff that way. It's butchery. Worse. Horrible."

"But they find stuff."

"Oh, yeah."

"What would a trained archaeologist do for them?"

"They scrape off the top with the dozer, then they send in guys with shovels; the moment they hit something, the trained guy moves in and does it just the way I do—trowel, on his knees, work, work, work."

"Ever hear of stuff like that in Palestine?"

She laughed. "Are there bears in the woods? The whole Middle East is wall-to-wall sites. Plus there's tons of people with no jobs and no money. It's a volatile mix. Same thing in Central America, western China, lots of places. It's a nightmare, in fact."

"Lot of Palestinian stuff on the market?"

She snorted. "I could take you to a gallery that has a ton of Roman and Greek stuff that it says is from Pakistan. You remember how big the Roman and Greek presence was in Pakistan, I'm sure. I think maybe Pakistan is code for Palestine. Or maybe North Africa. But yes, there's stuff of Palestinian origin out there for sale even as we speak, as they say. For big bucks."

Dukas asked her if she knew of any recent illegal digs in the Palestinian area, but she said it wasn't her field. She gave him a couple of names and phone numbers and said she'd ask around, but these things were held pretty close. He asked if she'd known a student named Salem Qatib, but she hadn't been there that long. She'd check to see who had.

He tried her two contacts, but one was in class and one was out of the country at a conference. He noted down the conference—Madrid, the International Society of Practical Archaeology—and wondered what impractical archaeology would be, and then he called Pigoreau in The Hague again. Pigoreau was "in a meeting," but a young woman with a delicious Dutch accent said she'd be sure he got the message, which Dukas dictated: *Ask around about a recent illegal dig in Israel or the Palestinian areas.*

Then he called Triffler.

"He's out." The speaker was one of the special agents, a guy named Bilson. He jumped to Triffler's defense. "But he's working on a case."

"Did I say he wasn't?"

"You checking up on him?"

"Tell him to call me *subito*."

He leaned back and looked at the undecorated wall of the borrowed office. Whoever had had it before him had left a lot of nail holes and, right above the desk, a patchwork of marks from sticky tape. Photos, maybe. Or notes. Phone numbers.

He was thinking about the Peretzes, then about Abe and Mrs Gurion, then Salem Qatib and what sort of man he must have been to train in a difficult, kind of far-out field and wind up with no job. But maybe—*maybe*—pursuing his field illegally. First the Navy—nothing bad on his record, but he'd have to get that checked—then two years as a graduate student, no suggestion that he'd overstayed his visa or broken US law. Then home, and in a few years he's living with a woman in a pretty nice apartment and he's tracking in a lot of mud.

He made a note on his pad: *No archaeological tools in the apt.—trowel, brushes. Where they?*

When the phone rang, he was still staring at the wall, making the odd note.

"Dukas." Expecting Triffler.

"Sergeant Gurion here."

"Sergeant! Mrs Gurion."

"Call me Miriam." She didn't sound very friendly. "We can visit Jaffa at four if you can make it."

"Great!" He didn't check to see if something had been scheduled for him; Jaffa would be more important than anything they could lay on.

"My friend is very nervous. He wants to know why you

201

are coming." She sounded like a scold. Mother hen protecting her chicks.

"Should be obvious."

"Not to him. He is *scared*, okay?"

Dukas hesitated. There was nothing he could say over the telephone that would mollify either the man at Jaffa or Miriam Gurion. "I'll get an embassy car and a driver." In fact, he'd get an embassy security man as driver. He didn't want to end up like Al Craik. "Want me to pick you up?"

She would take her own car. She would meet him there. She gave him directions, an address. She still wasn't friendly.

Dukas went back to the snack bar and got another slice of pizza and a package of Ho-Ho's and a large coffee; when he got back to the office, Triffler had called once and was trying again. There was also a message slip from "Mister Shlomo" asking to meet him at five "where they met before." He called Triffler.

"*I* was working," Triffler said. "I've been chatting up the experts."

"In something relevant, I hope."

"Are you eating? You sound as if you're talking through a knothole."

"Snack."

"I bet. Okay—experts in stolen artifacts and the illegal antiquities trade. Naples is a center, did you know? They manufacture about thirty percent of the world's antique art objects, right here. Less big in Middle Eastern stuff than Western European, Renaissance and middle ages preferred, but if you'd like a nice, newly made Greek statue with the patina of millennia still on it, I can find you one about three blocks from the office."

"Not what I'm looking for."

"As for the real stuff coming out of places like Gaza, my experts tell me to try Athens. Very big in the business, both real and fake. I got some names."

"What I think we're looking for, Dick, is a very recent dig,

202

because maybe that's where our guy got killed, or maybe it's *why* he got killed."

"My experts tell me that if the Palestinian Authority or Hamas catch you at it, and you haven't paid the chai, getting killed is the best you can hope for."

"But our guy wound up dead in the hands of Mossad."

"Do we know that for sure? Anyway, if he was connected with the trade, maybe Mossad would knock him around to find out who was behind it. I was told that both the PA and Hamas finance some of their terrorist activities with profits from the antiquities trade—a good reason for Mossad to be all over it."

Dukas grunted, then said *Mmm.* "Ask your pals about recent activity. Illegal, I mean. I want a place, the people involved."

Triffler asked if that was all, or would he like the moon as well, but he said he'd get on it, and then he said he had an idea. Dukas groaned—purely pro forma, as Triffler was in fact a source of good ideas—and Triffler said he wanted to go to Athens.

"Stop trying to get out of the office."

"Mike, it's a short flight. I can be there tomorrow morning. There's six people I'd like to see—I got names, addresses, contacts. A day, and I may have something."

"We have an NCIS office with real, live agents in Athens."

"They're not as well-informed as I am."

"The telephone doesn't work to Athens?"

"They won't talk on the phone, I was told."

They argued. Dukas wanted somebody as good as Triffler in the office, and there was nobody else as good as Triffler. Still. "Okay. One day. You're back tomorrow night, right?"

"For sure. We have tickets to *Madama Butterfly.*"

"I'm glad you see where your responsibilities lie."

Dukas called the CIA station chief's office to ask if he could get some time with her and was told he could have five minutes around three. In the interim, he tackled the paper-work he had been avoiding, got something to eat, shmoozed with Peretz, and presented himself at the chief of station's office.

"Antiquities," he said to her. "Palestinian territories."

"Big business," she said. "Big headache for the Israelis."

"How big?"

She didn't have the figures but she could cite facts to prove that a lot of suicide bombings and rocket attacks were being paid for that way. "The Palestinians would deny it, and maybe it's true that the actual cash that buys some specific thing comes from some other source. But that's a matter of accounting. A lot of the money comes from the trade, legal and illegal."

"Guys skim it?"

"Sure—it's the PA, right?"

Dukas was sipping coffee from a cardboard cup. "I think the death I'm investigating could be connected."

She raised her eyebrows to suggest that she wasn't surprised.

"Who's in charge on the Palestinian side?"

She chuckled. "They call him 'The Tax Collector.' That's how much money he brings in. Guy named Mahmoud Rahman Hamal. Used to be a Fatah foot-soldier, worked his way up, got into the PA security apparatus. Got some solid training in the KGB schools in the seventies. I'll send you a bio."

"Any chance of talking to him?"

She started to say something—probably "none"—and caught herself and said instead, "In his own bailiwick, he's an important man. You meeting him is like an Israeli cop asking to meet John Ashcroft. Not to mention how leery they are of meetings."

"If we offered money?"

"Don't even think it! Hamal, I believe, is a proud man—from his point of view, a straight shooter and a man of honor. I wouldn't insult him."

Dukas looked at his watch, saw his five minutes were up. "I'd settle for somebody farther down the line if he knew about recent stuff over there." He stood, leaned in. "It might be in their interest, too."

"Not if they killed your guy."

"And then got Mossad to handle the body for them? I don't think so. Could you at least maybe put out a feeler to them?"

She looked at him with the sort of look she might have given a fish that wasn't quite fresh. "I'll evaluate the situation. But no matter what, Mister Dukas, I don't want you meeting with a high-level Palestinian. You don't speak Arabic, do you? You don't know the situation here really well. You don't have our constraints or our goals. A country clearance doesn't make you an official." She, too, stood. "Maybe I could send a message or get some questions asked. But you'd have to work through a proxy who met my specifications."

Oddly, she didn't piss him off. Agency people often did, but he believed what she told him. He held out his hand, "All contributions gratefully accepted."

Somebody new called him from Michigan, this time a deep-voiced academic named Joe Bernstein, who sounded as if he ought to be out riding a Harley or fighting forest fires. "Salem Qatib was a student of mine. I was supposed to be his thesis advisor, but he never wrote the thesis."

"How come?"

"He couldn't write. He could learn the stuff, pass tests, talk, but he couldn't write. In the field, he was great—good eye, great at getting stuff out of the ground. But he couldn't put down a paragraph that made sense. No thesis, no degree; no degree, no job. And no PhD later."

"That why he came back to Palestine?"

"They like degrees there, too."

Not for illegal digging, they don't, Dukas told himself.

Jaffa

Dukas's driver-cum-tough-guy got him to the decrepit naval facility in Jaffa a few minutes early, giving him time to look the place over from outside the gate. He understood better what Craik had reported about the layout and the look of neglect. He reviewed what else Craik had said: the guy he was going to meet was named Mosher, a lieutenant, old in rank; Craik had speculated about some serious mistake in the guy's past that had made him a time-server here. What the military used to call a Sad Sack.

Mosher. Dukas free-associated about Jewish names. There had been somebody named Moise Oisher—a cantor? Dukas had grown up in a partly Jewish neighborhood where his father's Greek bakery had learned to make non-kosher Jewish pastries. The high school had been full of Jewish kids, a lot of them pushed hard by their parents to be brainy, to achieve. Dukas had got along, heard the talk, absorbed names like Moise Oisher, tried to get the brassieres off some Jewish girls until their mothers got wind of it. *Assimilated Jews*, he thought. Last night, Bea Peretz had said the words as if they were an insult, and Dukas had said as a joke, "I didn't think there was any other kind," and she had spat, "A lot of us are returning to being real Jews!"

A lot of us are returning to being real many-things, he thought. *Real Christians, real Muslims, real Jews, real Hindus.* He, for example, was trying to be a real cop.

"This yours?" the driver's voice said. He was leaning against his side of the car, a big and deliberately menacing figure in mirrored glasses and a black polo shirt whose tight, short sleeves made his arm muscles look like mountain ranges.

Dukas looked out and saw Miriam Gurion pulling in a couple of car-widths away. He got out. "Yeah, I'm meeting her."

"You want me to come in with you?" The driver knew what they were there for.

206

"You'd never get a weapon past the gate." The guy was wearing a belly-pack, the practically standard-issue announcement to the world that he was carrying. Not such a bad statement to make, in fact. He looked along the fence and said, "I bet you I could toss a gun over and pick it up in thirty seconds and they wouldn't know."

Dukas looked at the gate, at the uniformed kid on guard. He looked about thirteen. Even his H&K assault rifle looked older.

"You got a hideout gun?"

"I might have."

"Ditch the belly-pack and come with me." He didn't see a metal detector. Dukas doubted the kid had the chutzpah to try a body search of the security man.

Dukas smiled—*chutzpah*. He'd learned a little Yiddish in high school, too. *Shlemiel, shlemozzle, zaftig, chutzpah*. Not words that had proved very useful in Israel, he thought. He leaned back into the car as the security man was pushing his belly-pack under the driver's seat. "I want you to be a silent menace, okay? Keep the shades on, look grim, fold your arms, say nothing. Got it?"

The guy straightened. "My name's Roger."

"Roger."

Miriam Gurion led them to the gate, mumbled to the kid, who asked to see their passports and waved them through. Miriam pointed the way with a barely lifted finger. No attempt at chitchat. Dukas tried to look at the place with Al Craik's eyes, remembering what Craik had said. The Fourth Royal Marines. Next door, a second-floor office in an otherwise unoccupied building, an office Craik had seen with the windows open, now apparently closed. He'd seen a guy in shorts in that doorway, now closed, and he'd thought maybe he was one of the guys who had snatched him.

Then Lieutenant Mosher—it had to be Mosher—was coming toward them with a scared grin on his face. A small man, bent into an unmilitary curve. A *shlemozzle*. Dukas let her introduce them; he shook hands, didn't introduce Roger. Miriam said she had another appointment and walked away. Mosher looked panicky.

"Somewhere we can go to talk?" Dukas said.

"I don't understand why you are here."

"It's better if we sit down someplace." Dukas looked around as if a place to sit down might materialize on the scruffy grass.

Mosher led them around the corner of a building on their right and up a flight of stone steps. The building was stuccoed, probably built by the Brits, maybe as old as WWI. Inside was a corridor that creaked under their feet and, at a corner, Mosher's office. Roger sounded like a buffalo coming behind them.

No receptionist, no secretary. Other than the three of them, Dukas thought that the building was empty. "What d'you do here?" he said.

"I administer the facility."

Mosher had a computer that might have been six or seven years old, with an ancient monitor that was about fourteen inches beyond flat-screen. A couple of metal file cabinets, c. 1950. A view of the building opposite out one window and, at right angles, the defunct parade ground out the other.

Dukas looked at the parade ground. "The ammo bunker out there?"

"Uh—where we found the—?"

"Where you found Qatib, yeah."

"Yes, out there."

"I don't see it."

"You cannot hardly see it from here."

Dukas moved right to the edge of the window and looked out, his cheek against the wall, and he made out a grassy mound with a shadowed cleft in front of it. "Yes, you can," he said.

Mosher was sitting behind his desk. Dukas pulled a chair away from the wall and sat in it—not the situation he'd have liked, with the interrogator in the bad chair and the one being interrogated ensconced behind a big piece of protection, and on his own turf, as well. Roger leaned against the wall opposite and scowled at Mosher.

"If your friend would like to sit down—"

"He's fine."

Dukas put a micro-recorder on the desk. "Mind?"

"I—ah—I don't—" Mosher was confused: "Mind?" didn't make sense to his non-American ear.

"Do you object to being taped?"

"Well—yes."

Dukas looked at him until Mosher's eyes fell away. Dukas put the recorder back in his pocket and made a face— eyebrows raised, chin out—that says, *Okay, be it on your head.* In fact, because there was no prosecution involved, taping didn't make a lot of sense. But it was a nice piece of theatre. Still, he left the machine on in his pocket.

"Tell me about finding the body."

"I didn't find it. They did."

"You found another body two years ago."

"Yes." Mosher seemed to be gaining a little strength—like the guy in Greek myth who gained strength from contact with the earth, he gained it from contact with his desk. "A bad kid, a gangbanger, shot to death, dragged under the fence." He pointed out the window with his chin.

"Out beyond the ammo dump."

"Far out beyond what you call the ammo dump."

"It isn't an ammo dump?"

"Ammunition *bunker*, I think you say in English. Very long ago." Mosher was gaining so much strength he was daring a little superciliousness.

Dukas wrote down "ammunition bunker" and muttered the words as he did so. "He was dragged through the fence?"

209

"Yes."

He wrote and muttered "dragged through fence" and said, "Who by?"

Mosher dared a smile. "If we knew, we would have prosecution."

"Well, you said 'dragged inside,' so you seem to know something about how he got here, so I thought you knew something about who did it."

"No." Mosher smiled again. "No."

"Funny place to dump a body."

"Very wild and isolated." Mosher gave the chin gesture again. "Back there."

"Hole in the fence?"

"No, certainly not. It is wire back there. The bottom strand was cut and the body dragged through."

"Somebody must have been inside to drag him."

"I told you, the wire was cut! They came in and dragged the body in. It was two years ago! What has this to do with me?"

Dukas pretended to consult his notes. "You said this first body had been there for several days."

"Exactly."

"But—" He leafed through pages in the notebook. "You told Commander Craik that your guards patrol the fence every day." He looked up. "True?"

"Of course! But—they are boys, reservists—the weeds are high back there. They missed it, is all."

"That was in—" he was guessing—"February?"

"No! August!"

"Oh. Hot time of the year. Body lying out there for several days, it must have smelled pretty bad."

"That is how they found it, of course."

Dukas spent a long time turning pages and looking at notes about, in actual fact, a spousal-abuse case in Naples. "How long have you been in charge here, Lieutenant?"

"Six years in March."

"Six years!" Dukas smiled. "That's a long time in one station."

Mosher dared to smile again. "It suits me."

"I can see that." Dukas closed the notebook. "What did you do?"

Mosher stared at him. "Pardon?"

"What did you do, Lieutenant, to get ordered to this godforsaken hole for six years? You got no staff, no command, and a vacant lot full of weeds and some buildings that are falling down. In the US, this kind of duty goes to what we call the colossal fuckups. You a colossal fuckup, Lieutenant?"

Mosher's eyes widened. "I don't have to— This is insulting!" He tried to stand, at the same time reaching for the desk phone. Dukas looked at Roger and jerked his head, and the big security man took two strides and picked the telephone off the desk and carried it along its cord to the wall and unplugged the jack. Then he went and stood with his back against the door, arms folded.

"What did you do?" Dukas said.

Mosher's strength had deserted him again. "I will file a complaint!"

"You made a colossal fuckup and they sent you here, fucking Siberia. Then a dead guy turned up and you had an affair with Sergeant Gurion and she sort of swept it under the rug."

"This is very offensive!"

"You a married man, Lieutenant?"

"I did not have an affair with Sergeant Gurion!"

"Yes, you did. She told me all about it." Dukas opened the notebook again, began to leaf through the pages. "She feels guilty. Because of your wife." He waited. Mosher had sat down again, was gripping the edge of his desk. "And because of her responsibilities as a policewoman. In fact, she's reopening the investigation." The last was true, anyway. Maybe it all was true. "What did you do? To fuck up?"

211

Mosher looked at him, at Roger, at the building opposite. His mouth looked like a deflating rubber raft. He went through something that pained him and seemed to pull himself together, and he said, "I was in the crew of a submarine that ran aground."

"On the bridge?"

Mosher shrugged.

"Duty officer?"

"No!" Mosher allowed himself to be angry. "I had nothing to do with conning the ship. I was on the bridge, a matter of, of duty assignment—" He set his jaw, which was threatening to go off on its own. "Two men died. There were courts-martial. *I* didn't get the court-martial."

"You got sent here."

"I was exonerated."

"You gave evidence for the prosecutions." Dukas could say this with a lot of assurance. He knew how modern navies worked.

Mosher chewed his lower lip. "This interview is over," he said.

"Lieutenant Mosher, do you know the expression 'one-trick pony'? Do you know what a one-trick pony is? What you got here is a one-trick pony. People who kill and know only one way to get rid of the body. See, I don't believe in coincidence. Neither does Sergeant Gurion. Neither will your navy's judge advocate general." He held up two fingers. "Two bodies. One cause." One cause, one finger. Dukas waited. "Inside job."

Mosher held his eyes, twisting a rubber band in his fingers, licking his lips.

"Who did it?"

Dukas waited. Mosher looked away. Dukas waited again, like a timpanist counting a long rest, and then he threw himself forward and crashed a fist on the desk and screamed "*Who did it?*" Mosher jumped and looked terrified and scrabbled in a pocket for a cell phone. Dukas still had his fist on the desk, hunched forward, glowering, and now he put his head and shoulders right over the desk and into Mosher's face and he growled, "Make that call and I'll have you in an Israeli navy brig tonight."

Mosher hesitated with the phone in his left hand and his right poised to punch buttons. He leaned away from Dukas but didn't make the call. "I didn't do it," he said.

"But you know who did."

"No!"

"You know who hid the bodies."

"No, no—"

"Lieutenant, I don't care about you. Either way. I don't want you for my case, but I'll squash you if you stand in my way. You know who hid the bodies and you're scared shitless about it. What are you scared of? That they'll take your crappy job and your pension away? Lieutenant, if you don't help me, I'll see that your job and your pension and your wife all fall off the edge of the world! Who did it?"

Mosher licked his lips. "Who hid the body?"

"Both bodies."

"I don't *know*. But I might—suspect."

"Keep going."

"There was a—an office here. Over there." He bobbed his head toward the window on his right, toward the building where Craik had seen the office and the sign and the guy in shorts. "Maybe they—had something to do with—some things."

"Who?"

"Office-workers. You know."

"What office?"

Mosher combined a squirm and a shrug. "It was called— I have to translate from Hebrew—the Branch of Water—no, Marine—Examination?"

Dukas looked over his shoulder at Roger, but Roger was as

213

expressionless as a statue. "The Branch of Marine Examination. 'Examination' doesn't sound right."

"Exploration?"

"Were they scientists?"

"Uhhh—I do not think so."

"How many?"

"Four. Four guys."

"A secretary? Any women?"

"No. Just four guys."

"Uniforms?"

"No. Civilians."

"Four civilian guys, not scientists, in something called the Marine Exploration Branch. Were you ever in their office?"

"It was restricted." Mosher swallowed. "Sometimes they were away."

"One, two—all four?"

"All four."

"No visitors, restricted, but they must have communicated somehow. Open telephone?" Dukas was sitting back a little but his eyes never left Mosher's face. Now he saw a hint of guile, and he slapped the desk. "Lieutenant!"

"I think there is a, an, uh, antenna on the roof."

"Satellite?"

"Maybe."

Dukas sat back and turned the pages of the notebook. "Okay, we're almost done." He smiled. Mosher's face shone with sweat. "Who told you not to talk about any of this?"

Mosher licked his lips and blinked and wiped his hands down his cheeks. His fingers were trembling. Twice, he started to speak and stopped. His head moved aside as people's will when they are about to make an admission. Finally, he whispered, "Telephone. I know the man a little. He was here early on, when I was new here. Then he came back when we found the first body. Then he telephoned me this time. He said something like—I understood what to do and what was at stake."

214

"Civilian?" A nod. "Name?"

Mosher shook his head.

"You won't tell me or you don't know?"

"I don't know. The first time, he came with an officer I knew. Retired now."

Dukas got the name of the retired officer but thought it wouldn't help much.

"Did the four guys in the Branch of Marine Exploration ever say anything to you?"

"They—" Mosher straightened as an old grievance found a voice. "They treated me like a joke. Always, it was a joke. Like they shared something with me dirty." He looked at Dukas with misery in his eyes. "I never shared anything with them!"

Dukas closed the notebook and got up and told Roger to put the telephone back. He shook hands with Mosher and patted him on the shoulder and said, "Now I'd like to look into their office."

Mosher looked as if he'd either expire or explode, but Dukas pushed and cajoled, and in the event they went to the office but found that it was locked with two deadbolts for which Mosher didn't have the keys. Dukas made him get somebody with a ladder, and he climbed up and looked through the window. There was nothing much to be seen in the office—no files, no computers, a couple of desks and a sofa and a phone. A refrigerator and a microwave. Scuba tanks. A lot of magazines—girls and sports figures—and a big TV. Then he went up on the roof and looked at the satellite dish.

When he was back in the car with Roger and they were speeding toward Tel Aviv, he said, "You know guys like that? The guys in the office, I mean? An office but no office work?"

"I might have."

"Ex-something or other." Roger's sunglasses looked at him in the mirror. "Maybe ex-military. Demolition? Like SEALs?"

"There's a lot of ex-something or others floating around in the world."

When they got to the embassy, Roger drove the car around to the back and showed Dukas the entrance there. They both got out. Roger took off his sunglasses and revealed the wise, weary eyes of an ex-something or other. He smiled down at Dukas. "You're good." He shook Dukas's hand. "A pleasure to watch." He laughed. "Unless you're Lieutenant Mosher."

Dukas didn't feel as if it had been a pleasure. He felt as if he'd like to find a shadowy place where he could mutter through a hole that he wanted absolution.

However, what he got was retribution. He was no sooner in his borrowed office than Peretz looked in and said, "Your forensics team has been turned down again by the Israelis. Ambassador says it's definitive—don't ask again."

Dukas looked at his watch. He was already late for the meeting that Eshkol had asked for. Before he left, he tried Pigoreau again at The Hague, got the delicious Dutch voice, was told that Pigoreau was unavailable but had left the message that somebody he knew in the UN arts-theft section had heard of some recent activity in Gaza. There was also some buzz about it in Athens. She read him a name; Dukas passed it to his Naples office to be given to Triffler. Then he was off to try for Eshkol.

Afghanistan

Alan had said that they would be in Kandahar, but in fact he and Fidel were in a nearby village that was really nothing but an ancient prison and some houses that had grown up around it. It had been bombed a month before, but it also had damage that the Soviets had done in the eighties and some from when the Taliban had swept in. The prison might have started as something else a couple of hundred years ago—a small palace, a mosque, a warehouse—but somebody who had understood despair had turned it into a prison. US army people now had a lot of "detainees," as anybody was called who so much as gave them the finger, herded inside. Not a happy place.

He thought that perhaps the British had had something to do with the prison long ago. Certainly the brick tower that stood separate from it reminded him of another he had seen in Africa, one he knew the British had built. This one, like the other, was simply a square, hollow structure three storeys tall, with a roof and an internal stairway and a partial floor way up high. It was for hanging people.

He and Fidel were camping in a house fifty yards away that might have belonged once to a village schoolmaster, or just possibly to a Brit. One corner of it had been knocked down, and the inside was pretty well gutted, but they had cleaned out one room and put down their sleeping bags and their gear, and it was better than a tent. One wall had some bookcases on which there were still a few books, some in Farsi, others in English, these mostly "young people's" books from the 1920s illustrated with blurry black-and-white photographs of geography and native peoples and things like rice cultivation. A few Victorian editions from Mudey's and Tauchnitz were there, too, so battered by time and bugs the pages had congealed into soft, holed slabs. Alan had brought his own time-fillers, but Fidel had had to dig through the books until he found an English copy of *The Iliad*, published in 1898, a label inside the cover that said "Saint George's Teacher's College of Peshawar Library."

"Would you believe I never read this?" Fidel said.

"Here's your chance."

"Improve my mind, right." Fidel looked at the first lines. "You've read it?"

"It's about the Trojan War."

Fidel read, in an over-emphatic manner that was meant to be satirical, "'Sing, O Goddess, the anger of Achilles, son of Peleus, that brought countless ills upon the Achaeans. Many

217

a brave soul did it send hurrying down to Hades, and many a hero did it yield a prey to dogs and vultures. . . .' Sounds like a war, yeah. Achilles is a god, right?"

"Um, I think half of one. His mother's a goddess or something."

Alan had a shitkicker he'd bought in Bahrain, one of those mostly unconvincing military novels that involve saving the world in the last thirty pages and putting the hero through more shenanigans than real military people see in a lifetime. Still, it would pass the time until the snatch team got there with the prisoner. If they did.

"Who's Agamemnon?" Fidel said. Alan had settled down to read, his back against a wall—there were no chairs—and, not minding the interruption because the shitkicker really was crap, he tried to explain what he remembered of a long-ago college course. That done, he settled to the book again, and in barely enough time for him to pick up the story, Fidel said, "This guy Achilles gets so pissed off over having a woman taken away that he throws the whole attack off. What the hell's that about?"

Alan dredged something up from long-ago Cliff Notes. "Honor?"

They read on. Fidel, without prelude, would now and then read a passage aloud. He seemed astonished by the story, the brutality, the bloodshed, the gore. "All this for a *woman*?" he said.

"I don't think it's the woman herself. It's losing face, losing status."

"You said honor."

"Well—honor was sort of public—how other people saw you."

"They're all the time bragging, too."

"Well, I guess that's part of it, yeah."

Fidel shook his head and went back to the book. After a few minutes, he said, "The whole fucking *war* was about a woman. Helen."

"Helen, yeah. Agamemnon was shamed by it. Shame's a big part of their idea of honor, too, I guess."

"Fuck, Commander, if somebody ran off with Mrs Bush, would you go to war over it?"

"We're different."

"I'll say."

"But— Maybe Helen was their Nine-Eleven." He leaned on an elbow, his book face-down, more interested now in Fidel's question than in fake military action. "I think it's the idea people have of themselves. Down right in the gut, who they are. When you attack that, you really rouse the beast. For them, it was Helen; for us, Nine-Eleven. Nine-Eleven attacked our idea that we're the good guys, we're invulnerable, God is on our side, and John Wayne will save us."

"We were blindsided, thousands of people, a ton of money. This was one woman!"

Alan reached for his book, stopped with his hand on the slick cover. "It makes you ask what's worth going to war for, okay?" He believed in war if it had great cause—just war, necessary war. War with laws, conventions, rules. But war that was hard to start. Homer's war, he had to agree, made no sense. Or, rather, it was fired by a different idea of "sense," not a national will or a national destiny or national necessity, but that personal "honor." He pulled something else out of memory. "It isn't like Homer is saying that war is a great thing, you know. I mean, the way I remember it, by the end it all seems pointless. Like he'd agree with you—all this over a woman?" He thought of saying, but didn't, *All this over Nine-Eleven?*, because the intel officer in him said that Nine-Eleven hadn't been as new as most people thought, or as terrifying, or as big a deal. And Tom Terrific hadn't prevented it in the last thirty pages. But that wasn't a popular thing to say, and he didn't want to get in a squabble with Fidel, with whom he'd had some troubles in the past.

They went back to their reading. Once, Fidel said with a

laugh, "Jeez, he's got that right," and, later, "Christ, I know a guy just like that."

The day wore on, cold, gray; Alan was half in his sleeping bag by then and it was starting to snow. They had some MREs and he napped and woke and read until the pages left between his fingers told him that the shitkicker was pretty well finished, and all that would be left was the utterly incredible bringing together of three or four plots and some terrific exploit by the handsome, white, smart American officer that would save the world or at least the entire Pacific Fleet.

"Hey, listen to this!" Fidel said. "This is really cool. No kidding." Without asking if Alan was interested, he read aloud:

Meriones found a bow and quiver for Ulysses, and on his head he set a leathern helmet that was lined with a strong plaiting of leathern thongs, while on the outside it was thickly studded with boar's teeth, well and skillfully set into it; next the head there was an inner lining of felt.

He looked up at Alan. "That's cool—boar's teeth! How the hell would you make a helmet out of boar's teeth?"

Alan didn't remember the passage. He thought that all ancient Greek helmets were metal. "Maybe it's symbolic. You know, like the stupid swords you see on fantasy novel covers—you couldn't cut a loaf of bread with one, but it looks cool."

"Maybe the boar's teeth stick out in all directions, sort of like the points of a crown. Would that work? 'Thickly studded with boar's teeth.' That's a lot of boar's teeth, 'thickly studded.' Wild boars, right? Mean mothers. Hard to kill."

"Maybe that's the idea—'Look at all the boars I've killed. The great Me.'"

"Nah, the helmet has been passed down from a lot of people, this one, that one, like it's really valuable."

220

"Well, Ulysses—that's the Roman version of the name; the Greeks called him Odysseus—" more Cliff Notes—"is an important character. He's always 'the wily Odysseus,' 'the crafty Odysseus.' The archetypal intel officer."

"Yeah, he's putting on the helmet to go out at night and spy. Maybe that's what you and I ought to have, Commander— boar's tooth helmets."

"People would notice."

He read half the pages left in the shitkicker and sighed, wondering if he should bother to finish it, because he knew what was coming. Whiz-bang, nothing like real military life, which was mostly sitting in a cold, empty room waiting for something to happen. He thought about Fidel's "cool" helmet. It was true, helmets were cool. Like getting into flight gear—the helmet was always the most important thing; that's where you put your name, the squadron logo. How about a flight helmet with boar's teeth?

He yawned, went back to reading. Fidel said, "Oh, shee-it." He looked disgusted. "So Ulysses and another guy go out to spy, they capture a kid coming to spy on them, and—get this, Commander—Ulysses says to the kid—where is it?— yeah, here. He says, 'Fear not, let no fear of death be in your mind.' This is an unarmed kid, right? He's a *prisoner*. So Ulysses interrogates him and the kid spills everything he knows and then—and *then*—the other guy kills him: 'Diomed struck him in the middle of the neck with his sword and cut through both sinews so that his head fell rolling to the dust while he was yet speaking.' This is *honor*? Christ, it isn't even good intel work—if you kill them after they talk, the next guy'll never talk!" He meant, Alan thought, that killing the prisoner was both stupid and morally wrong. Wrong *now*, anyway, whatever it was then. Now honor is keeping the contract: talk, and I won't kill you. And the implied contract, the moral contract: I won't torture you, no matter what. Not even for prizes, for glory, for praise—

221

"Well—" Alan was surprised at how much of *The Iliad* he remembered. "They didn't exactly go by the Geneva Convention, did they."

"'The crafty Ulysses,' my ass. He couldn't do what an E-3 does in a Marine tactical intel unit." Fidel shook his head. "These people were weird, just weird."

Half an hour later, Alan made his third trip of the day to the special-forces unit on the far side of the prison. They were handling his communications. When he got back, Fidel was still reading, a ferocious frown on his face, and Alan said, "Sorry to break into story hour, but the snatch team are out. They got him."

Fidel looked disappointed. "That was fast."

"They're in the air, headed here. Couple of hours. We got things to do."

"Right." Fidel put the book in one of the cargo pockets of his pants and scrambled up, stretching and flexing his legs after hours on the floor. One of his knees popped. He caught up with Alan, who was already on his way to the prison, where they had picked out an old office that they could use as an interrogation room. Fidel made a joke. "Promise me you won't cut the guy's head off when we're through with him, okay?"

Naples

Carol Triffler was a skeptic with attitude. She was nearing forty and philosophical about it, a rather angular, long-faced woman who had been a teacher and was working on an MBA now that the kids were almost grown. Like Rose Craik, she had become a kind of mother hen to Leslie—odd, in that Leslie was perfectly capable of taking care of herself in a hostile world.

"Do I want to come to dinner?" Carol was saying. "Sure, I'd love to come to dinner. Noreen'll be here, though." Noreen was seventeen and rather a pain in the ass.

222

"That's fine. We're all going out. Rose will have her two. She says the Neapolitans love families."

"Honey, the Neapolitans manage to control their love when they see skin color. They never got over Ethiopia, you know what I mean? Rose thinks Alan'll actually be back?"

"I don't think she's leaving Bahrain without him. They got thirty days leave. The Navy promised."

"Oh, the Navy promised, oh, good! You can take that right to the bank and get a nickel for it. Is your husband going to make it, too?"

"He said he'd be about a week, and he knows about the date. He'll try."

"Did you know he just sent my husband to Athens? You think they know something we don't?"

"Oh, Carol, come on! You gotta think positive!"

"I do. I'm positive the Navy will find a way to screw us if we're planning a good time. How's that baby doing?"

Leslie, a stickler for truth and an unaware feminist, muttered that it wasn't a baby yet. Then she relaxed and sat still for the lecture that was sure to follow. Carol Triffler had strong views.

Tel Aviv

Dukas was an hour late by the time he got back to his hotel, and the coffee shop was closed. At least he thought that Eshkol had meant to meet at the coffee shop, "where we met before." But six-fifteen on a hot evening, people didn't gather in hotel coffee shops—because they were closed.

Dukas glanced into the hotel's two restaurants, expecting and finding nothing. He had more hopes for the bar, which was below ground level and was meant to suggest, maybe, a pub. He stood in the sudden shadow and let his eyes get accustomed to the gloom and the cigarette smoke and, from the shelter of a mirrored Victorian hall stand the size of a colonial monument to empire, searched the room. Eshkol was sitting alone at a kind of banquette, easy to see from the door—doubtless his intention. Dukas watched him. Eshkol was smoking, sipping beer, looking around. Not a man in a hurry.

Dukas signaled to a middle-aged woman who was delivering drinks to tables, and she hustled over with a smile that meant she'd be glad of the tip but she was overworked as it was. Dukas had his notebook out, and he read her his version of the phonetic pronunciation of "Branch of Marine Exploration." He looked up at her. She said something in Hebrew.

"Did you understand what I said?" he asked her. She nodded, said something else in Hebrew that was a little less patient and smiley, and he gave her a bill and asked her to tell the man over there on the bench that somebody from the Branch of Marine Exploration needed to see him over here.

She grabbed the bill and gave him a more genuine smile and headed for Eshkol. Dukas withdrew behind the Victoriana and waited until Eshkol came into the entryway. He looked annoyed and maybe worried, a solid, stolid-looking man with shoulders a little hunched as if he was hoping to punch somebody out. His eyes did a three-sixty around the entry past the small bar, the armchairs, the two women and one guy waiting there, and finally to Dukas, who was leaning against the wall and waiting like somebody anticipating the moment when the other guy would sit on the whoopee cushion.

"Shalom," Dukas said. "From the entire Branch of Marine Exploration."

Eshkol came close, still looking as if he might punch somebody out. Somebody like Dukas.

"Let's talk," Dukas said, and moved past him toward Eshkol's banquette.

It's awkward, trying to get information from somebody

224

when you're sitting side by side. Maybe that was why Eshkol had chosen the banquette. Although, as he'd set up the meeting, it seemed likely that he wanted to give, not get, information. The awkwardness of the banquette, however, made Dukas think that Eshkol's might not be very good information. Still, he sat down, and Eshkol sat heavily beside him, their shoulders touching, and Dukas ordered a Maccabee.

"Waiting long?" Dukas said.

"You're what Americans call 'cute,' Mister Dukas."

"Nah, I'm ruggedly handsome. The girl over there with her navel hanging out is cute."

Eshkol sipped his beer and stared out at the room. "You play a childish trick on me."

"Well, like they say, you run something up the flagpole and see who salutes." Dukas tried the beer, found it tasty, said, "Okay, enough about me. What's your connection with the Marine Exploration guys?"

Eshkol picked at the label of his beer bottle. "I wanted to meet with you to tell you that it was unwise, going to look at a woman's apartment in Acco."

"That what Tar-Saloman told you to tell me?"

Eshkol lost a beat before answering, his only response to hearing his boss's name."That's what I am telling you."

"People had been there first. Lots of people."

"We had, of course." Eshkol turned his head to look at Dukas. "You think we're stupid? Of course we'd been there. I don't deny it."

"Why were you there? What's your interest?"

"You took down police tape to get in."

"The tape was already down, mostly on the floor. The door was unlocked."

"That policewoman, she's going to get in big trouble one day. She was out of her jurisdiction. Many kilometers out."

"You didn't leave much for us to find. In fact, it was pretty much a wasted trip. You guys find anything?"

Eshkol faked a laugh. "You know I wouldn't tell you. Anyway, we weren't there first."

"Who was?"

Eshkol picked some more at the label. "If you go on forcing your way into places, you're going to be thrown out of Israel. It can happen."

"That's the message? That's the reason for the meeting? 'Back off or we'll toss you out'?"

"You're here with the permission of the State of Israel. The demarche gives you a little cover, but don't think it's a warrant."

"No. I just learned you guys negatived my forensics team again. 'Welcome to Israel, please check all investigative tools at the border.' I'm going to complain, you know."

Eshkol faked the laugh again. "Sharon will be terrified."

"So tell me about the Branch of Marine Exploration."

"Never heard of it."

"Oh, come on!"

Eshkol shook his head.

"There's this office out in Jaffa—four guys and some scuba tanks and a stack of girlie magazines you could jerk off to for the rest of your life. Four guys with a sat dish and a big TV and a sofa and a lot of shit-for-brains reading matter. Four guys who use an office as a place to sit around and wait until they get an order."

"Sounds like a poorly managed business."

"Sounds like four rent-a-thugs."

Eshkol shrugged.

"Where are they?"

Eshkol signaled to the waitress, and when she acknowledged him he said something that didn't sound like another Maccabee. He threw some money on the table and slid sideways out of the banquette. "You disappointed me, Michael. I thought you were smarter."

"Is that your message?"

Eshkol was standing. He leaned down so nobody else could hear him. "My message is to stop pushing us so hard. We got real problems to deal with, Michael, really bad people; we don't need this pushing all the time from you." He stared into Dukas's eyes. "Let us do our job. We're trying to keep a lot of shits from killing innocent people. Don't get in our way." He made it a plea, not a demand.

Dukas said, "When do I get the body for an autopsy?"

Eshkol straightened, muttered, "Oh, Jesus!" and strode away. Dukas went up to his room and called his wife and felt horny, and then he ordered sandwiches and chocolate-truffle ice cream from room service and sat there with the television flinging images at him and the phone book open in his lap, looking for the Branch of Marine Exploration, a tough act when you don't read Hebrew.

Israel was full of what Ray Spinner's mother called "Jewish people," so as not to offend them by calling them Jews. Not only were there people who looked like American Jews, but there were also people who looked like Ethiopian, Yemeni, Russian, and Palestinian Jews. There were Jews in halter tops and butt-crack shorts, and there were Jews in black hats and ringlets. There were Jewish food, Jewish music, Jewish smells, and Jewish speech, which Spinner thought of as loud and somehow abrasive, even when he couldn't understand what people were saying. There were even lots and lots of people who didn't look Jewish.

The department had found him a hotel a little out from the with-it part of the city, a perfectly decent little place that you'd think was fine if you were from Denmark and just wanted a cheap tour package. McKinnon was probably showing his sense of humor in putting Spinner there—Spinner could imagine McKinnon telling the travel people to find something "not too American." Americans on official business had to stay in the really good places because of security; Spinner, not being

227

on official anything, had been put in a place where he could get blown up by a twelve-year-old with a pipe bomb. If anybody wanted to blow up such a place. The bathroom was the size of an old-fashioned telephone booth, no tub, and had been cut out of a bedroom that had been none too big to start with. There was a lot of plastic and a lot more veneer.

"Shalom and oy veh," Spinner said. He unpacked and got out his instruction sheet and went through enormous grief walking what was called a "counter-surveillance route" and doing a lot of rigmarole, and at last he came face-to-face with Habakkuk in a café where Spinner doubted anybody ever washed his hands after going to the john.

"I am Habakkuk," the man said, as if he was a celebrity. He was about fifty, sandy hair going gray, a suit and tie and an expression like a teed-off priest. Spinner remembered that McKinnon had said that Habakkuk was an academic, and the guy had that look. And manner—critical, condescending. Also as if he was too busy for anybody but God. "What do you want?"

Spinner thought that he should get up and walk out, because anybody could say he was Habakkuk, but who else was he likely to be—Yasser Arafat? So Spinner put his forearms on the table and looked as belligerent as he could and said, "Salem Qatib."

"You want somebody named Salem Qatib?"

"He was connected to the illegal trade in antiquities. I want to make contact with people who know all that stuff." Now that he was saying it, it sounded stupid. In fact idiotic.

But Habakkuk kept his focus. "Information costs money. Difficult contacts cost more money." To Spinner's surprise, he put on a wheedling tone. "My life is very expensive. This is an expensive country to live in. To provide the information I do, it isn't easy, you know. Or cheap! I make plenty sacrifices for you people as it is."

"We know about your needs." Spinner didn't know zip about

the guy's needs, but he realized he was supposed to sound confident. "We can, mmm, recompense you. Up to a point."

"I do this from my passion for freedom."

"Of course."

Habakkuk banged a fist on his left lapel. "In my heart, always the freedom of Israel is like a big bell! Freedom! Freedom! Freedom! I have given my life to this cause." He had good eye contact. Better than Spinner's. "But I have needs. You don't appreciate my needs; you don't appreciate what I sacrifice. I have two daughters, a son. A wife who is—a wonderful woman, but not a— She doesn't share my passion. She knows nothing of this life—" He made a gesture, fingers waving back and forth between them—this life, *you and me.* "Keeping up the façade of normalcy is vital to my work. The work I do for you, I mean. She cannot live on air! My wife, I mean. My children. Are they to be sacrificed to my passion? Are they to be in rags, uneducated, ill fed? No. They must be the children of the intelligentsia they seem, so that I may carry on our work." Again the finger gesture. *Our* work.

McKinnon had said the man was venal. And idealistic. Well, McKinnon was right. "We can pay. A certain amount."

"I need twenty-five thousand, US."

Spinner had ten thousand in hundreds in a belt under his pants. He could get more if he had to; McKinnon had winkled out the name of a cooperative bank from the neocons above him at DoD. "We'll pay for results," he said. He didn't want to have to go into the men's room and take his pants down to get at the money right then.

"I need twenty-five thousand."

"We'll see. I must be put into contact with useful people— people close to the illegal antiquities trade. Palestinians."

Habakkuk sucked in his breath as if Palestinians cost more. "Dangerous for me," he said. "I would do this for love—" he whacked his chest again—"but I have needs. My life is not easy. Huge tension. Enemies. The intelligence services."

"You'll be paid. But I have to have results." Spinner tried to look square-jawed and forceful. "Also, I want to be put in touch with Deborah."

The other man jerked. "Never!" He brought his fists down on the table, but softly, so that they made no sound. "Not for a million dollars cash would I give you Deborah!"

Spinner tried to argue, then to plead. No good. Habakkuk's limit had been reached; he said again that not even big money would budge him. End of conversation. They both sulked and then changed the subject.

Habakkuk asked some questions about exactly what Spinner wanted: actual dealers in illegal antiquities? the Palestinians who dug things up or the Palestinians who ran things? the police? "This man you named. Who is he?"

"Salem Qatib."

"That one."

"He's dead."

Habakkuk sucked in his breath. The price was going up. Spinner told him the bare bones of what he knew about Salem Qatib's death. Habakkuk told him he had contacts in the police—he had contacts everywhere; he was worth his weight in gold—and he would test the waters.

They talked about how to meet again, and Habakkuk said that all that spy rigmarole was utter crap, and he could always be reached through a certain cigar store by asking for Mister Ashplant.

"I thought you're the one who made up the rigmarole," Spinner said. "The plan."

Habakkuk shrugged. "I wanted you followed for a little. To see who you were."

They parted. Spinner felt drained by this first adventure into espionage, but drained in a way that elated him. *He had done it!* He had made an actual clandestine meeting. He had set things going. He would succeed!

Three Mossad people, two women and a man, followed

him from the café back to his hotel. Two other agents had already been in his room, searching everything.

An hour later, Habakkuk's report on his meeting with Spinner was vetted by a Mossad analyst and routed to Shlomo Eshkol's boss—David Tar-Saloman.

That day, a suicide bomber, presumably Palestinian, blew himself up in Tel Aviv and wounded more than twenty people. Israeli aircraft destroyed a Palestinian Authority compound and a security headquarters in Gaza. Israeli soldiers killed two members of Hamas.

14

Athens

Piat left Mara's bed in the first gray light of another wet winter's day in Athens. He was cold when he left Barry's apartment, and the cold stayed high on his back and in his spine as he walked south, away from the Acropolis, through the working-class housing and ugly high-rise apartments. He hesitated at the top of the escalator into the subway and turned away, hoping that a longer walk would burn off his revulsion.

It didn't.

He was still drunk when he started walking. Sobriety hit him as he plodded past the endless car and motorcycle dealerships. Then he was thirsty. Early-morning rush-hour traffic passed him, one of very few pedestrians in a vehicular world. Where the road was being widened for the Olympics, there was no sidewalk. Piat didn't care. He liked to walk. In Afghanistan and the Far East, he had made his name by being willing to walk hundreds of miles where other American officers would insist on transportation. Piat had once rescued an asset from the Chinese in Burma by walking sixty miles over the border, picking the guy up and walking him back while his COS debated helicopters and air support.

Thinking about the Far East made Piat think about George Shreed. George had been Piat's boss, then his hero and mentor, and he was dead now. *Bear, all the good ones are dead now. All that's left is manipulative creeps like me, and organized bureaucrats like Partlow, and patsies like you.*

Sitting on Lesvos, Piat had begun to convince himself that he could walk away from it all. He was sorry to see how easily he took it all back, the guilt and the power over others.

It made him want another drink. Instead, he walked nine miles through cold rain and leaded smog, made stops and turns by professional habit and was standing outside Mikhail's shop when the young man came to open it.

"Twice in two days!" Mikhail said. He smiled and offered Piat an embrace.

Piat accepted. Mikhail, the keys to his shop in his hand, shrugged and pointed up the street. "Me, I'd like to get a coffee. You?"

The coffee shop had a shining glass counter, etched glass windows, and paint so new its smell almost obscured the odor of coffee. The coffee shop had just opened and had a computer in place of a cash register, and the service was fast and efficient. It was like an advertisement for the European Union.

This early, the shop bustled, with workers coming in and leaving—men in suits, women in skirts, but also construction workers and artisans. Mikhail took his coffee to a table and motioned for Piat to sit.

"Listen, Sasha," he began. Piat had to adapt to this name change. He was out of practice. He *was* Sasha to Mikhail.

"I'm all ears." Piat leaned forward smiling, trying to hide his fatigue and the sudden tension he felt at Mikhail's reserve.

"All ears? Ah—so you listen well. Okay. That piece of paper—" He hesitated.

"Yes? I know," Piat said.

"You have a photo? Is this thing real?"

"You tell me."

"From a drawing?" Mikhail shook his head.

"It's a good drawing. I did it myself."

233

Mikhail looked at him, drank some coffee, took out the drawing—already much creased and a little dirty. Piat could see that Mikhail had spent a lot of time with it. He spread it on the table and then covered it with his arms and leaned close. "Is gold?" he asked.

"Yes. It says so on the drawing."

"So. I saw. Had to ask. Gold. With niello? Here, the dark?"

Piat narrowed his eyes. "Yes, Mikhail. Again, it says so on the drawing."

Mikhail looked unhappy. "Show me a photo."

Piat weighed the risks and took out his laptop, loaded the CD. Mikhail watched silently, but his mouth made a little "o" when the first picture appeared.

Piat let him look for a minute. Then he closed the laptop with a snap. "Okay, Mikhail. That's it. Fake?"

Mikhail shrugged.

"Could it be done?" Piat asked.

Mikhail looked at him unhappily. "Maybe. Maybe not. *Kriste*, it is a beautiful thing! Is it not, Sasha?"

Piat admitted that it was.

"Let me see it again."

Piat opened the computer. Mikhail drank it in with his coffee. Finally, he closed it himself. "Okay." He pointed at the drawing. "The gold? Five men in Athens, maybe twenty in Rome and Naples, maybe ten more in Morocco and Spain—all can do this. The gold, patina, polish, dents—you know?"

Piat did know. He nodded.

"Okay. The niello—maybe five people in the world. Maybe more—I don't know the Americas. Myself, I could do it if I could try some things, experiment, maybe screw it up two or three times until I had the feel for it—you know?"

This time Piat didn't know—it was the craftsman speaking, not the forger. But Piat respected his opinion, so he nodded again.

"Last I turn to the figures and the—how do I say? Letters? Symbols?"

Piat interjected, "The Linear B."

"You know that? Okay—good. Drawing the figures so that they are right—neat, clean, to scale, and just like everything we know about Mycenaean art—very small group of artists you get left with. The Linear B—I have no clue where you find some guy who puts that together."

Piat nodded again. "But it could be done."

"Sure," Mikhail answered, but he shook his head *no*. "For half a million US dollars, I could do it."

Piat winced. "That much?"

"It would take me six months, and so many people would have to be paid." Mikhail shrugged. "This is not for real, right? You just want to know if this could have been done? Okay. It could. But I don't think so." Mikhail got up, leaving the paper on the table with his coffee cup. "I got work to do, okay? Sasha, listen. I hear things. Things about things that come out of the ground, you know? I maybe hear something about this thing. You be careful." He gave Piat's arm a hard squeeze and then he was out the door.

Half an hour later, Piat boarded the ferry to Lesvos. He knew he was alone.

The Swain was waiting on the ferry. Piat spotted him in the passenger lounge. He was with two older men in windbreakers and designer jeans. The last fog of Piat's hangover boiled away under the impact of adrenaline, because the Swain had allies who were not teenagers, and that changed everything.

And somewhere, there were Israelis. On the same boat? Piat locked himself in his cabin thinking that crime and espionage had to be good for tourism.

Tel Aviv

The next day was wall-to-wall boredom for Dukas until Dick Triffler called from Athens.

Triffler had flown over the night before and had been at work at eight. By eleven, he had been through four of the five sources he had been given introductions to. He met the fifth, a woman, for coffee at eleven-fifteen, and at noon Athens time he had a report for Dukas and was ready to fly home to his wife, children, and *Madama Butterfly* at the San Carlo. Except for one shady character Dukas's pal in The Hague had mentioned but Triffler was sure he didn't want to bother with.

"A place called Tel-Sharm-Heir'at," Triffler said after they'd gone through the preliminaries. Triffler was pretty good at languages; his gutturals were great. Maybe it came from singing.

"What about it?"

"It's near the coast in Gaza. The word here is that there was a big score there within days, and the stuff is starting to come out. Or stories about it are, anyway."

"Spell."

Triffler spelled Tel-Sharm-Heir'at and pronounced it a few times so that Dukas could cobble up a phonetic version.

"Okay, what are they saying?"

"Ah, this is where it gets ver-r-r-y interesting. The word is—and this is rumor in the archaeological community, Mike; nobody's *seen* anything yet—the word is that— In a word, the word is *Greek*. Not Egyptian or whatever they expect to find down there, but Greek, as in—"

"Yeah, yeah, Alexander the Great and all that. So what?"

"No, not as in Alexander the Great—that's the point! Greek as in early Greek, Mike. *Early* Greek."

"I'm Greek. What the hell does early mean?"

"Nobody's sure, but they're saying early. Think, Mike— you have to think now; put the comic book down—you're in Israel, what have they got to do with the early Greeks?"

"Nothing, for Christ's sake."

"Exactly."

Dukas scowled at the phone. Sometimes he thought that Triffler was smarter than he was, and sometimes he thought that Triffler simply did these things for a joke. "Okay, give me the lecture: what am I supposed to see that I don't?"

"Don't feel bad. I had to have it explained, too. Just had coffee with a fascinating Greek woman. Fifty, rail-thin, eyes as big as doorknobs, and *smart*. I'll give it to you in a sentence, although it's an involved and elegant theory: if the Greeks were entrenched on the coast early, then a lot of Jewish history is bullshit." He waited. "Was that simple enough?"

"In what way bullshit?"

"As in bullshit. As in never happened. As in conservative Jews, not to mention Christians, have built their claims to Israel on sand. As in, the 'God gave the land to us' line is moot and the Palestinians have an equal claim."

"As in dynamite."

"You got it."

"But all this is pie in the sky."

"Yes and no. Everybody I talked to has heard the rumor. Three of them, most of all the fascinating lady with the big eyes, have got some details. She says she has 'a source,' and her source says that somebody's rumored to be translating something from a language that may be Greek before it got to be Greek. She says maybe another guy saw a picture of something from the dig. You put two and two together, you get something being found that has an inscription that's written in dynamite."

"But it's only rumor."

"So far."

"But it's connected with this—" he looked at his scribbles—"Tel-Sharm-Heir'at?"

"That's the gossip."

"And the Palestinians?"

"Three of my people say the dig was done illegally by the Palestinians 'as usual,' but the ones who know about it say the talk about Greek is coming from other places. They're cagey about that. Some of it's right here in Athens, I'm sure, but the lady implied that there's some sort of international network and the buzz there is an inscription. Can I go home now?"

"You hit everybody on your list?"

"Well, there's the guy your pal Pigoreau gave you the name of—'Barry'. I asked my super-bright lady about him; she laughed—she says he's a hash hound, very shady—it'd cost money and take time—"

"You better talk to him."

"I don't think it's worth it."

"What you think is, you might miss the opera. Go talk to him."

"You're ruining my cultural life."

"You can sing *Madama Butterfly* lots better than some Italian broad, anyway."

Athens

Athens was rainy and cold, no matter what the travel posters said. It was January, after all; Naples had been pretty cold when he had left, too. *The sunny Mediterranean.* Triffler looked again at the slip of paper with "Barry's" address on it and stood at an intersection, looking at street signs in letters he couldn't read. However, a nearby taverna solved all his problems—lunch, English, and directions he could follow. The waiter seemed to find it a bit comical that a light-skinned African American in a thousand-dollar suit was looking for somebody in that part of town, but, for a good tip, he helped him.

Triffler found himself walking uphill, the neighborhood suddenly changing from the anywhere architecture of the 1960s to European nineteenth century and then to scruffy medieval, or maybe BCE. *It's like walking out of Athens and into Greece*, he thought. He liked it up there. Was he on a slope of the Acropolis? Winding alleys, low roofs, closed-up windows. *Nice.*

He knocked on the door of what was supposed to be his man's house. Silence answered. Deep, heavy, wet silence. Triffler knocked again, then found a bell-push where you'd expect to find a peephole (*Who was stupid enough to put a bell-push in the middle of a door?*), pushed but got nothing, finally realized it wasn't a push but a twist—speaking of stupid, why had he been stupid enough to think somebody was going to wire up a bell across a hinged opening? He twisted. He could *feel* the bell as well as hear it, a chattering clang.

After enough time for him to think nobody was home and if he left right then he could still hear *Madama Butterfly*, there was clanking and clacking, locks and bolts moving, and the door opened and a tall, gaunt woman who hadn't smiled in several decades said something in Greek.

"I'm looking for Barry. Mrs Mercouri recommended him to me." Mrs Mercouri was the dynamic woman with the headlight eyes, and she hadn't recommended anything, but Triffler could hardly say that he'd got a hot tip from a guy in the war crimes business.

She looked at him. Some people have that ability—to look at others without expression, without blinking, without looking away. Triffler associated it with madness. He got out his wallet and held out one of his business cards. "Richard Triffler, special agent. Naval Criminal Investigative Service. US."

Maybe she didn't speak English. Maybe she was deaf. No, because her mouth was opening, and the words that came out were, "How much?"

"Excuse me, ma'am?"

"How much? Barry's busy. His time is money."

Triffler knew all about agents and money. Barry wasn't an agent, of course, but the woman reminded him of agents' wives and girlfriends and lovers he'd known, people who wanted to negotiate a better deal. So Triffler jumped in with both feet. "It depends on how much Barry has to tell me." While part of his brain was saying, *Or is Barry somebody's agent after all? He's got the wife for it.*

"My husband's an internationally known scholar. He doesn't have anything to tell you."

There was a dog in Greek mythology, Triffler thought, who guarded something or other. Cerberus. The woman was Barry's Cerberus. Somebody had got around the original Cerberus by giving him something. Oh, yes, Cerberus had guarded the door to hell. Somebody had given him cake and somebody else had sung for him.

Triffler didn't think singing would work here, and he didn't have any cake.

He got out his wallet and took out one of two American hundreds he kept there for dicey moments and handed it over. "That's for you. Barry and I will negotiate for more later."

Cerberus looked at the hundred. She hadn't looked at his card. Money talks; cards don't. She stood aside and let him walk in.

Barry was *very* like an agent, he thought.

Because Triffler knew agents, he knew Barry within a couple of minutes. That he was a hash-head was helpful, too, but what helped the most was experience. Five minutes with Barry and Triffler knew he was egocentric, insecure, and arrogant. Also deep-down pathetic, a fantasist who could never keep from screwing up his own best chances. Plus American, slovenly, smart, self-destructive, and vain.

"I'm very busy with an important, a *very* important, scholarly project," Barry was saying for the third time. "I can't have people coming here, interrupting me."

"I was told you were the only man in Athens who could answer my questions. Maybe the only man in the world."

Barry muttered something about that being a lot of balls, but he was pleased. "Who ever said such a thing?" he purred.

"I was told you were the only man who could set me straight about some early Greek things."

"I can hardly imagine what 'early Greek' could even mean." Said in the sneering tone of a don to somebody who'd made a terrible gaffe and was certainly below him in class, as well.

"You tell me."

"My dear chap, some people say words like 'early Greek' when they mean the Byzantines." He tittered. "Or that horrible Hellenistic stuff. Do these terms mean anything to you?"

"I was thinking more of when the Greeks were on the coast down toward Egypt."

Barry's eyes flicked away and looked back, slightly dilated; the corners of his lips twitch-smiled as if he had a secret. "'The Sea People,' I suppose you mean."

"You tell me."

"Mister, mmm, I've forgotten your name, I'm so sorry—I don't have time to give a course in early Greek history. Any good textbook would do. Happy to recommend one."

"But you're the world authority."

"I'm afraid I don't understand your interest. The interest of the—" He looked at the card that Triffler had given him. "Naval Criminal What's-It. Is it naval because it's the coast?" But it had been Triffler's impression that Barry had known exactly what the Naval Criminal Investigative Service was when he had first looked at the card, because his face had suffered a spasm of fear.

"We got very privileged information that something had turned up with really important data on the early Greeks and the Gaza coast." *Privileged information* was bullshit, but Triffler knew that Barry was too hungry for praise to see it. "I've been all over Athens, finding the one man who can help us." He smiled, pointed. "You."

241

Barry gave a falsely modest moue, a coy tip of his head.

"The word is," Triffler went on, "that there's a new find that's going to blow early history sky-high. Maybe—the era of the Trojan War—?"

Barry erupted in anger. "Who told you such a thing? Who's blabbing such, such—"

"It's a story we got." He made a guess, based on a hint one of his Athenian sources had dropped. "The internet—"

"Those fools!" Barry struck the arms of his chair with his fists like a petulant child. "Fools and liars—I'm surrounded by fools and liars!" Red-faced, he stared at Triffler. "I'm about to make a major contribution to scholarship. I'm in negotiations with Cambridge for a professorship! And they all want to steal it from me!"

"That's terrible; that's disgusting! How can people be like that?" Triffler made a little speech about scholarship and the sanctity of knowledge, and he said he was only a layman and all he wanted was information, only a little of Barry's knowledge; he'd promise confidentiality; none of those people who wanted to steal Barry's achievement would get a thing out of him, and he'd pay good money—expertise deserved reward.

Barry hit his fists a couple of times on the arms of his chair and then relaxed his hands and put his head back, closed his eyes and breathed deeply and then, with a sly little smile, looked at Triffler and said, "I suppose you've never heard of Linear B, have you."

Bingo, Triffler thought, and he began calculating how much money he could get with his ATM card and where the nearest cashpoint was.

But he said he hadn't ever heard of Linear B—although he had; Mrs Mercouri had mentioned it—but he wanted to know what it was, and he did his dumb-cop act, and one thing led to another, and fifteen minutes later Barry took him into another room and began to show him photographs of a metal vase-like thing and explain how he, and only he, had translated a Linear B inscription that was going to rock the world on its foundations.

Tel Aviv

Dukas made an appointment with the chief of station, then checked some books in the embassy library, and then he placed some calls to his recent contacts at the University of Michigan. At three, he telephoned Miriam Gurion, who was distinctly chilly but who at least listened.

"Tel-Sharm-Heir'at," he said.

"What is that?"

"In Gaza. A recent illegal dig. Maybe where Salem Qatib was working. Want to take me there?"

"I do not want to do anything with you, Mister Dukas. I wash my hands of you."

"You interested in who killed Salem Qatib or aren't you?"

"You can't get into Gaza. Your embassy won't let you."

"Wanna bet? I'll get back to you. In the meantime, find out where this Tel-Sharm-Heir'at is."

By four, he had the chief of station's permission to go into Gaza, and he had retrieved his old UN passport from the embassy safe where he'd stashed it. The chief of station had offered Roger's services again, but Dukas had turned them down. "A guy with a gun won't protect me against five million people. I'll take my chances." She said she thought that was probably wise, but most people were nervous about security.

"Me, too, but I can live with being nervous. How you coming with setting up a meeting with the Palestinian honcho—the 'Tax Collector'?"

She was working on it. The meeting would probably be in Cairo, and they were at the stage of working out a meeting plan, but nothing was set yet. Should she send one of the CIA people? Or did he have a candidate?

"How about Abe Peretz?"

"The LegAt? Kind of an odd choice."

"He's ex-Navy; his Arabic's pretty good; most important, I know him and trust him."

She cocked an eyebrow, gave him a grin. "Most important, he isn't CIA." She didn't commit herself but she didn't say it was the worst idea she'd ever heard, either.

He called Miriam Gurion back. Tel-Sharm-Heir'at was just over the border, she said—as, in fact, he'd suspected. An hour's drive, two if the border was shitty.

"Tomorrow morning?" she said.

"Now."

"I am busy."

"And I'm getting tired of Tel Aviv. Now or never."

"I am tempted to say 'never.'"

"Your call."

"You broke Mosher's spirit. He is a weak man, my God, do I know that!—but you were cruel to him. Now they've fired him and put in somebody else who's closed the facility 'for reasons of national security.' It serves you right—now you'll never get in there to have a look inside that office."

"Well, that doesn't change anything about going to this Tel-Sharm-Heir'at place. Now or never."

She made an angry, spitting sound. "Pick me up at Dizengoff Street."

Spinner had a message to call Mr Ashplant, which got to him via the hotel's front desk as Mr Assplan, but he figured out what it meant. He looked at his communications plan, first ripping off the pages with a lot of bullshit about telephones and an X on a kiosk and a cigar store; in a few minutes, he'd burn them in the toilet. Right now, he was looking for the telephone signal—yes. Mr Ashplant. In response, he was to go to a public phone and dial a number.

As good as done.

He burned the pages in the toilet and flushed them down; aflame, they floated on the water, endangering but not melting the plastic seat. Bits of charred paper floated on the surface when he was done, and he flushed again. He dressed and went out to the same public telephone as yesterday, called, and a voice said in English, "Yes, Ashplant."

"Mister Ashplant's flowers are ready." That's what he was supposed to say. He wondered who had made that up, what had inspired the flowers—why not shirts or his car?

"Meet him where he told you." The line went dead.

Spinner walked to the cigar store Habakkuk had named. Habakkuk was inside buying cigars.

"Ah, there you are," Habakkuk said. "Do you smoke?"

"No—no, never have."

Habakkuk exchanged a pitying look with the man behind the counter. A box of cigars changed hands, then a good deal of money. *No wonder you're holding us up for more.*

"Back way." Habakkuk led him out, past a smelly toilet, across a parking lot. They went into a supermarket and Habakkuk began pushing a cart around. As it turned out, he really was shopping. He liked expensive food, too. "You are meeting somebody in an hour," he said. "This is a real coup; I didn't think I could pull it off. You know, contacts are like fish—you wait and wait, and then they nibble, and you pull a little and pull, pull, pull, you bring them in. Difficult, but worth it. I need five thousand dollars."

"What, now?"

"Yes, yes, you don't think they do this for free, do you? *I* can be put off; *I* can be told to wait for my money, but not these people. He demands five thousand to talk to you."

"Who is he?"

"Intelligence. Fairly highly placed. Disenchanted with the cynicism of his trade. Willing to help the cause of truth and freedom. Five thousand." He eyed Spinner. "You have five thousand?"

245

Spinner still had the belt on. He looked around the store, which was exactly like a big supermarket at home. "I have to get someplace private—"

"Over behind the lettuce. Behind the man with the hose. And bring some back for me, please."

Spinner thought he might just as well, as Habakkuk was delivering the goods. Or seemed to be, anyway. He went into the single stall and dropped his pants and wiggled the belt around so he could unzip the pocket, and he counted out ten little packets of hundreds and zipped up and pulled up and tucked and put five thousand in each side pocket of his sport coat and went out. He had to look in every aisle before he finally found his man.

"How do we do this?" he said.

"Just give it to me. Don't be squeamish. What, you think there are hidden cameras?"

In fact, there was a security camera at the end of the aisle. Spinner turned his back on it and, keeping his elbows close to his sides, fished out the packets of bills and dropped them into the cart, muttering, "For him; for you."

Then they went to the checkout and, while Habakkuk was packing his car, he told Spinner the mumbo-jumbo of identifying codes by which he and the fairly high-level intelligence person would recognize each other. It was Mickey Mouse but quite exciting.

The contact was an unhappy-looking man in his forties with the face and stance of a boxer. He was wearing a golf jacket and rather baggy chinos. He listened to Spinner's identifying code sentence with what seemed to be distaste and then delivered his own in a tone that sounded suspiciously like mockery. Spinner took this as a sign of self-disgust, the angst of the seasoned intelligence professional.

The man said his name was Shlomo. "You want to know about Salem Qatib?" He laid it all out for Spinner without a lot of side issues or backtracking: Salem Qatib had been murdered by people from the Palestinian Authority because they had tortured him beyond recovery, trying to learn the secrets of American cryptology. The Palestinian Authority was desperate for money—there was so much corruption—and was gathering information about American codes and selling it to al-Qaida. They were getting millions for it. Certain elements in Israeli intelligence were trying to hide what was happening because they didn't want the US to think they'd fallen down on the job; therefore, they were saying that Qatib had been killed because of some sort of archaeological business, but that was all smoke and mirrors.

"So it isn't archaeology!"

"It was never archaeology. It's cryptology." Shlomo turned sideways to look at him—they were sitting next to each other on a park bench—and said, "Tell your people to go after the Palestinians. In the name of God, don't they understand what's going on?" And he got up and walked away.

Spinner thought that was great. That was just great! Espionage was a lot more fun than analysis.

Gaza

Dukas's car came up a low rise that must once have been the last berm before the sea, and at the top they could look down a mile-long plain with the Mediterranean at the far end. Directly in front of them on the road, a hundred yards away, were six Israeli soldiers and a vehicle and two rows of metal spikes laid on the tarmac.

"Stop!" Miriam Gurion had a hand on his arm, her voice sharp with irritation and perhaps alarm. Dukas braked too hard and the tires squealed. Miriam turned and said something to the man in the back seat, a Palestinian they had picked up at the border who was some sort of liaison between Israeli cops and the PA's security force. Miriam had made a face and said, "They're our enemies, but we have common

247

problems. We have to work with them. Anyway, today we need him."

Now, the Palestinian ducked his head to look through the windshield. "Tel-Sharm-Heir'at," he said, pointing ahead.

Dukas put the car into low and went slowly to the checkpoint. A brusque young Israeli soldier looked at his passport and Miriam's police ID, and, after some chatter back and forth, she said that this was as far as they could go. They could pull the car off here and look, but that was all.

A faint slope rose from the road to their left. They climbed it for a few strides and looked down. Below them was Tel-Sharm-Heir'at: two mobile homes and a water truck on a three-acre site that had been bulldozed flat. Three civilians with assault rifles were standing by the trailers, watching them.

"What does the sign say?" Dukas asked.

"'The New Jewish Community of Sharm-Heirat.'"

"Ask our friend if this was here yesterday."

"He says no."

"Ask him if this is where the digging was done."

Words, nods. "Yes. Last week, this was an excavation."

Dukas nodded. "Figures."

The Palestinian pointed at half a dozen bulldozers parked a hundred yards away. He said they might know something over there.

Dukas dropped Miriam Gurion at Dizengoff Street and headed for the embassy. By the time he had got rid of the car and reached his office, she had already called once and had left a message marked "Urgent" for him to call back. When he reached her, she said, "Salem Qatib's remains have been delivered."

He knew from her tone that something was wrong. "Can your people do the autopsy?"

"He's been cremated." She hung up.

248

Tel Aviv

Spinner woke after midnight. He felt loose, relaxed, as if somebody had opened a tap in his foot and let all his juices out. Then he remembered Elana. He felt in the bed but she wasn't there.

There was a sound from the bathroom. Spinner smiled into the dark.

Elana was a cryptologist in the counter-intelligence section of the Ministry of Defense. She needed money, Habakkuk had said, the reason that she was willing to meet with him. She was a single mother, her husband killed in a car bombing. "Don't be rough with her; she's vulnerable," Habakkuk had said. The meeting with her had turned into dinner and then bed—and sex, as Spinner told himself now, to die for. She had wept after her first orgasm. She had said he was the first man she had been with since—since—

It was all great, except that an inner voice he didn't like kept saying it had been too easy. He tried to tell the voice that he was an attractive guy; she was horny; they had hit it off. The voice said, *It was too easy.* The voice went on to say that everything was being too easy, and he told it to shut up.

He drifted off, trying to ignore the voice by planning the report he would send to McKinnon. Opening with a quotation from Strauss on the state of perpetual war in which the purified state finds itself: "Justice in 'peace' is the allied individuals' conduct toward neutrals; there is never simply peace." Dynamite.

Too easy, the voice said.

The Aegean

In his cabin on the ferry, Piat couldn't sleep, and he couldn't read Greek, and he couldn't look at the cup anymore because it made him think about Barry. He decided that one drink, maybe a glass of wine, would settle him. He went to the bar.

The glass of wine turned into Scotch. He had a couple. Various scenes still chased themselves through his head.

"Mister Furman?"

Piat looked up from his empty glass to find that both of the men in designer jeans he had seen with the Swain were standing over him at the bar. They were big men, and the bigger one took the stool next to him. The other lurked too close.

"Yeah?" Piat focused on the bigger one. He was wearing an aftershave that stuck in Piat's throat.

"We need a few minutes of your time."

"Yeah?" Piat beat his thoughts into order. *Arab or Palestinian. Friends of the Swain.* And then, *This is trouble.* Adrenaline charged to his rescue.

"This is a delicate matter." The man standing at Piat's elbow had almost no accent. "Perhaps we could go to your cabin?"

"I don't think so." *Stupid to have come to the bar,* he thought. *Should have stayed in my cabin to start with.* "What's this about?"

The one with the aftershave responded. "We think you may have something of ours, Mister Furman."

"I don't think so. Who the hell are you guys, anyway?" Piat was good at outraged drunken innocence.

"We're businessmen, Mister Furman. And we have reason to think you might have something of ours." The man standing at his elbow had the hair of a television personality, as carefully managed as a golf green.

Piat christened them Cologne and Hair. "No idea what you guys are talking about. Want a beer?" He raised his glass to Cologne.

"No, Mister Furman. We would appreciate your cooperation. We are prepared to pay you to cooperate."

"Hey, is this a survey?" Piat thought he might get away with bolting, but he wasn't sure, and so far it wasn't worth the risk. "How do you know my name, anyway?"

Hair leaned over him. "You deal in antiquities, Mister

250

Furman. You were contacted by Miss Saida Frayj. We know that. She sold you something, I think?"

Piat straightened up as if focusing for the first time. "What the fuck are you talking about, bud?"

"No need to become angry, Mister Furman."

"I'm not angry. I just don't know you, or what the fuck you are on about." Piat turned his head to Hair. "You're standing a little too close, buddy. Back off."

Hair did not back off. He leaned over. "Mister Furman—" he began.

Piat stood up.

Hair backed away. It was that or get knocked over. His reaction was slow.

Piat sat down again and held his arm out so that Hair couldn't approach him without walking into the hand. All posturing. "Right there is good. Okay? Now who are you guys again?"

Hair was angry. Cologne tried to cover it. "We're businessmen, Mister Furman, and we would like to pay you for some information on Miss Frayj. Okay?"

"Gents, I have no clue what you're talking about." Piat was in action mode now. He was trapped on the boat with them and he didn't need to get arrested on a ferry for getting into a fight, which would lead to a lot of questions he couldn't answer. On the other hand, he couldn't see any good coming from talking to these guys. And he really didn't want to be alone with them. They had violence all over their body language. "No idea who you are talking about." He shrugged.

Cologne looked at Hair.

"Hey, could you just sit down?" Piat pointed at the bar stool beyond Cologne.

"I prefer to stand." Hair gave a small, careful smile.

Piat felt Hair was escalating—moving toward violence. Piat was trying to figure out who they really were and what they were really after. The cup, obviously, but why? They might be organized crime, but—organized crime and Arab came together. Palestinian Authority. Hoods from the hood.

And Israelis on the Swain. That made some sort of sense.

Cologne held up a hand for Piat's attention, a forceful gesture that made Piat flinch. "Mister Furman, let's not let this become adversarial. Did Miss Frayj sell you something?"

Piat decided that he needed out of this. The boat was not very full, but the passenger decks had people on them and Piat couldn't believe that these guys could survive police scrutiny any more than he could.

On the other hand, the continued absence of the bartender suggested that someone had paid him to stay out of the bar.

Piat placed his glass on the bar with exaggerated attention and started to stand up again. This time, Hair put a hand on his shoulder and pushed him down. Piat went with the push, apparently tangled in his bar stool, and fell heavily. Somehow, his drunken spill and his attempt to grab Hair for support ended with him kneeling behind Hair with Hair's right arm pinned against his back and his right hand twisted at a very painful angle.

Piat's left hand brushed along Hair's waistband and removed the small, flat pistol there. His adrenaline spiked. He hadn't expected them to have guns. Now he knew they weren't thugs. They were somebody's government's thugs. He stood up, releasing Hair and working the slide of the pistol. A cartridge fell to the floor, thudding against the thick pile of the carpet. He thumbed the safety, wondering what kind of idiot had a cocked pistol with a round up the spout in his pants. Stupid people scared him. Piat was thoroughly scared.

"On the fucking floor. Both of you." Piat's voice shook.

"Mister Furman, you are making a serious mistake." Cologne spread his hands wide. Hair's face was a mask of rage and pain. He held his right hand in his left.

Piat stepped farther from them. "Whatever." He took

252

another step away and lifted the bar's courtesy phone. "Get the fuck on the floor or I get ship's security to come look at your papers. And your goddam guns." His voice shook and his shoulders trembled, but the business end of the pistol was quite steady. Piat's body was as habituated to fear as to alcohol. He could function very well while he was terrified and drunk.

Hair sputtered something in Arabic. Cologne didn't move.

"Okay, Mister Furman. I don't really want to get down on the floor. I think we went about this incorrectly. Please accept my apologies."

"On the floor."

"No. You won't shoot us. This is a Greek ship; you'd spend the rest of your life in prison. And you don't want security any more than we do."

Piat weighed the risk of leaving Cologne with a gun against the risk of actually starting something just to make the man lie on the floor. He made his decision rationally. He'd outgrown the need to live on macho.

He took a step backward, whirled, and walked out through the bar's swinging doors, pocketing the gun as he went. In seconds he was among passengers and staff. He stayed among them for an hour, until the worst of his fear was past. Then he forced himself to go to his cabin.

He had to do it. Everything he needed to live was in the cabin, and there was no *good* time to go if they wanted him. He had to bet they didn't want to get him that badly. Yet. It all hung on the name Furman. If they knew him only as Furman, it was because that was the name on the door of his cabin, and it meant that his other fears about his past and about his position were groundless. Furman would be a dead end. Piat had built the identity of Furman on the acquisition of an Athens Museum reader's card and some luck. Furman had no credit cards, no passport, and no tax records. Furman wasn't tied to Molyvos. Furman was a simple false front for business transactions and had been built with something like this in mind. Piat told himself this twenty times, like a mantra, and unlocked his cabin door. Paranoid, he opened the bathroom door and checked the bunk before he locked the door behind him with shaking hands.

Then he got out a piece of scrap paper and wrote on it.

Girl in Molyvos = Saida Frayj

Saida + Swain?

Thugs want Saida's item

Saida's item = cup

That gave the cup a certain provenance. He wrote again.

Palestinians want cup?

Israelis? Want Swain? Or cup?

He wondered where the hell the Israelis, if they were Israelis, were. He didn't think they were on the boat. He wondered if they were all mobsters. It had a certain logic; he had done business with some of the digging cartels in Palestine before. It was all about the money there.

Except that the men at the Acropolis had had all of the slick, well-equipped look of men outfitted at the expense of a government to look like civilians. He knew the look well, having worn it for more than twenty years.

In fact, he didn't know much, except that he'd walked into it, and now he needed out. He had planned to move on in the spring, anyway, using his last safe passport and the funds he had raised in the black antiquities business. But at his desk in his stateroom, Piat weighed the matter and decided that it was time to go soon, perhaps even immediately. The question was, with the cup, or without it?

He looked at the photos of it again. There wasn't anything about it that he could see that would lure a government, unless it was stolen from a major museum, and he dismissed that, because if that item had existed in the museum world he'd have known, and so would Barry.

Good old Barry.

It would take him a day or two to get ready to move. He already knew where he was going. By then, Barry would have something. Piat decided to wait for Barry to make the call.

Piat hadn't slept in twenty-four hours, and fatigue, adrenaline and alcohol were combining to give him a serious headache. He ate an aspirin and drank a bottle of water while he took the time to strip the round out of his stolen pistol, replace it in the clip, and safe the weapon. Then he curled up in his bunk with his sweater as a blanket and the pistol under his pillow. The boat moved with the sea, and he slept.

15

Tel Aviv

Dukas was angry. It wasn't a hot anger but something depressed and somber. He'd been stiffed and stiffed good, and he was in a country run by the people who'd stiffed him, and right then there wasn't anything he could do. He knew it looked—even to himself—like running, but he had decided to go home.

First, he went to the CIA chief of station. He told her about the new settlement at Tel-Sharm-Heir'at, about the cremated body of Salem Qatib, and he reminded her that Israel had refused to let his forensics team into the country.

"What do you want me to do?" she said.

"Nothing. It isn't your fight."

"Not so far, but I could get interested."

"This is a criminal case. I'm here to investigate a death. You guys aren't involved." He was sitting in an armchair too small for him, his hands folded over his gut like a Buddha's. "It isn't that they destroyed the archaeological site. I don't care a rat's ass about archaeology or art or history. They can steal every goddam coin and statue in the Middle East, for all I care. I don't care if the Palestinian Authority gets rich breaking Israeli law. What I care about is one guy who used to be in the Navy and got wasted."

She had her head tipped on the fingers and thumb of one hand, looking at him. It was the beginning of her work day;

256

she didn't look her age yet. He did, of course—Dukas had looked forty-five when he was born. And right then, he didn't care how she looked, except that she looked interested and intelligent. "What do you want from me?" she said.

"I want this meeting with the Palestinians' antiquities guy—the Tax Collector. I'm not getting jack-shit from the Israelis; I want to see what I can get from him."

"You're not going."

"We established that. I suggested Abe Peretz. What d'you think?"

She adjusted her legs, her head. She had a silk scarf—Hermès, ten years old, souvenir of a tour of duty in Brussels—knotted on one side of her throat, swagged across and pinned. She bought her hair-coloring to match the scarf. "I can live with it. I'm not enthusiastic." She smiled. "I'm very seldom enthusiastic." She propped her chin on a hand. "The Palestinians have given a tentative go-ahead for the meeting. Cairo or Amman; I'm pushing for Cairo because there's less 'unpredictable factors' there. I haven't got a comm plan yet but I'm hoping we work one out today." She picked something from her skirt. "They like a long surveillance route so they can make sure the Israelis aren't following. We'll ask for the same, but it won't really be needed."

"You trust the Palestinians?"

"God, no, but I trust the situation. They've got nothing to gain by messing around. Anyway, I'll put two of my guys there—they need the training, anyway—and the Egyptians will do a good job. Better than the Jordanians, which is one of the unpredictable factors. You told Peretz?"

"Not yet. You hadn't okayed him."

"Now I okay him. Okay? You want to brief him?"

"Sure."

"I want to know exactly what he's going to say—what he's going to ask for. He's not to depart from those questions.

Okay? I don't want to hear he's made some shit-for-brains deal with the Tax Collector that leaves me hanging out in the Israeli wind."

"No deals, I agree. All I want is information, for which all we're going to offer is gratitude and the fact that the Israelis have shafted us, so I'm pissed and in the future will look on the Palestinians with more warmth."

"I don't think they'll be too impressed."

"The US Navy is pissed and will look on the Palestinians with warmth if they cough up some info, how's that?"

She grinned. "At least they've heard of the US Navy." She stood. "I think it'll be Saturday. You get your guy and make sure he's on board; then I want to meet with the two of you. Then you can brief him on your time. Once it's set, we'll do the travel arrangements and set him up to meet the local guys when he gets there. This is going to be kept simple, and I want it to be quick. The Palestinians know what we want to talk about, so there won't have to be a lot of throat-clearing."

"You think they'll answer my questions?"

They were moving toward the door. She said, "I've sweetened the pot a little with some help in beefing up their security in Gaza. I think you'll get something. Not everything. Never everything."

He stopped with a hand on the door. "I'd be grateful, but I'm suspicious of why you sweetened the pot."

"Illegal antiquities. There's a lot of chatter. I've been told to listen up." She put some weight on the door and it closed on him.

Dukas went back to his borrowed office and found two messages—to call Dick Triffler at the Naples office, and to call the head of NCIS in Washington on a secure line. He had to borrow another office to do that; people looked at him as if he was becoming a pain in the ass. As in fact he was, he knew.

He called Triffler first, hoping he'd have information he

could use with Kasser. He had to sit through Triffler's bitching about missing the opera, and through a recap of what he'd said yesterday—early Greek, Gaza, rumor.

"Then I went to see Barry, as you ordered, oh, great massa. I think he's a spook."

"Oh, shit."

"Maybe ex-spook. He's got the moves and the vocabulary, and he behaves like he's been down the agent route. He also, and this may mean nothing, mentioned 'his American contact,' who's a very important guy and, I think from context, is the source of what Barry has. 'Very important guy' should be taken with a dose of salts; Barry's the kind of pathetic loser who has to keep telling you how important everybody he knows is. But—big *but* here, Mike—"

"I like big butts."

"*But*, Barry's got a grip on the tail of something, and it may be important. He showed me some photos of a thing like a vase, which he called a cup. It has an inscription that he says is Linear B, which is an exotic pre-Greek that almost nobody in the world can read. He says he can—but he'd say that, right? so it may be bullshit—and he wouldn't translate any of it for me or show me anything in English, but he's one of those guys who can't keep from talking about what they're obsessing about at that moment. He made it pretty clear that the inscription is what the buzz is about. Somehow, it's going to rewrite Jewish history. He says. This cost me the afternoon and the opera and two thousand dollars from my own bank account, so I'd like to think I could recover at least the money. Hello?"

"How about my undying gratitude?"

"How about my two thousand dollars?"

"Put in a chit. Maybe the Special Agent in Charge will okay it when he gets back." Dukas hung up and spent a few seconds thinking about rewriting Jewish history, which didn't seem to him monumentally important—but, then, he didn't think history was monumentally important, anyway —and then he called the head of NCIS.

"This is Kasser." The dry voice was quiet, unperturbed.

"Dukas. You called."

"Yeah. Well, here's what I called about. I'm getting real pressure now to sign off on getting the Navy recoded. CNO's office is worried; NSA is going ballistic. Their view is they can't take the chance of being wrong about this guy Qatib, and they can't sit around while we try to prove otherwise. It's shit-or-get-off-the-pot time, Mike."

"Yeah, it would be nice if I could pull some proof out of my ass. But I can't."

"How bad is it?"

"Bad enough that I'm going home for at least the weekend. Good enough that I've got a guy going to meet somebody high up in the Palestinian antiquities rackets. Maybe he gets some answers—but maybe he doesn't." He ran quickly through what he had learned in Jaffa and at Tel-Sharm-Heir'at, and what Triffler had learned in Athens. "Triffler thinks this ancient Greek connection is important, maybe getting the Israelis' balls in an uproar. And I can see it—if somebody's about to pull the rug out from under your country's whole idea of itself, maybe you do things like killing a guy and turning an illegal dig into a brand-new settlement and stiffing me with a cremated body."

"Or maybe you do those things because of crypto."

"Maybe you'd do some of those things because of crypto, but not erase an archaeological site and throw up a settlement, and not involve Section Sixteen of Mossad, their arts and archaeology guys. No, Ted, I think it wasn't crypto. I just don't have all of it yet."

"Are you ready to say for *sure* it wasn't crypto?"

Dukas looked at somebody's picture of his kids and the dog. "No. Not yet."

Kasser was silent. Kasser trusted him, he knew. Dukas was

effectively the number five in NCIS now; he wasn't to be taken lightly. But Kasser, Dukas knew, was a man who knew exactly how much pressure from above he and NCIS could bear. "I'll hold them off if I can," Kasser said now, his voice grim. "But you've got to come up with something or let them go with the recoding, Mike." His voice changed, became almost kindly. "Finally, if they do it, it's only money. If they don't do it, it could be lives and ships."

"And then there's the truth," Dukas said.

"Oh, yeah. And then there's the truth."

Washington
An Israeli businessman who shuttled back and forth among Jerusalem, Washington, and Los Angeles asked an Assistant Deputy Secretary of Defense for a meeting on very short notice. He could do that because the two men were old friends, even old allies, in fact old business associates until the Assistant Deputy Secretary had had to divest himself of all conflicts of interest before taking the post. The businessman's name carried a lot of clout, anyway. He had connections. And money.

They met for a drink at a surprisingly modest bar in Northwest Washington—not the sort of place that Assistant Deputy Secretaries usually went to. But it was discreet. With no media people. They chatted, got the preliminaries out of the way—your wife, your children; my new job, my headaches; the goddam Democrats, the next three years. Nine-Eleven. Then:

"I had a phone call from Jerusalem, my friend."

Slightly wary eyes.

"It seems there's a small embarrassment in Tel Aviv. They asked me to share it with you before—" Gesture of hands and head, suggesting repercussions. "Not to put too fine a point on it—mmmm—" Smile, keen glance under the eyebrows. "Your people, that is your office, seem to have sent over somebody without a country clearance." Rapid acceleration of speech, an apologetic hand gesture. "This person, this man, named, umm, Raymond Spinner, is in Tel Aviv, I'm told, asking questions and seeking information. Now, you know and I know that information is important, but there are ways and ways to get it. You understand perfectly, I know, the situation in which Israel finds itself—imagine, if you will, if you found that Israel had sent an undeclared agent without even a country clearance from his own country over *here*.

"Well. The point is that we are friends. Not only you and me, but our countries, yes? And more particularly, your office and certain, mmm, elements of the intelligence picture in my country. Am I right about this? With this new administration in Washington, we know that we have sympathetic friends in—shall I say important places?—and most particularly in your area of responsibility. The last thing anyone would want to do is upset the apple-cart or frighten the horses. Mmmm?

"So. We find ourselves with this person who has so mysteriously—so *remarkably*—appeared among us. Some persons in Israel might be inclined to arrest this man—oh, yes, and they could arrest him, no question. Arrest and imprison. They could declare him 'persona non grata,' meaning—You know what it means. Try him in a court of law for espionage—a great embarrassment. Perhaps ask to trade him for—oh, for example—Jonathan Pollard. Mmm?"

The Assistant Deputy Secretary frowned.

"Unattractive possibility. Cooler heads prevail. So far. The thinking is that here is a splendid opportunity. Presented with a lemon, we make lemonade, mmm? Opportunity to make new connections, to share. Between you and me and the sheep-well, some persons are not content, not *happy* with—let me call a spade a spade—with the CIA. With their attitudes. Underlying assumptions."

The Assistant Deputy Secretary nodded. "Liberal."

"Mmm. Whereas, your office contains people closer to, let me say certain minds in Tel Aviv and Jerusalem. An affinity, as it were. A sympathy. So what I wanted to explore with you, at the suggestion of some friends at home, is the likelihood of our turning this Mister Raymond Spinner to good account rather than bad. Not to arrest him, but to have him instructed from home to enter into consultation with, mmmm, appropriate persons on matters of mutual interest. For example, the quest that has brought him to Tel Aviv, on which some people are more than willing to help him. In aid—let me be candid—of letting him and you get in ahead of other US elements already on the ground. We see a win-win situation here. And, to show Israel's bona fides, I was asked to let you know that certain information about Iraqi weapons of mass destruction could be made available if we see eye-to-eye. New information. Concrete information." Smile. "Rather than, God help us, arrest and a trial."

The Deputy Assistant Secretary said he thought they could jumpstart something important here, and would he have another drink?

Afghanistan

Alan and Fidel were running through the black night, the air cold and as lightless as a cellar. Alan could hear their feet pounding on the dirt road, his own breathing and Fidel's like the panting of dogs. Their breath made puffs of steam. Ahead, the gallows tower rose, blacker against a sky made charcoal gray by the faraway glow of Kandahar. They were running because a frightened female E-2 had just shouted into their house, "You better come! They got your guy!"

He had put in two twelve-hour sessions with the prisoner, sessions of nothing but a relentless and boring repetition of questions: what is your name? how old are you? how many sons do you have? did you work with the Taliban? what is your name? did you work with al-Qaida? why did you run away to Iran? what is your name? Between the sessions, he had got some sleep but the prisoner had not because they left the lights on and played loud music.

He was an old man with a long beard and a smell of sweat and spices and the colorless face of a cardiac patient. He wore a head cloth and long robes, from which his hands and feet stuck out like roots, deeply veined and lined and brown. A pious Muslim (or so he said), he had asked for running water to wash before he prayed; there was no running water, but Alan had got him clean water in a bucket.

Alan had made himself the old man's father, his god, who could give and take away. When Alan needed a break, Fidel became a stern replacement, a lesser god with less patience. But neither of them had touched the old man or threatened him.

Alan knew that the situation provided all the threat required.

They had made progress. Alan had told Fidel he thought they would need three more days with him. Alan wouldn't get to Bahrain in time to help Rose pack, he realized; he'd miss the first days of leave in Naples, too. He'd miss the dinner he'd planned with old friends. But it didn't matter, because in another day or at most two, the old man would start to give him answers.

And then the frightened young woman had shouted, "You better come; they got your guy," and he and Fidel had hauled ass out of their sleeping bags and headed for the prison at a sprint. The woman had stood behind them in the darkness, screaming, "Not there—the brick thing—the tower thing—!" She was one of the prison guards Alan had learned to recognize; she had, he'd understand only later, risked a lot to tell them what had happened. And so they were pounding over the snow.

Alan flicked on his Maglite. The brick tower turned dull yellow-brown. At ground level, an empty doorway was black;

the door, he knew, had rotted away and was lying in the weeds. Fidel got there ahead of him and plunged through to be silhouetted as his own light caught the walls inside. Coming in behind him, Alan found his eyes led immediately to the top because of a spot of bright light up there, white-hot—a gas lantern. And figures, seen mostly as shadows on the underside of the roof, over-sized and inhuman.

A soldier was waiting at the bottom of the stairs. Fidel's light was in his face and he was wincing. Alan saw that he was a kid; he should have been somewhere with a skateboard and baggy Levi's festooned with cheap chains. Now he was here, caught in the middle of something. Fidel growled, "Outa the way."

"You can't go up!" The boy's voice rose, less with fear than with excitement, Alan thought.

Alan plunged forward, said, "Commander Alan Craik, US Navy, get out of the way."

"Sir, you—"

Fidel growled, "Kid, shut up before you get in some serious shit." Alan went past him, and then both of them were pounding up the stairs. Above them, a voice was shouting and, even over the sound of their boots on the brick stairs, another voice screamed. Alan thought it was the old man's, then was *sure* it was the old man's. His own breath was painful, rasping in his throat; it was like finishing a marathon uphill. Fidel was moving up beside him, would pass him, but Alan barred his way with the flashlight and went on, up and up, turning at each corner of the square tower as the stairs spiraled up the inside. When they got to the level below the top, he saw a noose dangling out in the nowhere, saw the rope going up into the bright light above them.

He came to the top and panted for breath. Even breathless, he knew he had to take command right then, and he gasped out, "That man—is—my prisoner! Stop what you're—doing!"

Two more young soldiers were holding the old man by the arms. His headdress and his clothes had been pulled off and lay across the floor and spilled over the edge into the darkness. His hair, long and gray, hung around his head and down his face, wet, soaked, and over his naked chest. A white plastic bucket stood near the wall, water splashed over the floor around it.

"What the fuck is going on here?" Alan roared.

A fourth man crouched by the outer railing. He was big, bigger than Fidel and older, maybe pushing fifty. He wore camo fatigues but no sign of rank. *Ex-something*, Alan thought, *contract heavy, rent-a-thug.* "I asked you a question," Alan shouted.

"Go fuck yourself."

Alan pushed down his rage. "Alan Craik, Commander, US Navy. This is my prisoner. Who the fuck are you?"

"Beat it."

"Name, rank and number—you're under arrest—"

Alan moved forward, shifting his grip on the Maglite; its beam, moving over the black gulf beyond the railing, caught the rope that hung there; he thought, *They were threatening to hang the old man, a horrible death for a Muslim.* He moved to within contact distance of the big man, saying over his shoulder, "Put those two people under arrest, Fidelio. And see to our prisoner." He was staring into the other man's eyes. They didn't flinch.

The man was in a defensive position, a way of announcing that they weren't going to talk this over. On his left, the empty shaft of the tower yawned; the railing, removable at that point, had been taken down and leaned against the bricks of the wall. "You," he said. He stabbed a finger at Alan. "Get the fuck out of here. You'll be a lot better off if you just go away and forget the whole thing."

"You're breaking the rules about the treatment of prisoners!"

"He's a terrorist! *The fucking rules have been changed!*" The

266

man's face was contorted. "You weren't getting jack-shit out of him. Now get the fuck out of here!"

Then things happened quickly. Alan was aware of movement behind him and to his left, something about the old man, and there was a terrible groaning sound, like nails being pulled out of a board; and the big man came toward him in a lunge, meaning to catch Alan's face and then the back of his head and take him down, but they had gone to the same schools, and Alan blocked one arm and swung the Maglite. The big man grunted and sidestepped and chopped sideways, knocking Alan toward the gap in the railing. He saw that he was pitching forward into the void, reached for the solid part of the railing and dropped the Maglite, which fell spinning down the shaft and banged on the bottom and went out. Alan caught a wooden upright and swung around it on his right arm; he felt himself start to go over, his left foot actually stepping out into nothing, pulling back with his right arm and grabbing wood with his left hand and hanging there, his left leg sticking down into blackness.

The big man was headed down the stairs by then. Fidel started to follow, came back when Alan shouted, and then the two soldiers were running down, two, three steps at a time, Alan shouting at all of them to stop, that was an order, they were under arrest. For all the good it did.

The old man lay on the floor in the puddle by the white bucket. His naked body looked dead white in the glare of the gas lantern. The old skin was pathetic, wrinkled and baggy, the muscles slack. Alan bent over him, and his eyes flickered, recognized him. There was no relief or welcome in the look he gave.

"We need those guys' name and number," Fidel said. "The guy at the foot of the stairs is gone, too. We'll ream their ass."

Alan was feeling for the old man's pulse. "He's got to have a doctor. Christ knows what they did to him."

"Well, the water treatment for sure. And tried to scare the shit out of him with the rope."

"You know that guy?"

"Never seen him before."

The old man's pulse was rapid and faint. He was breathing through his mouth, shallow, quick breaths that caught and became little gasps. When he met Alan's eyes, he reached across his own chest with his right hand and patted the left side, then moved the hand to his upper arm.

"I think maybe he's having a heart attack. Jesus Christ."

Fidel bent down and the two of them moved him out of the puddle and put his rolled-up headdress under his head. Fidel was saying he'd go for a medic when there was noise below them and then lights, and Alan went to the railing and looked down and saw half a dozen people rushing up the staircase. "We need a doctor!" he shouted. "Somebody go for a doctor!"

Nobody turned back.

"We've got a heart-attack victim up here! Go for a doctor!"

The first one to reach them was an army lieutenant who looked scared. Behind him, laboring up the last few steps, came the woman whom Alan recognized as the prison commanding officer, a lieutenant-colonel. Her face was ugly with the anger that comes from being afraid you'll get caught. Her first words were, "Get the hell out of here! That's an order!"

"My prisoner is having a heart attack. Get him some help." Behind him, Fidel was working on the old man's chest, the sounds like somebody beating a rug.

"Get out."

"Colonel, my prisoner was being tortured. He's dying!"

She rapped out an order over her shoulder and one of the men behind her ran down the stairs. "Leave it to us," she said to Alan and stood aside.

"I want the four men who were here."

268

"I'll take care of it." She was insistent but also deferential, as if she had just understood who he was. And as if, perhaps, she didn't know what was going on, either.

"That guy refused to give me his name or his rank! Who was he? CIA? Civilian? And what the hell was he doing, torturing my prisoner?"

She thrust her face toward his. "I said we'd take care of it! It's out of your hands!"

"We're supposed to work under strict rules with prisoners."

"He's a terrorist, or he wouldn't be here."

Then Alan would have said something he'd have regretted later, but Fidel called him, and he went and knelt beside him over the old man.

The woman came toward them. "Just leave it to us, Commander," she said. "We'll find out what happened. We'll see that the rules are followed. Your prisoner will be okay." She was pleading with him now; she was wise enough now to be frightened.

"No, he won't." Alan stood. "He's dead."

She looked down at the dead old man. "We can cover this," she said. "It's natural causes." She started to give orders to the others, and Alan held out an arm to stop them.

"Colonel—this is a crime scene!"

She stared at him. And then her face twisted with fear. "Oh, Christ," she said. "Oh, Christ—"

Tel Aviv

The papers piled up on Dukas's desk because he liked paper, distrusted the electronic magic of the computer. Still, he used one when he had to and knew that messages would go fast—to Naples, to other people in the embassy, to Washington. He spent part of that day, then, writing complaints and objections, mostly about the cremation of Salem Qatib's remains. The destruction of evidence. The obstruction of an investigation (the bulldozed site in Gaza). Coverup.

He grabbed Abe Peretz between meetings—Abe, as liaison with local authorities, was the point man on some of the complaints Dukas was making and was already meeting with people in the police—and hustled him to his office and shut the door. He explained about the meeting in either Cairo or Amman.

"Saturday? That's the day after tomorrow!"

"It's important."

"It's the Sabbath, Mike."

"There's gotta be a special dispensation for important work. Every religion has special dispensations; otherwise, they don't last."

"Bea will kill me!"

"Abe, it's easy-on, easy-off—short flight, bop into town, meet your backup, bang, it goes down and you head home. Abe—trust me. This is important."

Peretz smiled, sniffed his fingers, said okay but his wife would kill him. What was it Dukas wanted him to do?

"Meet with a Palestinian, ask some questions. They're going to be vetted by the nice CIA lady. See, I'd go myself, but she won't let me."

Peretz laughed. He thought it was pretty funny that Dukas had even thought he'd be allowed to make such a meeting.

Late in the day, they met in her office. She was in a hurry; it became a cursory, good-enough-for-government-work exchange. She eyeballed the questions Dukas had had printed out—*What do you know about the death of Salem Qatib? How was Salem Qatib killed? How did his body get from Tel-Sharm-Heir'at to Jaffa? Do you know of any violence done to Salem Qatib? What was Salem Qatib's role in digging antiquities in the Palestinian Territories and Gaza?*

"Redundant," she said. She looked at her watch.

"We won't get an answer the first time."

"Lot of assumptions—that they know a lot. They're touchy."

"People who send out suicide bombers—and they're *touchy*?"

Peretz had questions about security. She ran through the comm plan very fast, gave Dukas copies, one for each of them, their names penciled at the top, told them the contact arrangements with their own security. The meeting was on for Cairo, five p.m. local. She had Peretz's tickets and handed them over. "I gotta run." She had another meeting.

Peretz caught her before she could leave. "I'm going in clear, my own passport, official business—right?"

"You're a diplomat. This is a diplomatic mission." She smiled. "Another reason Mister Dukas couldn't do it." She started out, came back. "But it's covert, so don't blab to friends and family. If you have to say anything, say you've got a liaison job in Cyprus and you can't talk about it." She was gone.

They walked back to Peretz's office together. "I feel a little underwhelmed," Peretz said. "I think I'd like a rehearsal and about three more briefings. What the hell's all this about, anyway?"

When Dukas tried to tell him, Peretz said he didn't have time. "Come home with me," he said. "We can take a couple hours after dinner."

Dukas said he didn't think that descending on Bea on such short notice was a wise idea. "How about after dinner?"

They settled on nine o'clock, a time when Dukas had hoped to be curled up in bed with a television set and a beer, but he accepted what had to be. As it happened, by the time he'd talked to Leslie and gone out to the Mexican restaurant that had been recommended by the chief of station, it was after nine before he got to the Peretzes, anyway. Leslie had wanted to talk about meeting the Craiks and the Trifflers for dinner on Saturday, and she was pretty insistent that he be there. But he was ahead of her: he'd already decided that he was fed up with Tel Aviv and was heading home. "Maybe I'll come back here, maybe not. Right now, babe, I'm outa here as soon

271

as I can get my shit together." He didn't mind if Mossad was picking that up on his hotel phone, as he assumed they were.

He walked into the Peretzes' apartment to find the air thick with the smell of onions, and the last of dinner on the table. Bea, surprisingly warm, embraced him and said he had to have dessert, at least; he pleaded the meal he'd eaten at Chimichanga, but she said she had a nut cake she'd made herself and he couldn't say no. Bea was a funny woman, he thought, up one time you were with her, down the next. Right now she was up. She didn't talk about wanting to stay in Israel or Abe's supposedly lax Jewishness. Maybe they were getting along better, Dukas thought. Maybe his fling with Miriam Gurion had made things better at home. That happened sometimes.

"More, Mike?"

"I'd bust."

"Why don't you get fat? One piece of this cake, I look like the Goodyear blimp. You, you look like a really healthy wrestler."

"Sumo wrestler, you mean. Anyway, Bea, you don't want to look like a healthy wrestler."

She laughed. Their daughters laughed, polite to the adults; they scooped up the dirty dishes and carried them away. Dukas told Abe and Bea he was leaving the next day. "Got better things to do. People to see."

"Don't tell me you don't like Tel Aviv!" But she caught herself and held up a hand and told him not to say anything; she didn't want to start one of her tirades. She laughed. "Bea Peretz, the one-woman Tel Aviv chamber of commerce. My friend Esther says I should apply for a job." Bea asked about his wife, the as yet unborn baby. "Mike Dukas a papa! I never thought I'd see the day." She patted his hand. "You and I have had our spats, Mike, but that's just me. I'm glad you're happy."

Dukas hadn't said that he was happy. What the hell, maybe

he was. He and Abe went off to Abe's study, a large closet with room for a small desk and two chairs and—odd home furnishing—a shredder. Dukas briefed him on the whole Qatib case, then explained exactly what he wanted to get from the Palestinians. "If you get fifty percent of it, I'll be ecstatic." They went over the comm plan in detail; so that he wouldn't carry his copy back to the hotel, Dukas left it on the desk and told Peretz to shred it.

Dukas left before eleven. Abe Peretz went right to bed, saying he had a lot to do next day. Their daughters were in their rooms, probably online. Bea waited half an hour, then went to the bedroom and made sure that Abe was in bed. In fact, he was asleep; he opened one eye, muttered something, closed it.

She went down the long corridor to his study and stepped inside. She had the excuse of the coffee cups she knew she'd find in there, both Dukas's and her husband's. Abe was a sloppy man; he was used to her going in there to clean up after him. She stacked the cups—mugs, actually, no saucers— and stood by the desk, her eyes searching over the surface. She turned papers in a pile, saw nothing new, then lifted a dictionary and an atlas and pulled out the three sheets of paper whose corners had peeked out underneath.

In the upper-right corner of the top sheet, somebody had written in pencil, "Dukas."

The rest was printed, probably from a computer. "Communications Plan for Cairo meeting between US representative and designated Palestinian Authority representative."

She lifted the pages and glanced through them only long enough to understand that these were instructions for a clandestine meeting in a Cairo shopping mall.

She turned on a printer, which served also as a scanner and a copier.

She made a single copy of each page.

She replaced the papers under the atlas and the dictionary.
She picked up the cups and left the room.

Mytilene, Lesvos

Piat woke with the change in engine noise that told him that the ship was in the straight between Lesvos and Turkey. He stripped, showered and shaved, and packed his few belongings. He was the fourth person in the queue to leave the ship at Mytilene. He didn't see the Swain or either of the thugs.

It was late night in Mytilene. Despite the season and the rain, every bar and dance club on the waterfront was open and loud, so that when the sound of the ship's engines died away their muffled rumble was replaced with a cacophony of bass thumps and high-pitched laughter. Piat went down the boarding ramp directly to the street and headed around the harbor to his Mytilene bar, which had everything he needed; booze, a pay phone, and three exits. He would *not* be taking the bus to Molyvos.

At the western edge of the harbor he turned left and took a long look back to the boarding ramp. There was the Swain, alone, hurrying after him. Piat gritted his teeth. The Swain was so inexperienced that he'd just stay this close and stay on him at all the wrong times.

Piat turned to hurry across the base of the harbor. The motion of a man in a taverna turning his head alerted Piat, who put his own head down, natural enough in the rain, and moderated his pace. That was Redcoat, last seen on The Acropolis, enjoying a quiet ouzo in Mytilene.

How did they get here so fast?

It was clear to Piat that he now had to lose the Swain as soon as possible. *Airport. They flew here from fucking Athens because the Swain booked a return reservation. Because I did. I have to get out of here, and not on the bus where I'm easy to find.*

Piat modified his travel plans as he walked. He didn't like

274

being pushed; he didn't know whether he was actually under threat himself, but instinct said he had to assume that he was, or would be. Sooner or later, Redcoat and his people would make him. He moved quickly along the waterfront to the Athinos Hotel and went into the ground floor bar through the patio, straight to the pay phone just outside the cleanest men's room in Mytilene.

Piat read the number off a slip of paper and dialed.

No one answered. He waited ten rings and went back to the bar. He bought a glass of ouzo, assured himself it was just for cover, and discovered that his glass was empty. He walked across the bar to the phone and called again.

Nobody. Piat had some friends on Lesvos, but his travel plans required one busy criminal to be available, and it wasn't looking good. Piat wondered if he could pay a cab to run him over to Molyvos. It would cost him a small fortune, but he could, up to a point, afford that.

He went back to the bar and ordered Scotch. He began to feel angry at all these people and their foolish games. And of course, the Swain chose that minute to push through the door to the bar.

"Christ," Piat said aloud. He realized that he was on the edge of being angry and drunk, a bad professional combination.

He slid off his stool and went back to the phone.

The man answered on the eighth ring, when Piat was beginning to lose hope.

"Who is this, please?"

"Andros? It's Georgio."

"Hey, Georgio! What can I do for you?"

"I need a ride."

"Enhh? Call a cab."

"I need you to take me around to Molyvos by sea."

"Jealous husband?"

"Five hundred euros. Right now."

"Where are you?"

Piat let out a long breath. "At the Athinos."

"I have a boat full of people. Enhh, I'll make the trip part of the party. Yeah, okay. Okay, Georgio. Fifteen minutes. Right there."

"Half an hour, at the castle. Please? *Effkaristo*?"

"*Parakalo*, good buddy." The connection went dead.

Piat knew Mytilene intimately. He walked out the back door, leaving his glass sitting on the bar. Unfortunately, he didn't leave the Swain, who was right behind him.

Piat growled. He ran it around his brain, whether he could now duck the Swain somewhere without alerting the Swain's various keepers and pursuers, trying to balance that against—

"Fuck it," Piat said aloud. He drew the captured pistol out of his waistband, rammed it into the Swain's midriff and dragged him into the doorway of a closed net-rigger's. The Swain didn't let out a sound.

"Stop following me, okay?" Now that he had taken this step, Piat knew it was wrong. Somehow, this kid was central to the whole deal and anything he did now would simply drag him deeper. Piat considered one option—shooting the kid and walking off. In Afghanistan or Southeast Asia—he actually turned his head away for a second, trying to avoid the memories. He wasn't that hard anymore.

The kid just looked at him. Maybe expected to be shot.

Piat felt a deadly spark of pity. "You know you have three, maybe four Israelis following you? Huh?" That was drink talking. Giving away that he could read such things, giving away too damn much. But the kid was brave and had done his best, and at some remove of irritation and drink, Piat liked him.

Israelis got a response. The kid's eyes flicked to the back door of the bar.

"I don't want you, and I don't want the bozos following you." This was taking too long. Piat didn't see a good choice. He slid the pistol back into the waistband of his jeans. Time to make things up as he went along. "You're coming with me."

"I saw them." The kid cocked his head at the door to the bar. "Two big men."

"More than two, kid. What's your name?" Piat started walking, his right hand close to the butt of the gun.

The kid followed. He didn't say anything, but he followed along.

Piat cut north, across the modern square behind the waterfront and into the old residential area, along streets lined with tenements that had once been grand houses with overhanging wooden balconies in the Turkish style, up the hill and away from the water and the Israelis. When he had climbed a few blocks, Piat turned north, parallel to the waterfront, and the houses became smaller and closer and meaner. It started to rain again.

Halfway up the big hill that hung over the north end of the harbor, the kid spoke. "Rashid," he said.

"What?" Piat whirled, hand on his gun, looking down the curving, cobbled street that was now their back trail.

"My name. Rashid."

"Call me Jack." Piat was used to being called Jack, and it wouldn't do any more damage. While he walked, he tried to figure out what he would do with the kid. *Rashid.* "You Palestinian?" After he asked, he turned his head to watch the kid's reaction.

"Yeah."

The kid was good at keeping his mouth shut. *Better than me.* Adrenaline and walking were pushing the alcohol through his system. Piat stopped and looked at his watch, the glowing phosphorus barely visible. He was going to be late.

Top of the hill. Piat turned east, toward the coast. A Byzantine fortress towered above them, a looming bulk of stone in the rain, showing black against the dark gray sky.

Byzantine, Genoese, Turkish, with Roman and Classical and Bronze Age all buried beneath. Piat turned off the street on one of the muddy paths that passed around the walls.

"Watch your step," he said. He paused to let the kid go first.

It was black under the trees that grew below the walls. Piat could barely see the boy's dark coat moving ahead of him. They slipped in the mud and made poor time. After five minutes, they emerged from the trees, and the street-lights along the seawall began to provide illumination. They moved faster.

"Where are we going?" the boy asked. He sounded terrified.

It occurred to Piat that the kid still expected to be killed. This was a good spot for it. Piat scanned the seawall and spotted a Zodiac tied up, its color a slick, lurid yellow under the lights.

"Head for the boat." Piat picked his way down the mud and gravel of the steep hill, slid down the last bank to the road that ran along the seawall, and grabbed the boy by the arm. "I can leave you here, kid. You just walk back into town. Just turn your back and walk, and don't look back."

"What did Saida give you?"

"What? Listen, Rashid, I'm in a hurry, here."

"You saw her, in the other town. She gave you something."

Piat could see a wet woman standing with a cigarette— probably marijuana, given the reek—looking impatiently at the pair of them and holding a mooring line from the Zodiac.

She could wait. This was too good an opportunity to pass up. Piat turned to face the kid. "Who is she? Your sister?"

The kid almost spat. "No."

Piat's picture of the situation started to fracture. "Don't you *know* what she gave me?"

"No. But—" Rashid lapsed into Arabic.

Piat didn't speak any Arabic, but he could see that the kid was crying, trying to hold on to himself but losing it.

"Whoa, son. English? Okay?" Piat grabbed the kid's arm, trying to steady him. The kid was trembling.

"She stole things—from Salem—I know she did. I'll find her—"

"Salem?" Piat looked at the woman smoking. She was only a few yards away, and she raised an expressive Greek eyebrow.

"My friend—is dead, yes? And she—" Rashid's hands were working and he began to speak quickly. He was incoherent.

Piat had no idea what the kid was talking about, but the babble had enough clues that Piat changed his mind. "Okay, Rashid. You want to come with me?"

The kid flinched, pulled his arm away, but he didn't run.

"You want to find Saida? That right?"

"Yes!"

"Okay. I do too." *And we'll see what you know about her and her cup.*

Rashid hesitated. Piat walked off and left him. He could live with either outcome. He crossed the road to the woman with the joint.

"Sorry to keep you waiting."

"He is too young for you," she said. She took a long drag, offered the butt to Piat and, when refused, threw it in the sea.

"It's not like that."

"Oh?" She smiled, clearly convinced of her own version of things.

Piat made her out to be twenty-something, pretty like all the girls of Lesvos, even when swathed in yellow nylon. One of Andros's harem, Piat guessed.

"Is your friend coming?"

"That's up to him." Piat climbed over the railing of the seawall and stepped down into the inflatable.

Rashid followed him, and the girl dropped neatly into the stern and brought the engine to life. In a few seconds, the harsh glare of the streetlamps became a dull glow through the rain, and they were moving with the swell of the channel, the hull of the Zodiac flexing with every wave.

Rashid was soaked in the first spray from the bow. He didn't have a raincoat.

The engine roared, cutting off all conversation, and they flew out into the channel where the swell got heavy enough to require the woman to do some serious piloting. Then they had weathered the point between Mytilene and Thera, the next town up the coast, and she headed back in. By that time, they were all soaked to the skin. Piat was freezing. He assumed it was worse for the kid, although he had an old US Navy peacoat.

She throttled down after half an hour and brought them alongside Andros's heavy powerboat, a sixty-foot-long cigarette boat hull with big engines and enough speed to outrun anything else in these waters. She moored the Zodiac under the stern and swarmed up the ladder. She stopped at the top and reached back to help Rashid.

"Get his head—he's going to be sick. That's it. I thought he was a local boy, eh? No, I think not. He's soaked." She went on in Greek. "*Esti kalos, eh?*" He's very pretty.

Piat didn't see why, with the kid spewing his guts into the water and over the sleeve of Piat's cheap yellow raincoat, he should find the kid to be pretty. The kid's sickness went on and on, so that Piat had to shift on the slippery baseboards of the Zodiac.

"Pass him up."

Piat raised his head to see Andros, two girls, and a big Greek man all crowding the stern of the powerboat above him.

Andros waved. "Pass him up, buddy."

Piat eyed the swell, the vomit, and the weight of his inert fellow passenger and contemplated refusal. Macho won. He got the kid over his shoulders, waited until a trough was almost under him, and stood. He got the kid up in one motion, and strong hands grabbed him and pulled, taking the weight and keeping the Zodiac pinned against the hull of the bigger boat.

As soon as the weight was off, Piat grabbed the ladder and started up behind. He managed to get aboard Andros's boat without collapsing on the wet companionway. Loud music with a heavy bass pounded out of the main cabin. Rashid was already vanishing below deck, carried by the woman who had piloted the Zodiac.

Piat changed into borrowed dry clothes in the main cabin. Andros didn't watch him, but he sat on one of the bunks, rolling a cigarette back and forth in his fingers. The music beat heavily through the deck.

Piat had paid Andros to move a few things, and he'd purchased some stuff from Turkey; Barry's hash, for instance. Enough transactions to get a ride to Molyvos; not enough that he could now avoid an explanation.

"Who's the boy?" Andros asked. He looked up. "Is he hot?"

Piat shrugged, trying to get a small sweater over his head. "It's a long story."

"I have time." Andros popped the cigarette between his lips and lit it, snapping his Zippo shut with a flourish.

Piat had decided to stick close to the truth. He might need Andros before this was over; and if the cup was real, there would be enough money for everyone. "I'm negotiating to purchase an item."

Andros shrugged as if this were a commonplace. "Sure."

"There are a lot of people after this item."

Andros stood up. He was a short, thin man, smaller than Piat, and he didn't threaten; he wasn't that kind of crook. But he leaned forward and put a hand on Piat's shoulder, now encased in one of his old sweaters. "Sure. Listen, Georgio. Tell me the story. I smell serious trouble, enhh?"

Piat wished he had a cigarette. "The kid's Palestinian. He's been tagged by Israeli goons, who are in Mytilene right now. I don't know *why*. He's following me. I decided to pick him up and carry him along so that I can learn something. You're just my taxi to home, and I hope it all ends here."

Andros took a deep drag. "What's the item?"

"Art. Greek. I haven't seen it yet. After I got involved, I began to see that there were other people involved."

Andros nodded slightly. "And you end up on my boat. Okay, Georgio. If this comes back on me, I'll send them straight to you, okay? Since you haven't told me *shit*." He took another drag. "And my daughter thinks he's pretty."

"This won't come back on you." Piat couldn't see *how* it could come back. "Listen, Andros, I don't know anything yet, okay? There might be money in this before it's over— a lot of money. And some of that money might go for transport costs."

"Sure. Where?"

"I don't know. Me to Turkey, for instance."

Andros sat and smoked. "Okay, okay. I've got a party, enhh? Friends of my daughter. Come and make yourself useful. We'll put you down in Molyvos in the morning."

Piat pulled out his sodden wallet and started counting out five hundred Euros.

Andros waved him off. "Save your money. It's not enough for a serious problem and too much for a little favor, okay? Join the party."

Piat looked at his image in the mirror on the back of the hatch; a thin man in clothes that were too small. *Party animal.*

The party consisted of a dozen people in their twenties and two of Andros's crew. Despite the pounding music, it wasn't what Piat had expected—drugs, girls, something sordid— instead, there was good food and everyone kept dancing in the tiny confines of the bridge cabin. Everyone spoke Greek; Piat did, too. People had shouted conversations that sounded like arguments; George Bush, Greek politics, the European Union.

At some point they got under way, and dancing became more acrobatic as the boat moved through three axes. Jerry found himself wedged in a corner over the pilot table with two very young women and Andros's daughter, now introduced as Maria.

"How's the kid?" Piat shouted across the pilot table.

She smiled radiantly. "He's good! Sick again, now, but good."

One of the other girls laughed. "She's in love with him!"

They tussled, hugged, laughed, and drank more wine and danced.

Piat confined himself to seafood and mineral water. Dancing was beyond him; just staying upright took effort.

Maria came back to his corner. "You are American?"

"Yes."

"You Americans have a lot of hang-ups, you know?"

This came out of nowhere, leaving Piat conversationally defenseless, but it was true, so he shrugged. "I know," he shouted back.

"Not all Lesbian girls are lesbians!" she shouted in English.

"The women of Lesvos are all beautiful," he returned in Classical Greek. Sappho, he thought. He had wanted to quote that for four months.

She laughed. So did her friends. They drank more wine, and he ate more food. He saw lights over toward Turkey, and Andros pushed past his daughter to use the pilot table and announce that the weather was breaking.

"Get that boy off my boat before he steals my daughter!" Andros said. He looked at Maria with mock anger. "How anyone could want a boy covered in vomit—"

"*Pater!*" Maria shrieked.

"Germans are the worst," said another girl. "They think that it's so serious—"

"—why can't they just have fun?"

"—do they think they just *discovered* that men are idiots?"

"Why do they have to use the name of *our* island?"

"Americans are the worst," said Maria, pointing her finger at Piat. "They think it's about politics. Worse than Germans. Do Americans ever fall in love?"

"It's been known to happen." Piat was no longer sure what the conversation was about. The general topic seemed to be that tourists were irritating. Beyond that, Piat's Modern Greek fell short.

"Same-sex-marriage," they all chanted in English and broke into giggles.

Piat wondered if this was the Greek version of Alice's tea party.

The woman closest to him put her arm around his shoulder when the boat lurched. "Do they really have protests like that in America?"

"I haven't been home in a long time."

She snuggled against him. "That's too bad."

"What are you all talking about?"

"Lesbians. Foreign girls who come here and want us to be *activists* and *follow Sappho*. And want to talk about *gay rights*. But never about *love*. It must be terrible in America if people spend so much time worrying about who can have sex."

Piat agreed and extricated himself. He pushed through the cabin to Andros, who had the wheel, his lined face lit from beneath by the green light of his instrument panel. Off to the right, there was a pink line over the Turkish coast.

"It will be a beautiful day," Andros said. "I'll land you in an hour."

Piat watched rosy-fingered dawn spread her hands over the wine-dark sea.

Tel Aviv

Ray Spinner was surprised—stunned, in fact—to get a message from McKinnon to "consult and cooperate" with

284

Mossad, who would, he was told, be in contact with him shortly. Just like that—no explanation of how the contact had been made or what they wanted. McKinnon's email was perhaps deliberately flat—no jokes, no sarcasm, no implication. It was as if cooperation with Mossad were something they'd discussed before Spinner left Washington, and he'd know all about it. At the bottom of the message, McKinnon had added "Keywords: cooperation, sharing, consultation." *These words will be on the final exam.*

"Consult and cooperate on what?" Spinner said out loud to his hotel room. He sent off a message to that effect. The answer didn't reach him until the next evening, when it was too late, but all it said was, "Use your best judgment but don't commit us to anything."

By then, he'd had a restless night and a great day, which started when a woman with a youngish, pleasant voice called him before he'd had breakfast and invited him to a tour of Mossad headquarters. "And lunch in the executive dining room; you could make that, we hope?"

They were taking all the fun out of being a spy. On the other hand, it was nice to fly with the eagles.

That day, a Palestinian woman blew herself up in Jerusalem, killing herself and one Israeli and wounding almost a hundred others.

16

Molyvos, Lesvos

Piat woke to the sound of his telephone ringing. It took him seconds to identify the sound and almost a minute to locate the handset, because he'd had less than three hours of sleep and because he seldom used the phone. He lifted the handset from the receiver. "Hello?" he said with a question in his voice, already starting to make coffee in his closet-sized kitchen.

"Jack? Jack, is that you?" Barry's New England rich-kid accent was particularly annoying without coffee.

"Yeah. Barry, it's what, ten a.m.?" Hearing Barry added overtones of guilt to Piat's fatigue.

"Some people are working at this hour, Jack. In fact, most of us are working at this hour. Besides, I thought you wanted a progress report. Don't you even have an answering machine? I've been calling you for a *whole day.*"

Piat felt a little spark of excitement. It was communicated down the wire from Athens. Barry was like a kid; when he got something going, he couldn't *stop.* And he had that tone— that, and the hour, told Piat a great deal. "I hate answering machines, Bear. But I want the report. Of course I do."

"Hey, Jack, if it's too early, I'll just twiddle my thumbs for a while."

Piat got the kettle on the Bunsen burner that served as his single stove element, got a filter into the top of his carafe, and heard a noise in his front room that froze him. *The Swain.* He'd brought the kid home with him.

"Jack?"

"Sorry, Bear. Lot going on at this end. Okay, shoot."

"I think it's genuine."

"You thought it was genuine Tuesday night."

"Did I? I really don't remember much about it, except that it's the best time I've had in three months and it made me feel alive again. I want in on this. I'm going to write a paper—"

"—whoa, Bear! Hold on, boy! I said we'd talk when I knew more. This is pretty fucking delicate and I *don't want to discuss it on this line, okay, pal*?" Piat found that he was breathing hard—instant morning anger, lack of coffee. Excitement. Barry really believed. Piat took a big breath, let it out. "Hey, sorry to bite at you, Bear. No coffee, man. Okay, tell me something."

"Jack, I really don't know where to start. The symbols are—difficult. At least one isn't in the standard Linear B lexicons. It's a loan symbol from Phoenician. You know what that means, Jack? It's like—Jesus, Jack, it's like Leakey discovering the missing link, Jack."

"Couldn't somebody fake it, Bear?"

"Who? Who the hell knows the vowels in Linear B so well that they can decide where somebody *might* have borrowed a letter from the Semitic alphabet?"

"You do. Somebody else might."

"Bullshit. I might, but I'd—no, Jack. No, I don't think I could do it. I don't think Michael Ventris could have done it. Anyway, who would have thought that the Semitic alphabet actually made its way into Greek through a colony? Herodotus says the Phoenicians came to Greece."

"Bear? What are you talking about?"

"You said Palestinian, right? I remember you saying that. Please tell me I remember you saying that."

"You remember right. Then you said *bullshit* with all your usual authority." Piat's water was boiling. The kid in the other room was snoring. Piat poured the water over the coffee grounds and inhaled the magic.

"I was wrong. There's a word, right near the top. *Pe-la-se*. Peleset, Jack. And the Semitic loan letter—Jack! We're going to be famous!"

Piat seriously considered taking the first coffee straight from the filter. He resisted the temptation, but he was having a hard time following Bear, which was hard enough in person.

"You said the word you could read was something about the Danae, Bear."

"So I did. And there aren't forty people in the world that could sight-read that. It's right there; Danae, and Peleset. I've got a—the structure of about a third of the words, Jack. Of course, I can't read the rest of it, where it vanishes around the curve of the cup. Do you have more photos, Jack? Tell me you have more. I need them."

Piat poured coffee and looked out his building's twelve-pane window, which allowed him to see out over the town and down to the north all the way to the Turkish coast. On a clear day, he could imagine that he could see Ilium. Today was a clear day, with the sea shining the color of new blue jeans.

"What does it say, Bear?"

"I—don't know yet. I have a feeling—"

"I can settle for a feeling." Piat drank his coffee. He wasn't seeing the sea anymore. He was already selling the cup. Barry's enthusiasm convinced him. It might still be a fake, but that scarcely mattered. If it could fool Barry—

"It's a treaty. Or the memory of a treaty. Some people and some Greeks, and a king."

"The Peleset? Who are they?"

"It's what the Egyptians called one of the Sea Peoples. They were probably Greeks."

"So it's a treaty between these Peleset and the Danae?"

"No. Well, perhaps. I certainly thought so. But it looks more like this king, he's in a picture, you know?"

"I know. The top of the cup."

"Exactly! The king, and the Peleset, and the Danae. They're making the treaty with someone else."

"I'm sure that's fascinating, Bear."

"Don't give me that patronizing shit, Jack! It is fucking fascinating. I want those pictures!" Barry was very emotional now. He was shouting.

"I don't have any more pictures, Barry." He was lying, but not by much. He'd held back the one photo that showed the whole cup. He didn't think Barry could even identify the symbols from that resolution.

"You do too!" Barry whined. "And you fucking went behind my back with them, didn't you. This is mine! Jack! Jack, please!"

Piat's world started to slow down, as if he was in combat. "Bear, what are you talking about?"

Silence, and heavy breathing on the line.

"Bear! What the hell?"

A small voice. "I saw one. From some bible thumper in Texas who probably thinks it's a struggle to read Koine. Jack. Jack, I'm so much better than he is."

Piat took a gulp of coffee. "Bear. Stay with me. You saw another photo from *Texas*?"

"Don't pretend to be surprised."

"Bear, I'm totally fucking surprised. And not very happy. How did you come to see this photo?"

"Somebody sent it to this joker in Texas. He runs a very well funded department at a *Christian* university. He labored at it and then passed it to—to someone I know. At Cambridge. Who passed it to me because *I'm the only one who can do this, Jack!*"

Piat regretted that he had not waited in Athens. Barry

needed a lot of handling even at the best of times; he had always been one of Piat's highest-maintenance agents. Confronted with twin crises—loss of agent confidence and someone else with a picture of the cup—Piat didn't hesitate to deal with the agent issue first.

"Bear. Hey!" Piat was talking to more silence and more heavy breathing. Perhaps a sob. "Hey, Bear? This is me, pal. I have *not* sent any pictures of this thing to *anyone* but you. Okay? Think about it, Bear. I want this secret, right? I wouldn't fuck around with it."

Small voice. "You'd cut me out."

"No, Bear. I wouldn't. Jesus, Bear, just because I said I might not be able to let you publish—"

"—so some Agency friend in fucking Texas can take all the credit! Yes, Jack! That's just what I think. You think I've forgotten how it all ended, Jack? Remember *Afghanistan*, Jack? I even know what *quid pro quo* means."

"Bear!" Piat raised his voice too much; he heard his own shout and remembered the boy in the front room. *How much of this was he hearing?* "Damn it! I am not shafting you! I did *not* send other photos to Texas." Bear had always had this persecution complex to excuse his own failures. Piat had rarely been on the accusation end. He didn't like it. He wondered how Mara dealt with it. "Bear, I swear to you. You're my man on this and it matters."

"Yeah? And someone else has the photos? Maybe I need to talk to them? Because I want this, Jack. This is my ticket back."

"Bear. Get a grip. Okay. Look, can you find out who sent these photos to the guy in Texas? I would really like to know."

Petulant. "Maybe. You have to promise me, though."

If only it were that easy, thought Piat. "Promise what, Bear?"

"Promise me I can publish. Or I'll help the guy in Texas."

It dawned on Piat that Barry was really very intelligent,

and that he had just been conned. Barry wanted the cup and the academic prize it represented. He needed whoever had the cup, and Piat had just admitted that there was another player. Barry's anger was real, but he had led Piat to admit that the Texas photos were from a separate source. Piat knew his Barry. Barry had no morals when something was important to him. The chance of keeping the cup secret was fading already.

Rule one of agent handling—never make an agent a promise you can't keep. Unless it's really, really important. Then promise him the moon.

"Okay, Bear. It's a deal."

"I get to see it. I get to know where it's sold to."

"Absolutely."

Long sigh. "Okay, Jack. I really thought—"

Piat's hands were trembling again.

Piat got off the phone with Barry after going through all the rituals of pacification he could manage. It was poor phone security. Piat didn't give a rat's ass, because if he lost Barry now, he could see ramifications spreading out into the future. Sometimes, for days at a time, he could forget that he was a wanted man, but he was, and if Barry said the wrong thing in the wrong corner—

Jerry Piat would spend the rest of his life in an American jail.

Next crisis. The boy on the sofa.

"You drink coffee, kid?"

Rashid actually smiled. "I'm an Arab. We invented coffee."

Looking at his smile, Piat could see what Maria saw. He was a very handsome young man, with sleep and without vomit. That face would be hard to hide. Something to keep in mind.

Piat handed him a cup. Rashid drank a few sips and made a face. Then he smiled again. "Sugar?"

Piat pointed at the kitchen and sank into his chair. "On the counter."

The boy came back stirring his cup. "We're safe?"

Piat nodded. "For a while."

"Won't they look for your house?" Rashid kept looking out the window.

"Look, kid—" Piat stopped on the edge of letting the boy into his confidence. If anyone ever trained this kid as interrogator, he would be deadly. Something in the face and the demeanor. Piat had seen it before. He had some of it himself.

For all that, why not level with the kid? Piat didn't believe that the kid represented any threat at all, except as a marker that other people would eventually use.

Rashid looked attentive.

Piat leaned forward. "You said last night that someone killed your friend."

."Salem. Yes. I want to know who killed him."

Piat nodded. "You think Saida killed him?" Piat was very close to sending her an email, and he wanted to know what kind of person he'd be dealing with. She'd looked to him like a self-absorbed sexpot, but she could hide a lot of things with that as outer armor. Men rarely looked beneath sexpot.

Rashid shook his head. "No, not really. No. But she knows things. Yes? She can tell me things."

Piat looked at this statement from various angles, trying to feel his way to the real question. He didn't see it yet. "What about the police?"

The word *police* went into Rashid like an arrow into a target. He flinched. "I am Arab. Yes? In Israel? And Salem? The police—"

Piat thought he was getting some bullshit. "How did Salem die?"

Pay dirt.

* * *

292

It took the rest of the morning for Rashid to tell his story. He tried to hide from Piat that he was working for someone else. Piat had the advantage every interrogator relishes; he already *knew* that Rashid was working for someone else, because he had seen him with the two men on the boat. So Piat was patient. He let the kid ramble about Salem and he asked helpful questions about Salem's activities, and he waited for his moment.

When Rashid started to wind down, Piat struck.

"How did you follow Saida from Israel?"

Rashid looked at him blankly.

Piat leaned forward, as if sharing a confidence instead of extracting one. "You found her apartment empty. So how did you find her again? And follow her?"

Rashid's eyes widened a little. He crossed his arms, leaned forward—and said nothing.

Piat waited. He sipped cold coffee. He thought about smoking. His thoughts drifted away from the boy, to Saida, and Barry, and the men on the boat—

"I want to find the men who killed Salem," Rashid said quietly.

Piat leaned back and sighed. "Look, kid—I don't really care, okay? I mean, I'm sorry for your friend. I don't really care who you're working for. But you didn't get here without help. Right?"

"I just want to find the men who killed Salem."

"Right." Piat shrugged. He thought of the men on the boat. He looked at the young man on the sofa and decided that he had neither the time nor the enthusiasm to break him. It might matter, and it might not.

Mostly, what mattered to Piat right then was that the cup was probably real. He considered leaving the kid behind while he went out to make contact, but he couldn't lock the kid in, and he didn't want him wandering off. Like everything else, taking the kid out was a calculated risk.

"Okay, kid," he said, getting to his feet. "Let's go find Saida."

"Where are we going?" Rashid asked after they had climbed the last of the stairs to the citadel.

"We're going down to the water."

"It's down there."

"Yeah."

Rashid suddenly looked behind him and then had to hurry along to catch Piat, who was now starting down the first switchback of the road that wound from the back of the citadel all the way down to the sea. "Are—people—following us?"

"Nope."

Rashid glanced back at the citadel. "How do you know?"

"Stop looking behind you. Never look behind you, okay?" Piat walked a dozen meters and relented. "Okay, kid, listen. We walked out of the house and went up, right?"

"Ah—yes. Up to the castle."

"And then we walked around the citadel—the castle. Very open, right?"

"So you see if anyone was following!"

"You're a quick study. We stopped at the café, right? So that going up first made sense to anyone watching. And we never had to look behind us, right?"

They walked on down the hill. A man riding a small donkey passed them, apparently asleep. Rashid watched him as if he were going to burst into flame. After they had passed another switchback, he said, "Why does it have to make sense? You said there wasn't anybody."

Piat sighed. Stony indifference to Rashid's questions would probably have been the right course of action. Piat had never liked explaining himself. On the other hand, he had always liked teaching new agents the ropes. The great game. "I didn't say there wasn't anybody. I don't think there's anybody, but there could be." Piat pointed with his chin at the peak of the hill that loomed behind the citadel, half a mile away. "See that hill? Don't stare at it. There could be a guy with a scope—you understand scope? Binoculars, then. One guy, sitting up there, could cover the whole back side of the hill, right? Every car, every donkey. Us. And we'd never know he was there."

Rashid's face froze, and he stumbled.

Piat grabbed his arm. "Hey! I didn't say there really was a guy. I'm pretty sure there isn't. But you act like there's always a guy, or ten guys. You act like it's for real, all the time, and you act like it's never occurred to you that anyone might watch you. If there is a guy watching, you want him to feel very secure that you haven't a clue."

Rashid was now walking closer to Piat, almost inside his space. The kid was afraid. Piat thought he was good at dealing with fear—they had that in common—but that the creeping fear of always being watched was a new thing.

Rashid was now trying not to look at anything. Piat could see his eyes, and how hesitancy had replaced curiosity.

"Why?" Rashid's voice was almost a whisper. "Why do you pretend you don't know?"

Piat thought of the cocky men on the Acropolis. He smiled. "Because when you want them—you have them."

The young woman behind the counter of the internet café was surprised to see that Piat had acquired company. She raised an eyebrow at Rashid.

Piat smiled in return. He didn't have an explanation that he could make stick, and in a town this small, they'd draw their own conclusions. Wrong but harmless. And better than any half-baked story he'd cook up.

"Nescafé, *parakalo*?" Piat held up two fingers. He put enough money on the bar for an internet connection.

She shrugged at him.

Piat could already hear the gossip wires humming. He sat at a computer, logged on, and wasted time deleting spam.

There were four emails from Barry, all from before the phone call, and each increasingly shrill.

The man in South Carolina had answered and encrypted his reply. Piat read his reply with satisfaction. South Carolina was Piat's most amoral client, an art collector with money and no concerns about legality or origin as long as the pieces were good. Piat didn't know who he was, or whether he resold the items. The South Carolinian was already willing to make an offer. He wanted pictures and provenance. Piat nodded and started writing his instructions.

"This is the worst coffee I've ever tasted," Rashid said.

Piat raised his head from his screen. The kid had a half-smile on his face, and the woman behind the counter was trying to look stern.

"That is Nescafé," she said. "Instant."

Piat thought they'd be undressing each other in a minute. So much for the easy cover that he'd picked the boy up.

"You make real coffee?" Rashid asked.

"Where are you from?" the woman asked.

Rashid smiled. He got up and walked to the counter. "Israel. I'm from Israel, but I'm Arab, yes? I'm Rashid." He held out his hand.

She shook it. "Irene," she replied.

Piat had known her for three months and never learned her name. He went back to crafting his email. It took him half an hour, by which time Rashid and Irene were old friends, busy talking about nothing. Rashid mentioned that he had passed through Cyprus. Piat caught it.

Then he wrote a much shorter message to Saida. His email said, "I'm interested. I need to see the item. Let's meet."

She answered before his second Nescafé was cold. Piat read her reply and looked at his watch.

There was a fisherman just down the street, Stephan, who sometimes rented his tiny, ancient Nissan pickup to Piat. It was eighty kilometers of mountain and gravel to Skala Eressos, where they set the meeting for dinnertime. Piat left Rashid talking to Irene at the bar, another calculated risk, and took a short walk down to the pier. Arranging for the pickup took less time than finding the fisherman. As a bonus, the fisherman mentioned that a police roadblock was active in the mountains. Piat added twenty euros to the rental price and was back at his computer in fifteen minutes. Rashid gave no sign that he'd even noticed Piat's absence.

Piat sent Saida a response, confirming the meeting. Then he pried Rashid loose from the café. "We're going to meet Saida," he said when they were outside.

Rashid looked stunned. He had been in another world, a nicer world. Now he was back.

Piat looked at his watch again. "You have ID, kid?"

"Ah—yes? A passport?" Rashid's hesitancy turned his answer into a question.

"There's a police roadblock we have to pass. That a problem for you?"

Rashid looked furtive. But he shook his head no.

As soon as they had the pickup moving up the first hill, Piat started lesson two, how to pass a roadblock, and lesson three, how to spot surveillance in a vehicle.

The roads of Lesvos were surveillance hell. There were no alternate routes, no parallels, no alternative turns, and no places to stop. Through most of the trip, there wasn't even room to pull a car off the road. Less than half an hour out of Molyvos, Piat was absolutely sure that they weren't being followed. He made this point to his pupil.

The two young policemen at the roadblock were conscientious and a little interested in two foreigners driving a local vehicle with two iced boxes of red snapper in the back, but they knew the vehicle and they were disarmed by Piat's Greek. As it turned out, they barely glanced at Rashid's ID.

The senior cop commented to his partner that it was their day to see a lot of Israelis.

Piat's breath caught in his throat. He forced a smile, killed the impulse to ask questions, and got a wave. He had trouble getting the truck into gear.

This road only went to one place. That was the place where Saida, and the cup, were waiting.

It was dark long before they reached Skala Eressos. The dark fell fast, and now Piat could watch for headlights and see potential surveillance at an even greater range, and he started to plan strategies to evade—well, to evade whomever he had to evade.

"How well do you know this girl, Rashid?"

"I'm sorry?"

"Saida. How well do you know her?"

"Well. I know her well."

"She going to be scared of seeing you?"

Rashid grunted.

Piat couldn't read his face in the dark cab; the lights on the instrument panel were too faded to give any light at all. "Listen, kid. She's probably in trouble. If we're going to talk to her, we may need to—take her away with us. Okay? Can you hack that?"

"Saida? In trouble? This I would like to see."

"No, you wouldn't. Those cops? You weren't the first Israeli they had seen today. Do I need to spell this out?"

"Why do they care about Saida?"

Why indeed? Piat thought he knew. "Can you two get along? Or are you going to spit at each other?"

"Spit?" Rashid shuffled in the dark. "Like cats, sure. No. But I have many questions to ask her."

"Me, too." Piat shifted gears as he made the last switchback before the flat country around Skala. "You can identify her?"

"Sure. But—"

"But?"

"She might run off if she sees me."

Piat nodded to himself. "I'm counting on it."

Lesson four—offensive tactical intelligence. Lesson five—operational daring.

Skala Eressos is, in the summer, a busy tourist location; the birthplace of the poetess Sappho, it has become a center for European and American lesbians to vacation. The locals are tolerant, or uncaring; the women who come are good guests.

The town is small at the best of times. A single wooden boardwalk studded with restaurants runs along the beautiful volcanic beach; the town is defined at the south end by a Bronze Age mole that runs out to three small rock islets, and on the landward side by the bulk of the hill of the ancient town's acropolis. Like all of Lesvos, history is impossible to avoid in Skala Eressos.

In the winter, the town shrinks to become a fishing village. A few tourists still come, and a small population of resident foreigners occupies some of the old villas behind the acropolis. All the restaurants along the waterfront close, except one, the Taverna. In the summer, the Taverna serves mostly locals. It doesn't offer trendy coffee or tofu or food aimed at the tastes of outsiders. In the winter, it's the only restaurant in town.

Piat was familiar with Skala in winter. His familiarity with the town and the fact that his truck looked local were the cornerstones of his plan. As he drove down the tunnel of olive trees that forms the last few kilometers of the road from Eressos into Skala Eressos, he reviewed the plan for Rashid and considered that the whole thing was foolhardy, or just plain foolish. He knew that he should probably drive back to Molyvos and try a different contact.

Except that he could feel time running. And he was here.

Skala was empty and dark. The lights from the windows of

299

the Taverna and the handful of streetlights provided the only illumination. Most of the buildings were closed and shuttered.

He pulled up to the T intersection that constituted the town square and turned left, noting a red jeep parked beside the boarded-up tourist agency with a statue of Sappho in front. There wasn't another vehicle in sight, except a few bicycles leaning against the Taverna. He had to assume that if the Israelis were here, that was their ride.

He passed it, turning into the narrow street that ran behind the boardwalk restaurants. His small truck filled the street from mirror to mirror. Rashid was silent in the seat beside him. The harsh glare of a streetlight made his skin look dead white against the shiny black of his hair. He was sweating hard.

Piat didn't blame him. Rashid was about to walk into the lions' den.

"You know what to do?"

"Yeah—"

"Don't let it get to you. Just do it. If she moves, keep her moving and let me do the rest. If she doesn't move, tell her to go with you and that I'll explain. Just keep going, kid. All we have is speed and surprise. Don't slow down." In the part of Piat's brain that never stopped working, it occurred to him that the Israelis could be fifty kilometers away and he was doing this all for nothing, jumping at shadows.

Always best to be sure.

He pulled the pickup to a stop on the sidewalk behind the brightly lit Taverna. "Ready?"

Rashid rotated his head as if his neck was sore. Tension. "Yes."

"Let's do it." Piat opened his door and got out, walked to the back of the truck and lifted a crate of iced red snapper and carried it to the back door. He didn't knock, simply walked in and called a greeting in Greek.

A short, thickset woman appeared with a stained apron and a heavy spoon.

"Red Snapper," he said in Greek. "Red snapper. Okay? From Stephan?"

"Okay, okay." She waved at him, pointed to a counter and responded in fast, idiomatic Greek, something about money, pay, a verb he didn't know.

The red snapper had been a last-minute thing, cover for the roadblock. No big deal. "Pay him," Piat tried. He was already worried that he was taking too long.

She shrugged. "Okay."

He went out for the second box. Rashid was gone. He should be around the Taverna, coming in the front from the board-walk. Piat hurried. He grabbed the second box and carried it in, setting it on the first one and almost upsetting both in his haste.

He heard movement. He looked up from his boxes to see the girl step through the door to the kitchen looking over her shoulder. He backed through the door behind him and she followed him as if she knew his plan herself.

"Saida?" he asked quietly.

She whirled on him, shifting her focus and already panicked. He grabbed her wrist and she slammed an open palm in his face. His head went back, but he didn't let go.

"Saida! I'm Jack." It was hard to look reassuring and benign while avoiding her strong left arm. "Damn it! There's men here trying to get you. *Get in the car.*"

She was still fighting him and he didn't see any alternative. He whirled her so her arms were pinned, lifted her and pushed her through the cab door. Something ugly was happening in the Taverna behind him, raised voices and movement and the sound of footsteps.

A shout.

Piat leaned over Saida, whose slumped form filled the bench seat. "I'm on your side. I'll buy the cup, okay? Just don't scream!" This was not the way he'd planned it.

Rashid was now very late.

"Fuck you," the woman on the seat said.

Piat rolled over the hood and landed on his feet by the driver's side door and got in. "There's a lot of people after you," he said.

Rashid was running down the street from in front of the car, the last direction he should have come from. Piat didn't question providence. He turned the key and gunned the car. Saida let out a stifled scream when she saw Rashid pile in next to her.

"Let me alone!" she screamed. Even over the sound of the car, that scream carried through the town.

Piat pressed the accelerator down, backed sixty feet, scraping stucco several times, and did a reverse bootleg turn in the T intersection right under the unlit headlights of the red jeep. Twenty seconds later he was going a hundred kilometers an hour out of Skala Eressos. Thirty seconds later, there were headlights in his rearview mirror.

"What happened to you?" Piat asked Rashid and risked a glance at his passengers. They were jammed against each other in the cab and they didn't like it.

"The Israelis were there. At the next table. They saw me. I ran." Rashid's voice shook. "They had guns."

"What Israelis?" the girl spat. "What Israelis?"

"The ones after you." Piat was already in the outskirts of Eressos proper, the larger farming town, with old-fashioned wooden doors flashing by on both sides. He had to make a one-hundred-and-twenty-degree turn in the town square up the first mountain switchback. As he entered the empty square, he downshifted savagely so that the engine roared and the whole truck vibrated like a jackhammer. He let the rear wheels skid and pulled them up with an up/down motion on the parking brake, and then he was accelerating up the switchback. The headlights in his rearview were, temporarily, gone.

Piat turned off his own. He had to slow down, but not by much.

Both of his passengers screamed together.

"Shut up!" he said. He made the first hairpin turn at a little over thirty kilometers an hour and identified the pale notch in the rock ahead where the road went through a narrow pass. He pushed the accelerator down, satisfied that he could see the next hundred meters. "We're in this thing, now. Saida—"

"Who set these Israelis on me? You? Or this boy?" Saida's voice was shrill. "You hurt me, you idiot."

"How did Salem die?" Rashid asked.

There was a harsh exchange in Arabic. Piat crossed the crest and had to slow down; there was a curve here somewhere. The torrent of Arabic washed back and forth next to him. He found the curve and had a narrow escape from a section of stone guardrail before he located the center of the road. The sound of their rear bumper grating on stone silenced the passengers, but only for a few seconds.

"Shut up!" Piat roared.

"Why do you have Rashid?" Saida asked. "He knows nothing."

"He knows a lot more than you think," Piat said. The village of Eressos was below them now, and Piat could see the headlights of the other car halfway up the first switchback. He hoped it was stopped, but he couldn't count on it. He tried to watch it and drive in near-perfect darkness, and twice the steering wheel bucked in his hands as the front right wheel caught the edge of the tarmac.

"How do I know you won't just steal the cup? You've kidnapped me." Saida was already recovering from adrenaline shock.

Piat downshifted hard, fourth to second, and the truck tried to skid. Then they were coming out of the last hairpin on this mountainside, headed for the crest. "I didn't kidnap you. I rescued you. I'll buy the cup. I want to see it first. Rashid—that's a long story. What I need now is for you two to cooperate and act like boyfriend and girlfriend so that we

303

can get past the roadblock in twenty kilometers. Saida, your scream in Skala might have got someone to call the police."

"They all hated me there, anyway." She let it go at that; the dislike of an entire community delivered as if it scarcely mattered. "None of them will call the police."

"Don't bet on it. Boyfriend and girlfriend. Got it?"

"With him? He's a child."

Rashid said nothing. He was staring out of his window at the darkness.

"Dozens of Greek women disagree with you there." Piat squinted at the dark road in front of him.

"Pssht," said Saida.

Piat came to the crest. His last view of the other car was its headlights on a switchback halfway down the ridge toward Eressos. He crossed the crest, rolled twenty meters and turned his own headlights back on. Driving became easy again.

Piat had hoped that the roadblock would be gone. He had counted on laziness and manning difficulties to pull it in at night. In the worst case, he had imagined that the same officers would be there.

None of these hopes was answered. Instead, two older cops examined him, their flashlights ruining his night vision.

He showed them a fake Maryland driver's license and the real international license he had obtained with it. They looked at the two documents for long enough to worry him. The senior cop had sergeant's stripes and he kept rubbing the Maryland license with his thumb.

"You speak Greek, eh?" he asked. "Why's that?"

Piat could almost feel the headlights of the red jeep coming. They couldn't be far behind him, however long they'd taken in Eressos. "I'm a writer," he said, as if that explained everything.

The other cop pointed into the cab past Piat's head. "You should tell them to get a room," he said with a laugh.

Piat turned his head and found that Saida and Rashid were

locked together, their mouths clasped on each other as if giving mutual artificial respiration.

Piat shrugged and raised his eyebrows. The two cops laughed, returned his license and waved him on.

Piat had a hard time breathing for several seconds and his hands shook on the wheel. Saida disentangled herself from Rashid and giggled. Rashid stayed silent.

Piat turned to look back. The roadblock was still visible at the bottom of the valley. Far above the roadblock, at the top of the mountain they had just descended, a pair of headlights appeared.

Piat began to drive very fast.

Piat drove to Molyvos the long way, all the way around the island, and pulled the Nissan on the wharf at Molyvos just before sunrise. His greatest fear, that the red jeep would be waiting at the bottom of the town, went unrealized.

Piat shepherded his passengers up the hill to his house through cold, empty streets. Saida slumped along silently under the weight of her bright pink backpack, lurid even by starlight, and Rashid seemed completely withdrawn.

Piat thought it was for the best. He was too tired to think and far too tired to talk, argue, or deal with Saida's demands. He got them into his house, filled Saida's arms with the last of his clean bedding, and fell into his own bed. No sense of chivalry prompted him to offer it to her. She was a little over half his age, and he needed sleep.

Sleep did not need him. Exhausted, he lay in his narrow bed watching the scenes of the day and projected scenes of the future play out on the backs of his eyelids. His inability to sleep finally made him angry at his body's failure to realize its own needs.

He decided he needed a drink, and he padded into the kitchen on cold feet and got one. He looked at the phone on the wall and made his decision—a whole series of decisions, each nested inside the last like a set of Chinese boxes. Before he'd finished thinking, he had picked up the phone and called the number Andros said was safe. Andros answered. He wasn't pleased at the hour or the subject, but in five sentences Piat had arranged to leave the island. Monday was the best Andros could do. They set a time and a signal. Piat placed the phone gently back in the cradle, already wishing he'd made it sooner—Sunday, at least.

From the sounds, he assumed that Saida and Rashid were fucking in the front room. He felt a new flare of anger and a vague desire to protect Rashid from Saida, which he dismissed as middle-aged jealousy. He shook his head, mostly at his own failings, and got back into bed as quietly as he could.

He hated that he felt responsible for them. He hated all the things he didn't know. He was afraid, as afraid as he had ever been in his life, and when he slipped into sleep, it was only to dream of fear.

Bahrain

Alan Craik and Fidel landed in Bahrain a little after three, local time. Their faces were grim. They acknowledged nobody but went straight to the legal office to file papers against the men in Kandahar whom they had tried to arrest. Then Alan went to his own CO to explain why he had been thrown out of Afghanistan.

Mike Dukas flew out of Tel Aviv at four-thirty that afternoon. He was in Rome by nine, local time, and in Naples a little after eleven. Curled into Leslie's warmth in his own bed, he thought that this was where he should have stayed the whole week.

An hour later, Abe Peretz left for Cairo. He told his wife he was going to an emergency meeting in Cyprus.

17

Tel Aviv

On Saturday morning, Ray Spinner was again invited to Mossad's local offices. He was surprised; it was the Sabbath. But Israel was full of secular Jews who did all sorts of things on the Sabbath, so perhaps it wasn't so strange. And it was flattering to be invited to tea with the "head of our liaison team," who had "expressed an interest in chatting with him." Maybe chatting wasn't work, hence okay on the Sabbath.

He was taken to a pleasant, modern room on the fifth floor, where a table had been set up on a balcony that gave a magnificent view of the city and the Mediterranean. The white tablecloth gleamed, the bright sun muted by an awning that bellied lightly in a breeze from the water. Silverware gleamed. Trays of sandwiches and cakes made colored islands in the white-and-silver expanse.

"We can of course offer you something stronger than tea, if you prefer," the head of liaison said. He had a grip on Spinner's right elbow, not proprietary but protective. Another man—heavy-set, fifty, quiet—stood back in the shadow of an inner room.

"No, no—tea is fine." Spinner had no real views on tea, but then he had little interest in food or drink.

They sat, Spinner and the head of liaison facing each other, the heavy-set man between them facing the glare and the ocean. "We have friends in common, I think," the head of liaison said. A young woman, who had appeared from nowhere, was pouring tea while another followed with cream, sugar, lemon—all the wealth of the Indies. "I am acquainted, of course, with your Number One." He meant, it turned out, the Deputy Assistant Secretary who was so many levels above Spinner that Spinner had never even seen him. "We see very much eye to eye." The head of liaison had a guttural but perfectly understandable accent.

They chatted about Washington and about American politics. The heavy-set man contributed little, but the head of liaison was charming and led the conversation. He asked Spinner questions about himself, always flattering. Spinner told some of the funnier stories that floated around his office about The Democrats. Everybody chuckled. It was all very civilized and, as contrast to the night that Spinner had just spent with Elana, very relaxing.

"I wonder—" the head of liaison said. He looked at the heavy-set man. He looked at Spinner. "I wonder if we could impose on you, Mister Spinner—"

"Ray, please—"

"Ray, thank you, yes, I wonder if we could impose on you to—may I say 'advise us'? Maybe too grand a term. You must have an expression?"

"'Share our perspectives'?"

"Exactly! Precisely. 'Advise' is too formal and sounds too much like work." He told a joke about a man who is scolded by a rabbi for beating his donkey on the Sabbath. Then he ate a cake and turned partly sideways so he could take in the view, and he said almost sadly, a little conspiratorially, "We have a dilemma, Ray. Dilemma, is dilemma correct?"

"Dilemma, yes." It was a word that Spinner had never used in his life.

The head of liaison breathed out a big sigh. "We have found that one of the most dangerous of the leaders of Palestinian terrorism has been contacted by an American."

He seemed genuinely grieved and genuinely puzzled. He picked with a fork at crumbs on his plate. "This is a dilemma for us, because we thought we had an understanding with our American friends—our brothers, Ray, let us face it: we are closer than friends—and it hurts, it hurts to find this going on. This man may be a rogue element, but— He has official status." He looked up. "You know something called the Naval Criminal Investigative Service?"

"Oh, yes." Spinner knew it all too well.

"This man is a special agent, as they call them. He has been here making trouble for us; we have had to go to all kinds of lengths to satisfy him. And it seems he is not satisfied, because now he is meeting with our enemies." The head of liaison shook his head. "It hurts, Ray, it hurts."

"Is his name Dukas, by any chance?"

The head of liaison looked at Spinner; the heavy-set man looked at the head of liaison, then at Spinner. "You *know* him?"

"I, mm, know of him."

"Is this meeting, this—forgive me, but I call a spade a spade—this *betrayal* typical of him? Is he that kind of man?"

Spinner thought of the Dukas who had pushed him out of the Navy, the Dukas he'd sent the message to about Salem Qatib. "I'm afraid so, yes."

The head of liaison looked at the heavy-set man, made a gesture of resignation, said to him, "You see?" In English, which might have been thought a bit odd if Spinner had bothered to notice. The head of liaison turned back to Spinner and leaned in, dropping his voice. "Here then is our—" He waved one of the young women away, then waited until the heavy-set man had closed the terrace door. Still, he kept his voice so low that Spinner had to lean in, too. "Here is our dilemma. We cannot allow even our friends, our brothers, to endanger our security. It cannot be tolerated. We must make a gesture, you understand? Do you say 'send a message'?"

"Yes, send a message."

"We must send this Dukas a message. And his superiors, if he is not simply a rogue element. But—" He pursed his lips and made a sound with tongue and teeth, *ttt.* "We want our real friends to understand what we have done. We want them to know we trust them enough to go ahead and do what we know is right. So, you see, my friend, we would like your advice. Can we go ahead and send the message to this Dukas and still have you and our good friends everywhere understand?"

"Absolutely." But Spinner didn't sound quite absolute—there had been a fractional hesitation.

"You think?"

"It depends, sure, on what sort of message you send. I mean, you're not talking about—"

"Let me be candid." The head of liaison glanced at the heavy-set man. "The Palestinian he is to meet is a terrorist. He is on our list of dangerous criminals who are to be executed whenever found. If we can kill him, we will. Does that shock you?"

Spinner shook his head. He had been trying to think like a neocon, and he knew he was supposed to believe in such summary killings. *Evil must be eliminated,* as he had heard McKinnon's boss put it. And yet— Somewhere down in the engine room of Spinner's mind, gears were grinding as if the smallest amount of grit had got into them.

"If we can grab this Palestinian when the meeting takes place, we will. If we can't, we will kill him."

The head of liaison stared into Spinner's eyes. Spinner thought he knew what was being asked, and he said, "I understand." Then he saw the other man's dilemma more clearly and saw what advice was really being asked of him, and he said, "What about Dukas?"

"Ah, the heart of the matter. We don't want to harm him. Far from it! We will go out of our way to protect him.

But—" A long eye-to-eye stare. "You know how these things go. Things can go wrong very quickly. I can't predict the future; I can't make Godlike promises. He might get hurt."

"That's a risk he takes, isn't it? He's a professional."

"That's well said, and it's our view, but we don't want to offend our friends and we don't want to lose their friendship. We might, you know, if something went wrong."

Spinner was on automatic, saying what he thought the other man wanted to hear, a technique he had perfected. "Not if they understand the situation. Not *my* people, anyway." But he was aware of those distantly grinding gears.

"You put my mind at ease. I feel better, talking to you." He looked at the heavy-set man. "Don't you?" The man nodded. The liaison head leaned toward Spinner again. "You agree, then, that we can go forward as our self-interest guides us—capture or kill the Palestinian, do our best to avoid harming the American?"

Again, Spinner hesitated. He was thinking of where he was, of whose turf he was on. He was thinking that things that were said in conversation weren't binding. He said, "Absolutely." But he was thinking that it was just possible that, in the nicest possible way, he was being set up. He'd been a naval officer for ten years; mostly, he'd been the equivalent of a personal assistant or a public relations wonk, but some of the Navy had inevitably rubbed off—hadn't there been lectures about contacts with foreign agents and the rudimentary signs of attempted recruitment?

"You agree, then, that we have your—forgive me, you are a younger man, and the word may amuse you, but you sit here as a representative of all our friends in America—your permission to act?"

Spinner really hesitated this time, aware that something underfoot had shifted. What had McKinnon said? *Don't commit us to anything.* But he wasn't committing anybody—except himself. He saw that he wasn't really in a position to

311

grant "permission;" he hadn't the status. At the same time, it was deeply flattering to be noticed in that way, to be recognized as a man who had come to Israel with a mission of a new kind. And it would be one in Dukas's face. But "permission" was a weird word to be used here on this sunny afternoon. Weird if they were talking about killing somebody. How do you cover yourself and commit yourself at the same time? You don't.

"I'm afraid I'd have to get back to my boss for that," he said.

"Of course, of course! We have your *understanding*, then. It is the same thing. I feel better, immensely better!" The head of liaison laughed; the heavy-set man opened the door; the women appeared and cleared the table and set out sweet wine and liqueurs. "Enough work for the day!" the head of liaison cried. He raised a glass. "To friendship!"

Spinner left half an hour later. One of the women retrieved a tape recorder from under the table. The head of liaison and the heavy-set man looked at each other and the heavy-set man shrugged.

On a nearby street, Ray Spinner was walking, not with any goal and not with much awareness of where he was. Not usually a reflective man, he was conducting a somewhat painful tour of himself and not knowing at all clearly what he found. At the heart of his doubt was the suspicion that he was being recruited by Mossad. Not nastily, and not brutally—not with offers of money and not with threats. But in a friendly, almost open but insidious way. He went over and over the scene on the terrace with the head of liaison and the other man, and he always came up against their request for his *permission* to do something. His *permission*. Even he, in the most self-deluded moments of his egoism, knew that he had no status that justified his giving permission for anything in a foreign country.

312

And there had been the VIP treatment. And the classified briefing. And the guided tour.

He was doing good work here; he didn't doubt that. He'd used Habakkuk to make contact with two people who'd sold him top-notch information about cryptology. He'd been able to send McKinnon a report showing that there was no doubt that Salem Qatib had been killed because of cryptology. The antiquities thing was bogus, a smokescreen.

But nothing in that justified the Mossad head of liaison's asking him for *permission*. In fact, the two things weren't connected; what he'd found about cryptology had been done as a spy, and the treatment he'd had from Mossad was just the opposite. Because he was an honored guest. Because he was—what? Because he was a gentleman, because he was one of the special ones who *understood*. Or at least that must be what Mossad thought—and wasn't it true? But wasn't it also true that he was a low-level munchkin who'd been sent by McKinnon as a kind of poke in the eye to the CIA?

Something was not right. Real life was not this contradictory. Was it?

Where was the clarity that Strauss saw in Plato? Where was the reasoned, talked-out, philosophical order? Why did he feel that he was on the receiving end of that justice that helps only friends and is "nasty"—Strauss's word—to all others in a world where "peace" is always in quotation marks?

Molyvos, Lesvos

Once again, the jangling of the phone pulled Piat awake. He cursed, looked at his watch, and rolled heavily out of his narrow bed. The floor was cold on his feet and he moved as if he had been drugged. He felt old.

The door to the front room was open. Through it, he could see Saida asleep on the couch, snoring lightly with her curled hair covering both pillows. Rashid was asleep in a far corner of the room, curled into a fetal ball with his back to the couch.

Piat picked up the phone.

"Yeah?"

"Jack?"

"Hi, Barry." Piat rubbed a hand over his face.

"I can barely hear you, Jack. Speak up!" Barry sounded excited, even frenetic.

"I have guests, Bear." Piat kept his voice down and started fumbling for coffee.

"I've got it, Jack. I've got it!"

"That's great, Bear." Piat had found the Medaglia D'Oro can in which he kept his coffee. It was empty. He looked into its shiny depths as if expecting to find enough coffee to save him.

"The inscription, Jack. I've solved the inscription."

"That's great, Bear." Jack had already filed Barry's knowledge as completed business—Barry said the inscription was genuine. What it actually said was of mostly academic interest. And he had no coffee.

"Damn it, Jack! Jesus, I've sweated bullets for days. And—" his voice changed, became almost teasing—"I know where the other photos are coming from, Jack. What's that worth to you? Hmmm?"

Piat hadn't given much thought to the other photos. He should have. "Sorry, Bear. I'm waking up."

"One of your bimboes, Jack? Shame on you. This is important! I'm going to be the most famous linguist in the world!"

Jack realized with a sinking feeling that Barry was high on something. His feet were freezing. There were stirrings from the front room. He tried to focus on the issues at hand. He turned his head away from the phone and tried to stifle a yawn. He forced some enthusiasm.

"That's great, Bear. Great. What does it say? And how—" realization dawned on Piat as he spoke— "how—where— where did you get the rest of the inscription? You said you

314

only had one side?" Piat pictured the photos he'd given Barry. "I don't have any photos of the other side."

"I do, Jack." Smug. "I have pictures of the whole inscription. I'm the only one who has the whole thing, Jack." Barry laughed with unsuppressed adolescent triumph. "I'm going to slay them at Cambridge and Yale. Hah!"

Piat wondered how many people had shared Barry's triumph in the last few hours. He was already looking out the window. He'd slept too long. "Where did the other pictures come from, Bear?"

"Fair is fair, Jack. I owe you an apology, okay? I went off half-cocked about that. To be honest, I'd hold on to this tidbit and get a little more moolah out of you, but I accused you unfairly." Barry's tones had taken on a familiar arrogance.

Jack thought that Barry was preparing himself for his new role as a famous linguist. "I appreciate that. I wouldn't hold out on you, Bear."

"My concern in this matter," Barry said carefully, "is that my other sources might have better access to the object than you."

Piat could see where this was going even without coffee.

Saida's head popped around the kitchen door. She smiled. She looked very good for a woman who had just woken up in a strange bed. Piat found that he had smiled back. Her head vanished and he heard her walking barefoot to the washroom. He wondered if she were naked.

"I doubt it, Bear. In fact, I'd say it was pretty unlikely."

"You have it? Gawd, Jack! Do you have it?"

"Later today, Bear." In fact, Piat thought he knew where it was already. The realization hit him that second.

"That's grand, Jack. You've put my mind at ease. Well, that's great. Perhaps—" Barry was going to get cagey, Piat could hear it in his voice. Piat discovered that he was fed up with Barry.

"Where'd the other photos come from, Bear?"

"Why don't you just call me when you have the object? And then we'll talk."

"Bear, I'd like to know now."

"You haven't even asked about the inscription."

"I'd like to know that, too."

Barry was smug again. "I think I should save that until we have equal bargaining positions, Jack."

"Bear," Piat spoke as forcefully as he could manage. "Listen to me, Bear. This is the bargaining position. I know where the cup is and I can arrange for it any time I want." Bare feet in the corridor outside the kitchen. They stopped, probably just at the closed kitchen door. *Screw her*, thought Piat. And hoped she didn't bolt or hadn't heard his last sentence. "I can buy it today and resell it tonight. I don't need the inscription or the other photos or anything, Bear. You want access to the object. You need me. I don't need the inscription to sell the object, Bear. You understand?"

Too damned harsh. Piat listened to the silence at the other end and waited for Barry to hang up. He shook his head at his own ineptitude.

"You—wouldn't do that, Jack?"

"No, Bear, I wouldn't." *I would if you pissed me off enough, compadre.* "You pissed me off, Bear."

Adolescent hurt. "I guess so. I guess so. Gawd, Jack—this matters so much, okay? This is my ticket out. Our ticket out. But I ought to tell you, anyway. I'm sorry, Jack. I was out of line—"

"Forget it, Bear."

"There's a set of photos with a classical hack at a Christian university in Texas."

"You said that."

"Yes. Well. It came to me from a friend at Cambridge. And the Texan got it from—you ready for this, Jack? From Israel. Government."

Piat nodded silently. "How do you know?"

"The guy's first email to my colleague included the entire original post as a forward." Bear sounded contemptuous.

Piat laughed with him. "That's very interesting."

"I thought so. But there's another set of photos going around."

Piat was alive and kicking now. "Shoot."

"They're pornographic, baby! Seriously. There's what we would have called a 'wicked-cute' chick in the buff with the cup. She's got tits! And a view of the cup that had the piece I was missing. I had most of the inscription—I actually guessed correctly what one of the missing words had to be, Jack, I'm that good. But there were four words and a name and a complete picture panel gone, just not visible. Gawd, it was frustrating! And then another acquaintance came to me with these three photos. Kismet, Hardy!"

Piat thought he knew whose tits were in the photos. She had been listening at the kitchen door. He had a puerile temptation to jerk the door open. "What acquaintance, Bear?"

"Chap I knew at Yale. Spanish gentleman. Not a serious historian or linguist, but he buys things; he's an aristocrat. He sent me the photos. And he got them from an academic in Egypt."

He buys things. Piat could read Barry's mind on that subject. He let it go. Egypt meant the University of Cairo, where Yasser Arafat had received his education. Palestinian U.

It didn't make Piat want to yawn, but it didn't change anything, except to add another potential buyer for the cup. If he could get the cup from Saida. Piat put his icy right foot on the top of his left foot.

"What does it say, Bear?"

"I thought you'd never ask!" Barry had already forgotten that he had intended to hold out. "I don't suppose you want to know how I cracked it or what dialect it's in—"

"Over a beer, Bear. Save it for in person."

"It was the best work I've ever done, Jack. It was all just

there. I dreamt about it, Jack. I feel like I've held it in my hands and drunk from it."

Piat had dreamed about the cup a few times, too. He didn't say so.

"It's a treaty, all right. Oh, Gawd, I wish I could see your face when I say this, because it's just so fucking amazing, Jack. It's a treaty, with a king who might, quite arguably, be Odysseus—"

Jack could suddenly see why Barry was so excited. "You're shitting me."

"I shit you not!" Barry's voice was happier. Jack had just sounded involved. That was what Barry wanted.

Odysseus! Now you're talking. Piat laughed. He didn't really believe Barry, but it was a pleasant myth.

"This cup is just one miracle after another, Jack. Semitic symbols in with Linear B. Odysseus. And the treaty—well, it's in honor of a war, or a fight, a battle. Allies. The Danae and the Peleset—"

"I remember this part, Bear."

"And the people of Yahweh, Jack. Against Egypt. And the people of Yahweh give this land to the Greeks and the Peleset."

Piat had a roaring in his ears. He didn't hear a word of Barry's literal translation. He forgot about wily Odysseus. He forgot his cold feet and his craving for coffee. Because he could see it all, the whole thing, the agents and the thugs and the hurry and now he knew the stakes.

Armageddon, today.

He snapped back and cut off Barry's flow.

"Suicide Kings, Barry." It was an ancient code word from their first comm plan.

"What? Jack—oh, fuck. Okay, bye."

The phone went dead.

Piat had to wonder who else Barry had told of his linguistic feat. He looked at his watch and out the window. The sun was shining. He opened the kitchen door. She was gone, if she had ever been there, and when he looked into the front room she was pulling a top over her head with every intention of provoking Rashid, who lay with his back to her.

Her breasts really were very good. Piat coughed.

She didn't jump, just turned. "Good morning."

"Where's the cup, Saida?"

"You said something about seven hundred and fifty thousand dollars."

"That's my bid, yes. But my conditions are that I see it first."

"Something tells me you don't have that kind of money, sweetie." She smiled at him nonetheless.

Piat didn't return the smile. "I will when I sell it on. Listen to me, honey. I'm willing to give you a little less than half of what I can get for it. No one else in the world will give you as much. Don't get greedy on me."

"You are in a hurry, now. That was the buyer on the phone."

"No, that was my authenticator. But I have a buyer."

"It's not hers to sell." Rashid was awake, sitting up, his arms crossed against his chest and his face haggard. "It's Salem's."

Saida barely glanced at him. "My fiancée. Rashid told me he has been killed. I knew it before I left."

Did you now? thought Piat.

"It was Salem's. It is not yours, you—" a stream of Arabic from Rashid, interrupted and out-shrilled by Saida.

"Did you think of Salem when we made love?" Saida asked in English. She flashed a smile at Piat.

Rashid slammed his fist into the wall.

Piat didn't feel very authoritative, standing barefoot in his boxer shorts, but he had plenty of anger to use and he used it. "Get some clothes on, Saida. Look at me, both of you. *Look at me.* We have a few hours, maybe less, until somebody

319

figures out where I live. I don't think they'll hesitate to shoot their way in. Got me? Saida, you can take my offer or leave it. I'm out of here in an hour, with the cup or without it."

"I may have a better offer." Saida pouted as she jerked her jeans on. "Where are these Israelis? I think you make them up to scare me."

Piat retreated to the doorway. "Okay, have it your way. I wash my hands of you. But you've got the fucking cup *in your pack* and when they catch you they won't even have to torture you for its location."

Rashid's head whipped around to look at the pack.

Saida burst into tears. "You bastards!" She wrapped her arms around the pack. "I want *out*. Out! Away from the fucking Israelis and the Hamas and the Islamic Jihad and the settlers and the Palestinian Authority. I want out! I want to go somewhere and live a pretty life. Not in a war. With *nice things*. Salem was going to take us away. The United States! This is mine. You fuckers. You—" back to Arabic. A little French, which Piat understood all too well.

He didn't reply. He went to his own room and started putting things in a bag.

It took him less than five minutes to shave, dress, and pack what he would take. He needed to pick up a package he had buried. That would take another hour. He needed to firm up his arrangements with Andros about getting off the island.

He still wanted to see the cup. It wasn't greed; he could live broke. It was something else. Something he could live without, but he'd be sorry.

And he wasn't ever going to run to Thermi. His running shoes sat in a corner, discarded as unnecessary at this point, with his shorts still sitting in the dregs of a bucket of washwater in the kitchen.

"Why should I trust you?" Saida asked from the doorway.

Piat shrugged. "You shouldn't. But if I had to answer, I'd

say that I have a gun and I could have had the pack anytime I wanted it."

She was slumped against the wood of the doorpost, her arms wrapped around the pack, all her armor gone. "I have other things, too. Salem said they were our 'travel fund.'"

Piat's stomach gave him a little jolt when she said "other things."

Rashid pushed past her into Piat's room. "They aren't hers."

"Whose are they?" Piat asked quietly. "Let's get serious, Rashid. Who do you want to give them to?"

Rashid didn't have an answer. He looked as if he didn't have anything at all. "She's like poison," he spat.

Piat pointed at the pack. He couldn't stop himself now, not if every officer in Mossad came through the front window with a pair of Uzis blazing. "Let's see it, Saida."

She went to the bed and opened her pack. She took out a brown paper bag, a mailing tube, and a cardboard box. The mailing tube's shape had given the game away to Piat's subconscious, that and the faintly metallic noise the box made when she moved it.

She opened the box and held up the cup like a gift, like a plea for Piat's attention. "Salem said it was the greatest find since Troy." She smiled crookedly, and shrugged. "Please?"

Piat didn't see anything else in the room. It was smaller than he had expected, although he knew its measurements. There was a shiny spot on the base where the stem had rubbed against the cardboard of the box. *She carried it on a bus.* He let out his breath.

The niello was almost perfect, running in a slightly uneven spiral around the brim and down the bowl, with symbols engraved in a band of gold between the niello panels. There was the king, clearly a Greek king, sitting on a chair with a spear in his hand. There was the same man dragging a warrior from a chariot, his spear through the other man's jaw like a salmon gaff. That piece of brutality was lovingly, realistically rendered. Near the bottom, three men fought a lion together; one had a shaggy beard and long robes and a tiara and the other two wore Mycenaean tunics, one of them wore a helmet of boar's teeth and the other a helmet of bronze with horns, and they all carried heavy figure-eight shields.

"Is it—wonderful?" she asked.

"The greatest find since Troy." Piat reached out and took it from her. It was heavy. Gold was always surprisingly heavy.

"They killed Salem for that?" Rashid asked.

Saida took a deep breath. "They killed Salem—oh, Rashid, they killed Salem for stealing from them."

"How do you know that? You didn't even know he was dead."

Piat decided that he didn't want to hear the revelation he thought this other Saida was going to make. Once she said it—

"What else is in there?" he said brusquely. He wondered what could be "traveling money" next to the cup.

The paper bag had a collection of pierced boar's teeth. It took Piat a few seconds to see that there were too many for a necklace. "A whole helmet." He shook his head. "As good as the one from Dendros." He dumped the paper bag out on the bed; dozens of matched teeth, each tooth pierced at the top and bottom. And a tiny, beautiful golden owl to close the top.

There were fewer than ten boar's-tooth helmets in the world. Most were in private collections; they were impossible to fake, and any dealer would buy one in a heartbeat. *This Salem guy knew his stuff.*

In fact, Piat knew where he could sell the helmet without leaving Lesvos. And, like Salem, he needed traveling money.

"I can get you twenty thousand US for the helmet," he said to Saida. Seeing her expression, he said, "For the teeth. In the bag."

She nodded. "Okay." All the life seemed to have gone out

of her. She was looking at Rashid, who was looking at the wall, not the cup, not the boar's teeth.

"What's in the tube?"

She shook her head. "Salem wrapped it." She held it out to him.

He took it and popped the plastic end off the mailing tube and removed something hard and metallic wrapped in bubble wrap and an old bag. It was eighteen inches long.

It was a sword. Bronze, with niello inlay like the cup's and a heavy hilt made of carved, milky stone. The bronze was green and black where the silver inlay had leached into the metal, but the gold and silver were bright. Someone had wiped it clean. It had three deep notches in the blade and a big chip out of the stone of the pommel.

Piat could guess that the same artist who put the figures on the cup had done the blade.

He shook his head and sat heavily on the edge of the bed and looked up at Saida. "We'll never get what any of these things are worth," he said with more honesty than he'd intended. He pointed the sword at Rashid. "Maybe—maybe he's right."

"Right how?" she asked, the hardness in her mouth flowing back over her face.

Piat looked back at the blade. He couldn't resist putting his fist around the hilt. "Just give me a minute to let my natural greed reassert itself, okay?" The blade balanced the pommel perfectly. "I was thinking that they belong together, in a museum. But that's not a luxury that we'd be allowed even if we were that kind of people." He thought of what the cup said, and his arms and shoulders trembled.

No cup with that inscription would sit quietly to be pored over by academics in a museum. People would die. Conveniently, Piat's needs and the greater good coincided.

Saida didn't even try to understand what his comment meant. "Only if they pay."

"Salem wanted the Palestinian people to have a great museum," Rashid said. "We used to talk about it."

"Salem told me that we'd live like rich people in the United States," Saida shot back. "I'm tired of talk. That's all we Palestinians do is talk. How much?"

Piat nodded for a while, his head bobbing up and down. They needed to get out of this town and off Lesvos. He could do it alone with the money he had; he could do it for all of them with twenty thousand dollars.

"You want to trust me to sell this stuff? Or not. Like I said. Take it or leave it."

"Okay, I'll take it." Saida was recovering; she gave Piat a big, fake smile.

Rashid grunted in pain or disgust.

Piat bored straight on, his eyes resting on the blade of the sword.

"I have to run an errand. I'll leave it all right here with you in your pack. Then we take a little trip together, and I'll get some money for the helmet. The boar's teeth. Okay? And then I arrange some transport and set up the deal for the cup and we get out of here. You two can watch the deal. I get half the cash." He nodded again. "Just like that."

"Where are we going to go?" Saida asked.

"Does it matter?"

"Tell me." Saida stamped her foot.

Rashid didn't participate at all. Piat was still too dazzled by the sword to pay him any attention.

"We'll get a boat ride from the Ypsilou monastery to Turkey. Ypsilou is on the coast—a friend of mine picks up passengers there. We'll do the deal in Izmir or Istanbul. Then we all go our separate ways. Good enough?"

Saida cocked her head to one side. "How soon?"

Piat hesitated—and told her the truth. "Monday. Monday night—we'll have to hole up until then, okay? I can't get transport before then." *Although I'll try.*

She nodded as if she understood.

Piat wrapped the sword, slid it into the tube, and popped the plastic cap back into place.

"I'll be gone an hour. If you wander off, I'll assume that means you're on your own."

Saida smiled. "I'm not going anywhere without you," she said. It sounded like a line from an American soap opera. Piat wondered if she had said it to Salem. He looked over at Rashid. "You okay, kid?"

"Sure." Rashid took a deep breath as if he was going to speak, and then he let it out. "Sure."

Piat was tempted to ignore precautions and move fast, but that was one temptation he never gave in to, and he walked a careful route, purchasing a Cadbury bar from a shop, crossing the middle range of the hill and making two deviations to see who might be watching him.

As best he could tell, he was alone.

Sooner or later, last night's Israelis would find a way to trace him or his borrowed truck. It was a small town.

Time to go. Time to go. Time to go.

He went into the internet café and paid, sat at a computer and read his messages. He replied to three. He sent two of them a new email address.

He went to a pay phone and called Andros, now hoping to move the trip off the island forward, but of course no one answered.

He walked around the headland, the cold wind plastering his hair against his face and making his ankles cold through his socks. He stuck to the rocks of the beach until he saw a drainpipe, and then he climbed a natural trail to a small field protected from the wind by big, old trees. The town rose in front of him, row on row of tiled roofs ascending like a red staircase to the sand-colored walls of the citadel on the acropolis. At his feet were huge slabs of volcanic rock, by art or nature joined into a single floor that covered twenty square meters. A threshing floor. One corner of its foundation remained, and Jerry reached into a natural fissure and removed a tin box.

The box was open. Piat's heart began to pound.

The plastic bag that protected the contents was intact, except for a small, round hole. Inside the bag was a nest with tiny field mice bedded down in the carefully shredded paper and plastic that had once been Piat's last clean passport. He struggled with a surge of frustrated rage, saw himself grinding the contents of the box under his heel, flinging them into the sea.

He didn't.

Piat put the bag tenderly back into the box and put the box where he had found it. The little naked mice made a thin wailing sound that seemed to carry on the wind all the way back to town.

When he reached his house, Saida was crying, a thin, wild noise, like the mice.

Rashid was gone.

Rashid boarded the bus for Mytilene, feeling the weight of all the possible invisible watchers on his back. To which he had just added the American, Jack. Jack, who talked to him like he was a small boy but told him so many things he wanted to know. Jack, who was about to be another victim of Saida. Even when he was on the bus, Rashid was tempted to get off, go back and do—something. For Jack.

In effect, he was running away on Jack as he had run away on Salem. That's how it felt, and his betrayal of the American seemed worse. What had Jack done to him? And he, Rashid, the king of hypocrites, had fucked Saida—*Oh, the glory of it*, said one part of his traitor brain, remembering her, and *Oh, the betrayal of Salem*, said the other.

When the bus set him down in Mytilene, he made his way

to a pay phone and called one of the preset numbers he had been given. Ali answered on the first ring. He was angry and forgiving and then angry by turns, which reminded Rashid of his mother. He ordered Rashid to remain where he was until another agent came to meet him. He suggested that Rashid would be punished for his absence. Rashid felt that he deserved to be punished.

And then Rashid began to explain where he had been.

Saida had a license and a credit card, so Piat sent her to get them a rental car at the Avis storefront down the hill. He had to assume that all her transactions were being watched, but his present needs out-balanced the risk. He was aware that he had reached a plateau of crisis where he was taking so many risks that eventually one of them would come back to bite him. In fact, he was aware that he was now simply reacting to each crisis without ever getting ahead.

It was a familiar feeling.

He started on the bottle of ouzo he had in his house while he waited for her to come back, wondering if she would come back. He thought that it would be easier, really; without Saida or the cup, his escape would be simple, and he would merely be poor. He had time to think about the inscription on the cup and what it would mean in various different hands: Israeli hands, Palestinian hands, American hands. Other hands: Hamas, Iran, Russia, China. All the hands that stirred the pot of "Middle East Peace." He drank the last glass of ouzo neat.

He really ought to tell somebody. He laughed to himself, imagining calling the Agency desk officer—*Hey, remember me? I murdered one of my colleagues? Yeah, anyway*—Yeah. Anyway. Those bridges were burned.

He thought of various men and women he knew in various posts around the world. None of them seemed very useful, and few of them would have anything to do with him. And somewhere in the ouzo he thought of Rashid's peacoat, now gone from the kitchen chair, and the symbol. Pen and a lightning bolt. Piat knew where he had seen that badge, over and over again. *Navy cryptologist.* Salem Qatib had been a navy cryptologist.

Piat thought he knew whom he could call. And how he might yet be rid of the kids. The dark side of his mind suggested that if he got rid of the kids at the right time, he'd have the cup all to himself.

Saida came through the door, all smiles and curly hair. "It was easy!" she called from the doorway.

He had really liked this house and this town and the run up the mountain. He had enjoyed sharing his home with Sappho and Alcaeus and Achilles and Briseis. And then he thought *I'm coming back.* At first it seemed like a stupid thought, but the more he looked at it the simpler it seemed. Without the two kids, he would not be of interest to anyone. He'd lie low. Hell, he ought to have money soon enough; pots of the stuff. *I'm coming back.* He felt better every time he thought it. It could be done. With just a little luck.

He left all his books, his running shoes, his shorts. He took three sets of clothes, some underwear, and his copy of *The Iliad.*

"Let's go," Piat said.

He drove. The car was small but new and had all the acceleration that the old Nissan had lacked, and he passed the aqueduct at Thera and turned west toward the center of the island. By three o'clock, he was in Kalloni. As far as he could tell, no one was following them.

He parked the car in the parking lot of a modern supermarket several streets short of the business district, next to a heavy Mercedes SUV with Spanish plates; a late-season EU tourist. The combination of ideas reminded him of how much EU money was in Greece; suddenly, it was part of modern Europe.

He led Saida to a nightclub that served breakfast all day. His only rival in the antiquity business on the island was there before him, a serious older Englishman who pretended to the manners of the British upper class. Piat thought that Teddy had been born in Essex or even London's East End. Not that it mattered to him.

"Odd taste in restaurants, old boy," Teddy said. "We could do a lot better."

Piat shrugged. "I like it," he said. "You must be enjoying the weather this winter; good for your boat." Teddy had a small sailboat, to which he referred constantly.

"Smashing. Simply brilliant. Been all around the island. Those poor sods in the channel don't know how lucky I am, really. You? Been out on the wine-dark sea, eh?"

Piat thought of the trip by Zodiac with Rashid vomiting. He tried not to think about what Rashid's desertion meant. He nodded. "Just a little. Managed to catch the rough weather." Piat realized he was mimicking the studied cadence of the other man's speech.

Teddy paid no attention to Saida, which confirmed Piat's long-held assumption that despite being married, Teddy was immune to the charms of women.

Teddy leaned forward across the table. "Is this—helmet— I mean, really, George."

Piat opened Saida's pink backpack and took out the brown paper bag. He removed the teeth a few at a time, building concentric circles of three-thousand-year-old boar's teeth on the round table until only the owl was left in the bag. Finally, he placed the golden owl in the center.

Teddy couldn't hide his gasp of awe.

"Fifty thousand. US. Cash."

Teddy looked at him. "I—was going to bargain, old man. Can't do that, I suppose?"

Piat tried to hide his contempt. "It's worth half a million dollars. I don't have the time to sell it. Fifty thousand, cash."

Teddy nodded. He couldn't take his eyes off the helmet. He was about to make a great deal of money, and he clearly thought there was a catch.

"Where's it from?"

Piat shook his head. "You don't want to know."

Teddy nodded as if that made him important. "How do I know it's genuine?"

Piat shrugged. "I don't know how anyone could fake one, Teddy, but if you don't like it—"

Teddy held both of his hands up in surrender. He reached into his raincoat and pulled out a used brown envelope. "Some of it is in pounds. Sorry about that. But the count's right—got the exchange off the laptop two hours ago. You're leaving, aren't you?"

Piat raised his head from the cash, surprised that he was so transparent and more surprised that he was transparent to Teddy.

"You've always been square with me, George, so I think I ought to tell you that there've been some enquiries."

"About me?"

Teddy nodded, clearly embarrassed by the whole subject. "You, and other—other things." He nodded minutely at Saida, who was mesmerized by Piat's piles of bills.

Piat felt his hands begin to shake. He waved over the lone waitress and ordered a Scotch and soda. Teddy ordered wine. Saida continued to watch the growing pile of money.

The waitress had seen too many drug deals to be especially interested. She moved off lazily in the direction of the bar.

"What did you tell them, Teddy?"

"Me? Not a thing. I don't even know where you live. In fact, the questions they asked left me wondering—about how little I really know about you." Teddy had started to collect the teeth. He left the golden owl in the center of the table where he could see it. He looked up at Piat and shrugged.

330

"None of my business. As I said, old boy, you've always been square with me."

Piat finished his count. The last four thousand was in small bills. He had scraped Teddy dry of cash, but Teddy wouldn't have to worry about that ever again. Piat thrust it all back into the envelope, pushed the envelope into his tweed jacket, and rose, offering his hand. Teddy had been "square" in return.

"I'm off to Turkey in an hour," Piat said.

Saida gave a little start. "You said—" She waved her hands. Then she caught the look on Piat's face. "Oh. I wanted to shop."

Teddy nodded and shook his hand. "Good luck, George."

"Thanks, Teddy. The helmet won't bite you; that much I can promise. Goodbye."

He shepherded Saida out into the winter sunshine and steered her toward a phone kiosk.

"You told him we were leaving for Turkey. Tonight. You told me Monday!"

"He'll talk to someone. Get it?"

Saida blinked once and gave him a long look as he walked next to her. Piat didn't like the look. It implied that she'd just decided he was cleverer than she had thought.

She stood outside while he tried both numbers he had for Andros and got no answer. She pouted while he dialed international information. It cost him six euros in change to find the number he wanted and reach an automated recording that informed him that the Naval Criminal Investigative Service Headquarters was closed for the weekend and he could reach them between nine and five on Monday. Just as he was about to hang up, a different electronic voice indicated that in the event of an emergency, he could reach the duty officer at another number.

Piat leaned out to Saida. "Got any change?"

The duty officer answered on the first ring. He sounded young and enthusiastic. Piat thought that it was about time he got a break.

"Naval Criminal Investigative Service Headquarters Weekend Duty Officer this is not a secure line may I help you?" he said.

"I need to reach Special Agent Mike Dukas." Piat spoke rapidly, because only speed would work. "It's an operational emergency."

"Wow," the kid on the other end said.

Naples

"Al Craik's bad. Rose is real worried."

Mike Dukas was home, a little disoriented from the change, disgruntled because he felt he'd mostly wasted a week. He wanted to tell her his troubles, but she told him Al Craik's instead. "How bad?" he said.

"Something that happened in Afghanistan; she thinks he's depressed—I mean, you know, the real-thing depressed."

"I'm not a lot of laughs myself. I'll talk to him at dinner. That's tonight, right?" They were all going out to a Naples restaurant, Craik's treat. Dukas sighed. "Now do I get to pour out my heart to you?"

"What are wives for?"

He told it all to her. Leslie was a good listener, a good questioner.

"You've got a case but no proof," she said.

"You got it. I think the four guys at the office in Jaffa were rent-a-goons who somehow got hold of Salem Qatib and killed him, but I don't know how and I don't know why. And I don't know who they are or where they are now. Some case."

"Why would they kill him?"

"Probably they didn't mean to. I don't know. When I went down to the site of the illegal dig—the one that had been magically turned into a settlement, two trailers and some AK-47s—I wound up talking to the guys that drove these bulldozers. They looked like frigging antiques—the dozers, not the guys. They'd done the first pass in the illegal dig, scraped it down to the layer where stuff was."

332

"They told you that?"

"Not right away, and not for free."

"And then they're putting all the dirt back so the Israelis can build a settlement?"

"Yeah, equal-opportunity heavy equipment. I guess if you're a Palestinian you take work where you can get it. But they were pretty up-front about it. They'd bulldozed it the first time for some guys from Hamas. Digging is no biggie—the Authority gives out the licenses to dig. But this was Hamas, which isn't the PA's best buddy. Anyway, after they'd dozed it the first time, they'd pulled the dozers out and a lot of local guys got to work with shovels, and the dozer guys hung around because they were supposed to close it up when the dig was over. But then in comes the Israeli military, and there was a big blowup and the dig was closed down. Then a couple of days later, the Israelis come back and pay them to cover everything up and grade it for the so-called settlement."

"That's it?"

"That would've been it if I'd run out of money. The dozer guys wouldn't give me anything about specifics—who, why. I showed them Qatib's Navy photo from the file—never saw him, never heard of him. I had this Tel Aviv lady cop and a Palestinian police guy, some kind of liaison-translator, with me; they were about as welcome with these guys as a blizzard at a beach party. I wandered away and said thank you, thank you, trying to put some distance between me and the other two in hopes that one of the guys would come after me. But instead, this little Palestinian shows up sort of from nowhere; he's got a kid with him about twelve years old, but the kid speaks English. Sort of. They're very direct—for a thousand dollars US, he'll tell me everything."

"What kind of everything?"

"I go, 'Who the hell are you?' and he says, I was a digger. I saw everything. Okay, but I don't give a thousand US just for that. Tell me. So we haggle and carry on, and the kid is really pretty good. Finally, three hundred down, the rest if the info is good."

"A thousand dollars? You were walking around with a thousand dollars on you?"

"Honey, I was in a place where people would kill me just for being there; why would I worry about how much I was carrying? Anyway, it wasn't my money. So the long and the short of it is, the little guy saw the Israelis come in and start beating the shit out of people. He and his buds were running all over the place. Israeli soldiers, they're following the diggers and chasing them off and whacking them with rifles. My guy says he jumped into a trench and crawled along it and got to a corner of the site where the guy who was in charge of the dig wouldn't let anybody go but himself and a sexy young woman."

Leslie smiled. "His word, 'sexy'?"

"The kid translated it as 'godless,' and the guy jabbered and I think the point was she didn't wear a headscarf and had a lot of skin showing. So I showed the guy the photo of Qatib, and he says, 'That's the guy. That's the guy who was telling us where to dig.'

"Now, this makes a kind of sense, because Qatib was an archaeologist. But at the same time, it was the only photo I had, so he could have been bullshitting me." Dukas sighed. He looked at Leslie, winked. They hadn't made love because her doctor thought it would be better now for the baby if they didn't; the wink was a kind of joke about doing all this talking and not fucking. "If I'd had five photos, I could have done a sequential lineup, got an honest reaction."

"You get what you pay for," she said.

"Oh, yeah, right. So, I ask him why the corner of the site was off-limits. Much jabbering and pointing. By the way, we're now behind a sort of dune so nobody can see us; the guy is really worried about the Palestinian liaison man.

334

Anyway, the gist of it is—if the kid can translate well enough; who knows?—that the one he IDs as Qatib had found a separate thing he wanted all to himself. It's round and it's got a pointy top, and the bulldozer knocked a piece out of it. That's all the guy knows about that, except that Qatib, if it was Qatib, and the godless woman have been inside it a lot, and the chatter among the diggers was they were taking stuff out. No idea what the stuff is. No idea how much stuff. But it must have been important, he says, because three Hamas guys showed up *before* the Israeli raid and started whacking Qatib around. His reason for thinking Qatib had walked off with some stuff—it was a Hamas dig, he was supposed to be Hamas's man, and he's stealing from them, so they beat the shit out of him. Biff-bang-whack! The Israelis showed up and some of them went right for this pointy thing where Qatib and the Hamas guys were, and they dragged the guy—Qatib—out, and the old man says he was bloody from head to foot. But walking. Looked like he'd been through a meat-grinder, but he was walking. And the Israelis drove off with him."

"Not great information."

"Well, yes and no. After I got back to Tel Aviv, I called this babe I know at the University of Michigan—we're having archaeological phone sex—and I describe this round, pointy thing and she says, 'Oh, a tholos.' Which means, a one-man tomb from, for example, *The Iliad*."

"My God, Greek!"

"My-God-Greek, indeed."

"Like what Triffler told you about."

"Very much like what Triffler told me he found in Athens, you got it. Yeah. I didn't know any of that then, but I talked to him on the phone yesterday before I left; it's intriguing. Yeah, Greek is big right now.

"So, anyway, there's the little guy crouched down in his trench by this tholos, and the Israeli goons and some bigwig—my guy thinks he's a bigwig because he's kicking ass in all directions—they drag the guy who may be Qatib *out* of the tholos and they beat the shit out of him, too. Right there. Then they drag him to a car and drive away."

"Where's the godless woman?"

"He doesn't know. He didn't see her. He's now hiding under a tarpaulin and hoping nobody drives over him with a dozer. Although what happens is, by late afternoon, people are back to digging, but they're different people, and the Israeli guy who was kicking ass is now in charge. My guy waits until it's dark and runs away, by which time they've got a generator and some police lights going and they're hard at work."

"What happened to the tholos?"

"He doesn't know. People went in and brought stuff out, but he doesn't think they got a whole lot. I think he made this part up because in fact he was under the tarpaulin by then."

"Did you give him the thousand?"

"I thought it was a thousand bucks' worth of creative story-telling even if it wasn't the truth; if it was the truth, it was worth a lot more than that." Dukas had her feet in his lap; he was massaging her calves. "A lot of it fits. The woman—we got a missing woman from that apartment I went to. The Greek connection. Qatib with the shit beaten out of him, which he certainly was when Al saw his corpse. The chatter in Athens about a big Greek find, and the guy Triffler talked to that was so cagey about an inscription."

"But why does Qatib show up dead in an Israeli facility in Jaffa? At the very least, it sounds like the Israelis killed him."

Dukas was silent. He swayed his head back and forth. He made *mmmm* sounds. "I'm starting from the Jaffa end. That's where the body was found. That says to me some not very bright guys killed him onsite—Qatib was already there

336

somehow, alive, and he died. They wanted to cover it up. I think they got him at the dig. And they knew who he was." Dukas shifted position under her legs. "It's thin; I know it's thin. But this guy I was with in Bosnia, Eshkol, he works against the PA in the illegal antiquities field. I think these were his guys—his muscle. Eshkol might even be the honcho who took over the dig. So they would have tried to get information from Qatib, even if they found him all beaten up by the PA. Although I'm not sure Eshkol would have told them to risk killing him; he's got a kind of moral sense."

"Is that why he came to see you, his moral sense?" For a twenty-one-year-old, she was surprisingly willing to accept the idea of a moral sense.

Dukas thought about it. "Maybe, yeah. I got the feeling— I was mad as hell when I had breakfast with him, but I felt— he was sort of torn up. Pulling in opposite directions. Like he loves his country and he's loyal as a sonofabitch to Mossad, but he hates that they're doing things he knows are wrong. Like he wanted to help me, but he couldn't be a traitor."

"So he gives you hints, but he also raids the dig and has Qatib beaten up."

"We don't know that. Whatever sent them to raid the dig—an informer, air surveillance, luck, who the hell knows?— they weren't in time to get whatever came out of the tholos, because the talk about that is in Athens, and it isn't coming from the Israelis. So I think somebody—let's say the woman—is out there with some stuff that's taking on a lot of importance." He squeezed her thigh and raised his eyebrows. "If I knew where the woman and the stuff were, it'd almost make it up to me for no fucking."

She leaned forward and kissed him. "I can maybe make it up to you, anyway."

He laid an index finger on her lips. "Nothing makes up for no fucking." He was an old-fashioned man. "Still—"

And then the telephone rang.

He groaned; Leslie said she'd get it; he said let it ring; she was already heading for the phone. And of course she said, "For you."

"Dick?"

She shook her head. She had the mouthpiece covered. "Not a voice I know. American. Guy." She handed him the phone.

"Dukas."

"Mike, this is Jerry."

Jerry. He didn't know any Jerrys. "Jerry who?" Like a knock-knock joke.

"Last time you heard from me, I sent you a postcard with a Mustang on it and a photo of a diner."

Oh, *that* Jerry. *Oh, Sweet Jesus—Jerry Piat.* The postcard had come, with no signature, from someplace like Singapore, and all it had said was, "I didn't know she was your girl." Because Piat had spent the night with a woman Dukas had been seeing, and she had got killed by somebody who thought she was Piat. And because Piat had been in NCIS custody and had skipped when two agents were dumb enough to let him loose on the street without noticing that he had the body to outrun both of them.

That Jerry Piat. Ex-CIA, ex- and probably current crook, specializing in antiques. Probably murderer of a creep who had deserved killing, but it was still murder and had been done on CIA property. "Oh, yeah," Dukas said. A distinct lack of enthusiasm.

"I need a favor."

"We tried that once before. You screwed me."

"Hey, hey, you got what you wanted. There was nothing personal in any of it."

"Oh, yeah, that makes all the difference. Sorry—I don't do favors for guys on the lam."

Brief silence. The voice then angrier, terser. "I've got something you want."

338

Well, that had to be bullshit. No way Jerry Piat could know what he wanted. "Bullshit."

"Don't blow me off, Dukas! I've got something goddam important, and you or somebody you can be in touch with wants it. Dukas—this is *big*."

"Big like what?" Again, a silence. It was an open phone; Piat was no fool. In fact, Dukas remembered a grudging liking for Piat. "Okay, so tell me."

"I can't tell you much, and you know why. This is a thing, an object. It's the same culture as your ancestors. *Those* guys. But it came out of a surprising place—over there where Samson came from. You read the Bible?"

Dukas didn't read the Bible. He didn't even own a Bible. But a phrase came to him—no, a book title. *Eyeless in Gaza.* Where the hell did that come from? Was it about Samson? "You mean, where a lot of Biblical stuff went down."

"Some of it."

Greek. Gaza. Holy shit. "What kind of object is it?"

"It's a valuable object. A very valuable object. But its real value is in the inscription on it, which is going to do for certain countries there at the end of the Mediterranean what the golden tablets did for the Mormons. Think international repercussions, Mike."

He had said to Leslie, *the woman, the stuff from the tholos.* Triffler had talked about the inscription and rewriting Israeli history. "Is this object a recent find?"

Piat's tone changed, became both suspicious and admiring. "You know more than you let on."

"Did a woman come with it?"

Silence. Then: "I may end this call right now. You jerking me around?"

"Yes or no is all I want. Maybe I'll do you a favor, after all."

"Yeah, there's a woman. So what?"

"Where are you?"

339

Piat laughed, not very pleasantly. "Oh, sure! Look, my friend, you know better than that."

"Give me a meeting, we'll talk about a favor. More than that I don't do by phone."

Piat hesitated yet again, then muttered, "Shit." His voice got suddenly louder, as if he'd taken a new grip on the phone. "Okay. Day and time?"

"That depends. I'm in Naples. You know that."

"Monday. You can make it to the meeting place by Monday."

"Where?"

Piat was silent, probably wondering, as Dukas was, how dangerous the open phone might be. Piat would be at a public telephone someplace—pretty bug-proof. He wasn't stupid enough to use a cell phone. So it would come down to Dukas's phone, and he'd be thinking that Dukas's phone would be vetted pretty regularly and so the risk was pretty low. And he apparently decided it was worth it. "There's a town called Kalloni, on the Greek island of Lesvos. It's near the center of the island. In the middle of the town is a square, kind of a park. At one end is one of those bandstand things— a gazebo. At the other end is an excavation, all cleaned up for the tourists. I'll meet you in the excavation. It's small; you'll see me."

"What the hell?"

"Unh, there's some other people interested in me. I'll need a no-go signal and a fallback, too."

So he was in trouble. Of course, why else would he have called? On the face of it, Dukas was one of the last people the Jerry Piats of the world would turn to, but in fact the logical choice if somebody was right on your ass and meaning no good. Dukas said, "No-go signal is a ball cap. If we're wearing one, it's no go—if either of us is wearing one, it means he's hot and the meeting is off. What's the fallback?"

There was a long pause. The phone line was so silent that Dukas said, "Jerry?"

"I'm still here. I'm thinking."

Dukas thought, *It's a game of trust. Even after making this call, he's trying to figure out how far to trust me.*

"Fuck it. Okay, listen. Fallback is a night meeting, on the beach at Ypsilou monastery," Jerry said. "You'll find it. If you have to. It's on the maps. Get one at the airport." He snickered. "And a day after that—I'll be moving. Izmir. In Turkey. You know it?"

"I've been there."

"The old Turkish fort—on the harbor."

"Okay. I'll find it if I have to. Times?" asked Dukas.

Another pause. "Okay. Fourteen oh four first meeting, five-minute window. Nine hours on the button at the fallback. Twenty-four hours later in Izmir, and then every twenty-four in Izmir until we link up."

"It better be worth it."

"It's worth it."

"Want to give me a hint what the favor is?"

Piat laughed. "We'll talk." The phone went dead.

Dukas looked at Leslie. She had been listening to his end of the conversation, frowning at what she thought she'd heard. "What now?"

"A voice from the past. I'm afraid he's part of my future, too."

Molyvos, Lesvos

When Piat got off the phone, he felt better. He'd babbled—that wasn't so bad, all things considered. He'd done something like the right thing, and he might even benefit from it.

Saida had grown bored with pouting and had begun preening. Piat left the phone booth and sat next to her on a park bench across the street.

"When are you going to give me the money?" she asked.

"Anytime you like. Now, if you insist."

341

She turned and gave him a steady look from under her heavy, dark brows. "You do not always do what I expect."

"You want it now?"

"I want to shop. But I know that is stupid." She raised both hands defensively, as if to fight off his expected reaction. "I need some things. So—what do we do now?"

Piat thought of all his tenuous plans—the meeting with Dukas, Andros, the buyer in South Carolina. Selling the cup. Selling Saida. "Now? Now we wait." He took her hand and raised her from the bench. "We need to disappear for a couple of days."

Her eyes widened, and she squeezed his hand and smiled.

Piat resented her assumption. Even while he knew it was accurate.

He led them back to the car by a complex route that included her stop at a pharmacy. He resisted buying cigarettes. Again.

By five o'clock, they were back on the road, the narrowest track on the island, heading slowly up the shoulder of the island's own Mount Olympus. Let Rashid and his friends and the Israelis search the island. Piat didn't think that they could find him in two days. After that—after that, every action would bring a danger.

"Where are we going?" Saida asked brightly. She was now playing the role of his beautiful assistant.

"The twelfth century," he said enigmatically, and accelerated into the curve.

As Piat parked the car at his destination, Shlomo Eshkol landed at the airport in Mytilene with a team. Piat would have recognized the men who met Eshkol, and he would have been terrified by the reinforcements who were arriving.

But he wasn't there. And he didn't know. And he was plenty scared already.

Naples

Dante e Beatrice is on the Piazza Dante, out of the tourist flow of Naples but very much part of the real city. It has been there a long time, a neighborhood restaurant that is a good deal more than that. Alan Craik had been taken there as a child when his father was stationed in Naples, and the place was part of his personal myth—a place where he had sat like a grownup, had his first sip of wine, watched his parents try to be decent to each other and find the love that had disappeared. They failed, but not in the restaurant.

Rose had reserved a table for nine that took up the middle of one part of the place. Alan had been there off and on a dozen times since his childhood; either the owners remembered him or they faked it beautifully. Stern-faced, sagging, he was greeted at six with, literally, open arms; his children were admired, his wife flattered. Two pregnant women at the same table were a very good thing. Carol Triffler's dour prediction that dark skin wouldn't be welcome was wrong; if there was any reaction, it was suppressed.

Alan, trying not to be grim and failing, had ordered a meal that was to have been memorable—mixed antipasti, then a risotto with scallops, followed by osso bucco with chard in garlic and oil, and then an insalata italiana. Four bottles of wine stood on the table, two each of Est! Est!! Est!!! and Gattinara. It could have been great.

"You look like hell," Dukas said—his way of being sympathetic.

"I'm okay."

"How long since you had some sleep?"

"I'm okay, Mike."

"You sleeping at *all?*" Craik really did look terrible to Dukas. Old, worn. "What's going on, Al?"

"Let's have some wine."

"No, tell me what's going on." Dukas stood, pulled Alan up. "We have to go to the john," he said to their wives, and he led Alan off, stood him against a high-gloss, caramel-colored wall in a dark space beyond the toilets. "You're whipped," he said. More sympathy.

Then Alan told him about Afghanistan, the old man who had died during torture, a brick tower for hanging people. A torturer in US battledress who wouldn't give his name or rank. "Yeah," he said, "I'm whipped."

Dukas chewed his lower lip. "Maybe you should bag this party, get some sleep."

"They tortured an old man to *death*, Mike! His heart gave out, he was so scared. Scared to death. That's our famous war on terrorism?"

"After Nine-Eleven, Al, people are—"

"Nine-Eleven, for Christ's sake! You know what the guy who killed him said to me?" His grimness turned to rage. "I said they were breaking the rules of war, torturing the old man; you know what he said? 'The rules have been changed.' *The rules have been changed!* All of a sudden, everything we've had drilled into our heads is changed? Torture is okay, fuck the Geneva Convention, if they can do it we can do it?" He hugged himself. "You know you don't get information that way."

"People are scared."

"Yeah. Bullshit."

"It's a war, Al."

"War, my ass! A flea bites an elephant, the elephant declares war and says the rules are changed?" He pointed a finger at Dukas. "Look at the Israelis—*they're* fighting a fucking war. The more they fight, the worse it gets, the more the Palestinians hate them. You want us to be like that?" He jammed his hands into his pockets. "Afghanistan, yes, we were right to go in there, except we didn't go in hard enough; we should have pulverized the bastards and got out. You know that now

344

people are saying we're going into Iraq? For what? Perpetual fucking war?" He shot Dukas a look again, his face contorted, almost crazed. "'The rules have changed.' Well, not for this sailor!"

"You going to get out, then?"

"I don't know what I'm going to do! I don't—" He put his right hand over his eyes. He leaned against the discolored wall, his breath shuddering. "We fought the Cold War, and the stakes—" He paused, drew a long breath. "The stakes were the lives of everyone on the planet. Nuclear winter. Right?" He looked at Dukas. "Why the fuck have the rules changed because of Nine-Eleven? What's at stake?"

Dukas let him go on for a while, and then he said, "Let's get you home. Get you some sleep."

"No!" Craik forced himself up. "I planned this dinner. I'll go through with it. It's important to be—to be—"

"Normal?"

Craik's eyes swiveled around the small space. "Normal," he said, as if he'd never heard the word before. "Normal." He seemed to gather himself, an effort, and then he smiled and touched Dukas on the shoulder. "Yeah, let's be normal." He laughed a little wildly.

At the table, they started drinking and eating and laughing, Craik's laughter faintly manic. Even the Trifflers' teenaged daughter joined in, converted, perhaps, more by the laughter and the excitement than by the food. Dukas and Rose babbled about the food and the cooking and at one point had to go into the kitchen to see how something was made; Triffler, still full of his trip to Athens, talked about *The Iliad* and then about heroic movies. Carol Triffler and Leslie talked about babies, Bush, babies, Nine-Eleven, babies, and money.

And it worked until, at thirteen minutes of seven, a waiter appeared with a man most of them didn't know, and the man pointed at Mike Dukas. The waiter came over and whispered

345

in Dukas's ear, and Dukas turned around and looked at the man and, still chewing, tossed down his napkin and excused himself.

Rose looked at Alan, who raised his shoulders and shook his head. Leslie looked grim but gave a tight smile and said, "One of Mike's girlfriends, probably." She knew that he was going away again on Monday—she even knew he was going to a Greek island called Lesvos—but she didn't say anything about that. If she thought anything right then, it was that the guy named Jerry had called back.

The talk and the eating started up again, and things were pretty much normal, although, as Dukas's absence got to be longer than five minutes, uneasy silences began to slice their enjoyment into pieces. Triffler was trying to perk things up with a joke he'd heard when another waiter appeared and headed right for him. Alan, across the table, saw the waiter whisper in Triffler's ear, and Triffler folded his napkin, put it next to his place, said, "Punch line in a few minutes," and followed the man out.

"When he takes *your* husband, it's okay," Carol Triffler said. "When he takes *my* husband, I worry."

"Where's Dad going?" the teenager said.

"If I knew that, I wouldn't worry. Or maybe I would." She turned to look through the archway where both men had disappeared.

"That's life in the Nav," Rose murmured. She winked at Leslie. "NCIS business, I bet."

They got the talk going again, although the Craiks' oldest child, Mike, didn't help matters by asking where everybody was going. He liked both Dukas and Triffler, had in fact been sitting between them and was now an island between two empty chairs.

"They'll be right back," Alan said. "Eat your chard."

And at that point the waiter appeared again and murmured in Alan's ear, and he looked stunned and then panicked, and he tossed his napkin down and made a *How do I get through this?* face at his wife and went out.

That left three women, a teenaged girl, and two kids. The youngest started to whimper. Mike Craik said he didn't like the chard. Leslie started to cry.

Rose patted her hand. "Just get used to it," she said. "You just have to learn to enjoy life without them." She grabbed her wine glass. "Hey, let's drink to something!"

In an alcove off the restaurant's entrance, Dukas and Triffler were standing with an American who turned out to be the NCIS duty officer. They all looked grave. Alan joined them, looked from one to the other, saw that Triffler and the duty officer were waiting for Dukas to start things. Dukas looked at him and said, as carefully as if he were a physician telling a relative that the operation had failed, "Abe Peretz has been shot. They don't know if he's going to make it."

Alan didn't get it. "In Tel Aviv?"

"In Cairo. He went to a meeting about my case because they wouldn't let me go."

"Meeting with who?"

"A Palestinian."

Alan winced. Dukas, defensive, said, "It was supposed to be in-and-out. We had surveillance, a safe meeting place. Nobody knows what really happened, but it looks like there was a shooter in place before anybody got there. He shot both of them."

"Jesus."

"Dick's going to Cairo." Triffler looked disgusted but nodded. "I gotta go back to Tel Aviv." Dukas appealed to Alan with a look, his eyes soft, concerned. Abe Peretz was his friend as well as Alan's. "The comm plan was secure. Only me, Abe, and the chief of station knew about it. Either the Palestinians did the shooting themselves, or—" His mouth was grim. "We've got a leak."

"Could have been the Egyptians," Triffler said. Aside to Alan, he muttered, "They were doing our surveillance."

"That's why you're going to Cairo. You know the Cairo cops; you've worked there."

"I know *one* Cairo cop. Anyway, yes, Mister Dukas, I'm going to Cairo."

Dukas said to Alan, "I'm supposed to make a meeting with a guy on Monday. On one of the Greek islands. I can't go now." He hesitated. He looked into Craik's face, his uneasy eyes. "Can you make the meeting for me?"

"Why?" Meaning *Why me* but really meaning *I just got back from hell; I'm on leave, and I deserve it because I'm going crazy.*

"Because the guy's hot and he's suspicious as hell and it's got to be somebody he knows on sight. He knows you." Dukas didn't bother to smile. "You'll remember him. He tried to shoot you in Jakarta a couple of years ago."

It took a second. "That guy." There really had been somebody who had tried to shoot him in Jakarta. In a kind of overgrown greenhouse.

"That guy." Dukas looked insistent.

"I never saw him, Mike."

"But he saw *you*. A lot. He scoped you out for half an hour. He'll remember you."

"But I—" Craik shrugged, frowned.

But Dukas was intent on the shooting of Abe Peretz and getting back to Tel Aviv, and he wasn't going to take no for an answer, no matter how whacked out Al Craik was. It was his case, but it was also his powerful sense of justice. Somebody had leaked information, and a friend of Dukas's had got shot on his nickel, and he wasn't going to take it calmly. He looked at the duty officer. "Commander Craik has a reserve NCIS badge. Activate it ASAP."

"You going to brief me?" Alan said.

Dukas looked at his watch. It was too late for a flight to

348

Tel Aviv that night. "I'm going to brief everybody." Dukas sighed. "Tell your wives after you get home, guys. I don't want to be pounded to death in an Italian restaurant."

That day the Israelis, using tanks, made a raid near Bethlehem, wounding four Palestinians.

Part Three

18

Tel Aviv

Spinner was wakened on Sunday morning by the telephone. He had spent a bad night—dreams, fugitive worries, imaginings. For perhaps the first time in his life, he understood self-doubt. Now, the ringing of the telephone pulled him from a deep sleep like the sleep of exhaustion and saved him from a dream of failure that he instantly forgot.

"Yes?" His voice hoarse.

"Mister Spinner, good morning. Sorry to come so early, but— I am a friend of the friends you have spent time with these last days. My name is Asher Rabin; we didn't meet, but I know of you, know such good things of you. I wonder if we could meet?"

Friends of friends. Meaning either Habakkuk or Mossad. Right then, he didn't want to see any of them. He was trying to shake off the after-effect of the dream, a logy weight like grief. "Meet when?" he said.

"Now, if you can. I have something important to tell you."

"Uh—I just woke up, I'm not—"

"My apologies for waking you. This is *very* important."

Spinner agreed to meet him in the lobby as soon as he could, but he took his time showering and shaving. He felt ill, he thought, but he didn't have much for comparison; he was usually healthy. He dressed without interest, even turning his back on the mirror. Most days, he liked to admire his slimness, the muscles emphasized by weight-lifting. Now, he pulled on a yellow polo shirt and chinos without looking and went downstairs.

Asher Rabin was a slender, youngish man with black-rimmed eyeglasses that to Spinner looked like something out of the 1950s. He seemed too emaciated and too intellectual to be from Mossad, so he must be a friend of Habakkuk's, but he grasped Spinner's hand and said that the director had sent him personally. *The Director. Therefore Mossad.* He had a dry, cool hand; he spoke American English with hardly an accent.

"Coffee," he said. "We both need coffee, right, Ray? Can I call you Ray? Not in the hotel; their coffee stinks."

He led the way out to the street, around a couple of turnings and along behind the Mann Auditorium to a café called En Avant, which very distinctly wanted to be a French bistro.

"French coffee," Asher said. "I hope you like French coffee. I drink it by the gallon. If you don't, they have americano, machiado, whatever. You drink juice? They do it fresh here—orange, papaya—I'll order; hold on—"

He was playing the host. Spinner was grateful. He muttered that he'd take americano and sank into a chair at a sidewalk table and stared along the street. The day was overcast but warm, the colors oddly bright despite the lack of sunlight. Sunday was a busy day here, Shabat over, a feeling of release. Three spectacular girls walked by; one eyed him, said something, and all three looked. Spinner felt better. *They* thought he was okay.

"Coffee, coffee!" Asher Rabin said. He put down two big cups, two glasses of papaya juice, and a plate of croissants and brioches. The crockery was heavy and white, probably authentic bistro stuff. The pastries looked right. Asher offered jam or honey, butter, but Spinner shook his head and drank a third of the coffee, waiting for its jolt. He sighed.

354

"The reason I came so early," Asher said, "is, I'm sorry to put it this way, but it's not such very good news."

Spinner looked up, a croissant almost in his mouth; catching his own over-reaction, he crammed the food into his mouth.

"Nothing about you!" Asher hurried to tell him. "Everything's okay, totally okay. You're our valued friend, nothing changed—that's the reason I'm here. We didn't want you to hear this from somebody else first." He stirred his *noir* and picked up a brioche. "It's the meeting in Cairo that you were told about. Asked about. You know." He pulled the brioche apart; the odor, rich, bready, reached Spinner. "It didn't go off right."

Spinner, chewing and trying to swallow too big a bite of the croissant, felt a shiver between his shoulders. "What does that mean?"

"You were told that we wanted to take action. You approved that idea. Not that it was your idea or that you bear responsibility! My God, Ray, believe me, we take all responsibility! It's only that you were informed and you said okay."

"I said okay to sending a message to Dukas." He remembered his qualms. "I didn't give any permission! I'm in no position to do that."

Asher broke off a piece from the brioche he was holding. He hadn't yet eaten any of it. "I'm sorry to tell you that the American was injured."

"Dukas?"

Asher shook his head but didn't explain. "These things are always a risk. We have very definite rules of engagement, and, you have to believe me, they were kept. The shooter knew precisely what her target was, and how far away from the target and at what minimum angle the American had to be for her to shoot. Unfortunately, the bullet took a bad track after it hit her."

Spinner had put down his food. "How bad was it?"

"We killed the target. The American was hit in the body. He's in intensive care."

355

Spinner closed his eyes. He felt sick. "It wasn't Dukas, though?"

"Another American, from the embassy. Look, Ray, this isn't your fault. Don't identify, okay? We hate that an American was injured. We took all the precautions—our guidelines are the same as the US military's guidelines—but bullets do crazy things when they hit bone. The target was wearing a protective vest, we think with plates; maybe one of the plates deflected it. We'd give anything to undo it, Ray! Believe me!" He stared into Spinner's eyes. "You do believe me, right, Ray?"

Spinner threw up. Right there, on the bistro table.

Mytilene, Lesvos

Eshkol's Mossad team spent the night in an unassuming hotel right on the waterfront in Mytilene. None of them got much sleep. The stakes were high now, and, to the immediate necessity of finding the girl and the cup, Eshkol added another layer, a layer he didn't want to bring to the attention of David Tar-Saloman—the necessity to control the four men from the Department of Underwater Exploration.

He was sitting in his underwear with his head down over his laptop, going through classified message traffic that he had just downloaded, trying to make sense of the operations and investigations that had led to, or been spawned by, the death of Salem Qatib.

A sharp rap on his door freed him.

"Shlomo?" Viseman leaned into Eshkol's room.

Eshkol waved for Viseman to enter. "I'm not even dressed yet," he muttered.

Viseman couldn't contain his triumph. "I have a hit on the girl's Visa card."

"And?"

"Yesterday noon, here on Lesvos. She rented a red Renault L5 from Avis in Molyvos."

Eshkol was pulling on his trousers with one hand while placing a cell phone call with the other. He looked up at Viseman. "Good work. Get your coat."

Tel Aviv

Dukas arrived back in Tel Aviv a little after noon and went straight to the embassy, lugging with him an STU from the Naples office so he could make secure calls without having to beg a phone. The embassy seemed to have an electric buzz in its atmosphere, maybe because of Abe Peretz's shooting—more people than should have been there on a Sunday. It also seemed chillier. People he had got accustomed to nodding to in the halls looked back with expressions that were no longer friendly, that now may have been suspicious or unsure or even hostile. They probably knew by then that Peretz had been shot in his place, so maybe it was blame. It was also siege mentality—he wasn't one of them.

Dukas didn't even get to sit down: there were four phone slips saying that a Mister Spinner had called, and a sheet of copy paper with "See me *now!*" on it in Magic Marker, with the name of the CIA chief of station. So she was in, too. He might have hesitated over her directive, but a guy with pale eyes and no smile appeared at his door and repeated that she wanted to see him *now.*

"I wish you hadn't come back," she said. She looked tired, older. "I almost canceled your clearance."

"I'm sorry about Abe Peretz. That's why I'm back."

"We're all 'sorry.' Look, I like you personally; you've been up front with us and you've got a job to do. But this one's ours. He's a US diplomat. This isn't a Navy matter, Mike; it's mine and the Bureau's."

"He's ex-Navy."

"With a nickel, that'll get you a cigar. Read my lips: US diplomat. US pride. International incident. Stay out, okay?"

He asked her if Peretz's wife had been told. Of course, was

357

the answer. Was she flying to Cairo to be with him? Not that they knew of. Dukas frowned, exhaled noisily, picked at a bit of lint on his trouser leg. He looked up at her. "He's a personal friend."

"Another nickel, that'll get you another cigar. Sorry to be hard-nosed, but our concerns are a lot bigger than friendship. Depending on who the shooter was, we may be looking at a shift in the way we deal with either Israel or the PA. Okay? I'm sorry, Mike, truly sorry—but you have to butt out."

"I'm still investigating Salem Qatib."

"I think that may be over."

"What, I'm going to get in your way just by being here?"

She moved a couple of things on her desk. She rubbed her forehead. "We sent Peretz because you asked for him. It was your meeting."

He didn't say the things he might have: you vetted it; you guys planned it; I was handed a done deal. "You mean people blame me. The Bureau guys? Okay. I'd react like that, too. I'll keep a low profile, okay?"

She was sitting now with her right elbow on the desk, her head supported at forehead and cheekbone on fingers and thumb. "Why did you come back?"

"Peretz is part of the Qatib case. That's my responsibility."

She was exhausted, too, he thought. Tough job. She said, "Stay out of the line of fire. You raise your head, you're dead." She lifted her eyes from the desktop. "Israelis are muttering about tossing you out."

"Why?"

"They know it's you behind Peretz, is my guess. What they're saying is that you're quote-unquote disruptive." She gave him a rueful smile. "I'd give a lot to have you one of my own people, Mike. But you aren't, and we're circling the wagons."

"'Butt out,' as they used to say."

"As they used to say."

He went back to the borrowed office and looked at the message slips about Spinner and wondered what the hell he wanted. It was odd for anybody like him to be calling on a Sunday from Washington. He looked at the message times—hell's bells, they'd been made starting at two-thirty a.m., Washington time, and had gone on until half an hour ago—still only six-thirty in DC. Well, Spinner was very small potatoes. The hell with him.

He sat behind the desk, wondered what he'd say to Bea Peretz. He hated such calls. But you had to make them. He did the moral equivalent of gritting his teeth and dialed the Peretzes' number. He let it ring, on and on. Then, when he was ready to quit, it was picked up and a female voice he didn't know said, "*Shalom*, Peretzes."

"This is a friend of theirs. Can I speak to Mrs. Peretz, please?"

"She is in seclusion, I am sorry. Your name?"

He told her, asked whom he was talking to; after an odd moment of hesitation the voice said, "A neighbor. My name is Esther." He remembered the dinner at the Peretzes, Abe's talking about Esther. "I remember," he said. It sounded stupid. But Abe had thought that Esther was part of the trouble between them.

"Try calling maybe Tuesday. Maybe if the news is good."

"If she needs help—anything I can do—I thought maybe she'd be going to Cairo—"

"Everything is up in the air. I will tell her you called, Mister—Du-kas."

He was left frowning into a dead telephone. He was angry that Bea hadn't gone to Cairo. But to do what? What was stupider than sitting around a hospital? She had two daughters to think about. Still—he was angry.

Cairo

Dick Triffler's foot hit the floor of the exit corridor from the Naples-Cairo aircraft, and he was pulled out of the way of other passengers and smothered in the hugs of a small, excited Egyptian. Triffler had known Police Sergeant al-Fawzi-al-Mubarak on another case; they had got along, but not so well as the hugging suggested. Still, there were advantages to having a local contact who thought they'd got on like gangbusters.

"My friend!" al-Fawzi groaned. "My friend!" Triffler, despite being taller, was afraid he was going to be kissed; however, all al-Fawzi did was push his chin into Triffler's collarbone on each side, a gesture somewhere between an air kiss and what French generals do as they're pinning medals on. "My good friend Triffler!"

"Good to see you, too." Triffler's idea of an effusive demonstration of friendship was a firm handshake. It was also too early in the morning for enthusiasm. He let himself be led out of the traveling corridor and down the external stairs to a black car that was parked in the shadow of the aircraft. Al-Fawzi was waving his hands at two other men, also cops, also bearing names, presumably, but Triffler never really got them, and nobody acted as if he was supposed to. One of them got into the driver's seat, the second one beside him; al-Fawzi held the door for Triffler to go into the back.

"You got luggage?" al-Fawzi said.

Triffler patted his shoulder bag. "Travel light." It wasn't so light, actually—Triffler always dressed well—and he had a laptop in the other hand. Al-Fawzi bellowed something and both of the other men jumped out of the car as if they'd found a snake in the front seat with them; one threw open the trunk and the other took Triffler's luggage as if he was going to run off with it.

"These are what we get now'days," al-Fawzi said. "Ignorant." He shouted at the two and they looked embarrassed.

"In, in, my friend." They settled themselves in the back; the car started with a screech of tires, and al-Fawzi bellowed, and it stopped with a screech of brakes. Al-Fawzi shouted, and the car went forward at about the pace of a crawling infant. "They think it is the super-highway, not the aerodrome." He asked if Triffler had eaten, if he needed sleep, a bath, a digestive mint?

"Tell me what happened," Triffler said. He didn't want to spend any more time in Cairo than he had to.

"Bad." Al-Fawzi made a face that included pushing his moustache up into his nostrils. "Your embassy is all over everything. I am told personally by my commander to lie off. In my own speciality, homicide!"

For a moment, Triffler thought that by "homicide" he meant that Peretz had died; then he realized al-Fawzi meant the Palestinian victim. Triffler knew by then that the Palestinian had been a woman and not the head honcho Dukas had hoped for—the Tax Collector. "You guys first on the scene?" he said.

"Of course, three cars there within two minutes. Uproar! This is in a shopping center, terrific crowd, late in the day, many shopping—this Palestinian woman explodes like a fountain in the desert, blood everywhere. Then your man is down, also bleeding. People think maybe a bomb, but no explosion. Here we go again they are thinking, al-Gama'at al-Islamiya again and so on. Big nonsense—two people, they think a bomb? Hysterics. So yes, somebody calls and we have three cars there in two minutes, but my guys can't get to the bodies because the security service has people already there, like chickens with no heads. Guns out, shouting, cell phones in their ears—chaos big-time, my friend."

"You know what was going on?"

Al-Fawzi made the face again. "I know *now.* I knew nothing until midnight, when I got briefing that was mostly laughable. Nothing to insult you, my friend, but what I am told

361

is it is your country making meeting with the Palestinian Authority in my country and bringing bloodshed. Was I told before it happened? No. Was my commander told? No. Who was told? The Minister for the Interior was told. Why, because of respect for integrity of Egypt? No, because your man required protection by Egyptian security services. Were the police brought to speed on it? No." He shook his head. "I go to the shopping center, security men are looking like lunatics, I direct the setting up of police barriers and the calling of a medical man. Ambulances come as I arrive. Chaos, my friend. Then I find there are also six Palestinian Authority security men, also running around. They are looking for the perp. In fact, the perp is miles away by then, already heading for Israel."

"An Israeli shooter?"

Al-Fawzi laughed without a hint of humor. "It took an hour to sort out. Plenty of time for twenty perps to get away. First, the security services mixed up the bodies—the Palestinian and the American—and for the first half hour, at two different hospitals, I am getting reports that an American woman is dead. If she had been a guy, we'd still be mixing it up!"

They were well clear of the airport by then and heading for Cairo. Al-Fawzi said, "You want to see the crime scene now?"

"Tell me as we go."

"The shooter was in a high-rise, eight hundred fifty meters away. Straight line of vision, I mean. Angle looking down, but necessary to see into the courtyard. In fact, the shot would have been impossible but for chairs and tables put out that morning around a food kiosk. They had been meaning to meet where the—what, roof?—the wall, the roof, gave them protection."

"In the lee of the wall, right. But what—they had to meet out in the middle?"

362

"Out from the wall, yes. So there is no sound of the shot heard where the bodies were hit. This is Cairo; the city is noisy. Vespas, cars, buses. Airplanes overhead. One shot eight hundred meters away, who hears?" He used his fingers on his heavy thigh to make a diagram. "Here is the kiosk; here, this finger, is the Palestinian. Over here, three meters away, is your American. The shot comes in *this* way—" he used his whole hand, fingers joined, to indicate a line from his left armpit across his left thigh—" and hits the Palestinian woman in the left back, up pretty high. She is wearing vest armor with, mmm, you know, extra strength—"

"Plates?"

"So, yes, we think a plate changed the bullet path. Probably coming out of her body, not in. Major damage. The entire heart, more or less, blown out. Then the, mm, plate, and most of the bullet—a piece went other ways in her body, no matter— hit your man in the right side, first rib."

"He had to be wearing armor, too."

"Yes, also with, mm, plates. Major trauma from impact. Armor saves your life but ruins your body, yes? Three smashed ribs, part of rib number one completely torn through. Bullet divides again and one piece—what do you say, turning like a gymnast—?"

"Tumbling."

"Ah, yes, tumbling into organs. Right lung, liver. Major part of bullet removes an organ—the English word I don't know—" He gestured at his abdomen, shouted a question at the front seat. Nobody up there knew the English word, either.

Triffler, however, muttered, "Spleen?"

"Internal bleeding! Damage! And so on! This big part of bullet ends inside a rib on the left side, just missing heart and various veins and things like that."

"Fifty-caliber machine gun cartridge, right?"

Al-Fawzi nodded. "We have the weapon. Left behind. I

show you first where the shooter was, okay? Very competent assassination." He dredged up a term from his videos. "A real pro." He nodded with bitter vigor. "Israeli."

Tel Aviv

Dukas called the Naples office and asked if somebody named Spinner had telephoned him there. The answer was no. He was puzzled about the message slips from Spinner—how had he known to call him in Tel Aviv? He tried Leslie at their Naples apartment; no, nobody named Spinner had called him there, either. "How you doing?" she said.

"I'm not. I've been told to butt out."

"Well, butt this way."

He got some coffee and found, next to the coffee machine, two things that had started existence as some sort of breakfast pastries but were now dry and lumpy-looking, as if somebody had sat on them. Still, they looked as if they were full of good stuff like fat and sugar, so he took them. Then he munched and tried to avoid thinking how wasted he was and made a list of things to do and started on the first thing by calling a number in Athens. He wouldn't get the man he wanted, but he got the duty officer at the National Security Office and said he'd like to talk to Colonel Kritikiou on a matter of priority. Dukas's modern Greek was ratty but serviceable, learned from a grandmother who'd thought English was what street people spoke. The duty officer said that it was Sunday but if it was urgent, he could contact the colonel and—

Somebody would call back.

Dukas looked at his list. There were really only two things he wanted before he gave up on Tel Aviv—who had shot Abe, and how the shooter had known about the meeting. He was sitting there, thinking about that and how slim his chances were, and then wondering if he should call Miriam Gurion and tell her about Abe—what were the ethics of calling a married friend's girl to say he'd been shot?—when the telephone rang, and he expected it would be Kritikiou from Athens and so was disappointed when it was Spinner. Surprisingly, he was crying. More to the point, he was in Tel Aviv. Across the street from the embassy, in fact.

Agiassos, Lesvos

"I just thought it would be more—" Saida waved both hands up and down as if she were in great distress. Her towel fluttered as she did so, displaying her thin sides and a flash of her breasts.

"Modern?" Piat asked. He was sitting on the bed in his boxer shorts, reading the local Greek paper and savoring the last of the coffee.

"Romantic?" she said, turning her head as if the question were an answer.

Bingo. Piat thought that a night in one of the best-preserved old towns in Greece would be romantic, too. He looked up from his paper to regard Saida, standing in a towel, framed against the winter sunlight on the screened balcony of their room. The screen, and the balcony, had all been done in the eighteenth century. What was under her towel had been done more recently, but the combination of Saida and the room and the balcony should have been endlessly romantic. Or something like it.

Piat was tempted to ask her what she thought of as romantic. But it was questions like that and his need to ask them that had made the last hours hellish.

"Jack?" she asked, throwing her head back to look at him over a mostly naked shoulder. "Jack? I should be a little more interesting than the local paper, I think."

When she stood just like that, her long leg presented like a fashion model's, he was most aware that she was pregnant. It was no one thing, except that her bras suggested her breasts hadn't always been so large, and the creaminess of her skin matched his memories of other pregnant women he had known. Her belly was a little round. That might just be a deficiency of exercise.

Last night at dinner, she had asked him when she could shop.

After dinner, they'd walked up the steep cobblestone streets. She had shown no interest in the old shop fronts, the textiles, the pottery. She asked question after question, every one of which might have been summarized as "What do *you* think about *me*?"

By the time they were sharing a bed in their antique hotel, Piat couldn't imagine having sex with her.

Actually, he could imagine it. His hands burned to reach out and grab her breasts, thumbs working her nipples, leg catching hers and rolling her over—

"Tell me again how much money I will have?" she had asked in the dark.

"Twenty million dollars."

"Hah!" she had said triumphantly, and slammed her mouth over his.

None of him would respond. She established this with remarkable patience over the next hour. "I have heard that this can happen to men," she had said a few times, as if, up until now, she hadn't believed it.

She looked good.

She smelled good.

Piat's body had wanted no part of her.

Eventually, they had slept. Piat found that he flinched and woke up every time he touched her. She, on the other hand, rolled against him, seeking contact. And twice he woke to find her crying, very quietly, in her sleep.

So that now, lying on the bed in his underwear, watching her cavort, if that was the word, in front of the balcony in a towel *should* have been more exciting than the local paper, with its nineteenth-century tales of robbery, revenge, and human kindness.

"Let's get some lunch," he said.

Athens

Two small men and a tall woman in a motorcycle jacket waited outside a door on the steps of an Athenian house. The narrow street smelled of urine and garlic. The tall woman kept breathing through her hand.

"No one's coming to the door," the older man said.

The woman pushed to the front, knelt, and pulled a ring of tools from the pocket of her coat. "Give me some space here."

"Just get it open," the younger man muttered. The thought of a forced entry in broad daylight made him sound shrewish. She rattled the knob and then turned it.

The two men were through the door like smoke blown by a fan. She pulled her tools out of the lock, wiped the knob and the lock with a rag, and only then stepped into the apartment, which smelled, if anything, worse than the street. It was a dirty place with cheap furniture and an odor of rot and hashish.

"Who lives like this? This guy's more like an addict than an academic," she said quietly as she looked around. Then she took a digital camera from her pocket and started to get images of every surface.

The older man emerged from the bedroom. "Gone. Cleaned out. I'd say yesterday."

The younger man pointed to the desk, where a line of empty pop-cans and the Styrofoam container of an ancient meal framed a large empty space that held only a bunch of wires. "Took his computer. Took most of his files, too. Want me to take the rest of these?"

The older man shrugged. "We'll be up all night going through them for nothing, but yes." He sighed and reached for his cell phone.

The tall woman glanced in two of the trash baskets. They were empty. "Strike you as odd, Raz?" she asked.

The older man was dialing. "What's odd? The smell?"

"The trash. This place isn't fit for pigs, but the trash is empty." She shrugged, and then snapped her fingers. "Give me fifty euros."

"For what?" he asked, but he handed her some bills as the phone made its connection. She took the money and left the house.

The older man got on his cell phone. He was doing a favor for a friend—had already dangerously exceeded the limits of a favor. "Shlomo? Nothing here. Cleaned out. Very professional." He watched the younger man pushing the contents of the desk, minus the Styrofoam container, into a plastic bag. "I doubt it. We'll take anything that looks possible. Sure. Shlomo, I've done this once or twice, okay?" He snapped the cell phone shut.

The woman was back in five minutes. "I just bought all the garbage in the alley. Get me someone to help me sort it."

Agiassos, Lesvos

Winter sunlight poured down from a high blue sky. Lunch consisted of excellent local cuisine, dismissed by Saida as "peasant food," in a taverna. After lunch, he took her down the steep hill to a Byzantine church that was the town's main reason for existence. She surprised him by producing a scarf and pulling it over her head as they entered.

Piat had never been to the church called the Panagia ti Vrefokratousa, the second holiest shrine to the Virgin Mary in Greece. Like his run to the hot springs, he had saved it. He entered the cold, incense-laden darkness of the interior and was momentarily blind. He stumbled and Saida took his hand. They walked together to the first row of pews while Piat's eyes adjusted. He started up the nave and stumbled again, looked down at the floor. It was formed of alternating squares of black and white marble, each one at least two feet across. In the central aisle a deep trough had been worn into the checkerboard, the steps of ten thousand pilgrims having cut into the thick marble slabs by three or four inches.

Piat had never seen such a dramatic physical testimony to the power of religion.

Saida knelt on a cushion and began to pray, surprising Piat again.

Piat left her and moved forward to the row of icons at the front of the church. Pilgrim season was far off, and the church's icons were displayed behind the altar. They had no security. He was alone with them.

In a breath he identified the icon that had, supposedly, been painted by Saint Luke. The so-called Jerusalem Icon. It was of a different quality from the others, a quality beyond mere age.

Magnificent.

It shared some quality with Saida's cup, art and craft and history. Richard the Lionheart had seen this icon. So had Frederick Barbarossa. And it sat on the altar of a church without even a trip wire to protect it.

Manuel Komnenos had ordered this painting to be moved from Jerusalem during his reign as Emperor, when Byzantium, however briefly, held the upper hand in Jerusalem. He had ordered it sent to his new church on Lesvos. A thousand years ago.

Piat glanced at the other three icons on display. None of them was of the same order, although they were all both ancient and very well executed. The Jerusalem Icon stood alone, a piece of art and a piece of history, with an aura that was almost palpable.

"My father paints a better saint than that," Saida said derisively in his ear.

When he turned, she had moved away across the altar and was lighting a candle. The sound of her two-euro piece ringing into the collection box echoed into the dome above. She shielded the candle from the winter breeze with one hand as she walked it to the shrine of the Virgin, the elegance of her motion betraying long practice.

She bowed her head for a moment, rose, and dusted her hands.

"You are a Christian," Piat said.

"My family is Christian. *You* are surprised? You know every piece of history that ever happened!" She laughed. "Many Palestinians are Christians. Everyone in my village."

"Your village?" he asked automatically.

"Bethlehem."

Piat winced. "Orthodox?" he whispered.

"Atheist. Pah, the time my mother and sisters spend on all this. But this church—listen, let's go, okay?" She moved down the nave, and he followed, leaving the one taper burning on the shrine.

He left her bemoaning the row of closed shops that represented the only opportunity for modern shopping and walked around the walls of the church courtyard, still blinking at the light, to the pay phone on the square. He called Andros three times. As he expected, no one answered. He left no message.

Above the town, a front was moving in, closing off the blue sky like a dark curtain. The temperature was dropping. Piat thought that he had let too much time pass. Out there, at the bottom of the hill, at the base of the mountain, there were people looking for Saida, maybe even for him. He had a feeling, a feeling he had lived on for his whole adult life. The feeling told him that the hunt was close, and he didn't have time to dick around.

He called Andros again. Then he called Andros's long-suffering wife. No one answered there, either.

He shivered in the cold wind and went to look for Saida.

Cairo

The shooter had fired from the eleventh floor of an office building whose front door was half a mile from where Abe Peretz and the Palestinian woman had been hit. Triffler, accustomed to modern war and its weapons, was not surprised by the distance. Standing at the window from which the shot had been fired, he said, looking down through the haze at the distant, low smudge of the shopping center, "They should have known a shooter could do it from here. I'd never have let anybody hold a high-risk meeting right down there."

Al-Fawzi didn't know that it had been a high-risk meeting; neither had Triffler, but he certainly knew it now. Al-Fawzi said, "Very professional." He kicked with a toe at a hole that the shooter had cut in a window, now blocked with plastic. The shooter, or the shooter's team, had also pushed two desks end-to-end for a platform to lie on. The barrel would have been supported on a bipod.

"Did they leave the gun?"

"Yes, yes. Your people got it. Only about three a.m. this morning, I am told. I—I, homicide, the Cairo police—am not allowed to keep it, but I have a quick report on it."

Triffler asked about the rifle, learned that it was American-made, the M82A1. *Your foreign-aid dollars at work.* He thought that probably al-Fawzi was right about its having been the Israelis.

"And nobody saw them?"

"Not one soul."

"I thought Saturday was a work day."

"For many yes; this place, no." The office was small, rather ratty. It belonged to a travel agency that booked overland truck trips for European kids who wanted to see Africa on the cheap. The internet, however, had made it redundant and it was going downhill fast.

"Anybody hear the shot?" A fifty-caliber machine gun round would have sounded like a cannon in this enclosed space, he thought. But maybe not if the flash suppressor had been out the hole in the window. Al-Fawzi said people had heard something but thought it was a car, a jet, a boom box. "You want to see the crime scene?"

"Definitely."

They were driven over by the same two plain-clothes cops; al-Fawzi continued to shout at them. He made them park in a space reserved for fire prevention, and he made them stay with the car while he and Triffler went inside. Triffler was not greatly surprised by the place; he'd spent three weeks in Cairo once and had some idea of what the city looked like. The shopping center had tried to recapture some of the feel of an open-air market; there was a lot of camel-and-palm-tree motif in the floor tiling and mosaic walls. At heart, however, it was a one-storey strip mall bent at four corners to eat its own tail, making an enclosed courtyard about two hundred feet long and fifty wide, neither upscale nor down, with a lot of elec- tronics and clothing and video stores. The eastern end of the courtyard had been taped off, and two uniformed cops stood just behind the tape. They raised it so al-Fawzi and Triffler could duck under.

Triffler made a little drawing of the place, marking the food kiosk and the café-style chairs and tables. He backed away from the end wall until he could just see the build- ing from which the shot had been fired, and he wrote down the distance from the wall, shaking his head. It was within that distance that they should have met. He was tempted to think that maybe the shooting had been done by the Palestinians themselves, because it was so stupid to have let the meeting happen out where it did unless you wanted the people to be easy targets.

372

The outlines of the two bodies had been made on the tiled floor with spray paint; they were, however, stylized, suggesting the bodies on medieval tombs—feet together, arms at sides, all very neat and rectangular. Al-Fawzi shrugged. "Security had taken them away in the ambulances before we could even do the outlines. Not by the book."

"So this is just a guess where they were."

"These drawings are accurate."

"More or less."

"More, not less."

Triffler was skeptical, but he paced off the distances and put them on his sketch. He stood about where Abe Peretz must have stood just before the bullet hit him and looked at the office building through the haze. The shooter would have been using a telescopic sight with a lens the size of a car headlight. Piece of cake.

Tel Aviv

Sitting across the desk from him, Ray Spinner looked pretty much as Dukas remembered from the only other time he'd seen him—like a huge ego who'd got his ass caught in the wringer. Now, Spinner had the same stunned look, but he was different—not so much angry as confused. And shaking.

Spinner started to speak three times before he was able to make any sound. Then he said, "I have to talk to you."

That seemed pretty obvious. Dukas nodded. He also glanced at the wall clock, because he was sure that he didn't want to devote much time to this.

"I've been—" Spinner frowned, as if a spasm of pain had gone through his gut. "I think I've been—" Looking at his trembling fingers. "I've been used."

"Who by?"

"See, I was sent here a week ago. To do things. By my boss. I've done exactly what I was told to do!"

Dukas didn't know what "to do things" meant, but he

373

knew that when you came to a foreign country "to do things," there were certain bases you were supposed to touch. "Your boss at DoD?" he said. He knew that after the Navy, Spinner had landed on his feet at DoD.

Spinner nodded.

"So this is US business? So naturally you have a country clearance."

Spinner shook his head.

"But you're declared, right?"

"What's 'declared'?"

"You better tell me what 'things' you came to do."

"Look, none of that crap matters now! What matters is I did something really stupid, really—oh, Jesus—they really did a number on me, and I've fucked up big-time. I got a guy shot!"

"What, here?"

"No, no, in Cairo. I don't know his name. An American. Embassy guy—"

Dukas moved so fast that Spinner flinched, but Dukas was heading not for him but for the door. When it was securely closed, Dukas pulled his desk chair around so that he could sit almost next to Spinner but facing him. "Say that again," he said.

"An American got shot in Cairo." He studied his shaking fingers. "He wasn't supposed to. But, they—I—" He turned his head away, his voice shaking. "Oh, shit!"

Dukas had interrogated many people. Liking or disliking them didn't matter. He disliked Spinner a lot, but he knew that right then the best thing was to go gently. He said, "Tell me about it, Ray."

Cairo

At the hospital where Peretz had been taken, Triffler was allowed to look at the wounded man from a doorway. He saw mostly tubes and machines. A doctor who spoke good

374

English told him that Peretz might make it but would be "a different man."

"Different how?"

"He has lost much internally."

Maybe a hollow man.

Al-Fawzi took Triffler to an all-male café, putting the other two cops at a separate table, and he said, "So what do you think?"

"Whoever it was knew all about the meeting. It was like shooting a cow in a farmyard." He said it could have been the Palestinians, assassinating one of their own.

"The woman was the mistress of a top Palestinian. Also his assistant. Not likely. It was the Jews."

"We don't have the evidence." Still, he thought, the shooting was done either by the Palestinians or by us or by a third party. *I don't think it was us. Was it?* He said to al-Fawzi, "Any chance there's a link to al-Qaida?" Everybody was looking for links to al-Qaida now. *It could have been us if she was connected to al-Qaida. I don't want to believe we do stuff like that, but I think maybe we do now.* But more likely it was the Palestinians.

Or the Israelis.

Which suggested an intelligence leak like a severed artery. But why? Why, for a rinky-dink meeting in a dusty shopping center where neither side was sending its top people?

He preferred that it be the Palestinians. Then there'd have been no intelligence leak, only the Palestinians using information they'd got legitimately, and he wouldn't have to adjust his ideas about his own side or Israel.

"We need more facts," he said.

Al-Fawzi gave him a look that meant *Dream on.*

Tel Aviv
Spinner's breath shuddered when he took deep gulps of air. "They wined and dined me, and they said there was this

375

meeting that was going to go down in Cairo. They said you were meeting with some biggie from the PA, and he was an enemy, a terrorist, and didn't I think that that was a shitty thing for an American to be doing? And I said—" He put a hand over his face. "Sure, that was a shitty thing. I mean, they made it an Israeli thing, a security thing, and you were giving encouragement, what the fuck was I supposed to say? You know, you were giving encouragement to their enemies. And so—" He didn't so much as glance at Dukas now. Maybe he would have been ashamed to look at anybody just then. "They kept pushing me. Like I was supposed to—approve— They asked me to 'give permission.' Well, shit, even I knew better than that!"

"Permission for what, Ray?"

"To send you a message. By doing something to the Palestinian while you were there. At the meeting. I didn't think they meant— Oh, fuck, I knew what they meant. But I thought this was some Palestinian scuzzball, a terrorist. And if you saw him blown away, you'd—I don't know—"

"I'd what?"

"You'd get the message."

"To get out of their hair?"

"I guess."

Dukas sat back. He studied Spinner, then his own hands. He pushed his anger and his disgust aside, like something on a plate he didn't want to eat. For now, the personal was meaningless. "Will you make a statement?" he said.

Spinner nodded.

"I'm going to put on a tape recorder." He got the little machine out of his attaché and put it on the desk. He told the machine the time and the date and place, and his own name and Spinner's. "Tell it to me again."

Spinner ran through it again, a little more quickly, without some of the emotion. This time, however, Dukas interrupted.

"Who?" he said. "Who used you?"

"The, uh— It's—it sounds incredible. Now that I think about it. Mossad?"

"Mossad used you."

"Yeah. At the headquarters here. I had lunch. Sort of brunch. With the head of international liaison and another guy. They're the ones that told me about the meeting. In Cairo."

"What do you mean by Mossad, Ray? What does the word mean to you?"

"Uh—the Israeli spy thing, right?"

"How long have you been in Israel?"

"I came in on Tuesday."

"To meet with Mossad?"

"No, that was later."

"What did you come to do?

"I can't talk about that."

Dukas wanted to shout at him but stopped himself. "Okay. Somebody who said he was the head of international liaison of Mossad and another man talked to you at lunch or brunch in Mossad headquarters about a meeting in Cairo. What meeting?"

Then Spinner went through it again, this time with less shaking but with a lot of stops and starts. Dukas said, "How did they know about this meeting?"

"They didn't tell me."

"But they asked for your 'permission.'"

"After they asked if I approved or agreed, I forget which, and I said— Shit, they made it seem so sensible."

"Ray, this is for the record, not for me. You and I had a run-in in the past. Did you agree or approve because you thought I had something coming to me?"

"Not getting shot."

"But maybe seeing somebody shot right in front of me. Maybe it would serve me right."

"Well— They didn't say it would be *shooting*."

"Why did they think it would be me?"

"They didn't tell me. They seemed pretty comfortable with it."

Then Dukas had him go through it all yet again, and then he said, "Who made the first contact—you or Mossad?"

"Mossad. They invited me."

Dukas tried to keep his incredulity out of his voice. "Ray, you were here without a declaration. How did Mossad know you were in Israel?"

"Oh, well—you know."

"No, tell me about it."

"Well, you guys—In the spy world, you guys know all that. Anyway, Mossad are the best. Best in the world. They picked me up at the airport, I guess."

They were back on both sides of the desk. Now, Dukas leaned forward and said in a low, quiet, paternal voice, "Ray. Ray—that's movie stuff. That's James Bond. People in intel and counter-intel are human, just like you. They put their pants on the same way, one leg at a time; they fart; they pay taxes. They aren't ten feet tall. Mossad didn't pick you up at the airport, because unless somebody told them, Mossad wouldn't have the chance of a turd in a toilet bowl of knowing who you were. So think about it, Ray—how did Mossad know who you were and why they should invite you for lunch?"

Spinner didn't know. He said so, and he said it with such force that Dukas believed him. So Dukas said, "Okay, good. What did you do in the days before they called you?"

Spinner dodged and weaved, but he couldn't get away from the question. It was like trying to make an end run in a hallway—Dukas was always there in front of him with his squat lineman's body in the way.

"Who did you see, Ray? Who did you talk to?"

"Nobody."

"Yeah, somebody. You didn't come to sightsee, Ray. You

378

came to get information for your boss, and your boss didn't tell you to stand in the middle of downtown Tel Aviv and ask passersby for it. He said go to X and talk to Y, didn't he, Ray? Didn't he? He gave you a contact, didn't he, Ray? What was the contact?"

Spinner said several times that he couldn't tell Dukas, but Dukas told him that he was part now of the investigation into the wounding of an American diplomat, and if he didn't tell Dukas he was going to tell people a hell of a lot less patient. The CIA and the FBI would both want to know all of this, and if Dukas didn't get it, they would. They'd make it part of the war on terrorism, if they had to, meaning that they could make it up as they went along and turn Spinner over to the Egyptians to get the information, if that's what suited them. "I'm your best bet, Ray. Spit it out."

"I can't. It'd be my job."

"Ray, if you don't tell me, it could be your front teeth. Or your balls. Ray! Look me in the eyes. Tell me!"

So eventually Spinner told him about a contact named Habakkuk, who was an Israeli patriot who sent information to sympathetic people in Washington.

"And did he ask for money?"

"A little. Some."

"And you paid him. You had money. From your boss? A good deal of money, in fact." Dukas leaned back and put his fingers together and gazed at Spinner. "Ray, I'm going to tell you something that only years of experience in what you call 'the spy thing' allows me to know. You'll be astonished. Habakkuk is a Mossad asset."

"No. Not possible."

"Yes. Inevitable."

"No. He works for a Jewish PAC in the States. He's an *intellectual*."

Dukas smiled, the way you'd smile at a fifteen-year-old

who told you that she'd fallen in love and this time it was the real thing. "What did Habakkuk sell you?"

Spinner hesitated but said, "Proof that the Qatib guy was killed because he was a cryptologist."

"Proof! Proof is rare. What kind of proof?"

"A guy who's in Israeli intelligence. He laid it out for me— the Palestinians were after US cryptology to sell it to al-Qaida."

"A guy."

"An Israeli."

"He had a name?"

"Shlomo. That's all, no last name."

Dukas was thinking about Salem Qatib and cryptology and a turncoat intel officer who would say that Qatib had been killed because of it. In fact, Dukas was sure now that Qatib had been killed because of archaeological artifacts, so why was somebody telling this confused amateur an outright lie? That led him to the people with a vested interest in withholding information on archaeology and artifacts, taking him back to Mossad and then to the only Shlomo he knew. "Describe Shlomo for me."

"Oh—kind of solid-looking. Light hair. Not bad-looking, but big features—strong. Sort of a broken nose."

Dukas searched through the papers he had left on the desk and came up with a printout of an old photo of Eshkol that Pigoreau had sent him from The Hague. He put it down across from Spinner. "Like that guy?"

Spinner's face said it all—horror, fear, shock.

"He's a Mossad special agent named Shlomo Eshkol. Who else did Habakkuk set you up with for this proof about cryptology?"

"A, uh, woman. Cryptologist. She needed the money for personal reasons."

"She go to bed with you?"

The face had got younger, decades younger, and looked scared and stunned.

"See, you were right, Ray. You were had. She was Mossad, too. She ever alone with your stuff—passport, papers, laptop? So it was after you spent the night together that they invited you to lunch, right?"

"Why?"

"Because they had a live one. Imagine—somebody so naive he wasn't declared, wasn't under cover, just walking around fat, dumb, and happy, and he's got his own personal pipeline into the new power guys at DoD. Jesus, they must have torn their hair out worrying that you were a set-up. Christ knows I would have. Too good to be true. But they kicked it around and they thought it was worth a try, so they fed you bull-shit and you sent it right up the pipe to your boss. You were a gift from God, Ray."

Spinner broke into sobs.

Agiassos, Lesvos

They sat in their room while the rain poured down outside. Piat sat in the one comfortable chair, trying to make out the Greek in a copy of *Aeneas Tacticus* he had found in the town's only open bookstore, but mostly reading the facing-page English. He was surprised that no one he knew had ever mentioned that this was the first book on spycraft. Written in 360 BC.

Saida had a stack of magazines—fashion, gossip, and five issues of *The Economist*. She lay on her stomach on the bed, her sodden sandals tossed into different corners of the room and her legs cocked up over her back, munching chocolates from a bag. She clearly felt that reading was a public affair, because from time to time she would read a paragraph aloud, tidbits that ranged from the status of Britney's and Justin's love affair to an acidic comment on America's policies toward Iran. Finally she looked at Piat. "What are you reading?"

"A classical Greek book on war," Piat said.

"Don't you care about what's happening in the real world?"

Piat swallowed several sarcastic responses and tried to see himself through her eyes. After a minute of heavy silence, he went back to reading. "No," he said finally.

Over dinner, she suddenly reached across the table and grabbed his hand. "You think I'm stupid."

Piat didn't know what to say.

"Listen," she said. "Listen. I don't care for your Greek books. Or the cup. Maybe a little for that icon in the church, okay? But I'm not stupid."

Piat felt unaccountably defensive. "I never said you were stupid." It sounded like a pitiful response to him even as he said it.

"All these things you like? This stupid little hotel with a leak in the ceiling, the cobbled streets, the peasants—I grew up with that, okay? Maybe not here, but I have had all the peasants I can stand. Okay? Pottery? Bethlehem does some beautiful pottery. I, myself, can turn a fine thin cup. So what? So that I can worship in an old church and my brother can get fried by the Jews?"

Piat leaned back, away from her. "Fair enough."

"You think I'm greedy, and I am. I want something different, shiny and clean." She smiled, a genuine look of amusement that went all the way to her eyes. "Okay, the hotel's not stupid, I admit. But you see what I'm saying?"

Piat leaned back in his chair, pounded back the rest of his wine and refilled their glasses. They were alone in the dining room of their hotel, the only guests, virtually the only people. "I worked in Africa once," he said. "No, listen, this is funny. And it's your point, too, I guess. I worked in Africa and I knew this guy, an old African, who guided for hunters from the UK and America. You know—white guys who wanted to shoot a lion or an elephant or some big antelope. Anyway, he used to laugh at them because they always had big, expensive hunting rifles, sometimes costly antiques. Heavy old express rifles with rare cartridges. And he would tell me that he would pretend to be impressed by their elephant guns and their big cartridges."

Saida nodded to indicate that she was following the story.

"And he thought they were idiots. He'd say to me that every poacher in the world knew that the best way to kill elephants was with an AK-47 and twenty friends."

"You killed elephants?" She was outraged.

"No." He shook his head. "Let me try this again."

"Okay," she said suspiciously. She was clearly happy to have him talking to her. He saw that. She poured more wine in his glass. But she didn't like elephants being killed.

"I used to work in the Far East."

"Anywhere you haven't worked?" she asked.

"I don't like to be cold. Anyway, I was in, uh—fuck it, I was in Burma. And I was working with some guys—tribal guys, okay? Who live like it was still ten thousand BC? And we had to move around a lot. Somewhere in there I learned enough of their lingo to tell them that in the US, people went on vacation and went camping." He started to laugh before he got to the punch line, and she started to laugh with him.

"I get it." She said, her head back.

"They wanted to hear that story over and over."

"Of course they did!"

"And one day, when I asked where one of the other families that had been traveling with us had gone, the head man laughs and says—" Piat sputtered, as he was laughing too hard already. Saida was pointing at him, obviously able to hear the punch line coming. "—says, in English, 'They're on vacation.'"

They both roared, bringing the owner in from his kitchen. He watched them with satisfaction and vanished again.

Tel Aviv

The third time through, Spinner gave more details—a description of Habakkuk, their method of communicating—but he danced around the subject of Elana, the woman he'd spent the night with. Elana was sex and Spinner's self-image was as an ass-man, and Dukas knew it cut deep to find that the woman who had found him so instantly irresistible was an agent. Otherwise, the story seemed coherent and complete, but Dukas was sure there was more. It was early; there was always more at this stage. Then Spinner said something about Al Craik, and Dukas's antenna vibrated.

"How'd you know Al Craik had been in Tel Aviv, Ray?"

"It was about the Qatib thing. Remember, I was a wiseass and sent you that email over my boss's boss's name?"

"Yeah, but that wasn't about Al Craik. How'd you know about Craik?"

"We just knew. We had some report, I guess."

"What report?"

"We get all kinds of reports. It's an intelligence office."

Dukas kept himself from reacting to that. "So you were getting reports direct from here."

"Well, yeah. That's how I knew about Habakkuk."

"So Habakkuk told you about Craik?"

"Uh, I guess so."

"How did Habakkuk know?"

"Habakkuk had sources. He didn't tell us everything."

"But for Habakkuk to know about Craik, he'd have had to be pretty close to this investigation. You said he was an intellectual. An academic."

"He picked up information."

"From Mossad, sure, to feed to you guys. But you knowing about Craik wouldn't have been a Mossad feed. Where did it come from?"

Spinner was sitting with his elbows on the arms of the chair, his fingers joined in front of him. He squirmed as if trying to get deeper into the chair seat. "Somebody."

"Yeah, somebody. Ray, I don't want to have to go through

384

it all again about CIA and FBI and embassy security. You're going to talk to them or you're not leaving the embassy. Everything's going to come out. Come on, Ray—you know something about this source, don't you? Tell me."

Spinner pushed his lips together. His red eyes looked haunted. "I want to do the right thing."

"Yeah, I believe that. I believe it's what brought you here. You were used; you'd fucked up; you'd done a stupid mission that nobody in his right mind should have sent you on. And now you want to make it right. That's good. Tell me, Ray."

Spinner sighed. "There's a source named Deborah."

"Good."

"I think it's a woman. I think she was close to Craik somehow when he was here. She had stuff you wouldn't know otherwise. The way she wrote, I thought she was probably American. But there's lots of Americans here."

Dukas put his hand on his throat, an automatic gesture because he felt that his throat was closing. "Yeah?"

"I thought she was maybe the girlfriend or the wife of somebody Craik knew socially. It was that kind of closeness. But Habakkuk wouldn't tell me anything about her. She was his prize. I wanted to deal with her direct but he wouldn't allow it."

Dukas could feel his face flushing, his heart pounding.

"Deborah," Spinner said. He twisted one side of his face in a kind of grin. "I looked it up on the Web. Jewish names. Deborah means 'bee.' Busy bee."

Dukas put his face in his hands. "*Oh, my God,*" he groaned.

Mytilene, Lesvos
"Who is this American, Shlomo?" Even on the telephone, David Tar-Saloman sounded shrill. Since he had been promoted past Eshkol, he had lost any ability to be careful and calm. He was always angry. His anger led him to error.

Shlomo was reminded of the scene in the rain in Albania. The same tone. The same anger. And no one to restrain him. *And I get to clean up.* He spoke patiently, as a father would lecture a teenager capable of dangerous behavior. "The American in Athens is a former academic, last name Oldfather, first name Barrymore. He used to be connected to the American School of Archaeology in Athens. The data sheet should be on your fax. The American here on Lesvos is last name Furman, first name Jack. Neither Tel Aviv nor Washington nor Athens can find any record that this man actually exists beyond some tickets purchased between Athens and Lesvos, hence I think the name is fictitious and he is the same as Oldfather, Barrymore. Do you copy all of that, David?"

"Ben-Raz says the apartment in Athens was cleaned professionally. Yesterday. And the team on Lesvos has informed me that they have told you repeatedly that this American is a professional and that you have ignored them."

Eshkol took a deep breath to calm himself and let it out slowly. "I'm sorry that you felt you had to go around me to my people, David."

"Shlomo, this is a national emergency! This thing, the thing you surfaced, is out there. And now there are Americans at every turn in this case! Don't you see it, Shlomo? Listen! The American here in Tel Aviv? Spinner? Walked into their embassy this morning. What does that tell you?"

Shlomo thought for a moment. "He needed a passport?"

"They are running this, Shlomo! The Americans are running it! Listen to me! Ben-Raz went through the trash in the American's apartment. He found drafts of translations of the characters on the cup."

Shlomo motioned to Viseman to bring him coffee. With his free hand he made a note. "How far had—"

"Too damned far! Farther than anything we've cobbled together." Tar-Saloman was shouting.

"What did it say?"

"You don't have the need-to-know for that information," Tar-Saloman said quickly.

"David. David, I'm leading the investigation on the case."

"It is not important to your investigation, whatever it may say. What is important is that this American had access to the whole cup. Or he had access to the same pictures we have plus other pictures. I think the latter, Shlomo! I think our man in Texas gave our pictures to the Americans. It is an American operation. To discredit—"

"David, get a grip on yourself." Eshkol was surprised at his own tone.

"Shut up! Shut up and obey! Get that cup. Get the girl. End this, do you understand me? End it and clean up the mess." *The mess you made* was the unspoken end.

"David, why, for the love of God, would the Americans be running an operation to discredit Israel?"

"To punish us for arresting their man. And now as revenge for the shooting of their officer in Cairo."

"Which you wanted, David." Shlomo's temper was slow, but the match was burning.

Tar-Saloman didn't falter. "Operational necessity, Shlomo. I want the girl, and I want the cup. Now. Any means necessary."

"Listen to me, David. When could the Americans have set this up? Look at the timing! Look at the motivation. The Americans would have had to be inside Mossad to know, in advance, who we would pick up and why. *You are jumping at shadows.* They would have had to plan their operation *before* we ever arrested their man. *It is not possible, David.*"

"Get the girl. Get the cup. Any means necessary. That's an order. Obey it, or I'll pass it straight to Dov and let him loose."

Eshkol winced. "As of right now, I don't even know where

the girl is. And David, Dov couldn't find her if she was naked in his room."

The connection was severed abruptly at the Tel Aviv end.

Tel Aviv

"It's Peretz's wife."

Dukas's face had gone from purple to white. He was standing with his back to the CIA station chief's door to keep anybody else from coming in. "I've got a guy in my office with an embassy security man. Mossad did the shooting, he says, and they got the information on the meeting from Bea Peretz." He told her about being at Peretz's apartment the night before the meeting. "I gave him my copy of the comm plan. You'd written my name at the top. Somehow, she got hold of it and passed it. They thought I was the one making the meeting."

She was leaning her elbows on the desk, her fingers tangled in her hair. She groaned aloud. She looked like somebody in mythology, some creature with snakes for hair. "Oh, Jesus." She threw herself back. "Are you sure?"

"I believe the guy. He's a self-absorbed asshole, but I believe him. Mossad's been jerking him around for days. He came to this morning when he heard Peretz had been hit." He told her what Spinner had done, where he had been. "He can show it was a Mossad hit; he ID'd 'Deborah' close enough for me to see it even before he did the 'bee' thing. No proof, but when do we ever get proof?"

She reached for the phone. "I'll have her picked up."

"She'll be gone." She met his eyes, her hand on the phone. He said, "Mossad aren't dumb enough to leave Spinner without surveillance. And he couldn't spot somebody following him in an empty bus. The moment he walked in here, they knew what was going down. They'd be crazy not to have pulled her." He slouched against the door. "I called her number this morning to say the crap you say—I'm sorry about Abe, sorry,

sorry, sorry—and there was this woman there, 'Esther'; my guess is she's a minder or a watcher. She'll have her out of there like grease through a goose."

"Even so." She made a call, holding up a hand for him to stay. When she was done, she said, "I'm grateful. Personally grateful. But now I want you out of here."

"I'm getting too close?"

"We're going to take your guy Spinner apart. We don't want you around. I told you that if you put your head up, you'd get it." She looked at a small clock on the desk. "I'm going to ask the ambassador to cancel your country clearance as of eight tomorrow morning. There's a bunch of planes before then. Be on one, okay, Mike?"

He half-smiled. "Okay."

By the time he got back to his office, two young men were there with Spinner. They had the Bureau look—sidewall haircuts, 1970s suits—and they were sufficiently dour to be the next J. Edgar Hoover. Spinner was already standing between them, about to be frog-marched out the door. Dukas stood in the way. He looked Spinner in the eye and suddenly felt sorry for him. His life was about to get very hard. "I know this was tough for you," Dukas said. "But it's the best thing you've ever done." He stood aside.

He set about transcribing as much of the interrogation as would be immediately useful to Kasser at NCIS headquarters. When he was half done, the phone rang.

"She's gone," the station chief said. "The two daughters, too." She hesitated. "Sorry it ended like this."

"Yeah—sorry, sorry, sorry." He told her about Miriam Gurion and asked her to call the policewoman when it was over. "She's a good guy. As a favor to me, okay?"

"Why me?"

"Because I guess I think you're a good guy, too."

He made a copy of the tape of Spinner's interrogation and dropped it in an envelope for her, and the phone rang while he was scrawling her name on it, and a voice said he had a secure telephone call in the communications office. It was Kritikiou from Athens; for a moment, he went blank, then remembered why he was calling.

"Colonel Kritikiou! Thank you for calling back. My Greek is very bad. Sorry to call you on a Sunday." He was watching a communications clerk frown because he was speaking a language nobody at the Tel Aviv embassy could understand. "I hope you remember me."

"If I didn't remember our weeks together in Bosnia, Michael, I would not let you bother me at home on a Sunday or any other day. Your Greek is quite good, although I will never teach you the difference between the formal and the intimate. You talk to me like a member of the family."

"That's all I ever heard at home."

"Well, it is fine. In our business, we are all one family." They both laughed. They were both cynics.

When they got down to business, Dukas said, "I want to declare an agent. It's only a matter of meeting on Greek soil. The subject is stolen antiquities, but not from Greece. From Palestine. This has nothing to do with Greek security." He told him about Al Craik's impending trip to Lesvos, assured him that it was pro forma, a matter of a meeting and a handshake. "No information, nothing like that. Simply a contact meeting." No, the person Craik was meeting wasn't Greek. Nothing was Greek.

"Why are you telling me, then, Michael?"

"Because this is the correct way to do things. 'By the book,' we say." They both laughed again.

Dukas went back to pounding notes into his laptop, then cleaned up the office, erasing any sign of his presence. He was looking around for the last time when Triffler called and told him what he had learned in Cairo. Dukas heard it all the way through, thanked him, and told him to go home.

"I thought you'd want me here until they'd squeezed every factoid out, Mike."

"It's over. Get your Cairo guy to send you stuff as he gets it. Otherwise, we're being shut out, so you might as well go home. We both might as well go home."

Last, he went online from another office and looked for flights to take himself back to Naples.

Eressos, Lesvos

Rashid was sitting on the floor of a two-room guesthouse in Skala Eressos. He regretted returning to the fold.

"We need guns," al-Dahgma muttered.

Rashid tried to ignore him, tried to stay inside his book so that he wouldn't have to become part of what was happening.

Franji, the older one, the one Rashid already hated—too much cologne, too much touching, too much anger—spoke carefully. "Someone is coming tonight, with guns and new orders from the colonel. That's all we need to know." What Franji clearly meant was *That's all you two need to know.*

Rashid couldn't decide which one of them he disliked or feared more. Al-Dahgma was angry and dangerous. Mr. Franji was older, more cautious, and far more ruthless. He had hit Rashid across the face when Rashid had returned.

Franji came and stood over Rashid. "Tell me again about your American friend."

Rashid didn't look up. "He's not my friend."

"You told me he rescued you from the Israelis. Why? Why would he do that? The Jews and the Americans share a bed, eh? So why, do you think, would this American save you? Unless he wanted you to work for him?"

Rashid kept his eyes on his book, although he hadn't managed to read so much as a sentence in the last hour. "I brought you the meeting site. I have told you what I know, okay? And if I was going to work for him, why did I come back?"

"To spy on my operation, you little shit."

Rashid looked up, but he was too slow and Franji's hand slammed the book against his cheek. Rashid's head snapped back against the wall. He grabbed it with both hands to stifle the pain.

"What operation?" he spat out. "If I hadn't told you, you wouldn't even have known where he was!"

Franji hit him again, an open-handed slap to his ear that made him scent copper blood in his nose and set off a ringing in his head. "Conveniently, he and the girl were gone when we got there, weren't they? Where are they? Where are they? Heh?" With each repetition, he hit Rashid again.

Rashid rolled into a ball on the floor and tried to protect himself.

Al-Dahgma got to his feet. "You are wasting your time. He doesn't know anything. He's the colonel's pet; he wouldn't stab us in the back."

Franji stepped away from Rashid. "Fa," he spat, an exclamation of disgust. "He knows something."

Al-Dahgma shrugged. "Whatever he knows, it's nothing. He gave us their travel plan. We need to be ready to get the girl."

Franji went back across the room to the only chair, sat, lit a cigarette. "We have another mission."

Al-Dahgma started. "What now?"

"Jewish agents killed one of our officers in Cairo last night. The colonel says that we are to kill the Jew agents here on the island." Franji waved his cigarette. "As soon as possible."

Al-Dahgma became excited. "That's what I've been saying. We will need guns. And where are these agents?"

Franji took a long drag on his cigarette and stared off into space. "We will have to find them." He took another drag.

The younger man started to pace. "They're here looking for the girl. They must be."

Franji nodded. "That's what the colonel says. We have to

392

bring them into the open." He turned and looked at Rashid.
"I think I know how."

Agiassos, Lesvos

After they finally made love, she pulled herself up over him,
so that her hair was in his face. "Listen to me, okay?"

Piat was still wondering why his body had changed its
mind so totally. "You have my complete attention."

"How much trouble am I in?" She sounded sober and cold,
as if sex had washed everything else out of her.

"If we can get off this island tomorrow—" Piat considered
lying and thought better of it. The circumstances were against
a lie anyway. "I don't *know*, Saida. But there are a lot of
people looking for the cup. And we've been in one place for
two days."

She nodded above him, swaying back and forth a little.
"Can I still pretend I'm going to get a lot of money? Or are
we pretty much done with that?"

"We aren't done. But tomorrow could be rough."

"And the cup? Is it really worth all that money?"

"There's a buyer meeting us in Izmir in two days, honey.
And yeah, it's really worth all that money." Piat compart-
mented away the thought that he might sell her to Dukas
for a passport and then sell her cup.

"I'm scared," she said, and burrowed against him. "You
really didn't make up the money just to fuck me?"

Piat tried again to see himself through her eyes. There was
another long silence while he evaluated the gulf between
them. And contemplated handing her over to Mike Dukas.
"No," he said. *Rather the opposite.*

She hugged him. "I'm scared," she repeated.

Me too, thought Piat. He craned his neck to look at his
watch on the night-stand.

Eressos, Lesvos

Rashid woke to the sound of a car outside their guesthouse. He wasn't sleeping well because he was terrified of his companions and because his face hurt however he rested his head.

Franji went to the window and looked out, then slipped through the door. There were voices outside in Arabic, the sound of a car door opening, being closed, and Franji was back inside, followed by a taller, heavier man.

"This is Gunaym," he said, pointing to the newcomer.

Al-Dahgma came and clasped hands. The newcomer didn't smile. "Who's that on the floor?"

"A little shit foisted on us by the colonel."

Gunaym came and squatted by Rashid. "It is rude not to greet a new comrade," he said. He put a hand on Rashid's face and Rashid flinched. "I think this one is in some pain."

Rashid looked up in time to see Franji wave a hand. "He is of no consequence. I think he may intend to betray us and I tried to instill a little discipline."

Gunaym looked at Rashid again and then stood up. "If he has betrayed us, he should be dead. If he needs discipline, he should read the Koran. I fail to see how hitting him accomplished either goal."

Franji began to protest, but the newcomer simply raised a hand.

"This is a combat operation now, my friends. I will take charge of it and take responsibility for all of its aspects. You understand?" He looked at both Franji and al-Dahgma.

Al-Dahgma nodded agreement.

Franji protested. "This is my operation."

"No," said the newcomer. "Help me get the rest of the bags." He turned to Rashid. "You too."

Rashid got to his feet and followed Gunaym out into the dark. There were two ski bags in the car and the big man handed him one. He took it by the handle and carried it inside, feeling the weight of it on his arm and the shape bulging against his thigh as he walked. He didn't have to wait for it to be opened to know what it carried.

The new man brought the other ski bag and the other two brought luggage from the trunk. Gunaym laid the bags out on the bed and began to open them. As Rashid had expected, the heavy ski bag held a rifle.

Gunaym laid the rifle on the bed with two Beretta military automatics and began to distribute clips of ammunition between them. "Have any of you been trained with firearms?"

Rashid shook his head numbly. Franji moved his head in a fractional nod, and al-Dahgma pumped his excitedly and began to demonstrate his familiarity by stripping one of the weapons on the bed.

"Ruger," he said enthusiastically.

Gunaym smiled. "Good. You and I will take the rifle and the pistols, then. You know where we will find the Israelis, I think?"

Franji pushed his chin toward Rashid. "He told us where the American and the girl intend to take a boat to Turkey. I know nothing about the Israelis. But I have an idea of how to find them."

Gunaym nodded. "You have been here three days and you have no idea where these Israelis are?" he asked. He began to strip the rifle.

"The Israelis were not the concern of *my* operation." Franji sounded very defensive to Rashid, who was balanced between joy and terror at the new turn of events.

Gunaym nodded again. "Refocus yourself, then. This is a combat operation. We are to kill the Israeli agents. If the cup can be recovered, so much the better. If not, so be it. That, as with all things, is in the hands of Allah." He concentrated on easing the heavy spring on the bolt clear of the receiver. "Tell me your plan."

395

Franji pointed at Rashid. "We tether him like a goat in the open and lure the lion."

Gunaym looked at Franji, and then at Rashid, and scratched his chin.

19

Tel Aviv

It was pushing toward four in the morning. Dukas was pulled up from sleep the way you pull a night crawler out of a hole. "Sixteen forty-three," he rasped—his room number.

"Stand by," a woman's accented voice said. It was authoritative, rather deep, but certainly female. "Stand by for an important caller."

Oh, smell me, he thought, contemptuous before he was fully awake. He assumed it was somebody in Mossad or the foreign ministry telling him to get the hell out of Israel. *Ha-ha, the joke's on you, I'm already going.*

"Special Agent Dukas!"

This time it was a male voice, more heavily accented, and as angry as a snake with a broken fang. The anger came through the phone line like poison. "This is Colonel Mahmoud Hamal! They probably call me to you 'the Tax Collector.'" Said with utter disgust.

Before Dukas could react, Hamal rushed on, the words gusting out. "You Mossad lackeys who are listening, do you hear me? It is Hamal! You have murdered my woman, my heart, you bastards, you swine, you shit-eating dogs! You *Jews*! Dukas, you hear me? You hear what I am saying to them?"

"I'm not a Mossad lackey, Colonel."

"Tell me you did not set up a meeting at which my woman, my heart was killed!"

"I don't know anything about a meeting."

"You know everything! Do you think I am stupid? An infant?" He was screaming. "You crossed the border and went to Tel-Sharm-Heir'at! You asked questions of the diggers! You are looking for the killers of Salem Qatib! What do you think, I let them make a meeting to talk about antiquities and I do not think it is you behind it?"

"What meeting?"

Silence. Then when he spoke again, Hamal's voice was much softer, as if he had forced himself to sound calm. "*You know*. The meeting in Cairo. Your man, the black man, was in Cairo today, asking questions. I know it is you, Special Agent Dukas. Now I have things to say to you, but I want you to say to me that you did not make up the meeting in order to shoot me or my woman. Say it!"

"No, I didn't set any meeting in order to shoot you or anybody."

"So you did not, and your CIA did not, and so the Jews did it. Well, I am telling them now, *now*, that they will pay in blood. For her, ten. Are you listening, Jews? Ten of you!"

Dukas heard the man's breathing, almost a panting.

"Ten," he said again, now almost a whisper. "And I will start with the four you have on Lesvos."

Dukas frowned at that. Could Hamal really know if there were Mossad agents on Lesvos? Jerry Piat had said he had people after him—were they Mossad? Dukas was thinking fast, wondering what it meant for Craik, who was headed for Lesvos.

"Dukas?"

"Yes, Colonel."

"Now I have a message for you. Now I will tell you who killed Salem Qatib. It was not me or my people. I am telling you this because I want you to see how things are done where you are. Salem Qatib was stealing from his Hamas bosses. He stole God knows how much in antiquities. We caught him, yes. We questioned him, yes. We beat him, yes. But he was alive when the Jews came and took him, and it was the Jews who decided that he would die. They think they are God."

Dukas was thinking how bizarre it was that Mossad were almost certainly hearing all this. Or would hear it, because they were probably taping it remotely, and they would hear it only tomorrow or the day after. Would it have the same crackle and threat then as it did now for him? Cautiously, Dukas said, "But you're not Hamas."

"Hamas sometimes make arrangements with us for our mutual benefit."

"They pay you chai." When there was no response, he said, "How did Mossad know about the dig?"

Hamal snorted. "A Mossad spy told them where he was. I admit it—we have Mossad spies. It is inevitable. This scum, this shit-eater, he knew about the dig and he had a special telephone number to call with information. And he called."

"How do you know that?"

Hamal screamed into the phone. "Do you think that after my woman was shot dead at the meeting, I would go on as if nothing had happened? There is a story in your Bible, Special Agent Dukas, a man who pushed down the pillars of a house because he had been wronged! I said, let my house collapse on me, but find the traitors and make them talk! One of them was the one who made the telephone call about Qatib. He talked."

"Who did he talk to at Mossad?"

"You think a little scum like this knew? You think Mossad *trusted* him? You know better, Special Agent Dukas. His control was some Israeli with no name or a false name. But I know that his control is part of Section Sixteen. You know Section Sixteen, I think."

Shlomo Eshkol. David Tar-Saloman. Yeah, I know Section Sixteen.

"Now I will give you that telephone number, Special Agent Dukas. I will give it to you and I will leave it to you to follow this thread until it leads you to the very man in Section Sixteen who killed Salem Qatib. And I tell you this—they came in a car, four of them, and took Qatib from the dig. And they killed him. They killed him with torture because he was nothing but a dog of a Palestinian. They tortured him because they wanted to know what he was finding. *And he died.*"

Then Hamal gave him a telephone number. Dukas wrote it down and read it back, and Hamal said that that was right. And then there was what sounded like a curse in Arabic and the line went silent.

Dukas should have got right on the blower to Ted Kasser then, but he picked up the telephone and dialed the number that Hamal had given him, the number that a Mossad informer had given up under torture. A woman answered and said something in what he took to be Arabic. She would be no more than an answering service, he thought, simply a way for an informer to make contact. She would, however, take a message. Dukas said, "This is Special Agent Dukas of the Naval Criminal Investigative Service of the United States. Tell Shlomo Eshkol he needs to talk to me. Tell him I want a meeting." And he hung up. Thinking that now he would call Kasser, and if he could convince Kasser of what Hamal had said, it would be over. And he would call Craik back from Lesvos, and Jerry Piat would have to take care of himself.

Kasser had an STU at home, one of the perks of office. But there was a downside—people like Dukas called when you thought the workday was over. (It was evening in DC.) Dukas laid it out for him, including Spinner and Mossad, and said categorically that the cryptology idea was bullshit. "Don't let them change any codes. It's a non-starter. It's crap. Cryptology isn't in it."

"Guys from DoD say they've got it solid, Mike."

"They've got it solid because one guy has been feeding them gold-plated dogshit courtesy of Mossad! Ted, they're just wrong!"

"You ever try to prove to a true believer that he's wrong?"

"Make them lay out their case. They can't do it."

"They're already giving everybody a lot of bull-ticky about 'better sources' and 'unfiltered intelligence.' There's a lot of people convinced by them."

"Ted, for Christ's sake, there's such a thing as truth."

"Truth is whatever gets fought for the hardest—you know that, Mike. These guys have the vice-president's office pushing their idea really hard. Can you, right now, right this minute, *prove* that the Qatib case isn't about cryptology?"

"Jesus, I can't *prove* it isn't about creationism, but I can sure show that it *is* about antiquities and money."

"Can you *prove* it? Rock-solid, courthouse proof?"

Dukas was exasperated. "We're not going to court with it!"

"But you've got to convince some very skeptical people."

"What the hell are they skeptical about? When have we ever had intelligence that's one hundred percent courthouse provable?"

"That's what they're skeptical about. They're saying that they have rock-solid evidence and we waffle. We *interpret*. We *speculate*."

"Like shit!"

"It's a new world back here, Mike. On this one, we got to have proof. Get me proof. Okay? Get me proof, or the Navy's going to spend a couple of hundred million on a very successful Mossad disinformation ploy."

Dukas sighed. "Well." He looked at his watch. It was almost first light. "When?"

"There's a meeting of what's called an 'intelligence appraisal group' day after tomorrow. Something else put together by the VP's office. I think that whatever comes out of there as the truth will prevail. You got to keep punching until that meeting, Mike."

Dukas had been going to suggest that they shit-can Jerry Piat and the Lesvos effort. But it would have to go ahead now. Lesvos and Jerry Piat might offer the final line that would connect all the dots, the final bit of logic, the final synapse.

Dukas put his feet on the bed and thought about Al Craik's making a meeting that had gone from a gimme to a high-risk because of one telephone call, and that was a repeat now of the supposed gimme that Dukas had given him in Tel Aviv and the one that Dukas had sent Peretz to in Cairo. If Hamal had meant what he said about killing Mossad people on Lesvos—and it made sense that the people Piat thought were on him were Mossad—then any meeting with Piat would be a high-risk one, and it wasn't fair to send Craik. Dukas sighed and put his hand on the telephone and, after a moment's thought about best-laid plans, called the NCIS office in Naples. It was four in the morning there and the duty officer sounded a little woozy. There was a cot in the back; he'd probably been sacked out. Dukas told him to find out Craik's flight schedule and then tell the Athens office to get somebody out to the airport to tell him to turn around and go home.

Lucky man.

Because Dukas's next move was to start looking for a flight for himself to Athens and then Lesvos, because it was his case and he was the logical one to go. What he found was that he could connect with a flight that got to the island at 1535 local, too late for the first meeting time with Piat but okay for the fallback. Dukas sighed some more and said some unkind things to the wall. The fallback was at night, meaning he'd have to hang around and hope to get out the next morning and get home by—it was disgusting.

He checked the schedules again, looking to see if there

was any way he could make the two-o'clock meeting. But there wasn't. The winter schedule for Mytilene, Lesvos, had planes coming in only at half past six in the morning and mid-afternoon.

And then he saw that to make the meeting at two, Craik would have to arrive in Lesvos on the morning flight, and that would be leaving Athens in about—oh, shit, twenty minutes.

He called Naples again. They'd already called Athens. They'd try to page Craik in the Athens airport.

Dukas checked his watch. He had an hour to pack and haul his ass to his flight to Athens. So that, if they didn't catch Craik in Athens, he'd make a high-risk meeting, and Dukas could arrive a couple of hours later to hear how bad it had been.

Eressos, Lesvos

Gunaym woke Rashid gently. He had laid out a mat on the floor next to Rashid after stripping and cleaning the guns and checking some communications equipment, and his presence, between Rashid and the other two men, had helped sleep to come. Now he shook Rashid's shoulder until Rashid opened his eyes.

"Do you pray?" he asked.

"I used to," said Rashid as he rubbed his eyes. He looked carefully for adult condemnation.

"Would you like to pray with me? It is a beautiful morning." Gunaym rose in one easy motion with his rolled-up mat, washed his hands at the sink, and walked to the door.

Rashid followed into the gentle pink of dawn. The light was everywhere at once, making the car and the house and the gravel in the drive all equally beautiful.

Gunaym walked down to the beach, which curved gently away to the north, vanishing out of sight more than a mile away. He kicked off his slippers at the beach, unrolled his mat on the edge of the damp sand, and knelt, sitting back on his feet. Rashid started to kneel on the sand, but Gunaym indicated the other half of his mat.

They prayed together, toward Mecca and the pink sky to the east.

When they were done, Gunaym rolled up his mat. "Come, walk with me," he said.

Gunaym walked fast on the packed sand, headed south toward the inlet of a small stream at the base of a ridge that rose a thousand feet above the sea. Rashid followed him along the beach.

"Why did you go off with the American?" he asked suddenly.

"First—first he threatened me. He said that it was because of me that the Israelis were looking at him."

Gunaym turned and looked down at Rashid. "And was that the truth?"

"Yes. I didn't even know they were there." Rashid drew a breath to go on, faltered, unsure what to say. Unsure why he was being asked. He shrugged. "I did. Okay, I was starting to know they were there. But I was following him—the American."

"So. And then?"

"I liked him. He showed me things. He showed me how he kept people from following him. He is a good man. He was nice to me."

Gunaym nodded. "Americans are nice people." He slowed his pace and looked out to sea. "And then you stayed with him?"

"Yes."

"And? Why did you come back to us?"

"He went and got Saida. You know—"

"Sure. Yes. I know who Saida is." Gunaym shifted his rolled mat to his shoulder and started to walk again.

"She—we—I—had sex. And she knew—all along—that Salem was dead. But it was wrong. And then—then I thought she would go to the American, that he only wanted us for money. Or perhaps I thought—" Suddenly it came to Rashid that what he had thought was that the American would prefer Saida to him, as Salem had. The thought made him feel small. He wondered if the American thought of him at all.

Gunaym watched him.

Rashid felt no urge to say any more. He had already said too much.

They were far down the beach, almost to the base of the deceptively distant ridge. Rashid stood up straight. "You are going to kill me," he said in a flat voice.

"No," said Gunaym. "No. Not now." He shrugged. "I might have. Will you work for us, now?"

Rashid nodded, slowly.

Gunaym looked away, his gaze tracking a gull. "This may be our last morning on this earth."

Rashid prepared himself for religious promises. He had heard them all from his mother's friends in Hamas. Gunaym looked the type.

"If that is so, I will miss it." Gunaym scooped a handful of sand and threw it into the wind.

As they walked back up the beach, Gunaym told Rashid what he wanted him to do. "Every day, you go to a different town. Molyvos, Eressos, Kalloni. Mytilene if we have to. And you sit in a café and wait. Franji is not a fool, Salem. You will draw the Israelis. They will follow you."

Just hearing it made Rashid tremble. "I'm the bait."

"Yes." Gunaym shrugged.

"What about the beach? Tonight?"

"Oh, we'll be there. But I don't really expect your American to just stumble down to us. I have to take some action to bring the quarry to us."

405

Rashid retreated into silence.

Finally, with the house in sight, Gunaym put a hand on the boy's shoulder. "These men, these four. They killed Salem. Not their kind, not other agents. These four killed Salem. They tortured him, and then they killed him."

Rashid cocked his head a little and stared at Gunaym, trying to read his face. "You know that? Or Colonel Hamal told you to say that?"

"He told me to say that. Yes. We captured a man who was informing to Mossad. He told us everything."

Rashid shuddered despite the bright winter sun. He had learned a little in the last few days about what that phrase might mean. *He told us everything.* Rashid thought, *The informer died like Salem died. For what?*

And then he thought, *They are all the same.*

Gunaym said, "Do this, and we will avenge Salem."

For the first time, avenging Salem had no interest for him. Had the informer avenged Salem? Did it matter? He tried to hide the thoughts on his face. "And Saida? The American? What of them?"

Gunaym shrugged.

Over the Aegean

Somewhere to the north in the haze off the port wing was windy Ilios, but Alan Craik couldn't find it. He saw a flotilla of frigates and antiquated landing ships steaming in formation through an archipelago; he saw Chios off the starboard wing, volcanic mountains rising stark above the white-capped sea, but he didn't see Troy. He would have liked to.

Alan had slept, eaten, moved through airports on automatic. He was angry—so angry that it was burning away at his view of the world. He had his copy of *The Iliad* open on his lap with a map, but he didn't want it—reading *The Iliad* seemed to him trivial. Everything seemed trivial.

Lesvos looked bleaker than the mainland, with a steeper

coast and less vegetation. Their flight path brought them over the island at Molyvos, and he craned his head to see the walls of a fortress rising clear and pink in the new sun. Beyond the fortress, the island was green even in winter, but to the south, over the starboard wing, he could see that the western half of the island looked like desert. His guidebook said the cause was the winds from Africa.

He put Fidel's copy of *The Iliad* back into his pack. He concentrated on keeping his ears from exploding, swallowing and holding his nose as he watched the Turkish mainland roll by his window, watched the boats in the channel grow closer, and tried not to let his mind fix on images from Afghanistan. *"The rules have changed."*

The cabin intercom crackled and delivered a message in Greek and German. Alan assumed it was a warning for landing. He had never taken his seatbelt off, so he continued to watch the world out of his window. It was not unlike the view from the back seat of an S-3, except that this seat was less comfortable.

He felt the crosswind as the pilot made his turn on final, felt the sluggish response of the plane through his seat. He could see that they were landing crabwise, the motion of the plane off angle from the vector of the landing. Mytilene did not run to multiple runways, apparently. He fought the urge to move his body in sympathy to the way he wanted the plane to land and tried to be an unconcerned passenger.

The pilot did the final approach like a pro, getting all the gear lined up and on the runway in one flick of the controls in the last seconds on final. *He's done this a million times,* Alan thought. *I need to relax.*

I need to be in Naples with Rose and the kids. Why am I here? The plane rolled to a stop with the low terminal building just off Alan's wing. *Because I told Mike I'd help him. Because I am the boy who can't say no. Because Abe got shot.* He didn't have any luggage beyond his carry-on, and he swept through the luggage-control area and walked into the terminal, looking for the car-rental counter, his thoughts wandering to shopping and how to fit it in. He had plenty of time; after he made the meet, he'd slip away and find the local equivalent of a souk.

The Avis counter was empty. It was 0732, and he was standing almost alone in an empty airport. He went into the café, ordered a pastry and coffee, and tried to read. Every few seconds, his eyes would flick over to the Avis desk, which remained obstinately empty.

Eventually, Alan watched a tall young man unlock the steel shutter with the Avis sign. Alan walked up, tossed his driver's license on the counter, and said, "I have a reservation."

The Avis man took the license and started the process of opening his register. At 0841, Alan put his luggage down with a sigh that indicated both his suppressed anger at being here and his tension. The end of the sigh caught in his throat. He was looking at one of the men who had abducted him in Israel.

After they had snatched him in the SUV, they had held him in a room with a cot and a window with a heavy metal shutter. He had been handcuffed to a pipe and left. Later, two men had come for him; a big blond man with a cut on his chin had stayed by the door, and a much smaller man with a big head and oiled hair had come in with a chair.

Both of them had been in the SUV. Alan's hands had begun to shake. He hated it, and them.

Very carefully, Alan straightened. The big blond man was twenty feet away, sitting in the waiting area, watching the television. The rental car guy said something about Alan's license, and Alan looked away, but not before the blond man had seen him. Alan flinched. He signed something that the Avis man passed him and his hand was difficult to control. He took a second look at the seating area, could feel his pulse slamming at the base of his throat.

Athens

An NCIS agent named Howard Greenspan was standing smack in the way of everybody rushing out of the Athens arrivals gate. Greenspan was short but wide, with exaggerated memories of his career as a high-school nose guard. He was there to meet Mike Dukas, and by God, nobody was going to push him out of the way.

Dukas saw him from thirty feet away, recognized him as one of his people, connected the name before they were within speaking distance, and was ready to say something friendly when Greenspan grabbed his arm and shouted, "We didn't catch up with Craik but he wants you to call him *right now!*"

This didn't make a lot of sense to Dukas, but they'd straightened it out by the time he'd maneuvered Greenspan out of everybody's path and to a public phone that another special agent was holding for him. Other travelers were giving ugly looks, but he didn't care.

"He's on the phone *now?*"

"Naw, he's sitting by one wherever he is. See, we missed him here in Athens—"

Dukas had already heard it once, didn't need to hear it again. He took the phone from the second agent, who said, "We figured a public phone was as good as we could do. Sir." He meant, there was no secure line, but in a crunch you took your chances. The guy already had a phone card for him; Dukas dialed the long, long number and heard the other end pick up after half a ring. *Sitting on the phone.*

"Yes?"

"Alan, hey, it's Mike."

"Oh, boy. We got a problem." Craik sounded like death warmed over, Dukas thought—tired out.

"No, now that I got you, we *haven't* got a problem. You're sprung. Go home."

"You don't understand, Mike. There's a new factor here.

409

I just saw one of the guys who grabbed me off the street in Tel Aviv. He's *here*, Mike."

Dukas had to think about what that meant. *At the beginning*, Craik meant, when he was in Tel Aviv and Dukas thought it was just a simple matter of checking a death. One of the Mossad people who had grabbed Craik at the beginning. "Saw him where?"

"*Here! In the airport at Lesvos!*" To Dukas, Alan sounded brittle. "He's watching for people leaving, not incoming. I think he saw me. So I know he's here. They know I'm here."

"You don't know the half of it." Dukas sketched in what Hamal had told him. "He said four guys, four Mossad guys on Lesvos, Al. That's a team."

"Like the four guys who snatched me in Tel Aviv."

"Fuck. Yeah, like the four guys who killed Salem Qatib. And you're sure of the ID?"

He was sure. Very sure.

"I'd give a small piece of my body to know if all four of them are there."

"If I can make them put a tail on me—"

"No, no—"

"—then I can ID them, or some of them, anyway. The more of them I can ID—"

"No, no, too risky—"

"—the better case you have with Kasser."

Dukas hesitated over that. Craik was right—IDs would make a case with Kasser. For form's sake, nonetheless, he said, "You're not a trained agent." What he meant was that he wanted the IDs but Craik hadn't been in very good shape the last time he'd seen him. "Al, it's the kind of thing I'd think twice about asking any of my guys to do."

"Nobody but me can ID them."

Craik would be running on adrenaline and nothing else; he wanted to get back at the people who had snatched him in Tel Aviv more than he wanted to go home and get some rest. Not for the first time, Dukas thought that maybe Craik was a little crazy.

"Mike?"

"I'm thinking."

"For Christ's sake, stop thinking and let's plan. How do I keep in touch with you?"

"You don't have to. I'm coming to Lesvos."

"What the hell for? I'll make the meeting with your guy."

"You've got a tail; the meeting's busted."

"So there's a fallback; what's the problem? Look, I'm going to go rent a car. Then I'm going to start to drive around, see who's on me. I'll leave you a message at the rental car desk, okay?"

"You know how to drive a surveillance route?"

"Jesus, Mike, what do you think I've been doing for ten years?"

"The object is to make it easy for them to follow you."

"Yes, Mom."

"You won't get much chance to ID them that way."

Dukas felt as if he was sending his kid off to his first day of school, which was stupid, because Craik had been in and out of all kinds of stuff. But that was the trouble: Craik got involved in *stuff*, violent stuff, and what was needed in this case was patience and tradecraft and the most careful, tactful kind of avoidance of anything exciting. "No inspirations," Dukas said.

"Does that mean you think *I'll* do something stupid?"

Dukas could feel the weight of anger under Craik's surface and he backed off. "Don't get fancy or aggressive, okay?"

"But you're saying it's okay."

Dukas sighed. "I'm saying it's not okay, but you can do it if you're goddam careful, and I feel like a complete shit for sending you there in the first place. Rose will kill me."

Then they arranged to communicate (cell phones, purchased by Alan at the airport, one left for Dukas at the rental car desk) and meet, and Dukas hung up and looked at his watch

411

and wondered what he'd do for five hours. Well, a quick visit to the Athens office would probably be good for morale. And he could call Colonel Kritikiou to tell him he had another agent to declare—Michael Dukas.

And Colonel Kritikiou had something new for Michael Dukas: if there were to be two declared American agents on Lesvos, he thought that things were perhaps rather serious, and he insisted that a representative of Greek intelligence meet Dukas when he arrived on the island.

Mytilene, Lesvos

Alan walked away from the rental car desk, having left a cell phone for Dukas. He took his keys and walked out the main doors of the terminal into the bright winter sun, trying *not* to look all around him.

The rental cars were parked in a long line just to the left of the main terminal doors, and Alan walked down the line, looking for his car and simultaneously trying to guess where a surveillant would be waiting to tag him as he left the parking lot. It was an open, treeless landscape, with nowhere to hide a car, and before he settled into his rental he already suspected a white Suzuki jeep that was parked alone less than a hundred meters to the north.

He took his time putting the luggage into the car, adjusting mirrors and stripping off his heavy jacket. Then he got in, started the engine and worked all the signals and the brakes.

The white Suzuki stayed where it was. There was a man in the driver's seat. That's all Alan could discern. If this was a classic bubble, there would be three or four more cars prepared to take a turn on him.

If he wasn't imagining the whole thing.

Alan put the Volkswagen into gear. He pulled to the main road, turned left toward downtown Mytilene, and accelerated slowly.

The white Suzuki pulled out of its spot behind him and began to accelerate.

Alan found he was humming under his breath. There were rules about detecting surveillance, and Alan's hunch about the white Suzuki did not meet the accepted criteria of a confirmed observation. Yet. He slowed for the airport traffic circle and followed the signs for downtown Mytilene. He had not planned to stop there, but the rules were now changed.

In the distance of two blocks Mytilene changed from a European town with broad thoroughfares and well-signed exits to a street plan that reminded Alan of Africa. Suddenly, the streets were so narrow that his Volkswagen seemed too big; every street was one-way for obvious reasons, and pedestrian traffic thickened to the point where driving was not the efficient way to travel.

By the time Alan rolled the car into a parking spot just west of the harbor, he had driven around the harbor twice, watched the town's public parking lot vanish in his mirror as he struggled to find the entrance. So much for *act naturally. Tourists naturally get lost,* he thought.

Once parked, he went into the first store that was open, a grocery and tourist shop just on the edge of the harbor, located to catch foreigners like him on their way downhill from the car park. He walked in intending to buy himself binoculars. One glimpse of a shiny digital camera and he was struck by a better, if riskier, plan and one that would have a bearing on Dukas's case. He also bought batteries, an English language magazine, and maps. Every inch of Lesvos and every town, no matter how small, had its own map, exact, colored, labeled in Greek and English. He thought that the island's tourism motto might be "Lesvos: an island made for espionage."

He also bought a yellow highlighter.

He put his new belongings in his pack and started to walk around the harbor toward the ferry dock. It was 0945. His

413

meeting with Piat was in Kalloni, forty-five minutes to an hour away by car, at 1400. Leaving slop time to cover contingencies, he had two hours and forty minutes to make his plans and execute them.

He intended to break every rule involved in dealing with surveillance.

Mike would not necessarily approve.

An hour later, he was sitting on a bench looking out at the sweep of Mytilene harbor, from a medieval-looking tower on his right, across several million dollars' worth of yachts and fishing boats, past the military base mentioned in his guidebook and the ferry dock on his left, to a massive fortification atop an ancient acropolis with heavily wooded slopes. The town hung above the harbor like a crescent moon.

A heavily built man in a canvas hunting-vest was watching him from the door of an open café across the street. He had been watching Alan for most of the hour, while Alan prowled along the waterfront and walked up the winding streets above.

Canvas Vest was the round-headed man from the snatch in Tel Aviv.

Round-head had leaned forward like a priest giving penance. His breath had been foul. He had said, "You've put us in a—well, a difficult position." The man's English had been clear, just slightly accented, his voice deep. "We want you to know that this—didn't— wasn't intended to involve you."

He had leaned even closer, the light from the room's single bare bulb reflecting from his bald head. "What's done is done. And we'd be most appreciative if you didn't—make too much of this. We're on the same side. We're in a war. Things happen, you understand? Mistakes are made. Rules change."

Alan knew him in an instant, a single flick of the eyes. *Two.* Of the four men who had snatched him, he had two.

He got to his feet, hoisted his pack and walked along the

414

waterfront toward the ferry dock until he found a taverna that was busy despite the season and the hour. He sat, ordered a croissant, and an espresso and mineral water and opened the map of Kalloni, where he was meeting Piat. Downtown Kalloni was a simple, modern grid, with a roundabout and a public park landscaped around some Roman-era ruins at the center and a gazebo. By the time the croissant reached his table, he had yellow-lined his route in, located a municipal parking lot west of the public park, and ticked off the route he intended to walk to the meeting, a simple series of left turns around the grid. He hoped that the grid would look like Mytilene, with tourist shops on every street to give his route substance.

Canvas Vest passed the taverna across the boulevard, on the harbor side.

Alan devoured his croissant. He had ordered it for cover, but it smelled, and was, delicious and fresh. The mineral water vanished in a long fizzy swig. The coffee was good.

Canvas Vest was now standing against a light pole by the harbor. Alan remembered staring at his shoes in a speeding vehicle in Tel Aviv. He finished his espresso smiling.

At the next table, two Greeks flirted and romanced. Alan leaned over during a lull.

"Excuse me?"

"Yes?" They both looked at him together, as if already one person. The girl raised her eyebrows. She looked very young to Alan.

"Could you watch my bag for a moment?" he asked.

They both laughed and nodded. He entered the taverna with the camera in his jacket pocket, sat in the washroom on one of the toilets and scanned the manual, inserted a battery, turned it on.

He tossed the packaging into a trashcan and walked back through the taverna with the camera hung from his neck. At the top of the steps down to the outside terrace, he paused, extended the lens to its maximum magnification, drew a bead on the round-headed man and his lamppost, and snapped two pictures. *Tap, tap. You want to change the rules? Me too.* He felt better already.

Canvas Vest saw him as he lowered the camera, and his face went splotchy red, his outrage visible from sixty feet away. Alan kept his face blank, walked down to his table and retrieved his bag. The two young Greeks asked him to join them in good, if accented, English, held up an unopened bottle of wine. He pleaded a prior engagement, thanked them, and left with his backpack on one shoulder, headed uphill away from Canvas Vest.

He made a wrong turn somewhere, found himself climbing away from the harbor in the wrong direction, a danger in an unknown town, but the harbor was a difficult landmark to miss and in thirty minutes he was at his car. His watch said 1121.

The white Suzuki was eight cars behind him as he made the last turn on to the highway.

Kalloni, Lesvos.
Rashid sat in a taverna in the main traffic circle of the resort town of Kalloni with a can of Coke and a magazine on his table. Off to his left in a car park screened by some scrubby trees was Franji, sitting in his car and smoking. Franji and his car represented Rashid's "evasion plan," a phrase that Rashid hated because of its implied desperation.

He had been tethered like a lamb. All he could do was bleat and hope for a miracle.

Nonetheless, his brain was still functioning and he had begun to make a plan of his own. In his pocket was a Swiss army knife he had bought on arrival in Kalloni. He took off Salem's peacoat and began to unpick the stitches around Salem's rank badge. As he cut and pulled, he thought of Salem, on a ship, carefully sewing the patch on. He was cold by the

416

time he had the patch free of the heavy wool. He put the patch in his pocket with the knife, as ready as he could be.

Then he used the taverna's one computer link to send an email to Saida.

The idea that he would be tethered here for days, virtually alone in a tourist town, waiting for some enemy to come and take the bait—

He pulled his book from his pocket and made himself read, despite the fact that le Carré and spying had lost much of their charm as fiction. After a while, he ordered lunch and more Coke.

Bleat, bleat.

Tel Aviv

After a night and part of a morning at the American embassy, Ray Spinner felt as if he had been dried out and hung in the breeze like the shell of a dead insect. Fatigue was only part of it—he had been kept awake all night answering questions—because some of it, he could sense, was mental, perhaps even spiritual. Humiliation was part of it, and a deep disappointment in himself. Surprisingly, the only good thing was what Dukas had said to him, that confessing was the best thing he had ever done. Nobody else had seemed to think so: stern, youngish men from the CIA, the FBI, and embassy security had taken turns ridiculing him, bellowing questions at him, calling him fool and sucker and even turncoat. He had realized early on that what they hated was what he stood for—his Pentagon office, which they called "James Bond Central" and "Amateurs, Inc." and "Intellijerks." The idea of doing an end run around the established intel agencies, which had seemed so attractive when McKinnon had talked about it, was jumped on, shredded, and buried.

Now he was in his hotel room, packing. One of the severe, youngish men from the embassy was sitting in the room's only chair, reading or pretending to read a free brochure on the delights of the city (English and Hebrew). Spinner was folding a shirt, ready to put it into a two-suiter that was open on the bed. He kept looking at the man, wanting some sort of human contact, wanting some sign that he wasn't, in fact, a dead insect. He cleared his throat. "How do we get to the airport?" he managed to say.

The man looked up. He was shorter than most, rather wide, his face perhaps Slavic. He looked at Spinner as if he had never seen him before and wondered what he was doing there. "Embassy car," he said, and went back to the brochure.

"They want to be sure I get there."

The man looked up again. "We're in a foreign country."

Spinner laid the shirt in the suitcase and picked up another. "A car followed us here, didn't it."

"One of ours."

"No, behind that one."

The man looked up again, this time apparently aware that Spinner was human. "That's possible."

Mossad. His friends from Mossad. He wondered what they would do if they managed to pick him up.

Spinner finished the shirt and then opened and closed the bureau drawers to make sure he hadn't left anything. He looked around the room. His copy of Strauss's *The City and Man* lay on the bedside table. He hadn't opened it since he had got off the plane, he realized. He held it out. "Need some reading matter?"

He gave Spinner the look again and scowled. "What's it about?"

Spinner tossed it toward him, but short so it would land on the bed and he wouldn't have to catch it. "Search me."

"What's the story?"

"It's a little short on story." He tried a smile. "You have to read between the lines to get it."

He'd sent McKinnon a message to tell him that everything he'd sent about cryptology was a mistake. He'd got an almost instantaneous answer: "We don't make mistakes. And when we do, they cease being mistakes." McKinnon hadn't said he was fired, but he thought he was.

The other man picked up the Strauss book and opened it to the title page. Spinner zipped up his luggage and checked the minuscule closet and the bathroom and slapped his pockets, meaning to make sure he had his ticket and his passport, and he remembered that the other man had them. He hauled the bag off the bed and dumped it by the door, then shouldered his carry-on and stood there. "Ready," he said.

The embassy man got up slowly, reading Strauss, then stood there for perhaps twenty seconds, turning pages and frowning, until, having flicked a page where Spinner saw some of his own yellow highlighting, he tossed it on the bed. "Not my kind of shit," he said.

Spinner picked up the two-suiter. "That was my reaction, too."

Odysseus Elitis Airport, Lesvos

The notion that his Greek ancestors had flitted through a sun-drenched landscape in their underwear made Dukas almost smile as he crossed the Lesvos tarmac. It was damned cold, and the sun, if it was up there, was not drenching anything closer than the top of a thick cloud layer. The wind that whipped in from Asia made him wish he'd dressed for Minnesota. He rounded his shoulders and lumbered faster toward the terminal entrance.

Although he'd expected as much, he was annoyed that a young man who had the good taste to be embarrassed was waiting for him at immigration. He was a dark Greek, dressed as an international movie star—blazer, nubbly T-shirt, jeans, space-alien sunglasses, two-day beard. Seeing him, Dukas felt old and seedy in his raincoat and Tel Aviv-style polo shirt; his own two-day beard somehow didn't seem trendy. The Greek's English was good but no better than Dukas's demotic

419

Greek, so they went back and forth between the languages. His name was Darcouri; he was a lieutenant in the Greek navy; he was billeted at the antenna array that looked toward Turkey from the eastern side of the island.

"Colonel Kritikiou said you'd be here."

The young man looked shocked. "Me? He said I'd be here?"

"He said 'somebody.'"

"Ah, oh, that's okay, then." A flash of teeth, a relieved grin. "Okay, I am somebody." A laugh, surprisingly deep from the young face under the shock of black hair.

"They tell you what this is about, Lieutenant?"

"This? Oh, this. A meeting, I am told."

"You intel? Intelligence?"

Darcouri nodded gravely, then gave his deep laugh again. "Electronic intelligence, yes. But—" He made a shrugging gesture, hands held out, then looked at Dukas with shrewd eyes that were not as naive as they had at first seemed. "I know a black cat from a white one in the dark, okay?"

"Good. If we need a cat, you're the expert. Otherwise— look, I know this is not easy for you, this situation—but I want to do my job and go home. Okay?"

"Me, too." A grin. "I am just married."

Dukas chuckled without humor. "Me, too." Darcouri was leading him around customs and immigration, down a concrete-block hallway where a middle-aged woman waited in an office doorway to glance at his passport, stamp it, look quickly at Darcouri, and wave them on. "You got briefed?" Dukas said, and, when the English "briefed" caused puzzlement, added in Greek, "They told you what is going on?"

What they'd told him, it turned out, was that he was to shadow an American officer who was making a declared meeting with another foreigner, and he was to see that nothing else happened and that the national interests of Greece were honored. "God, if you can do all that, you should be an ambassador," Dukas growled. Now he was leading, headed for the

420

rental-car desk; before they got there, he stopped and turned to face the younger man, bringing him up short. "I got somebody else on the island. You know that, I think—both declared. We're trying to meet another American who has information on a case of an American death in Israel. This is all purely about information. Okay?" He didn't mention Hamal or the four Israelis who were supposed to be there or Jerry Piat's dubious past. If it all went smoothly, Darcouri knew all he needed; if there was a screwup, he'd learn fast enough. Darcouri nodded, and Dukas started them going again.

He gave his name to the woman behind the rental-car counter and flashed his passport. Not pretty, but riveting—black hair, huge eyes, olive skin, tall. He put his credit card on the counter. The Greek intel man stood back as if commerce embarrassed him. The woman gave Dukas a mechanical smile and whipped data into a computer, meanwhile fishing an envelope and keys from a stack with the other hand. She watched the computer screen, took a pencil from her hair and scratched her scalp with it, put the pencil back, and took a package from a drawer somewhere under the counter. "For you," she said without looking at him.

Dukas signed something, waited while she attacked the computer again. He was looking for watchers, wondering if his new Greek minder could recognize them—black and white cats were one thing, Mossad agents another—then thinking about Colonel Hamal and the murderous bitterness in his voice. Dukas didn't want a disaster. He didn't want some international firefight, with his Greek minder calling in the cops and everybody spending time in jail until embassy flunkies arrived from Athens and sorted it out. *No violence, please, we're Greek.*

And why not? Why should a lovely little Greek island be a hunting ground for the black dreams of three other countries?

Dukas watched the tourists from his flight hurry past. Their

421

faces were hopeful, often smiling. A week in paradise. *If nobody starts shooting.*

He led the way to the rental car. One face had looked suspicious to him, and he watched for it as they walked. Darcouri, so far as he could tell, hadn't noticed. Or was he being cautious?

In the car, Dukas opened the package that Craik had left for him. A cell phone and a map of the island. A small circle had been drawn around the center of a tiny village.

"Good map," Dukas said in Greek.

"We make the best maps in the world." A nation of geographers, he meant—the heritage of Odysseus.

Dukas pulled out of the parking space and eased into the flow. When they had left the airport and were winding toward the sea, Darcouri said, "I think you are being followed."

"Maybe it's you they're following," Dukas said. "Some jealous husband."

That was thought very funny.

Mytilene–Kalloni Highway, Lesvos

The white Suzuki hung well back, often vanishing from his rearview mirror for minutes at a time in the twists and turns through heavily forested mountains. Alan drove carefully, just slightly over the posted speed limit, which should have made him the slowest car on the road, but the white Suzuki continued to stay back.

Alan stopped for gas that he didn't need where a side road curved away to the south coast of the island, facing Chios. When Alan left the station, there was no sign of the white Suzuki. He drove for twenty kilometers without being able to guess if there was another car on him. The road was straight and flat through olive groves and pastures, goats and sheep as it descended gradually to the coast near Kalloni, and a new car, if there was one, could have stayed far back on the nearly empty road and watched him from a mile or more away.

He looked for excuses to stop. There were none. The Kalloni coast was closed for the season, and, aside from gas stations, every shop, pottery, bar and taverna along the road was shuttered.

Now he wasn't sure whether he should go for his meeting with Piat or abort it. If he went as things were now, he'd be unsure of his surveillance status—definitely a no-no. If he didn't go, he'd be sending a clear signal—but the more he thought about it, the less clear that signal seemed. It was possible that Piat would simply feel he had been blown off.

Balanced against that, he might lead his own surveillance straight to Piat.

So much for Mike's "easy day."

The density of the shops, hotels, and tavernas along the highway increased until he passed a sudden inland bend to the road and both sides were suddenly full of residential buildings. He was in Kalloni. He looked at his map, open on the passenger seat, and tried to match Greek street signs to the English characters on his map. This absorbed him so totally that he realized five minutes later that he hadn't been watching for surveillance and that there was now a red Citroën C3 that had made the last two turns with him. At the same time, he saw the tell-tale blue parking sign that he had hoped for.

He had no time to be relieved, because the blue parking sign was only the start of his approach route to the meeting with Piat. The lot was so nearly empty that it was embarrassing to park there. Alan suspected that he had just made a mistake, because he must have passed through viable parking in the town itself, but he was committed now; leaving the parking lot would look foolish. He parked.

The only other car in the lot was a white Citroën. It had stickers for a local rental agency, and a single male occupant who avoided meeting Alan's eye.

The red Citroën was gone. It might never have been

involved. Alan hung his camera around his neck, shouldered his pack, and glanced at his watch. 1236; a few minutes too early for his intended start time on his route, but he had a whole town in which to use the time.

He thought, *I'm too tired to do this well.*

He started along his route, trying not to take too long staring at the unfamiliar street signs.

He got the right street out of the parking lot. At the first cross street, he found the red Citroën parking across the street, far too close for his comfort. A pretty, middle-aged woman got out, saw him, did a double take, and then leaned into the car to say something to a man. Neither the man, a lean young guy with a silly moustache (instantly christened "Moustache"), nor the woman was anyone he had seen before, but their reaction was as good as a sign. He put them behind him and took the first turn on his route, a simple left across the street toward the main business district.

He was careful not to look behind him. While trying not to focus on anything for too long, he tried to find himself a stop to anchor this leg of his route and make it look realistic, although after almost walking into the couple with the red Citroën he wasn't sure that subterfuge was called for.

Just across the street, a few buildings ahead, sat a sweet shop. And it was open. The smell of baking sugar carried through the crisp air and made Alan's stomach growl despite the early croissant. He walked up even with the shop and stepped to the curb, looking both ways. At the top of the street, ahead of him, stood the heavy blond man from the airport (Alan tagged him Big Blond) now sporting a camera bag and an expensive oilskin jacket. At the base of the street stood Moustache. Alan crossed the street, entered the shop, and took his time choosing cookies and cakes.

Alan left with a sticky bag in his left hand and the remnants of a honey-coated cookie crunching away in his jaw. He walked east, the actual meeting place now passing out of sight to the north somewhere beyond several streets of houses and shops. At the corner, he crossed the highway on which he had entered, pausing at the central meridian to extract a coconut macaroon and look down his back trail.

The middle-aged woman from the red Citroën was now west of him, walking slowly up the other side of the highway. Alan rolled up his cookie bag, put it in his pack, wiped his hands on a napkin and shot four pictures of the woman as she walked. She certainly noticed him. After the third picture she hesitated and flushed.

He was breaking the rules; he was announcing himself to his surveillants and daring them to do something. He found it satisfying.

When he started walking again, he noticed that she gave him a much longer lead. He had to stop to read every street sign. The two of them moved slowly.

Eventually, he reached his next turn and took it. As he approached another intersection, he slowed and snapped pictures of some older houses with projecting wooden balconies. His fourth picture caught Big Blond again, just peering around the corner. Big Blond walked away fast, headed east, his shoulders high and his chest out. Big Blond wanted to hit something.

Alan crossed behind him, headed north. He found a big, modern grocery store just off his route on the right down a major street, and he walked in because everything since the sweet shop had been closed. It didn't make much of a stop. Illogical. Hastily chosen. He picked out a bottle of San Pellegrino Limonata and walked back up to the gleamingly empty automatic cashier, where he pressed a few buttons and paid with carefully counted euros. All very high-tech for such a small town. Through the window, he could see across the parking lot to where Big Blond and the woman were arguing, their hands moving up and down, up and down. From the gestures, he gathered that one of them should have followed him inside.

425

He took a photo through the window and went back to his route. His anger was still there, coiled inside, but every photo helped.

Kalloni, Lesvos.

Piat drove to his meeting in Kalloni on nerves. It was broad daylight, and he was driving a car rented on a credit card, and he knew that somewhere on the island the noose was tightening.

He should never have given Dukas a meeting in such a constricted place.

He saw nothing on the drive down Mount Olympus. He watched every side road; he worshipped his rearview mirror; he talked Saida through the basic principles of surveillance detection; he saw nothing.

Nothing was almost worse than something.

He parked the car at the supermarket in Kalloni. His operational instinct told him that he had parked here before and should not do so again, but no other parking place in Kalloni offered the same ease of access and evasion.

"You know the drill, right?" he said. Saida was watching the street behind them.

"I sit here. You go do something dangerous."

"If I'm not back in twenty minutes by the car clock—twenty minutes, okay? You drive out of here. Go to the monastery and do what I told you. Okay?"

"Okay," she said. Her tone suggested that she had little intention of following his commands.

"Saida—"

"Listen, Jack. I can't do this without you." She leaned over as if to kiss him.

"Yes, you can. Damn it, we haven't got time for—" He leaned in the window.

She pushed him out. "Stay safe, Jack. I need you to sell the cup." She closed the window.

Piat walked to his observation point by a route he had practiced months before, because old habits never die, and every ramble through a town becomes the prep for a counter-surveillance route. He knew before he reached his spot that he was inside somebody's bubble. It wasn't instinct—just experience. He could feel the surveillance, and he knew that in a few seconds his brain would correlate enough data that he'd figure out how he already knew.

His observation point was the balcony of an internet café a whole street north of the meeting site, a café that had a back door for customers who knew where to find it. From the balcony, he could see a third of the downtown street grid. He looked at his watch. 1352.

He ordered a Nescafé.

A hundred meters away, a woman with an expensive shoulder bag stood indecisively on the corner of two streets. She hesitated only a moment, her eyes lingering on an object to her north. She didn't match her surroundings. Clothes too dark. Not moving enough. Piat glanced at her through his bird-watching glasses. *Earpiece.* Bingo.

He came to full alert. He snapped his binoculars back up to his eyes and swept north of her, trying to see what she was watching. The action, whatever it was, was invisible behind the bulk of a local church.

Piat pulled his glasses down. He glanced at the meeting site, a set of Roman ruins in the middle of the park. Still empty. He looked at his watch, crossed and uncrossed his legs, and risked another look at the woman. She had crossed her street and was now looking in the window of a closed shop. Her quarry, if he read this all correctly, was somewhere to her north, headed toward her.

Piat risked another sweep with his glasses.

Piat had last seen Alan Craik through the scope of a rifle in Jakarta four years ago. The image in the binoculars was not very different. Craik was walking too fast to avoid

427

detection and was wearing the ball cap that meant "under surveillance."

Piat knew that Dukas and Craik were friends. So Craik was coming in place of Dukas, and he knew he was under surveillance, and he came anyway. Trying to send a message?

Piat saw that his coffee had appeared on the table. He took a long pull. Craik was still well off the meeting site, and Piat no longer intended to make the meeting, anyway. But he wanted to see more of the people following Craik.

He raised the glasses again. Emerging from behind the church was a heavy blond man that Piat recognized as one of the swarm who had followed Rashid in Athens.

Time to go. Piat hoped that they all spent the day following Mr. Craik, because if they saw him or Saida, the game would change. For the worse.

Alan walked past the church, still a little too early, still moving a little too fast, and stopped in a stationery shop less than a hundred meters from his meeting site. He bought a pad and some pens and two books in English, because this was beginning to look like a long day.

From the steps of the shop, he saw a man across the archaeological park stand up from sitting on a bench. Alan knew him and his too-dark sunglasses—another of the men from Tel Aviv. Alan had stared at his shoes while he lay with his face pressed against the floor of the SUV. Dark Glasses had slugged the lady cop.

Without looking up again, Alan walked straight toward him, since Dark Glasses was now standing on top of the meeting site. In the pocket of his jacket, Alan turned the camera on and thumbed the lens to the greatest magnification. He walked past an outdoor café on his side of the street and noticed that the young man at the front table was reading le Carré's *A Perfect Spy*. Their eyes met for a moment and then both glances moved on.

Something else about the handsome young man stuck with him, but he didn't get it until it was far too late to take any action.

The young man was wearing a US Navy peacoat.

Rashid watched the tall American go into the pen shop and come out again. He looked out of place, more like a person on business than a tourist, although he was dressed like a tourist. He had short hair like a soldier. He wasn't even remotely an Israeli. Obviously American. The American met his glance and moved on, and Rashid's pulse, which had begun to quicken, subsided. Rashid went back to pretending to read.

He looked up, glanced at the back of the American now moving quickly away, and then looked in the direction from which the American had come.

One of the big men from the rainy night in Mytilene was watching the American walk down the street. Rashid wasn't sure. He couldn't be completely sure. But the man was big, heavily built, round-headed, and had on a heavy canvas vest, and even at fifty meters Rashid was—almost sure.

He wanted to hide. He quelled his first notion, to retreat inside immediately, and sat as motionlessly as he could, until the man in the canvas vest made a turn and disappeared from his view.

Then Rashid picked up his bag and fled.

Alan crossed the park without looking up to check his latest surveillant. He kept his eyes down on a tourist map, stopping once to check his watch. 1358. He was in the window, on the spot.

He started down the steps into the Roman ruin.

Piat walked a different route back to his car, swinging north to try and avoid contact with the bubble on Craik.

It should have worked.

Piat was getting into his car when he saw the well-dressed woman's back. She was on her cell phone.

"Fuck!" he said, and threw the car into gear. But training beat panic; he backed smoothly out of his spot and took his time turning left on to the boulevard.

"The woman?" Saida asked.

"Yes. You see her?"

"She is watching us. Now she is running."

Piat turned north on the first side street, choosing speed over stealth.

Alan walked across the Roman ruin alone. He hadn't expected Piat to be there and yet felt a sag when he reached the steps on the other side. He still had his hand wrapped around the camera.

He felt an illogical temptation to wait around or to make a second pass. Stupid. He was wearing the "no-go" sign. Why would Piat be there?

At the top of the steps, he made a guess at where Dark Glasses ought to be and swung forty-five degrees to the left. Bingo. He found himself looking at the man at a range of thirty feet. Dark Glasses had a cell phone pressed against his ear, his head ducked down, and he didn't appear to see Craik, his whole attention on his call. Even while Alan watched, he plucked up a bag from the bench and began to walk straight at Alan.

Alan raised the camera to his eye and shot the man four times, the last image at a range of less than ten feet. By the time the man realized what had happened, Alan was pushing past him.

Alan moved faster and looked back.

Dark Glasses stood frozen in the path, his face splotchy.

Alan walked very fast, the space between his shoulder blades burning. He could hear the other man shouting into his phone in Hebrew.

Alan waited for the sound of running. The moment he heard the other man's burst of motion, he was off himself.

He didn't bother with the rest of his route. He ran straight back down the boulevard to the car park.

He jumped into his car and turned the key. Dark Glasses was more than a city block behind him. Not a distance runner. Alan shifted into reverse and sped out of the lot. He never noted the interest of the man in the white Citroën.

He passed the white Suzuki sitting empty by the side of the road. Suddenly he was high on adrenaline and glad to be alive.

As he drove, he looked at the images on his camera. Three down.

One to go.

The tiny village that Craik had circled for the rendezvous with Dukas was on its own hill halfway down the island, north of Kalloni. There was the road coming in and six streets branching off it, and that was about it. Where the road met the two middle streets, a square had grown, like a bulge in a snake that has just had a good meal; the road came in, went around two sides, and left. Lieutenant Darcouri, Dukas's Greek minder, said that Greece was full of beautiful villages like this; Dukas said he hoped that some of them had wider streets, or the automobile was doomed. He managed to go a hundred feet up one of them, which narrowed even more after that and twisted away up a steep slope as if it was following an old goat track. "Picturesque," Dukas said, getting out and checking to see if he should find another parking place.

"Beautiful," Darcouri said. He meant the job of parking. He had had to come out Dukas's side because the passenger door was two inches from the whitewashed wall of a house. "Five-star."

They walked down to the square. Dukas explained that he was meeting his partner there and he'd like a few minutes alone with him. "You don't have to know everything we say, right?"

"No, no, Michael." They were on first names already. "I am only to oversee."

"Good. Wait here." Dukas pointed at a café with three tables and crossed the road to the center of the square. It was stark and mostly empty, a few benches and three small trees whose tops were bending in the wind. Craik was sitting on a bench. Dukas sat down and shoved his hands into his raincoat pockets and stuck his feet out. "You meet Piat, or did you bust the meeting?"

"Busted. They were all over me." Craik nodded toward the little café. "That your Greek nursemaid?"

"So Piat'll do the fallback, and I'll take over from you. You check into a hotel, go to bed."

"And do what—stare at the ceiling?" Craik's arms were folded over his chest; his chin was down.

"Al—go home."

"There's no plane until tomorrow morning."

"Al, I don't need you anymore."

"Maybe I need this." Craik held out his hands as if they held something small—a ping-pong ball, perhaps. "One good thing. One thing that goes right. I just want one thing that tells me that what I'm doing is useful and right."

Dukas stood. He looked down at his friend. "If this one goes the best it possibly can, it won't be much. We meet Piat, maybe he knows something, maybe he doesn't. Maybe he can turn over this girl, a witness. Maybe he won't. Maybe he won't even show."

"But we will have done our part *right*."

Dukas smiled. "We haven't changed the rules, if that's what you mean." He held out a hand.

Craik took it, pulled himself up, gave a smile that showed

432

a little of his old self. "I have." He gestured at his camera."I don't want to turn into *them*."

"I wouldn't let you." Dukas patted Craik's shoulder. "Let's go get some Greek coffee and maybe a dessert."

They started toward the café, and an Israeli watcher folded his newspaper and hurried up the road.

Southern Lesvos.

The wind blew from the southeast. It came from the desert, and it swept north over the marshes of the Nile delta, crossed hundreds of miles of sea and blew across a dozen islands without picking up a drop of moisture. In the summer, it could be hot, capable of changing the olive crop or withering the grapes.

In the winter, it was cold. The wind blew cold and hard off the seas against the southernmost headland on Lesvos, whistling through the volcanic rocks and the towers of a wind farm.

Piat sat with his back to the smooth metal base of one of the windmills, the white steel rising smoothly to the great blades high above him in the dark. The turning blades were just audible, but inside the pillar the turbine beat against his back, *thump thump thump*. Saida lay curled in his arms, her head on his shoulder and her back firmly against him, and he could feel her heart racing faster than the turbine. *Thump thump thump*.

"I'm cold," she said, not for the first time.

Around her head, he looked at his watch, trying not to move her or alert her to his interest in the time. She was already nervous enough for both of them.

"I wish I had a cigarette," Piat said. He was looking at a map of the monastery where he was supposed to meet Dukas. And Andros. If everything worked.

The monastery sat in the crater of a volcanic mountain that rose fifteen hundred feet above the sea, a giant headland

433

between two fine beaches. From the main road, an old gravel track, wide enough only for wagons, ran a third of the way up the mountain, and split, the left fork climbing on ancient stone steps to the monastery near the summit, the right fork wandering around the northern flank of the volcano, climbing and descending, until it ran down after a few hundred yards into the sand of the northern beach.

"I wish we were safe," she said.

Piat watched the last five minutes of their time at the wind farm tick away. It was like watching the alarm clock on a work morning. For five more minutes, they were safe.

Four.

Three.

Two. He folded the map away and stowed his flashlight in his pack.

One.

And then they were in the red car, with forty miles of island to cross, and a boat to catch.

They bumped down the last of the wind farm's dirt road and out to the main highway. On a steep curve, the second switch-back on the climb up the island's central spine, Piat stopped the car, cut the engine, and listened. Saida's eyes glittered at him in the dark. He smiled at her.

"Just us," he said, and started the car.

Fifteen minutes later, they came down the ridge at a sedate sixty kilometers an hour, the only car on the road, headed into the police roadblock that permanently occupied the crossroads at the base. Saida was driving now.

She had the rental car on her credit card. Piat had debated the roadblock a dozen times, considered the risk of driving all the way around the island to avoid it, debated who should be at the wheel. In the end, the simplest notion seemed best. Let her drive her own car.

Saida's nerves were infecting him.

She pulled to a stop too early and too fast, six feet short of the waiting police officer, and then edged the car forward against the clutch, running the engine too fast.

She rolled down the window.

An older officer leaned in. In Greek, he said, "Good evening." Then in English, to Saida, "Good evening."

"Too cold to be a *good* evening," she said in English. "Aren't you freezing?"

The change was that sudden. First she could barely drive the car, and then she was performing. Piat felt his own nerves recede a fraction.

The Greek cop laughed. He looked at Piat, and something in his squint spiked Piat's adrenaline.

Piat held the cop's gaze, forced himself to smile and nod. *That guy is looking for us,* Piat thought. *Bullshit paranoia. Maybe.*

The cop pulled his head out of the window and gave the roof a gentle thump. "That wind goes right through, eh? Drive carefully, okay?" He waved them on with his flashlight.

Saida accelerated smoothly away.

Piat watched the roadblock out the rear window, but he couldn't see anything except a blur of light as the cop with the flashlight moved away from the roadblock. He didn't see the cop get in his car, and he didn't see him place a call, not on his radio, but on a cell phone, but he imagined such things. He thought how he would search the island for himself.

Outside his window, scrubby pines gave way to olive trees. Saida drove too fast, took corners too hard.

As they approached the top of the next ridge, the first peak with a view of the sea on the north side of the island, Piat reached over and touched her shoulder. "Stop the car at the top."

She did so without comment.

He opened his door, the chill wind pouring over them. He got out and stood up and walked to the edge of the road, but he couldn't hear anything over the rush of the wind in the trees and rocks above him. The incoming weather front had obscured the moon, and it was *dark*. Lights sparkled in farmhouses below him in the next valley. The lights of the coastal towns glowed orange in the distance.

Behind him, two pairs of headlights began the long climb up the ridge they had just completed. As he watched, they were joined by a third pair.

They came very fast, taking the switchbacks hard. Three cars. All together, driving fast.

Saida put a hand in his. She pointed where two pairs of headlights had just vanished in a turn and the third pair was still visible toiling up a grade. "For us?"

"Yep." He didn't think it was paranoia. He was certain that the three vehicles were pursuit, and he was certain that he knew who was in them.

She shivered.

He slapped her backside, which she didn't like. "Cheer up," he said. "This is how we earn twenty-five million dollars." He took the keys from her hand, waited for her to close her door, and powered the car over the crest and down into the valley beyond. As he accelerated into a curve, he tried to imagine if the guys hunting Saida would have a car ahead of him. He didn't think they had the manpower, and there wasn't much he could do about it anyway.

Unless their only purpose was to push him into a sniper. Or a mine.

Anything was possible.

Piat had done all this before, and he knew that when the stakes got this high, people and nations forgot all the rules and did whatever they had to do to get their money and their power. Guns, bombs, collateral damage. He'd done it for years.

He downshifted from fourth to second, teased the edge of a skid, felt his stomach drop out the bottom of his chest as his car crested a small rise and started down the reverse slope. In his rearview mirror, headlights started to crest the ridge where he and Saida had stopped.

"Are they closer?" Saida asked. "They're closer!"

"No," he said.

"Can't you pull off and hide?" she asked. "Like you did before?"

"No," he said.

"Can you—" She was getting shriller with each question.

He put a hand on her knee. "Shut up, Saida." He snatched the hand back to upshift.

"—ambush them?" she continued. "They'll kill me!"

He pushed the car as hard as he could, but he wasn't gaining enough distance to kill his lights and drive away. And this time, he had to stay on *this* road. He glanced at his watch, the luminous dial taking too long to register on his tired eyes. He didn't have the time to evade. The tires bit gravel, and the car swayed, once, back.

"They'll kill *us*, honey. Not just you. There are at least three or four of them, and I'm not good enough to ambush them. They may suck at surveillance, but for my money, they're really good at killing people."

He glanced at her and saw her staring out the rear window at the empty dark road. He changed lanes, keeping in the oncoming traffic lane while powering into a long curve. Dangerous only if anyone else was on the road, coming the other way. "One way or another, it'll all be over in ten minutes," he said.

"Yeah?" she asked.

"No," he said. "I'm lying to make you feel better."

"Jack? Shut up. You're making me nervous." He saw the flash of her smile.

Two flicks of the wheel while he negotiated three sheep in the road, and they were slowing for the turn to the monastery.

437

"Jack? Did you see Rashid in Kalloni?" Words tumbling out of her.

He downshifted, downshifted again, cut the lights for the approach to the turn. "What? Rashid?"

"He wanted to come back to us. He sent me an email. I—" She hesitated as he swung the rental car into one of the five parking spaces at the base of the track to the monastery.

He got out, produced a flashlight from his pack, ran it over the parking lot and then crossed the road to where the track went uphill to the monastery and the beach beyond. The volcano that held the monastery rose high above them, blocking even the scent of the sea, and the cold wind struck it full force and bounced off in a dozen directions.

New tire tracks and new footprints, too many to mean anything.

"Rashid wants to come back?" he said suddenly, working it out. "You told Rashid we'd be in Kalloni?"

"You like him, too!" she said.

"Fuck," said Piat, looking at the road they'd descended. "Get your pack. We have to move." He stood there in the darkness, listening to the wind. He reached under the seat of the rental and took out the pistol he had carried since he wrestled with the two thugs on the ferry. He checked the magazine and the safety and put the pistol in his waistband.

"He thinks that they will kill him," she said.

"I may kill him myself. Come *on.*" Piat pulled her across the road and up the steep track. He chewed on the problem while he watched the night—Rashid, Saida, the Israelis. Palestinians. Loyalties. Twenty-five million dollars. Armageddon.

A hundred feet above the road, the track split. To the left, the track rose to become a steep staircase carved into the volcanic rock, steps just visible as a jagged line winding up and vanishing into the dark. A thousand feet above, the lights of the monastery showed like yellow stars. To the right, like the easy road to hell in a childhood illustration, the path ran smooth and easy down the seaward slope through high dead grass and scree from the slopes around the base of the mountain to the beach on the sea beyond. The sea was audible in snatches when the wind died and gusted again.

Piat stopped, Saida's hand still clutched in his own. He listened for engine noise, watched the darkness behind them for headlights. A gust of wind swirled around them. Something moved in the dark at the edge of his peripheral vision and he put the light on it.

A scrap of fabric pinned to a branch of wild olive blowing in the wind like an arm pointing. A scrap of black wool with three red chevrons, a white pen, and a lightning bolt.

Piat knew whose it was and who had left it and what it meant all at once. *Jack, don't come this way. From Rashid.* Or maybe *Save me, Jack.*

Saida grabbed his shoulder. "That's Salem's patch." Her voice trembled.

"I know." Professional courtesy, if nothing else, demanded that he do something for Dukas. "Don't move," he said in her ear. In his mind's eye, he could see Rashid's "friends" waiting on the trail.

He ran back down toward the road. He watched the road to his right all the way back, dreading the sudden appearance of headlights. They must be just over the ridge. As he reached their car, the first set of headlights crested the last hill and started down. He heard the gear change distinctly in the cold air, and then the wind swept by again as the second and then the third set of lights started down.

He pulled open the back door, and grabbed his ball cap from under the seat. He shut the door and pulled the cap over the antenna so that the adjustment strap caught. He flipped down the front sun visors for good measure, wished that he had time for a note, and trusted that Dukas, if he came, could read the signs.

Then he was off up the track again. The headlights seemed

close, but he reckoned that in fact they were half a mile away. Saida was waiting for him on the trail to the beach, and he caught her arm and pulled her back.

"This way," he said over the wind. He pulled her up the trail toward the monastery.

"But—Rashid—he must have left the patch." She was pulling against him.

"He's not alone." Piat pulled harder, got her moving, and pushed himself up the slope toward the steps. Below them, the first set of headlights was pulling into the parking area. The other cars cast enough light to throw Saida's shadow ahead of him on the steps.

"But you have to get him—he wants—where are we going?" Saida was already panting with exertion.

Piat pulled her down and put a hand over her mouth. They crouched on the steps.

"Listen to me. Rashid left the patch to tell us that he's here. He's here with a couple of badasses. Okay? They probably have guns, Saida. They're looking for you, too. And me. Now, when those headlights go out, we're going to move up the steps, as quickly and quietly as we can. When I say 'down', you get down. Okay?"

Her face was a paler blur in the dark, but her voice was acid with reproach. "You're going to walk off and leave that boy to those—pah!"

The last set of headlights went out on the road below them. Deep male voices floated up on the wind.

"Yes. Now move," Piat whispered at her, and pulled her to her feet.

They went up a long flight of steps to a landing with a stone urn full of flowers cut in the face of the rock. Piat crouched on the landing. He found that he had drawn his pistol.

Saida folded herself into the base of the steps.

Moving gravel, and a larger stone displaced into the gully

440

far beneath them. Then silence. Piat belly-crawled to the edge of the steps to get a longer sightline and a shot, if it came to that.

He could neither see nor hear anything moving on the hillside.

The wind dropped, and he heard a car change gears in the distance.

The stone landing under him was cold through his jacket, cold through his jeans, and his belly was colder than both. His teeth tried to chatter and he bit down.

A man moved, forty feet below him. He raised a hand, made a fist, punched the air. Two other men moved past him to the fork at the base of the steps.

Piat considered shooting them. He guessed that they were the Israelis he'd seen in Athens. They were combat-trained and it showed in the way they moved. He'd get one, if his hand didn't tremble too violently. Two if he was very lucky. Then the others would get him.

He didn't shoot.

Another gust of wind hit him. The wind direction was changing, heralding a front. He couldn't hear anything except the wind. The pistol in his hand felt like ice. The gust passed, and in the silence he could hear the patterns of the men's speech but not the words or the language.

A pale blur of a face peered up the steps. Piat's stomach pulsed.

The engine noise came with a new gear change, but Piat didn't dare turn his head to see if there were more lights.

The man at the base of the steps said something, and then all of the men moved away, down the path to the beach, the dead grass indicating their passage until the darkness hid them. Piat waited, counted slowly to a hundred, and then rose to a crouch.

"Up!" he hissed at Saida. He glanced at the road and saw another car with widely spaced headlights descending the last ridge, a few driving minutes away. And then a second car appeared from the opposite direction, moving fast, and skidded on the gravel at the edge of the parking area. A door slammed, unnaturally loud over the distance.

"Up!" he hissed again, but Saida was already moving up the steps, black against the sky-lit rock. She got to the next landing as another car door slammed behind them. Piat risked a look. A single figure ran across the road, a dark shape with a raincoat billowing behind him as he ran, and disappeared below him. The man ran heavily, his footsteps loud on the gravel.

Piat pushed past Saida and led the way, moving up the steps as quickly as he dared. A new gust of wind struck them, banishing all sound but its own roar, and this one continued as Piat went up two flights of steps, then a third, his heart bashing at the base of his throat and his knees burning with the effort. Saida lagged. At the fourth landing, he threw himself down and waited, watching over the edge. They were halfway to the turn around the mountain, where the steps would no longer be in sight of the trail to the beach.

Saida pushed past him, sobbed, and collapsed on the platform.

Piat watched the car with the widely spaced headlights pull into the parking area. He was now too far above to see anything after its lights cut. He hoped that the reverse was also true.

He turned to order Saida up and found that she had already pushed herself halfway up the next flight of stone steps. He followed her.

They made three more flights. Piat was dizzy with the effort. He was surprised at every turn of the stairs when Saida kept pushing on ahead of him, but she did, her breath coming in quick gasps. They reached a larger landing, a natural platform with urns for flowers and a trickle of water where a stream would run under their feet in the spring. Ahead, Piat could see the sea. *Thalatta, thalatta!* The line came unbidden from inside his head, the shouts of joy from the ten thousand escaping the Persians in *Anabasis*.

He took a great breath and the wind flawed. He scanned the sea, looking for lights, any lights at all, and there came the distinct crash of a shot from the beach. It sounded like the roar of a distant cannon, and then it began to echo off the mountain and the cliffs that lined the sea to the north. Then more shots came, a rolling peal of man-made thunder that mixed with the echoes until the seabirds, roosted for the night on the seaward face of the mountain, burst into flight at full screech, and the air was filled with violence.

20

Lesvos

Alan drove automatically, pushing the accelerator down to maintain speed in the Volkswagen as they struggled uphill.

"The monastery track is off to the left at the base of the ridge." The Greek officer in the back seat leaned forward. "You are driving too fast for these roads."

Dukas didn't turn his head. "We're in a hurry."

As they crested the ridge, they could see the lights of an oncoming vehicle in the distance. Alan slowed down for the switchbacks of the descent and geared down.

"What do we owe Piat?" he asked.

"Nothing," Dukas said. "Where'd that come from?"

"Just thinking aloud," Alan muttered.

"It's not about Piat." Dukas glanced at the man in the back seat, clearly weighing his words. "It's about a US Navy guy who was murdered."

Alan grunted, his attention on the oncoming car. It was still a half-mile ahead, and it was slowing or had stopped at the base of the ridge.

"That the monastery?" Alan pointed at the car lights in the distance.

The Greek officer leaned forward again. He pointed up, way up, nearly to the top of the windshield. "That's the monastery—"

Alan took his eyes off the road and saw a cluster of yellow lights high above them.

The Greek continued, "—but that car is at the turn."

The distant car's lights went out.

Alan negotiated the last three switchbacks, short stretches of straight with right-angle turns at the end, and they were down in the valley. He accelerated.

"Mike?" he asked.

Dukas stared out the windscreen. "Yeah?"

"You got a plan?"

"Find Piat. Talk to him."

Alan handled a gentle turn and slowed for the entrance to the monastery track. Three cars were already parked on the gravel shoulder, filling the tiny parking area. Alan fought the gearshift and cursed, forcing the car into a space left by a red car and the edge of a steep drop.

Dukas was out of the car as soon as he stopped. He shone a flashlight into the windows of the red car, shone it on a ball cap suspended from the car's antenna. Alan ignored the Greek officer and followed him.

"Engines are still warm," Dukas said over the wind. He pointed at the ball cap. "Piat's canceling the meeting." He hunched his shoulders.

Alan looked up the mountain. It was too dark to see anything. "We done?" he asked.

"For today, maybe."

Alan pointed at a Suzuki four-by-four. "I've seen that car all day. That's the muscle. Israeli."

Dukas nodded.

"And the rental with the ball cap is Piat?"

"It better be." Dukas sat down on the bumper of their jeep.

"So who's in the other two?" Alan walked over to a white Citroën parked next to the red Suzuki. "I saw this car, too. More Israelis?"

"No idea." Dukas was looking up the track.

The Greek officer got out of their car. Whatever he tried to say was lost in the wind. He started toward them, and the wind diminished, then dropped abruptly.

"Fucking Piat," Dukas said.

"I heard a shot," the Greek officer shouted. He pointed up the hill.

As he finished speaking, a volley of shots sounded, and an echo like summer thunder.

Dukas swore and stood up. He started across the road toward the track.

"Mike!" Alan called. "What the—Jesus—Mike!"

Dukas was already climbing the trail.

Darcouri said, "Who is shooting?"

"What do you think?"

The young Greek looked severe. "I think you have gone beyond anything that is permitted by the government of Greece." He pulled out a cell phone and started jabbering; the number must have been already keyed in. His voice was excited, tense, eager. Alan ran across the road, up the first slope, and came to a flat space with stone steps rising away to the left and a broad trail through beach grass to the right. Dukas was kneeling on the beach trail with his flashlight on, his fingers masking the light. He handed Alan a scrap of cloth.

"Navy cryptologist."

"Salem Qatib."

A flurry of shots, closer this time, and the scream of a man in pain too much to bear. The scream was repeated like a baby's scream for help when no one comes for it.

Alan crouched by Dukas on the trail. "What's it mean?"

"No idea."

Scream.

"The kid."

"What kid?"

"The Palestinian kid. This patch goes on a peacoat. I saw one today but I was too busy to get it. The kid left the patch—"

Dukas hushed him with a gesture, listening. The wind had fallen to a breeze, but the wave sound from the beach murmured and roared by turns. The screaming had stopped.

"Yeah, maybe the kid. Your Israelis are here. Piat's here. Why not Palestinians?" He turned the flashlight off. "I'm going down toward the noise."

Dukas got to his feet. He might have chuckled, or grunted, but most of the sound was lost in the noise of the sea.

Alan glanced back into the darkness where the parking area was. "The Greek guy's on his cell phone. The shit's going to hit the fan." He pushed past Dukas and started down the trail.

He didn't make it fifty yards before he found the first body. The man was dead, face down and full length. Alan didn't need a flashlight to identify him. He'd been looking at that red ball cap and heavy build since early morning. He patted the body down, rolled it over clumsily, saw the gunshot wound high in the chest, found the gun in the dead man's ankle holster. He took the pistol, checked the safety and the magazine, worked the slide as Dukas came up behind him.

"One of the Israelis," Alan said. "Ambush." He sounded hopeless. "What a fucking waste."

"They'll be on the beach."

Alan remained crouched over the body. "Is this really about making an arrest, Mike? You're here to arrest the guys who killed Salem Qatib?"

Dukas said, "In an ideal world, yeah." Then, "That's what it's about for us. They're here about some goddam cup."

Alan handed Dukas the man's wallet. "I'm sick of it, Mike. I think I'm through."

Dukas was listening to something on the wind. Flight decks had wrecked Alan's hearing. All he could hear was the sea, but Dukas was twitching like a bird dog. He heard something that made him lean forward. Suddenly, he cupped his hands to his mouth and bellowed. "Hey!" he called. He started down the trail at a heavy trot, and Alan followed him. Ten steps later Dukas stopped again and called. *"Eshkol!"*

Alan heard a sound in answer. Dukas must have heard something more, because he moved faster, leaving Alan behind.

Dukas bellowed again. "Eshkol!" He listened. "I'm coming down!" And then, in reply to something Alan couldn't hear, he said, "American officer! Don't shoot! Don't anybody be that stupid!" Then he shouted something in Greek and then in perhaps Hebrew.

He started forward and was lost in the dark.

Alan didn't follow. He was trapped now in his hopelessness, a deepening fatigue, the world blurred. Moving as if the air was as thick as glue, the pistol hanging forgotten from his hand, he made his way into the rocks and down toward the beach, moving, as it turned out, from corpse to corpse— four of them. Four dead men, waymarks to a meeting that had come too late.

Dukas made himself walk noisily down toward the beach, letting his feet knock pebbles loose and crunch down on the gravel. Twice, he called out, "Eshkol!" and paused until he heard an answer from the darkness. Behind him for the first few yards he could hear Craik's footsteps, as well; then he lost them as they seemed to move into the rocks to his left.

He came down to the beach, feeling the gravel change to sand underfoot, his flashlight held out at arm's length to his right side so that, when he turned it on, a shot might take his arm rather than his chest. The sand was firm, therefore wet; the tide was out. "Eshkol. I'm on the beach."

He flipped the light on, waited for the shot. Somebody shouted something; another voice answered. Both angry, the second hoarse and breathy. Dukas swept the pale, feeble light in front of him and saw a pair of feet, toes pointed up; beyond, a dim, standing figure; farther away still something lower, black, indistinct—a kneeling man or a rock? He pushed the light off and walked forward.

"Dukas. Stop there."

He stopped. A bright light came on, found his face, and he winced. The light probed him, head to feet, found no weapon. Went off. Then, feet whispered across the wet sand. Dukas tried to force his eyes to adjust, and he was barely able to make out the lighter pall of the sky when darkness intervened: Eshkol, in some enlarging garment—a raincoat?—standing a few feet from him.

"So," Dukas said. He could see the paler space where the head was. He could hear Eshkol's sigh.

"A hell of a thing, Michael."

"How many?"

"I think there were three Palestinians. Four of mine. I got one still alive, I know, but he's bleeding pretty bad."

"There's a Greek intelligence guy up at the cars, calling his people. You don't have long. Your guy bad enough he needs a hospital?"

He heard Eshkol sigh again, then breathe in heavily. *Somebody's bleeding, and he's running his options,* Dukas thought. Then he saw it: Eshkol was wondering how he was going to get himself and a wounded man and three bodies out if time was short. The dead Palestinians would have to take care of themselves. Dukas said, "I can help you."

"Oh, yeah, I remember how you help, Michael."

"I think it was you didn't help me."

"I don't want your help."

"Pretty messy for Mossad if you and your guys wind up in a Greek prison."

"Let me take care of my own business."

Dukas shrugged himself deeper into his raincoat. He was cold, on the verge of shivering. He understood better what

449

Craik had tried to express back in Naples, that sense of no hope that is like physical want, like being cold and wet and hungry and lost. He exhaled and thought that Eshkol would hear it as a sigh. Maybe it was a sigh. "You're not going to get what you came after," he said. "The guy was supposed to be here on the beach. He isn't—unless he's one of those bodies."

Eshkol said nothing.

"I think your cup has grown legs, Eshkol. I think it's time you kissed it goodbye."

"I don't know what you mean, my cup."

Dukas snorted. "Like fuck. Look, Eshkol, I got one goal in this shithouse mess, to write a report about the death of Salem Qatib. I don't care two-dogs-fucking about whether the Trojans or the Tribe of Dan or the Minnesota Vikings were into Israel when there wasn't any Israel and King Solomon was a guy with eighteen sheep and a mud hut and no temple! What I care about is what happened to Salem Qatib and whether you guys killed him because of the stuff he stole or because of US Navy cryptology. That's all. That's all!"

"So what are you saying to me?"

"I'm saying it's time to make a fucking deal."

Eshkol hesitated. The wind gusted, and Dukas heard a sob, not from Eshkol but from somewhere beyond him: the smaller shape he had seen, now just recognizable as somebody huddled on the sand. Crying.

"What for what?" Eshkol said.

"Israel's past for the four guys who killed Salem Qatib."

"Too late," Craik's voice said from behind him. "They're dead. All but one, and he's bleeding out."

Dukas moved a step forward. "That true?" He could see the shape of Eshkol's face now, darker patches where the eyes were. "The very four?"

"The Palestinians shot them."

"Oh, did they! Wasn't that convenient, though!"

"It was an ambush! They had a rifle! Fuck you, Dukas,

450

we came down with Glocks against that thing—you think it's 'convenient' that four guys died taking out a Palestinian sniper with a rifle?"

Dukas folded his arms to try to preserve some warmth. "Yeah, I think it's convenient. I'll see what my Greek pal's forensics tell me about where the bullets went in." He stepped forward again, this time close enough to have touched Eshkol, had he wanted, and he put a finger almost under Eshkol's nose. "The clock is running out, for Christ's sake! Deal with me! If you can't give me four killers, give me names! Give me reasons! Give me facts!"

He saw Eshkol's head move; was he listening to the sobs from the beach? Or was he looking aside? Dukas looked that way. Was there somebody else over there? Like, maybe, the guy who was hit and was bleeding but maybe still had a gun?

He turned to Craik. "See who's over there. Not the guy who's crying—there's somebody else." He looked at Eshkol. "Isn't there?"

"I told you, I got one guy is bleeding."

And, Dukas thought, *you're waiting for him to bleed out and leave you with no witnesses and no cleaning-up to do. Very professional.* "I think he's got a gun," he said to Craik. He heard movement behind him, then saw in his peripheral vision Craik's darkness move down toward the water. He looked again at Eshkol. "Deal."

Eshkol's voice was hoarse. "With what?"

"I told you—names, facts, reasons." Before Eshkol could answer, he said, "A signed statement. I'll see that you get out of here to a place where you can make it."

"Your office in Naples?" Eshkol said. He made one of his gestures, and probably some sort of face, too; Dukas didn't need to see them to read the man's bitterness. Eshkol went on. "What do I get?"

"The US will support any story Israel likes about the cup and the dig at Tel-Sharm-Heir'at. The easiest is that the

451

cup was a fake; the photos are fakes. We've consulted experts, yah-di-da, yah-di-da—'a clever fake but wouldn't convince anybody who knew the period.' The inscription is pure invention. We can plant stories in the media, also in the scholarly press if that'll make you happy. The cup never happened, and Israeli myth is safe."

Eshkol was smiling, he could tell, not with humor but with cynicism. "And the girl who has it? And the guy who is helping her? Some American—some American pro, Michael, as in I smell a rat and I think this whole thing is a put-up American job!"

"Yeah, right, and I'm actually a CIA veteran from the Bay of Pigs. Forget the girl and the guy."

"Yes, until they sell the cup and it's all over every TV screen in the world!" A dim flashlight beam shone down near the water, then went out; Eshkol's head swung that way, swung back.

"You should pray they sell it!" Dukas growled. "You know what the fucking thing is worth better than I do! You think for that kind of money—we're talking millions, you know that—you think somebody's going to announce he's the buyer and put the fucking thing on *display*? It'll disappear! The only thing you could do better is melt it down!"

"Just what we mean to do."

"Yeah, well—" Dukas was aware that Craik had come away from the blackness by the water and was now merging with the kneeling figure. He could hear the murmur of their voices, Craik's deeper. A sob.

"If we get the girl and the American—" Eshkol started to say, and then Craik called, "Listen!" Eshkol turned partway around; Dukas straightened. Craik was nearer the water, maybe had heard whatever it was because it was coming from there. And then Dukas heard it, too—the gentle *bump, bump, bump* of a Zodiac hull hitting the troughs between the waves, out on the dark sea.

"There!" Alan called. Maybe he pointed, but Dukas couldn't see him that clearly. What he did see was a pinprick of light, moving like a horizontal falling star, and another in answer well out on the water. The bumping sound of the Zodiac went on, and now the sound of its outboard, too. Going out to sea, not in.

"There goes your cup," Dukas said.

Eshkol stared at the moving light. His shoulders jerked. Dukas put a hand on Eshkol's arm, felt it tense, knew that, as he had thought, Eshkol had a handgun clutched inside a pocket. "If you take that gun out, Craik will shoot you," he said. "*Deal with me.*"

Craik and the other one were coming slowly toward them, a single, wide mass with legs. Dukas made out a face below Craik's, somebody smaller. The Palestinian kid? Eshkol seemed to ignore them and to focus instead on the place where his wounded man was supposed to be. Eshkol said, "You say you don't care about what the cup means, Michael, but I care. I *care*. Give me your word, your government will prove the cup is a fake."

"And you make a statement that gives me the truth about Salem Qatib." Dukas took his little tape recorder out of his pocket, the same one he had used to tape Spinner a million years ago. He turned it on and mumbled the date and place and their names.

The Zodiac sound had faded. Dukas thought he was still hearing it, nonetheless, because he was sure he could hear a rhythmic pulsing, which changed as he listened into the faraway chuffing of a helicopter. "You got about a minute. Say it and then get out of here."

Eshkol moved his left hand out of his pocket. Not the gun, but a flashlight. He said, "I am talking about Israel, and you are talking about a stupid case!"

"I'm talking about getting the truth."

Eshkol moved his shoulders, maybe huddling against the

cold wind. "The truth." He shook his head, then raised the hand that held the tape recorder and leaned toward it. "This is Special Agent Shlomo Eshkol of the Institute for Special Information. I declare that four men working under cover as the Marine Exploration Branch of the Israeli Oceanographic Service killed the Palestinian Salem Qatib. They did this while trying to get information about Qatib's illegal activities raising money for Hamas through archaeological digging. Qatib was a criminal, and his work funded terrorism, but he was not meant to die. But he did." He pushed the recorder away and took a step toward the water, and Dukas stepped in front of him and said, "Names! I want names!"

"I'd kill you both or be killed doing it before I'd give their names, Michael! They made mistakes, but I'm not going to have their names thrown back at us. Take what I've given you or go to hell."

"Say at least that Qatib didn't die because of cryptology."

"Oh, shit—cryptology! My God, that was a stupid decoy! Cryptology meant nothing! Okay? Okay? You'll let me pass now, Michael?"

Dukas took a step back. He said, "Okay—go chase your cup."

Eshkol's flashlight came on, a small, powerful beam that bored into the dark. He shone the light on Craik, then on the frightened boy with him, then took three steps down toward the water and disappeared into the darkness when the light snapped off. His shoes whispered in the sand and then the sound was lost in the wind, and, long seconds later, down near the water the light came on again, shining white-hot into the beach grass. There was one shot, and the light went off, and Eshkol disappeared again into the sudden darkness.

Craik came to Dukas with his arm still around the boy's shoulders, and the three of them stood there, the wind cold, the sea muttering, the helicopter loud now as it circled over the top of the path and looked for a place to land.

*   *   *

454

DIRECTOR OF MOSSAD TO RETIRE
Joshua Ben-Levi, Director of Mossad under two
administrations, will retire at the end of next month.
In making the public announcement, Ben-Levi cited
his health and a desire to spend more time with his
family. According to sources close to the Israeli
Intelligence establishment, Ben-Levi will be replaced
by Colonel Benjamin Galid of the IDF.

Jane's Defence Weekly, January 14th 2002

From the 2002 Supplemental Budget Authorization of the
United States Congress:
Item DoDNav547.1. For recoding of naval communications,
153.6 million

Coda

The Janissary fort that guards the harbor of Izmir on the northern point isn't really old, by Mediterranean standards. It was built in the late seventeenth century to satisfy an ambitious Agha, with a carved marble arch at the gate proclaiming the builder's allegiance to Allah and carefully built bastions illustrating the use of the most recent European advances in fortress design.

It hasn't been garrisoned or maintained since the time of Ataturk. The brickwork has piles of dark red dust at the foot of every wall; the western bastion has sagged away as the beach under it erodes, and the pier where the supplies for the garrison were landed is slipping into the sea, unused except by curious boaters and a few smugglers. The marble arch remains intact, and on a wet winter's night it is still dry in the sentry boxes built into the gateway.

It was raining hard.

"I'm surprised you waited," Dukas called as he walked carefully up the concrete path to the gate. He had a flashlight in his hand, and he moved like a man using his last resources of energy.

Piat offered his hand. "I'm surprised you came," he said. "Where's Craik?"

Dukas shrugged. "What have you got for me?"

456

Piat laughed. It was meant to be a chuckle, but it developed a shrill pitch too quickly. "Nothing," he said. "Maybe an apology."

"Yeah?" Dukas was intrigued rather than angry. "Where's the girl?"

"Gone," he said. Then he laughed, and this time the sound had some authenticity. "She took my laptop and left. She sold the cup to *my* fucking buyer for a lousy million dollars."

"Jesus," Dukas grunted. "I'd have thought ten million was more the mark."

Piat shrugged, the motion of his shoulders just visible against the pale gray of the arch. "The buyer told her it's a fake." He took another drag. "Or so I hear."

Dukas nodded to himself. "Will it come back on the market?"

"Not a chance in hell. If it were a fake—maybe. But it's not." Piat sat on the stone bench provided by the Agha of Janissaries.

"You don't know that."

"I don't know that the world is round, but I'm pretty fucking sure all the same."

Dukas could see that there was a long, low boat tied up on the slanting remains of the old stone pier. He watched the deck. "I'd be happier if you'd got ten million dollars."

Piat chuckled. "Me, too. But I'm not going to rant. I was going to sell her to you. She just got me first. And she left me a little memento—so here's to her. Fair's fair."

"What did you want?" Dukas asked. "When you called?"

Piat said, "My life back. Or rather, just to keep the life I had. I wanted you to take the kids, and give me a passport in exchange." He made a motion with his hand, lost in the dark. "And to warn somebody."

"Not much chance I'd give you a passport." Dukas raised a hand in the dark to forestall Piat's protests. "The world's

457

changed, Jerry. I doubt I could get a passport if you could give me Bin-Laden."

"Oh," Piat said. "Well, fuck that too, then. What happened on the beach?"

Dukas's turn to shrug. "The Palestinians and the Israelis wasted each other."

Piat drank from a bottle. Dukas caught the liquorice smell of Ouzo. Piat offered it to him, and he accepted it.

"Like a morality play," Piat said.

Piat laughed. "You going to drink the whole bottle?"

Dukas handed it back. "Not sure I see the moral."

Piat shrugged. "No? Well, you wouldn't. I have a boat to catch."

Two days later, Piat was back on the hill, running to Thermi.